Contaminant Six

Joseph R. Lallo

Table Contents

ACKNOWLEDGMENTS

I would like to once again thank Nick Deligaris for his continued excellence in cover illustration. Tammy Salyer's support and encouragement as an editor really helped me through the revision process. And as always, I would like to thank the readers who joined me in this experiment in steampunk!

Prologue

A cold wind swept across the dim landscape as Coop trotted across the courtyard. He pulled his filter mask a little tighter and peered up through the layers of toxic fug where he'd been doing most of his business for the last few months.

"Don't see why it's always gotta me doing this runnin' around," he muttered. "Gunner's the one who's supposed to be good at the wheelin' and dealin'."

His long, well-worn overcoat rustled, and the tiny huddled form of Nikita peeked into view. The little aye-aye was his only company on this journey. She reached out her spidery finger and tapped out a message on one of his buttons.

The captain said make many deals, she rattled.

"I know, I know, but ain't none of the same folks makin' deals these days," he griped. "Used to be a fella could poke around in Keystone and get all his goods bought and sold with time to spare for takin' in one of them fancy shows. Things ain't been near as pleasant since we started doin' business down in the fug."

He rustled his jacket. "The stink's liable to hang on to me for a week once we go up top again." He squinted into the distance. "You reckon that buildin' there's where we're headed? It's sure easy to get turned around in this soup if you ain't payin' attention."

His irritable trudge took him to the edge of the courtyard. The map called this place Graham's Junction, but the map was a leftover from before the fug showed up, just like the city was. Most of the buildings had been left to the mercy of hundreds of seasons with no real maintenance. The one exception was the building dead ahead. The place had once been a general store, judging by the shape, but time and use had modified it into something more akin to a jerkwater resupply station. A manufactured sign swinging in the breeze labeled it *Blanc's Depot: Food, Fuel, Water, Dry Goods.*

He pulled a bit of paper from his pocket and glanced over the contents. "We got a good sixty canisters of phlogiston left over. A dozen or so burn-slow bricks. Some doodads from Caldera. With any luck these guys will clean us out, and we can call it a week."

Coop stowed the page and snagged a paper-wrapped bit of breadfruit. He held it down to Nikita. While she daintily nibbled the treat, he squinted past the building. As he drew nearer, the dim light and thick fug finally revealed something he'd not noticed on the way here. The massive envelope to an airship was visible over the skyline. Unlike the speedy little two-seat airship that had brought him here, it was a cargo hauler. Coop's lips curled into a sneer beneath his mask.

"Someone's tryin' to poach another of my customers," he growled.

He quickened to a run, one fist clenched tight and the other unconsciously resting at the grip of his pistol. Nikita huddled a little deeper into the safety of his coat.

Coop kicked in the door. The inside was crowded. Pale green light from phlo-lights along the top of each wall illuminated the scene. Mr. Graham, a man he'd done business with for nearly a year, was in his usual place behind a counter strewn with the sort of goods designed to eat up the change left over from the larger purchases his customers made. From the expression on his face, the transaction he was working his way through with the other four men in the building was not going as smoothly as he would have liked. At Coop's sudden appearance, he and the other men turned. The owner of the place looked decidedly more stressed at the discovery of just who his new visitor was. The others weren't any happier to see him, at least judging from the three whose faces he could see.

Three tall, sturdy men flanked a smaller gentleman, who seemed to be their leader. The big guys had the paper-white skin and lanky-yet-solid build of "grunts." They were fug folk, the very sort of person who called the fug home, but grunts tended to earn a bit more respect from Coop than the smaller, scrawnier academic-types. For one, they were usually doing the same sort of honest labor he got up to. That was to say, not honest from a legal standpoint, as what he was doing was still smuggling by most measures. Honest in the way that meant they were actually getting their hands dirty and doing the jobs rather than looking smug and telling someone else to do them. A few years ago, Coop hadn't even known grunts existed. Now he called more than a few of them friends, and had a couple scars from the less friendly ones.

The leader was harder to read. He was probably human since, like Coop, his face was covered with a mask. The mask was a good deal fancier than a simple filter strapped across his mouth like Coop favored. This person had a full face mask that tapered into a downward curved beak of sorts. Large lenses of smoked glass let him see through the grimy white mask without betraying what sort of face lurked beneath. The overall impression it gave was of a seabird who'd donned a heavy black duster and decided to go into business for himself. Gloves covered his hands, and dusty black canvas pants

2

covered his legs. The only evidence there was flesh and bone beneath the outfit were the whispers of long, ratty hair sticking out from beneath the back of the mask and between its straps. The wide-brimmed hat in one hand suggested even that much exposure was rare.

"Hey, fellas," Coop said. "Ain't seen you around these parts."

"Ah! Mr. Cooper," Mr. Graham said. "I'd not been expecting you for another three days."

"Lucky me, I got in here early then, because that there ship out back ain't the sort to be doin' buyin' at a place like this. Which means these fellas are probably *sellin'*. I wouldn't mind so much. Free market and all that. But you and me, we had a deal. So I'd be obliged if you'd set my mind at ease about whether or not I'm going to be haulin' back my load on account of these fellas poachin' my buyer."

"Now, Mr. Cooper, I'm sure you'll understand if—" Mr. Graham began.

The masked fellow raised a hand to silence him. "No, no. Don't make excuses for this guy," the man said in a muffled voice. "Coop, right?"

"That's what my friends call me. Ain't too sure that means *you* should be callin' me nothin' but Mr. Cooper, though."

"Oh, no, no. You and me? We're in the same business. Sales, right? Tell you the truth, I been waiting for his little sizin' up for a while now. Surprised we didn't cross paths a long time ago, business-wise." He held out a black-gloved hand. "Name's Dr. Wash."

Coop shook the hand. "Wash. Well ain't you the busy fella. Been hearin' your name more and more. Mostly from folks we used to buy or sell from."

"What can I say? Ever since you did the world the favor of punching some holes in that Tusk guy, opportunity has been knockin' nonstop. Gotta get while the gettin's good, am I right?"

"Mostly I'd agree, 'cept in this case where what you've been gettin' is rightly mine."

"Now, Mr. Cooper," Mr. Graham objected. "My business is no more rightly yours than—"

"Shut it, Graham!" Wash snapped. "Me and my business associate are havin' a chat." He turned back to Coop. "They say the customer's always right, but they ain't had to deal with these dopes. Gettin' mouthy while business is gettin' done. Now what was I saying?"

"Somethin' liable to make me want to put a fist in your ribs, if what you said so far is any indication," Coop said.

Wash's heavies each took a step toward Coop. He held his ground.

"Boys, did I tell you to menace the guy? Back off," Wash said. "I been meanin' to talk to you, but you ain't so easy to get ahold of. Me? I got teams all over. To make a livin' in the fug, you got to be spread out. Or at least, you usually do. Seems like you *Wind Breaker* fellas run a pretty lean operation. Helps that you got suppliers for all the usual fug-exclusives, plus all the usual Caldera-exclusives. Must be nice."

"Gets us shot at more than most," Coop said.

"I bet it does. But listen. You must be sick of runnin' all around under the fug, snappin' up all the little nobody dealers like Graham here."

"Now really!" Graham scoffed.

"Luggs, do me a favor and give Graham a reason not to butt in when two men are talkin'."

The shortest of the three grunts turned to the counter and, without much regard for the target, dropped his fist heavily onto some of the merchandise neatly displayed beside the register. He brushed the pulverized sundries from his hand and turned back to observe the conversation.

"You're not liable to keep business, treatin' folks like that," Coop said.

"There's more than one way to keep business. One way's to give good service. Another way's to be the only one *givin'* service. And another way's to make these fellas afraid to find out what happens if they stop payin' up. First one's a pain, so I like to stick to the other two. That's where you come in. How's about I be your middleman? Hmm? With Tusk gone, all the organization at the top is screwy. All of a sudden there's all this slack in the rope, right? It's gonna get taken up. Sooner than either of us expect, I'm guessin'. So either we fight about it, or your crew can give me the goods and my guys can handle distribution. For a cut, you know? You make the same on the sales, and I'll set a markup on my end to make it worth my while."

"No, I don't reckon I'll be makin' a deal with a fella who thinks hirin' some folks to smash a bunch of candies and chaw is a good way to make some money. Cap'n sent me down here to find buyers and deliver goods. That's what I'll do."

Wash tensed a bit. Though his face was hidden, it sounded as though he was speaking with a tight jaw and a sour expression.

"Listen, you half-wit yokel. I *am* a buyer. You play your cards right, and I'm the last buyer you'll ever have to find. This here is the last chance you're gonna get to get in business with me without payin' through the nose. That's the *easy* way. Pass it up and you ain't gonna find a place to sell your stuff anywhere under the fug. That's the hard way. Got that?"

"Last chance?" Coop scratched his neck. "You sure about that?"

"Oh, I'm sure. I don't have the time to waste dealin' with dopes what don't know a good deal when they see it."

Contaminant Six

"Suits me fine. I wasn't lookin' forward to havin' to chat with a weird bird-faced fella and the three grunts it takes to make him worth takin' serious on the regular. I reckon I'll take the hard way. We should do this outside."

"Yes, please!" Mr. Graham yelped.

"*Shut it, Graham,*" Wash barked. "Boys, teach Coop a lesson. Graham, you watch good and close so you can tell folks what happens when Dr. Wash doesn't get his way."

Nikita squealed and bolted from her place within his jacket. As she scrambled out the door, the grunts descended on Coop.

He could have easily gone for his gun, but Coop had been in enough rumbles to know that pulling a gun only gave you the advantage if you were the only one *with* a gun. As poor as his odds were with fists and feet, things would be measurably worse once bullets started flying. Better to keep things in the realm of a barroom brawl. That's where he was most comfortable besides.

The grunts lumbered toward him. They were strong, but wrangling those ungainly bodies made for a slow and ponderous opponent. He gave the nearest grunt a boot to the knee, and the next a shot between the legs. If he'd been able to deliver an elbow to the gut of the third, he probably could have gotten off without so much as a bruise. Alas, long limbs meant long reach, and before he could get the proper force behind the intended body blow, he had a knobby-knuckled mitt wrapped around his face. A moment later he was soaring through the air and smashing through a carefully arranged display of hats and pocket watches.

He slid across the floor and thumped into the far wall. His filter mask was slightly askew, but Coop had been getting a considerable amount of below-the-fug combat experience, so straightening and tightening it had long ago become a reflex. Most of the fight that followed was a blur. No bullets were fired, but quite a bit of improvisational weapon-use was employed using the unfortunate Mr. Graham's inventory. After he'd used an umbrella as a snare, then as a bludgeon, a blow to the chest sent Coop stumbling out the door. He caught his footing and assessed the state of affairs.

"I reckon that's about as much negotiatin' as I can stomach for one day," he wheezed.

Coop's strategic retreat was a swift one. His opponents had wasted their time working his head and body while he'd spent most of his time working the knees. It meant that the pair of thugs interested in chasing him down were doing it with uneasy, hobbling gaits. He easily reached his airship and fired up the turbines.

"Get back here, you idiots!" Wash called from the doorway. "Back to the ship, we'll chase him down."

Coop squinted with half-blurred vision in the direction of Dr. Wash's ship. He was too far away to see it through the fug, but he tugged the image from his memory.

"Too big to be fast enough to catch up. But big enough to have the kind of cannons that'll make this getaway a short one," he reasoned. "I reckon there ain't much time to lose."

He unfastened the mooring ropes, then hauled himself up the second one as the ship started to drift. Halfway up, he rattled his fingers against a pipe that ran along the side of the ship. Nikita bounded out of the alley between two decrepit buildings and sprang to the same mooring rope. The pair climbed to the enclosed gondola. Coop slid into the pilot's seat of the little scout ship. The passenger's seat was loaded with unsold goods, a supplement to the meager cargo capacity of the vessel, so Nikita huddled into his jacket as she always did.

"Heya, darlin'," he said, stroking her with one hand while the other danced across the controls of the ship. "What'd you bring your ol' pal Coop?"

A little trembling hand emerged from his coat, clutching a rounded nut. He grabbed it and held it up to the phlo-light illuminating the compartment.

"Ha. That'll do 'er. That's my girl."

#

"Get in, get in!" Dr. Wash urged from the rope ladder leading up to his substantial vessel.

His three bruised bruisers hobbled their way up the ladder.

"I don't know why I pay you idiots. It was three of you against one of him, and the guy walks away."

"If you wanted him dead, we'd've killed him," Luggs rumbled.

"And if I wanted him dead, I'd've told you to kill him. There's a way we do things, Luggs. Broken bones and black eyes are negotiation. Bullet holes are a declaration of war. And the way you handled negotiation, I *know* you can't handle war."

"Then what are we going to do?"

Dr. Wash thumped up the stairs to the helm, Luggs in tow.

"Get your worthless carcass on the grapplers. I'm going to snag his rigging. Worst case, we reel him in and grab his cargo. Best case, the whole thing goes down and he dies."

"... And that wouldn't be war?" Luggs said.

"Faulty equipment takes folks out all the time. It can happen by accident. Getting shot to pieces, not so much."

"But wouldn't they be mad about us stealing the cargo?"

"I ain't got time to explain the nuances of running a successful black market smugglin' ring. Just be ready to tangle the hook up in the rigging." Dr.

Wash grumbled under his breath. "I don't know where Tusk got his guys, but if he could run this pit, he must've had some good ones. You'd think I'd've run into a couple looking for work…"

The cargo hauler lurched into the sky. Dr. Wash spun the ship's wheel to bring it about and target where he assumed Coop's ship had been moored. The ship began a sluggish, swaying turn. He slapped the wheel to peg the steering to starboard. There was a disquieting rattle, then a startling thud as the heavy wooden control harness dropped from the mechanism and rattled to the ground. He glared through the smoked glass of his mask at the shiny threads of a retention bolt that *should* have been topped with a domed nut. Without it, the ship would be stuck circling until a replacement could be found.

"Forget the grappler," he barked. "Get down to supplies and get something that'll fit this bolt."

Luggs nodded and hobbled into the bowels of the ship.

"Ichabod Cooper, thickest member of the crew. Ain't even the best shot of the crew. The *deckhand. And the pile of trash got a step ahead of me.*"

He listened to the rigging creak and complain at the stresses of the constant full-force turn. Dr. Wash raised his voice to shout at no one in particular.

"This is on you idiots. If you could be trusted to run these trips on your own, I wouldn't have to be out here buttin' heads with the competition."

He leaned heavily against the rail and stared out over the purple-drenched landscape "This ain't over."

Joseph R. Lallo

Chapter 1

Laylow Island was odd by just about any measure. It was small, barely sufficient to support a reasonable-size farm or a meager village. The location could not have been less desirable. More than a day's travel from the mainland of Rim, it would have to be self-sufficient because no one would be likely to run supplies to it. It even managed to be too far from the Calderan trade route to serve as a supply post. It was a hard-to-find, easy-to-forget patch of dirt in an endless sea. It would take a very strange type of person to want to settle down there.

The *Wind Breaker* crew was very strange indeed.

"Nita, darlin'? Did you get a load of this here whatchacallit?" called Lil, the youngest member of the crew.

She was dangling from a rope nearly as thick as her waist, trying her best to get at the bolts of a massive bit of machinery beneath her. Her hair was wild, and her white shirt had soaked up a few pounds of grease, but from the look in her eye, she was still having the time of her life.

"You'll have to do better than 'whatchacallit,' Lil," called Nita, the ship's engineer, from somewhere that wrapped her words in echoes.

"One of them long jobs." Lil coughed a bit. "The ones with the forked ends and pins so it can turn every which way."

"Which is *called*?" Nita prompted.

"You know what the dang thing is, Nita."

Nita emerged from below the deck. She was also smeared with grease, but dressed in a manner much more suitable for heavy-duty engineering. Her work gear included clothes of rugged canvas and leather topped with twin straps of assorted wrenches and a surprisingly utilitarian corset for helping keep the weight off her back.

"If we need to replace something like that, you're not going to be able to go to the trader and ask for a 'whatchacallit.'"

"I ain't gonna be able to ask a trader for *nothin'* on account of the fact that this is the sort of thing the fuggers'd be sellin', and they ain't doin' business with us. So it's a whatchacallit."

"A universal drive shaft," Nita called.

"Now how's a body supposed to remember a name like that?" Lil muttered. She cleared her throat.

"Are you feeling alright?" Nita asked. "You've been coughing a lot."

"This whole ship is dusty as all get out and stinks like the fug. I don't know how you *ain't* coughin'. Anyhow, I been working on getting the universal whatchacallit unstuck. You reckon it's just about ready to come free?"

Nita climbed up a nearby rope and peered over the top. "Have you got the bolts off the retainer on the other end?"

"Yeah."

"Then two more and you should be ready to go."

Lil took a breath and leaned a bit farther out to put her wrench to work. "I was hopin' you'd say there was a mess more bolts I was missin', because these are a bear to get out."

Nita peered about. "Where did you tie the supports?"

"The what now?" Lil asked, still heaving at the wrench.

"The supports. To keep this thing from slamming down once you finish unbolting it?"

"Uh..." She pulled the wrench from the bolt and looked up to the struts over the drive shaft. "You know, I had a feelin' I was forgettin' somethin'."

Nita's eyes goggled. "We've got to get some straps on it before—"

Gravity, always with impeccable timing, chose that moment to reassert its dominance. A drive shaft the size of a small tree trunk and dangling from two half-loosened bolts tore free and dropped. The distance to the damaged decking below was short, but it was more than enough to give the hunk of metal the force it needed to reduce the planking to splinters and continue its merry journey. The whole ship shook with the force of the fall. Lil was jostled from her grip and dropped to the edge of the jagged hole it had left. She started to slide, but Nita grabbed her arm and hauled her up.

Below, alternating splinters and slams told the tale of a piece of machinery punching through deck after deck in the darkness of the empty ship. Light poured in from the bottom of the pit of shattered flooring as the drive shaft plummeted through the hull and sent up a plume of sand from the beach below. Bits of wood and other debris rained down on top of it.

Lil looked sheepishly up from the spectacle. "To be fair, I only forgot one step. And at least we won't have to tote it down."

#

Gunner squinted into the distance, eyeing the rising plume of sand beneath the half-dismantled ship over the island's harbor.

"What was that?" called a voice below.

"Something fell from the bottom of the dreadnought." He pulled a spyglass from his belt and took a closer look. "Correction, something fell *through* the bottom of the dreadnought."

"Is anyone hurt?"

"It doesn't seem so." He swept his gaze up along the ship until he spotted Nita and Lil at the railing, each tapping their heads in the all-clear sign. "No, they are fine."

He turned back to his own task. A freshly installed platform dominated the rocky outcrop he had selected to install his pet project. The bulk of the device was wrapped in canvas tarpaulin, keeping the precise nature of the mechanism secret from anyone who didn't know who Gunner was and where his interests lay. Those who *did* know Gunner's proclivities would have been concerned by the fact that it was larger than a garden shed and smelled of fresh machine oil.

"A hand, my dear?" his partner called.

Gunner pocketed his spyglass and snapped open a parasol that had been set beside a hatch in the platform. He held it in place, then reached down through the hatch to take a dainty hand that was held aloft. With deceiving ease, he lifted Dr. Samantha Prist from the darkness. She sat on the edge of the hatch and took the parasol from him. The pair was dressed almost identically, with sooty leather smocks, goggles perched on their foreheads, and thick rubber gloves protecting their hands. The matching outfits underscored the otherwise staggering differences between them. Prist was a fug woman, quite pale and, to the casual observer, quite delicate. Her hair was in a neat bun, her outfit was in better repair, and overall she looked as though she should be supervising an operation such as this rather than crawling through its workings. Gunner was a human and, as his appellation would suggest, worked as the gunner of an airship. This had left both his gear and his anatomy in a decidedly less complete and pristine state.

"How does it look down there?" Gunner asked.

"The new blend of lubricant is working well. I do wish we had a bit more trith to use on matching bearing surfaces so we wouldn't have to worry quite so much about abrasive wear on the thrust bearings. Sand is *bound* to get into the mechanism."

"We've got to be economical with the trith, Samantha. We've got more of it than anyone outside of Caldera, but it still doesn't grow on trees."

"Understood, but you're just substituting materials cost for maintenance cost."

"I suspect the captain will approve. Particularly since he's able to delegate maintenance."

"Well then. I don't imagine there's much more for me to do."

"There's not much left for me either. I would prefer to make it easier to prepare for use. Automatic, to some degree, but that will require Nita's help, I suspect, and she's got her hands full with more-important projects."

"In that case, perhaps we can shift our attentions to your laboratory. I am quite keen on testing out the new beam splitter on the ray caster."

"The captain is less keen on it," Gunner said.

"We will take every precaution. When have we ever skimped on safety?"

A distant crackle drew their attention to the beach again. Gunner raised his spyglass again. Prist fetched a pair that looked a bit like opera glasses. Nita and Lil were dashing along the deck. They both hopped over the railing and hung from the mooring rope. A rolling, thunder-like grind and splintering became steadily louder until several tons of steam pipe came pouring out of the bottom of the ship.

"Dang it!" Lil's voice echoed across the landscape.

"I see the dismantling of the dreadnought is proceeding apace," Prist said.

Something akin to the ring of a church bell pealed across the island.

"That'll be the captain," Gunner said. "I'm sure he'll have many of the same questions I have regarding the ladies and their specific tactics for disassembly."

Prist angled her parasol to block the sun a bit better and fetched a set of smoked-glass lenses from her bag to perch upon her nose.

"It never ceases to amaze me how that man can make a bell sound angry," she remarked.

#

A few minutes later, Captain McCulloch West stood before his crew. Despite the fact that he was standing in a freshly built, quite cozy, and decidedly nonairborne cabin, he was dressed in the same aging military uniform he favored while at the helm. His jaw was clenched tight around a thin, sweet-smelling cigar, and his beard was rustling in the sea breeze through the open window. His ex-wife Butch, who served the roles of cook and medic while they were in the air, was busy working some lard into pie crust behind him. Wink, the ship's inspector, peered down from a rafter overhead, nibbling on a bit of dried fruit. It was a downright wholesome and idyllic scene, but his body language alone was enough to make it clear the business at hand wasn't going to be pleasant.

He marched back and forth in front of the assembled members of his crew. Lil, Nita, and Gunner each received their share of his smoldering gaze. Only Dr. Prist, who technically was not under his command, escaped the nonverbal tongue lashing he was dishing out. Finally, he stopped in front of Lil.

"You reckon you know why I called you in here?" he asked.

"I'm thinkin' it might be on account of the big heap of bits and pieces that fell out of the dreadnought," Lil said.

"Right you are." He kept his eyes focused on Lil but addressed the others in turn. "Ms. Graus, how come we're takin' the dreadnought apart?"

"Because it is too expensive to keep it running, and it would serve us better as a source of spare parts to build and maintain other ships," Nita said.

"And, Gunner, what's the status of the *Wind Breaker*?"

"Stripped down to the framework and the steam system," Gunner said. "Envelope drained, all hardpoints free of weapons. Fully decommissioned."

"Nita, *why* is the *Wind Breaker* decommissioned?"

"It was a patchwork of repairs, and its performance was suffering for it. We decided a full refit would be the best course of action," she said.

"Gunner, what do we *call* ourselves?"

"The *Wind Breaker* crew," he said.

"Lil, do you reckon as the *Wind Breaker* crew, we might want to do the best we can to get the *Wind Breaker* back in the air right quick?"

"Yes, Cap'n," she said.

"And do you reckon we're liable to *get* the *Wind Breaker* back in the air if you keep harvesting parts with a sledgehammer?"

"Will all due respect, Captain," Nita began, "she wasn't using—"

"If you're givin' me the respect I'm due, Ms. Graus, you're waiting until I'm through talkin' before you speak your piece. Now, *Lil*, you tell me what happened."

"We're supposed to put retainer straps on things before we unhook 'em. And I forgot."

The captain pointed to a conspicuous bit of fresh planking on the cabin wall. "And what happened there, Lil?"

"A valve came shootin' through the wall."

"And why?"

She coughed a bit. "I forgot to check it was tight before I put the spurs to the boiler."

"And what happened to the north mooring tower?"

Lil paused. She leaned aside to Nita. "What happened to the north mooring tower again?"

"I am asking *you*, Lil," Captain Mack barked.

"I forget. But seein' as how we're talkin' about all that other stuff I did, probably it busted on account of me forgettin' to do somethin'."

Mack took a breath and marched toward the window, eyes on the skeleton of the *Wind Breaker*.

"You know what makes for a good crew? A good crew is a mess of people who, when you tell 'em what to do, they get it done. Take Gunner for instance. Damn fine officer, burnt-off eyebrows and blown-off fingers notwithstanding. I point him at somethin' that needs holes blown in it, and he blows holes in it. Glinda here? Ain't no finer hand ever gripped the handle of a knife, whether she's slicin' up a roast or cuttin' a bullet out of a thigh. It ain't much of a stretch to say Nita here is the best engineer ever to take to the skies over Rim, and it'd be true even if she *wasn't* one of the only ones. Even Wink is a damn sight better of an inspector than any other ship could claim to have. And then there's you and Coop. Best deckhands I ever had. I can count on one hand the number of times I heard 'can't' or 'won't' out of you. I give an order, and you get it done."

He turned toward her. "Leastways, you used to. Somethin' goin' on with that head of yours I need to know about?"

"No, Cap'n!" she said.

He eyed her intensely. She coughed again. Nita pulled a handkerchief from her tool sash and handed it to her. Mack crossed his arms and paced back and forth through the room.

"I don't think it's too much of a secret to say me and Butch have been thinkin' about trading out our sea legs for a nice, easy bit of island life. That's what this here island is for. But it *also* ain't no secret that it would be a damn shame to take this crew out of the air just because the cap'n was gettin' worn out. You lot have got loads more livin' to get done before you put your feet up. You're fine workers, and together you're finer still. Funny thing is, when it gets right down to it, a cap'n's pretty near the least important part of a crew. Ain't no job that really needs doin' gets done by the cap'n himself. Not on a proper ship with a proper crew. So why am I here?"

He turned back to them. "I'm here to make sure the crew's doin' what it *needs* to do. I'm here to hand out orders, make sure they get followed, and to point the ship in the direction that serves us all best. And I can't rightly hang up my hat if I don't think you can keep things aloft on your own."

Lil stifled another cough and smirked. "That mean if I keep botchin' this and that, you'll keep bein' the cap'n? Because that's as good a reason as any to dump some pipes out of the bottom of a ship."

He fixed her in an uncomfortably intense stare. "You see me smilin', Lil?"

"No, Cap'n."

"We ain't at the supposin' and wonderin' part no more. Me and Butch are pretty near done. It ain't a matter of if we're handin' off the reins, it's when, and to who." He pointed a finger out the window to the dry-docked *Wind Breaker*. "When that girl flies again, it's with a new cap'n. And I ain't sendin' her out with a crew that I don't trust to do her right. No matter who I pick, we'll be needin' a new cap'n, a new medic, and a new cook. Until we do some recruitin', that'll mean a lean crew. A crew that ain't got *room* for someone forgettin' her orders or her procedures."

Contaminant Six

Lil produced a particularly unpleasant-sounding hack and held the borrowed handkerchief to her mouth.

"Or pertendin' she ain't sick when she is. Now, if there's somethin' keepin' you from doing what needs doin', Lil, you say so. And if there *ain't...*"

Again a long, raking cough shook the deckhand. She took the cloth away from her mouth and blinked teary eyes. "I reckon... I reckon maybe... I ain't quite right, Cap'n..."

Lil started to waver. Nita propped her up just as her legs gave out entirely.

"Lil? Lil!" Mack barked, as though he could snap her out of it through sheer force of authority. "Get her on a cot. *Get her on a cot!* Glinda, get your bags. Dr. Prist, you too."

#

If circumstances had been different, Nita would have been filled with pride and wonder as her fellow crewmembers went to work. It never ceased to amaze her just how thoroughly and efficiently they could shrug off fear and uncertainty to fulfill the orders Mack delivered. Until this moment, she'd believed she could do the same. From her time in the steamworks in Caldera all the way through to the endless misadventures she'd had with the crew, she'd gathered herself and set aside fear and dismay until the job was done. But in this moment, she couldn't. The instant she felt Lil's weight lean upon her, the moment she saw the light fade from her eyes and her body slump to unconsciousness, Nita's mind had been a blur.

She moved as if in a dream, shuffling along with Lil's arm across her shoulder, helping Gunner deliver her to a cot in the captain's room. Voices were muddy and distant, like she was underwater. Her thoughts circled in tight loops of fear and helplessness.

"Nita..." came a buzzing, indecipherable voice.

Lil was unwell. It wasn't the first time. They led a far from isolated life. Colds, flus, chills, and fevers tended to sweep through the crew from time to time. She'd seen Lil terribly sick more than once. But this was different. Her unfocused, unseeing eyes were fixed on the handkerchief she'd loaned to Lil.

"Nita!"

Hands on her shoulders shook her. She blinked and looked up to find Mack shaking her.

"Yes, Captain," she said.

"You been side by side with her day and night. Did you see anything like this comin'?"

"Aside from her forgetfulness, she hasn't lost a step. She was coughing a bit earlier, but the dreadnought is dusty, we both were."

Nita turned. Butch was bent over Lil on one side of the cot, dabbing cold water on her head. Prist was on the other side, inspecting her mouth and nose.

"Is she breathing?" Nita called.

"Hyperventilating. It's like she's suffocating," Prist said.

Butch wrangled a stethoscope and pressed it to Lil's chest.

"Lungs are clear," Prist assessed. "She didn't sear her lungs did she? Get a breath of steam?"

"The boilers on the dreadnought have been cold since it was delivered."

"No acid? Chemicals?"

"Nothing! We've been working so close, if something had happened to her, it would have happened to me too."

"Her lips are turning blue. We need to work fast if we are going to save her," Prist said.

Nita's eyes darted about, her mind slipping back into the wholly unfamiliar mire of helplessness and panic. She hadn't felt this way since her mother had been suffering from her own illness, but at least then there had been *time*.

She looked to the handkerchief. As if she were seeing it for the first time, she noticed the flecks of purple staining it.

"Dr. Prist! Look. This happened once before, after she'd been in the fug for too long."

The fug woman looked to the offered handkerchief. Her eyes darted, inspiration flashing across her expression. "Does anyone have any ichor? Quickly!" she said.

Both Gunner and Nita rummaged about. Nita was the first to reveal the vial of faintly luminous amber-colored liquid. The stuff had become an essential part of the crew's equipment, as it could push back the fug and offer a life-vessel of sorts if they were to be submerged in the toxic stuff without a filter mask.

Prist took it. "Captain West, give me your matches. And I want everyone out of the room."

"What's going on?"

"Lil's system is not responding properly, and I may know the cause, but I don't have time to explain. Out! And shut the doors and windows."

Mack handed over the matches. The crew hurried out the door. All but Nita.

"I said go!" Prist demanded.

"If you need ichor and a match, I know what you're planning." The engineer pulled a mask from her sash and strapped it in place. She took Lil's

16

hand in hers. "I'm not leaving until I know if it works."

"I won't waste time arguing." Prist popped the cork from the vial. "Hold it under her nose."

"Is this going to work?"

Prist struck a match. "We shall soon find out."

She held the match beneath the vial. In her shaky grip, it nearly singed Nita's fingers. As soon as the flame licked at the glass, bright purple fumes began to curl from the vial. The gasping deckhand drew in a lungful of the fumes. Nita's grip tightened around hers. She'd coped with what even a whiff of the fug could do. It was a horrid, stinging chemical sensation that seared her lungs. For days she'd been at the very fringe of the fug, breathing thin wisps of the stuff, barely able to endure it. Even with the mask in place, Nita's eyes teared as the fug stung them. Taking a deep breath of the stuff should have sent the weakened woman into fits of coughing and choking. Instead, she took a second breath. Then a third. Her breathing slowed. She calmed, no longer unconscious and on the verge of suffocation. Now she seemed to be slipping into something akin to sleep.

Prist shook the match out before it could burn her fingers. The purple fumes slowed. In their absence, Lil's chest fluttered a bit in half-suppressed coughing, but the moment passed and she was calm again.

Dr. Prist was a chemist, not a medical doctor, but for all their faults, the fug folk taught their professors well. She had a rudimentary knowledge of physiology and thus enough experience to know a stable patient from a critical one.

Nita looked up to her. "What does this mean?"

"I think you know what it means," Prist said, sympathy in her voice. "If you insist on staying here, keep the ichor handy. If she starts to hyperventilate, gentle heat, beneath the nostrils. And only until she calms. I will return shortly. There are some texts I've loaned to Gunner that may be of some help."

Prist stood and slipped out the door. Voices rose, demanding updates. Demanding answers. They wanted to know why they had to leave, why they smelled fug. As before, the voices seemed muted and distant. There was only Nita and Lil. She held Lil's hand tight.

"We'll figure this out, Lil. I promise."

Joseph R. Lallo

Chapter 2

Lil's wits sluggishly returned to her. Her eyelids felt like sandbags, too heavy to lift. The room felt uncomfortably warm. She shifted, weakly pawing at the sheet drawn over her.

"She's waking up," said Prist.

A hand was gripping hers. Somehow, even with the fog of unconsciousness only *just* parting, she knew it was Nita. The fingers around hers squeezed tighter. She returned the gesture and wrestled her eyes open. The room was dim. Night had fallen, and the only light came from a flickering oil lantern.

"What happened?" she said thickly.

Her mouth had an unpleasant acrid taste, like she'd been sucking on a filthy coin. The room smelled awful, like medicine, and like something else that was familiar but she couldn't quite identify. As her thoughts cleared, she realized a handful of things that were very, very wrong. The smell clinging to her nostrils was fug. There was a thin haze of it in the room. It wasn't nearly the thick rolling clouds that made most of Rim uninhabitable to surface folk, but it was enough that she should have been gagging. Nita and Butch were in the room with her, and each of them wore a fug mask and a worried expression. Prist and Lil lacked similar protection. Prist, at least, didn't need it.

"Wh-what's going on? Where's my mask?" Lil said, trying to sit up and grope for the missing bit of apparatus.

Nita eased her back to the bed. "You don't need it. In fact, you shouldn't have it. Not right now."

Prist nodded. "Open the window. Let's see if she's had enough for now."

Butch unfastened the shutters on one side of the room, then the other. A cool night breeze swept through the room, clearing it swiftly of the residue of fug. Lil took a breath of fresh air. It should have been pleasant, revitalizing. Instead it felt oddly lacking, like she'd blown her breath into a bag and breathed it back in.

Nita took off her mask. "How do you feel?"

"I feel like a mess of sand got dumped on my head. What's this all about? How come there's fug floatin' about on Laylow Island?"

"You coughed up something purple and fainted."

"… I don't remember that."

"That's likely to become more of a problem for you, but we'll get into that shortly," Prist said. "If you recall, during your time in Tusk's clutches you were subjected to the fug in fairly high concentrations for quite a while. You coughed up some purple that day as well."

"You sayin' I've had some of that gunk cloggin' up my pipes since then?"

"In a manner of speaking. You'll also recall, I hope, that you and Nita were tortured while in Skykeep, once again exposed to near-toxic levels of fug for extended periods of time."

"Don't remind me," she muttered. "All this reminiscin' and whatnot got a reason, Doc?"

"By now you're well aware that fug folk, and every other creature beneath the fug, either began as or was begot from something that began as a creature of the surface. Exposure to fug usually causes death. But in some, it causes a change."

"You better not be sayin' what I think you're sayin'…"

"I would dearly like to tell you that what's happened today is temporary or isolated, but when a whiff of the fug steadied you rather than worsened your condition, it confirmed it. You are changing, Lil."

Lil sat up, shrugging off Nita's attempts to keep her on her back. "No. That don't make no kind of sense. You're up here just fine, breathin' the air all the rest of us are. You don't *need* fug, so why should I? This is somethin' different. It's gotta be."

"Lil, we know very little about the mechanism of the change. Of the several thousand fug folk who live today, the vast majority were changed during the Calamity. It happened all at once for us. As you might imagine, with people dying by the cityful, we weren't precisely in the position to study the transition. And fewer than five out of every one hundred people who reach the critical level of fug toxicity survive. Combined with the knowledge of that toxicity and the requisite safety steps taken by humans, there has yet to be a thoroughly documented case of a human transitioning to a fug person since then. This is actually a tremendous learning opportunity."

"I ain't too pleased about bein' your opportunity, tremendous or not."

"I realize that. Now, you've been through a great deal. If you would prefer I give you a moment before we discuss the current matter any further…"

"No. If you're afraid of heights, you take a long look over the edge. Let me know what's in store."

"As you wish." Prist flipped open a small textbook to a marked page.

"This is not an area of expertise for me. At least, fug poisoning in humans and the resulting transition are not. But I did focus on the effects of the complex chemical compounds related to ichor. In the hours you were unconscious, I have drawn up a prognosis."

"I ain't askin' for a prognosis. I'm askin' what's liable to happen to me."

"… Yes, that is what a prognosis is."

"Well say it regular."

"I shall endeavor to do so. Bear in mind this is all speculation, but it is at least based on the firmest scientific foundation I can produce. You are now in what I would call the early stages of the transition. This should last not less than three days and not longer than three weeks. During this stage, all current symptoms will become more acute."

"Now what do you mean by *that*?"

"Episodes of shortness of breath will become more frequent and will need to be treated with doses of fug. Within a week, you will likely be unable to breathe properly without some concentration of fug in the air."

"I ain't likin' this prognosis so far."

"When you have reached the point that you *must* breathe fug, you will have entered what I call midstage transition. This, at least, we know a bit more about. Here you will see a marked increase in physiological changes. Your skin will lighten, your hair may darken. Depending on the nature of your final development, you will follow the anatomical template of a standard or 'grunt' fug person and become either leaner or taller. This development will bring with it some combination of advanced strength and increased mental acuity, with strength more prominent in grunts and mental acuity more prominent otherwise. You will likely not regain the ability to breathe outside the fug again safely until the physical transition is complete. That could take as long as two years."

Lil's expression became sterner. "You're tellin' me if this goes the way you think it's gonna go, I'll be stuck in the fug for *years*?"

"I… Lil, if it goes the way I *think* it is going to go, you'll be stuck in the fug forever."

"Oh, if you think I'm movin' into Fugtown just because of this nonsense, you don't know Lil Cooper."

"Therein lies the issue. It won't *be* Lil Cooper living in the fug."

Lil glanced aside to Nita as her friend's grip tightened more. The engineer's face had the distinctive flavor of strength that suggested if Nita let it falter for even a moment, Lil would see the grief beneath it. Prist continued.

"As I said, *all* of your symptoms will become more acute. That means memory loss as well. It is a near universal fact that the first generation fug folk, the ones created rather than born, lost their memories in the process. Nearly everyone retains basic aspects of education: language, learned skills, etc. To my knowledge only a small fraction of grunts have lost any intellectual capacity of that sort. But I've heard of no more than a handful of instances in our entire history where a fug person maintained any but the most basic anecdotal memories. All of the experiences will be gone. The first generation of fuggers chose to take new names, to quite literally bury the past."

Lil was silent for a few moments, the words trickling through the cracks of her mind like molasses. When she finally spoke, it was with unnerving calm.

"You could have saved a whole lot of breath by telling me I was going to die."

"No, no! That you've made it this far makes it a near certainty that you're one of the lucky ones who will *survive* the change."

"There's a Lil now, and in a couple weeks there won't be. That ain't what I'd call surviving." She kicked her legs off the side of the bed and stood.

"Easy, Lil. You're still recovering."

"I ain't recovering, I'm dyin'. And a Cooper doesn't take that sort of thing lyin' down. Now we done beat everything we came up against so far. We took down the man who's had his mitts around the throat of Rim since before any of us were alive. There was a cure for what was ailin' Mrs. Graus down there in the fug, so there's bound to be a dang cure for this. You just tell us what you know about it, and we'll *find* that cure, right?"

Prist straightened up. "Miss Cooper, there is no *cure* because the process by which my people were created is not a disease. I resent the implication that my kind are a consequence rather than an alternative."

Lil winced. "Doc, if there's still a me after this is said and done, I'll go through and even us up on anything I said that wasn't proper, but if what you said is true, then I ain't got the time or notion to be pickin' and choosin' words all careful-like."

Dr. Prist sniffed. "Fair enough. Now, as it stands there is no treatment. Certainly not an established one. A surface person transitioning to a fug person these days is a vanishingly rare occurrence and not one that we find particularly undesirable. It simply isn't an area that we've pursued. However, having observed the symptoms of the earliest stages of the transition, I have insight into the process that others who may have studied the process in passing lacked."

She flipped through the pages of her book, jumping from bookmark to bookmark. "I have done my best to understand ichor as fully as possible. Until you provided me with the opportunity to work with the Well Diggers—if I may depict those events rather charitably—I'd never had the opportunity to access the well at South Pyre. In the absence of hands-on experience, I devoured all of the literature available. As the backup for the head chemist, I was tested relentlessly on even the minutiae. It so happens I brought this book with me to aid in the formulation of a lubricant for the project Gunner and I are working on, and thus—"

"I ain't got much time, Doc," Lil said impatiently.

Prist tightened her lips somewhat and placed her finger on the page. "'Ichor: Impurities and Contaminants, Chapter 7: Severe Adverse Reactions. Incident seventy-three. A worker became ill following his lunch break. He became short of breath, gasping despite no obvious obstructions to his airways. Violent coughing produced copious amounts of indigo discharge. He collapsed and slipped from the catwalk over the primary outlet of the ichor source. Workers transported him to the nearest emergency medical station. With the exception of a brief subsidence of the hyperventilation in the minutes prior to medical treatment, the afflicted worker asphyxiated shortly thereafter.'"

"That's a whole lot of talkin' that didn't amount to much, near as I can figure, Doc," Lil said.

"A fug worker had exactly the same symptoms as you," Nita explained.

"Precisely," Prist said. "Specifically, he had the symptoms shortly after handling a known component of South Pyre ichor. We call it Contaminant Six. It is a known irritant. As I recall, the answer marked as correct on the examination was 'death due to acute allergic reaction.' But in light of the extreme similarity between his reaction and your own, there is the *chance* that his exposure to Contaminant Six returned him to a state that was vulnerable to the fug. This is further suggested by the brief recovery. If we assume the medical station was near to the main opening of the ichor well, it would be one of the few places in the fug that is kept *free* of the fug, as the ichor would push it back."

"Then we just gotta get a mess of that stuff," Lil said. "What are we waiting for?!"

"It isn't as simple as that," Prist said.

"It didn't seem all that simple what with me not knowin' what that stuff was or where to get it," Lil said.

"As it happens, those are among the lesser difficulties. Contaminant Six is present in South Pyre ichor. If nowhere else, it will be present in some quantity there. And I am quite familiar with the substance, at least insofar as the limited literature dealing with it. The issues are thus. If Contaminant Six itself was the cure, this wouldn't be an isolated incident. There would have been dozens, if not hundreds of exposures over the years. Not just one. Something else must have happened to activate it. We'll need to know everything there is to know about that incident if we hope to re-create its effects. And we need to be prepared for a cold reality. It may not work, or worse yet, it may work precisely how I expect it to."

"That's bad?" Lil said.

"If it is, effectively, a counter-reactant to the fug and its effect on physiology, then it will do its work with a similar success rate. The lottery you won to survive the transition to fug person shall need to be played again if you hope to survive the reversion."

"You say that like it ain't worth doin' because of that."

"For all we know, your chance of surviving the treatment could be one in twenty or worse. The only thing making it *that* likely is the relatively incomplete transition, meaning the reversion will be less severe."

"The way I figure it, you're tellin' me my choices are have a chance at stickin' around or have no chance of stickin' around. Ain't exactly a tough one for me."

"We don't know if it will work at all. If you *do* lose your memory, there's certainly no guarantee this will restore it. We don't know to what degree it will restore your body either. You might be left in some in-between state, perhaps appearing as one but functioning as another. You could end up with anything from immunity to the fug to even greater sensitivity to it. The risks!"

"Look, it'll work or it won't. That makes it fifty-fifty, far as I'm concerned."

A genuine smirk came to Prist's face. "Ignorance and optimism are a potent combination."

Lil jabbed her chest with her thumb. "It's what got the Coopers this far. Now we still jawin', or are we gonna go get what needs gettin'?"

#

Nita, Lil, and Prist took the situation to Mack and Gunner. From the moment a potential treatment was suggested, Mack's attitude matched Lil's. If there was a chance, then they would chase it to the end of the world and back. The moment there was a direction to point his prow, Mack snapped into action as though this was a mission he'd had to plan a thousand times before.

"First thing's first. If Lil here's going to need fug to keep kickin', then we're getting her to Rim right quick. That means the *Wind Breaker* ain't involved. The old girl's weeks from bein' anything that'll get a proper crew anywhere they need goin'. Gunner? What we got that's not a death trap at present?"

"I believe the *Rattletrap* is ready. It's that runabout Lil, Nita, Coop, and I pieced together out of one of the lifeboats from the dreadnought. It's

24

fully fueled and in proper repair," he said.

"There was the gig from the dreadnought as well, though I wouldn't trust it for more than two people at the range we need," Nita said.

"About how many people can we trust in the runabout?"

"Fueled for the Rim trip, assuming we're headed for Lock, I—"

"Aim for Keystone. It's a step closer to Ichor Well if we need to head that far, and most things worth knowing pass through that town at one time or another. Best chance we'll get to learn where we can learn what needs learnin'."

"I'd say four. Five if one of them is Wink."

"Get it loaded up. All the burn-slow you need. And grab the fléchette guns earmarked for the *Wind Breaker* refit to mount on the hardpoints."

"On it," Gunner said, hurrying off.

"Nita, it'll be you, Lil, Gunner, Prist, and Wink," Mack instructed.

"Captain, that will leave you and Butch alone," Nita said.

"Ain't neither of us on the verge of endin' up dead or empty-headed. Don't worry about us."

"At least keep Wink. Without an inspector you—"

"You're going to be airborne, you're going to need an inspector to get messages in and out. We'll be fine holdin' down the fort. The gig'll do us fine if we need to get movin'. Now *you* get movin'. I want you in Keystone in two days, and I want a message sent out to Coop, givin' him the rundown of what's been done and what's *to* be done. The boy deserves to know his sister's in a bad way. Him runnin' all about above and below the fug, he's liable to have a better handle on where the best info is at."

"What should I do, Cap'n?" Lil said.

"Keep hold of your marbles. And try not to get yourself killed. Seems that's about as much as you should have to worry about. Nita, on the other hand, this young lady is your responsibility. She's all our responsibility, but yours more than anyone."

"Captain, if you'd given me any task *but* keeping Lil safe, I'd have disobeyed your orders at my first opportunity," Nita said.

"Sometimes bein' a cap'n's about giving the orders you know'll get followed. Now get movin'. All of you. There's work to be done, and I'll be needin' both of my deckhands."

Lil saluted. "Aye, Cap'n!"

Joseph R. Lallo

Chapter 3

The *Rattletrap* sputtered its way through the sky, moving far faster than its designers had ever intended. The jagged mountainous coastline was in the distance to the east, but they were still far enough away that if the ship failed as spectacularly as it felt like it might, they were not very likely to be found and rescued.

Lil's head was tilted aside, her ear angled to try to track down the source of the rhythmic squeak she'd never heard an airship make before.

"This thing sounds just about ready to fly apart, darlin'. You sure you got all the bolts and valves where they belong?" Lil asked.

"I assure you, this is more airworthy now than it was when it was first built," Nita said.

"Then why's it so noisy?"

Gunner gave the wheel a gentle spin. "Because it is a lifeboat. They built it to keep people from going down with a ship. It was only ever supposed to make one trip, from the sky to the ground. We're pushing it harder and farther than it was ever intended to go."

"Guy, dearest, as accurate as your assessment may be, I'd really rather you'd kept it to yourself," Prist said, the tension dripping from her voice. "I'm less accustomed to entrusting my life to jury-rigged perversions of engineering than you and your associates."

"How's about I just climb up there and put a wrench to that strut?" Lil suggested, hopping up to grab the rigging.

"Lil, you get down here this instant," Nita snapped like an overprotective mother. She grabbed Lil by the belt and yanked her down. "What is wrong with you?"

"Ain't nothin' I ain't done before," Lil said.

"You've also never been at risk of suddenly running short of breath before."

"Maybe so, but I been at risk of being shot up by wailers and such," Lil said, hands on her hips. "I ain't dead yet, and I had a fresh whiff of fug not ten minutes ago. This here's still a ship, and I'm still a deckhand."

"And I'm still your friend, who, by the way, has been ordered by the captain to keep an eye on you."

"Who's stoppin' you? I ain't climbin' so high you can't keep an eye on me. Besides, Cap'n Mack ain't here, is he? Gunner's the skipper this time around. Gunner, permission to climb up and see if I can't quiet this ship down a tad?"

"Denied," Gunner said. "If you need an assignment, head below decks and see if you can even out the fuel mix. The gauges are running a bit high for my tastes."

"Can do."

"Nita, go with her," Gunner said.

"*I ain't made of eggshells,*" Lil barked.

She angrily stomped down the ladder to the cramped belly of the little vessel. Nita hopped down to join her. Between the food, fuel, and supplies stuffed into every available section of the runabout's interior, accessing the boiler was no simple task. It was no trouble at all for Lil, who had made an art of slipping through gaps and cramming herself into openings that should have been a challenge for anyone with a skeleton. Nita was no slouch at navigating tight spaces either, but her jangling gear and somewhat more substantial frame slowed her progress a bit. When she slipped into the charitably named boiler "room" in the belly of the ship, Lil was already tending to the firebox.

"Gunner was right," she called over her shoulder. "Dang thing's stuffed full of coals. Whoever loaded 'er up nearly choked 'er. Nothing to it but to cut down on the air flow until it burns down a bit. Who loaded this thing up, anyways?"

"You did, Lil. Half an hour ago."

Lil turned and gave Nita a sharp look. It faded when she saw that Nita's expression wasn't one of mischief but of concern.

"You ain't jokin', are you?"

"No."

Lil slammed the door shut. "This ain't right, Nita. Last week everything was grand. Got a nice island, safe and sound with solid ground beneath my feet for the first time in forever. Not just visitin' either, but a place I can call mine. Or at least *ours*. I'm helpin' get the old ship gussied up better than she's ever been. The cap'n was mutterin' about retirin', but he's been chewin' that one over for ages and ain't hung up his hat yet. Now I'm sittin' here wondering if I even said all this before, waitin' for the next coughin' fit and hopin' the fuggers got a cure for bein' fuggers."

She thumped her fist down on a bag of coal, sending a plume of black soot into the air. "And I didn't even *do* nothin'," she growled. "Used to be if I was going to be sore in the mornin', it was because I did somethin' to deserve it. I ain't had a dunk in the fug since that whole Tusk mess, and then, out of nowhere, I can't breathe without the stuff. It ain't fair. It ain't right."

28

"Life doesn't always play by the rules we wish it would."

Lil shook her head. "You remember back when we were visitin' Caldera? Your brother and sister dressed me up all fancy and got a crowd in to watch me swing around on rigging for no good reason."

"I remember."

"That was a good one. It'll be a shame to lose that one. Or how 'bout when we were locked up in Skykeep and I got all drenched and we—"

Nita took her hand. "Lil, let's not talk about the past."

"Well why not? That's the bit that's slippin' away."

"We are going to get you fixed up. Every memory you have will be there waiting for you when we're through. I know it. And even if I'm wrong and some of them fade, I'll spend every night telling you stories of the times you've forgotten. It will be glorious."

"You were there for some of the best times, but you weren't there for it all."

"Then Coop will fill in the rest."

"Oof. We better get me fixed up proper, then. I don't want to have to rely on Coop's version of how things went."

Lil smiled, but it was a brittle mask. She gripped Nita's hand a little tighter.

"You reckon... you reckon things'll be okay? If the fug gets its teeth into me deep enough that there ain't no me no more?"

"We won't let that happen."

"But if it *does*, you reckon there'd still be a place for me on the *Wind Breaker*? You reckon that other lady'd even want it?"

Nita gazed into Lil's eyes. "Lil, did I ever tell you the story of 'The Monkey and the Twisted Vase'?"

"I don't think so, but then, that don't mean much these days."

"Well then, let me tell it to you, the way my mother told it to me..."

#

There was once a monkey who gazed through the window of a glassblower's shop. Every day he would long to possess the thing of beauty proudly displayed there. Beside a twisted vase was a curtain like nothing the beast had ever seen. Every morning the sunlight fell upon it in a magnificent way, transformed into a glorious rainbow of colors as it fell on the curtain. Each day he would watch the sun rise and see the colors. And each time he saw those colors, he desired them all the more.

"I want that beauty for myself," the monkey said longingly. "But the glassblower will notice if it is gone, and he will chase me."

The monkey thought and thought. Finally, his little mind found the answer. He sneaked to the market and stole a curtain from a shopkeeper. That night he slipped into the glassblower's shop and took the curtain he'd seen take on such wondrous colors and replaced it with the new one.

"This curtain looks just the same as the old. The glassblower will not notice what I've done until I am far away."

Delighted at his cleverness, he dashed away and waited for the morning sun to fall upon the curtain. To his dismay, when the morning sun came, the curtain remained as mundane and drab as the one he had replaced it with. Yet somehow the new curtain had earned the colors he so desired.

"So it was not the curtain," he grumbled. "Then what could it be?"

He racked his brain and it came to him. The vase was filled with water. It must be the water that produced the rainbow. So the next night he sneaked inside again and poured the precious water into a bowl and replaced it. But sure enough, the next day when the sun came, though he saw a shimmer and a ripple, it was nothing compared to the rainbow he longed for.

"Inside the vase is water, and the water is not beauty. Outside of that water is glass, and the glass is not beauty. The curtain is just cloth, and the cloth is not beauty. The light that falls upon the glass is the same light that falls upon the tree. It is not the beauty either. It must be magic, a secret the glassblower keeps for himself."

#

When Nita was through, Lil blinked at her.

"That it?" she said.

"That's it."

"That ain't the best story I ever heard. For one, I got questions," Lil said. "That you're tellin' me that story means it's got somethin' to do with me. I ain't the monkey, am I?"

"No."

"Good, because near as I can figure, the moral of that story is 'there once was a dumb monkey.'"

"And just why do you think the monkey is dumb?"

"Because obviously the vase was the pretty thing."

"Oh? Even though it was emptied out and filled back up?"

"Well sure, because… oh, I see what you're sayin'." She punched Nita lightly on the shoulder. "You're sayin' it don't matter what's goin' on in this head of mine, you'll still think I'm pretty."

"What I'm saying is it doesn't matter what's going on in that head of yours, you'll still be *you*. Yes, your experiences, your memories, they're a part of you. But they're a *part* of you. So is your hair. Cut that off and you're still you. I didn't fall in love with your hair, I fell in love with you. I didn't fall in love with your memories, I fell in love with you. Not your skin, not your body, not anything the fug will try to change. *You*. And if the absolute worst happens, and all of the water is dumped out, I'll still be there, helping to fill it all back up. And when the sun rises, we'll both see the beautiful light."

Lil smirked. This time the mirth was genuine. "You could've just said that instead of all this jabber about monkeys and such-like."

"What can I say? I'm a sucker for a good story."

#

Gunner tapped a gauge. "The pressure's looking better," he said with a raised voice. "Keystone isn't far off. How does it sound, Wink? Are we near enough to send a message?"

The perpetually sour face of their one-eyed inspector glared at him from the rigging. His spidery fingers tapped out a reply.

Not close enough. Soon.

"Send the message to Coop just as soon as you can."

This one knows…

"And be sure to use the codes. Enough people know about the tapped messages, we don't want anyone eavesdropping."

This one knows!

Prist leaned heavily on the railing and took her place beside Gunner. "It is impressive how effectively Wink is able to communicate seething annoyance with nothing more than the *way* in which he taps. One would think that tapping would be a communication method devoid of inflection."

"Much as he's able to spot the tiniest flaws in the ship with just one eye, Wink continues to impress with his skilled use of limited faculties. He and Nikita are even getting better about using things besides past tense. Albeit in a hit-and-miss sort of way."

"Indeed." Prist wrung her hands a bit. "In that regard, I've noticed you have been rather taciturn during this trip."

"While I typically bristle at the implication that I am only useful when pitted against problems that I can shoot at, I must say I would feel far more comfortable if there was an enemy I could set my sights on. I'm out of my element."

"Having observed the sort of problems you've been forced to solve, your element is a particularly volatile one."

"We do what we have to do to keep the crew together, alive, fed, and happy."

"Noble."

"Not always, but thank you for the benefit of the doubt."

"Happy…" Prist mused. "Guy, forgive me if I tread upon an unduly sensitive topic, but I think it is best addressed sooner than later."

"If this is about Coop, I assure you, whatever it is, it is a matter of ignorance, not malice."

31

"No, no. I fully understand Coop is blessed with the innocence of a child, but unfortunately the tact as well. No, the subject is happiness."

"Are you unhappy?"

"Please, let me finish. Naturally, as we pursue this mission, we shall operate upon the assumption that we shall succeed, and Lil will be treated to recover."

"There would be no point in trying if we didn't believe we could succeed."

"Right, naturally. But I need to know. If we fail, what happens?"

"We won't."

"Guy, there are circumstances beyond our control at play. We can do everything precisely right and still not find ourselves with a treatment. A treatment may not exist. Or there may not be time to create one that can be safely applied. What happens if Lil becomes a fug person?"

He remained silent, hands tight on the ship's wheel.

"Guy."

"I don't have an answer for you, Samantha. You are asking me what I would do if someone I have served beside for years was suddenly a stranger. Someone with an unfamiliar face and no memory of our history. I suppose I would try to remind her of who she was."

"And if she doesn't know? If the memories are gone, never to return?"

"I don't know, and I don't intend to find out. I won't dwell on the worst-case scenario."

"Worst-case scenario? How many times have you and the rest of the crew nearly died? How many times have you willingly risked your lives? I've personally witnessed it too many times. But I have *never* seen the sort of trepidation that I'm seeing now. Her life is not on the line. What *is* on the line is someone like you becoming someone like me."

"This is about losing someone. I don't care how we lose her. She's equally lost." He looked to her. "I have very little love for the fug folk, present company excluded. But that has nothing to do with what they are and everything to do with the number of years I've had to live with their boots on my throat. If you mean to ask if, in our failure, I will hate Lil for what she has become, I will not. I will mourn her for what we lost."

"Yes, well… forgive the insinuation," Prist said.

"No forgiveness required. Your judgment would in virtually any other place be perfectly sound. I suspect the *Wind Breaker* crew is unique in that opinion of the fug folk."

"Which raises another issue. If Lil *does* lose herself, if she becomes a fug person…"

32

"Her past as a member of the *Wind Breaker* crew will be a tremendous liability."

"Indeed. One would hope she would still see her way to joining the crew. If not, it would be best to encourage her to sever ties entirely. There can be no between."

"Nor will there be. Because the cure... the *treatment* will succeed."

Wink rattled out a message above them. *This one hears the others. This one sent the message.*

"Excellent. Then the wheels are turning. I'm sorry that Coop has to hear about his sister this way. But not nearly as sorry as I am for the first people he decides to take it out on."

#

Coop kicked open the door of a small shack, startling the fug man seated at the table within.

"Good heavens, Coop! A bit of warning!" yelped the man as Coop approached.

The fug person looked a good deal too-well-dressed to be waiting in some forgotten shack a dozen miles east of the farthest reaches of Fugtown. An impeccable black suit, marred only by the general disarray caused by a lengthy trip, contrasted with a clean-shaven face of deathly white.

"Digger," Coop said by way of greeting, "Do you mind?"

The deckhand-turned-salesman tugged a capped vial of ichor from his pocket, not waiting for a reply from his associate before opening it and setting it on the table. The moment the ichor was exposed, the fug was pushed to the edges of the room, providing him with a pocket of fresh air in the sea of toxic stuff. Streamers and plumes curled from his clothes as he shook them out, and more of it whisked from his unruly hair as he tousled it. When the bulk of the residue was cleared, he unfastened his mask and dropped it on the table.

"You ever worn one of them, Digger?" he asked.

"Once or twice as a disguise."

"Really starts to kick up a bear of a headache after a bit."

He sat in the only other chair at the table and kicked his feet up. With the mask removed, Digger was treated to an unobscured view of his associate's face.

"You look much the worse for wear."

"Yeah. Bumped into some of that bird-lookin' fella's boys. Bumped into 'em real hard. Let me tell you, if I don't see another one of them fellas ever again, it'll be too soon. Poachin' our buyers. Cutthroat as anything. Better in a rumble than I'd like, too."

"That is unfortunate. I take it then that you failed to sell your share of the inventory?"

"What sort of a fella you take me for, Digger? Of course I got it sold. Just had to convince the next place they ought to stock up."

"You didn't... threaten them, did you?"

"Not as such. Might've suggested somethin' bad was bound to happen soon, but that ain't the same thing. One way or another, somethin' bad's *always* happenin' soon. So keepin' some extra stock for a rainy day? That's just good sense."

He reached into his pocket and tossed down a sack of coins. "A couple hundred victors. That's your cut of the last sale. There's a mess more in the ship, but I ain't puttin' that mask on again until I get good and drunk. You got my bottle?"

Digger picked up the sack of coins and estimated the contents. "I'm not certain I agree with your tactics, but I can't argue with your results. I'd say you earned a bit of a tipple." He took out a bottle from a crate beneath the table and handed it over.

"We'll start with a tipple and keep goin' until I got a better reason for my head to hurt as much as it does," Coop said. "How'd your bit go?"

"Considering I'm attempting to sell goods in Fugtown, a place where they consider the product of Ichor Well to be contraband, I've had to do my dealings with a bit more care. The good news is... well, perhaps 'good' isn't the proper word for it, but the *opportune* news is that things have only been getting worse with the supply lines between South Pyre and the rest of the fug as they are. I don't know how the death of one man can lead to such a breakdown of order, but the shipments are getting pillaged along the main trade routes with almost the same frequency as they had been out over the sea."

"We made our livin' fightin' off raiders and such-like. Well past time you folk had to do the same."

"It has created enough of a demand in the larger cities that even people in Fugtown are beginning to consider finding alternate sources to fill their needs." Digger sifted through the money and began making marks in his books. "I feel a bit fiendish profiting so heavily from lawlessness, but then, I suppose the Well Diggers have never technically operated within the bounds of law."

"When folks makin' the laws are more interested in workin' out what to do about you than what to do for you, them laws ain't for you anyways, and you may as well pay them no mind."

"That is revolutionary thinking."

"You know me." Coop opened the bottle with his teeth and spat the cap on the table. "I'm the thinkin' sort. You got anything to snack on? Not so much for me as for the little lady here? I'm fresh out."

Digger found a canister of nuts and uncovered it. Nikita hopped from Coop's jacket and scampered over to snatch a few to nibble.

Contaminant Six

"So what comes next?" Coop said. "And if you don't say 'you take some time off up in the mountains,' I'm liable to get real sore."

"It just so happens that's precisely what comes next. I've got to settle some accounts here, then deliver some orders back to Ichor Well so that we can be ready to supply the next batch. Your job is done until we are able to generate a surplus again."

"That's what I want to hear. I sold out of everything I brung from our last Caldera trip too. Time to set back, take a load off, and maybe take a gander if there ain't somethin' I can bring back to surprise Lita with next time we get to the islands. Seems like it's been forever since I got a letter out to her. Wouldn't want her to forget about me."

Nikita stopped nibbling a nut and cocked an ear. She reached out. *Message from the crew.*

She started to drum out the message. The system of taps was a tricky thing to follow, but spending every minute of every day with Nikita had given Coop a considerable amount of practice in deciphering it. He may well have been the crew's foremost expert on the language at this point. Digger resorted to jotting the message down word by word rather than trying to shoulder the dual task of decoding and comprehending it simultaneously. Coop just listened. And he didn't like what he heard.

Lil is sick. Fug poisoning. Won't die. Might turn into a fugger. Might lose her memory. May be able to stop it. Need information. Contaminant Six. Component of South Pyre ichor. Could make medicine. Need to find supply of it. Need to find research about it. Time is limited.

The message continued, indicating the timing and location of where the crew would meet up to collaborate, but Coop's mind was already clicking with an almost mechanical certainty.

"This is terrible..." Digger said as he looked over the words he'd traced out.

Coop sealed the bottle of booze. "You know what that number six stuff is?"

"No, I'm afraid I've never heard of it. My role in production is more on the logistical side."

"The doc's on the ship sayin' we need to find it, so she ain't sure where it is or she'd've said. So that means it's on me to go find some."

He stood and strapped on his mask. The liquor was slipped into one pocket, the ichor was capped and placed in another. Nikita grabbed a handful of nuts and burrowed into his coat.

"Where are you going to go?"

"Going to go find some of that stuff and what to do with it."

"But you don't know the first thing about where to find it."

"I don't know the first thing about darn near anything. Don't need to. Just need to know who knows the first thing about it and shake it out of 'em."

"And you know someone who knows about it?"

"I ain't never heard of the stuff, and I ain't never found none of it. So it must be pretty rare. If it's pretty rare, it's worth a mess of money, on account of that's how it works. If it's worth money, someone's liable to be sellin' it. And if it ain't me and it ain't you, that leaves one more fella on the short list."

"Who?"

"The bird-lookin' fella, Dr. Wash."

"But you just got through saying you never want to deal with him again!"

"My sister's sick. There ain't much in life that's about what I want and what I don't. But when it comes to family, want loses to need every day of the dang week. I ain't lettin' Lil down. If that means knockin' on the door of the devil and wringin' his neck to get what I need, then I'd best dress for warm weather, because that's just what I'll do. Comes with bein' a big brother. Nikita, when we get in the ship, you get up on your roost and send word I'm havin' a word with Wash and his boys. This close to Keystone, I reckon there'll be someone headin' back in the right direction to get the message to 'em."

#

The *Rattletrap* wheezed its way into port at Keystone. Despite Nita's tweaking and tinkering, it was none too happy about going long distances. With Gunner at the controls, they eased between two mooring towers at the north end of town and awaited the ground crew.

"Come on, now, gentlemen! We are on a schedule," Gunner shouted at the pair of men pacing toward the ship.

"I always knew that Coop and Lil were excellent deckhands," Nita said. "But you don't truly appreciate their particular style of mooring until you have to wait for the traditional way."

Lil crossed her arms and huffed. "If you'd let a girl do her job, we'd still be out of here in half the time."

"You're not well, Lil," Nita said.

"I know I ain't. And even while I ain't well, I reckon I could have both them mooring lines tied up before these fellas could do the first one."

"We'll just use the time to plan things out," Nita said.

"A wise decision," Gunner said. "Samantha and I shall pay a visit to the pubs."

"Like heck you will," Lil said. "I ain't lettin' you do the fun bit. Me and Nita'll hit the pubs. I could use a pint or two besides."

"Fine. Then we will go to the market district instead. We could use a resupply anyway," Gunner said.

36

"That's more like it," Lil said. "... Now what're we after again?"

"We are looking for anyone who has any insight into Contaminant Six, or anyone who might know where to find someone who does," Dr. Prist said.

"You reckon we ought to hit the whatchacallit? The cable car?" Lil asked.

The crew turned to the fug-facing cliff, where a towering strut supporting the huge cable for the funicular that had given Nita her first introduction to the fug dominated the section of the city.

"We may as well," Gunner said. "We'll meet up there when we're through. If there's anyone from down below waiting for a ride, they would have fresher information than most."

"Let's get to it, then." Lil clapped. "What're we waiting for?"

"The ground crew," Dr. Prist reminded her.

"Still?! That's all the patience I got. Time me. Bet I get mine done before theirs!"

"Lil, no! What did I just say?" Nita barked.

Lil nimbly hopped over the side with a mischievous grin on her face. In moments she was on the ground, hauling back the rope to tie it up.

Nita shook her head. "Saving Lil from herself is going to be a very trying experience," she grumbled.

Joseph R. Lallo

Chapter 4

The wheels of Dr. Wash's personal elevator squeaked above him. The cables jangled and groaned. There was a time when he'd done most of his business in a sturdy little shack at the base of the elevators, but that time was long gone. As was the time when he did most of his work on the east coast, near Circa. He just couldn't risk that sort of exposure these days. It was a funny thing. Right around the time someone was becoming wealthy enough to afford bodyguards, that was the time they needed to start hiring them. His heavies were crammed into the elevator with him. Each of them was nursing some manner of bruise or sprain from their clash with Coop. Wash himself had gotten off lightly, but the pain in his side served as a reminder that he was going to have to invest in some better security if he was going to continue to try expanding his territory into the nebulously defined slice of the fug supplied by the *Wind Breaker*.

They reached their stop, and the doors slid open halfway. Dr. Wash angrily kicked them until they finished opening.

"This whole racket is falling apart," he snapped, marching out onto the catwalk that led to his office. "The next time we get a quiet minute, I want one of you guys to get me the name of someone good with a wrench to straighten all this up. We're pulling in triple what we were making a month ago, but this whole hunk of the elevator network feels like it's about to slide off the mountain! It's no way to run a business."

He approached the office built into the mountainside. Ever since the Calamity happened and humanity took to the skies, the slopes, and the peaks to escape the fug, the art of building a relatively safe home or place of business onto a sheer cliff had been developing nicely. Nowadays anyone with a saw, a hammer, and a length of rope could build a city wherever they could find a place that spent most of its time free of the fug. In Dr. Wash's case, even that wasn't necessary. He'd built his new personal office just high enough along the mountainside to be lost in the fug from those looking up from below, and thus *well* out of sight from those looking down from above. The only people who could find him were particularly well-trusted business associates and particularly well-informed enemies. The latter would need to approach via elevator. That alone was enough to scare them off. No one wanted to be dangling seventy feet above the ground in a box controlled by the man you wanted to kill.

"You, out here, you two, in there," he said to his guards. "I've got some paperwork to do and then we'll call it a night."

Dr. Wash twisted a knob to illuminate his phlo-light and dropped a bundle of hastily written dispatches on the desk. Between balancing the ledgers, rooting out people who were stealing from him, and sifting through intercepted messages to find extortion-worthy information, the bulk of Wash's work was ink on paper. He snapped open a switchblade and cut the twine holding the messages. The wind whistled as he did his work. His shack swayed a bit in the breeze, a product of the "if it bends it won't break" style of engineering that had spawned it. All of it was a lullaby of sorts, the familiar and comfortable sounds of work being done. The business of intercepting messages had gotten easier once he discovered he could snatch them right out of the air with the help of an inspector, then harder as more and more people started using codes to protect their messages, then easier again once he got the services of a code cracker. The nice thing about codes being a relatively recent addition was the fact that the people making codes were also relatively new, and thus relatively poor at their jobs.

He marked down this and filed that. He was hungry, but the mask complicated meal times so he tried to avoid eating more than once a day. He could hear the sputter of distant turbines, but they matched up with schedules he'd subconsciously memorized. Everything was as it should be.

Until it wasn't.

A new set of turbines added their whine to the low-level din. These were out of place. Wash looked up and tilted his head, waiting for them to pass. They *should* be going up, or coming down. They weren't. Either this was someone badly off course, or it was someone who Dr. Wash was going to make certain was going to have a very bad day.

"Do we have eyes on the idiot headin' this way?" Wash called.

"It's up above us. Fug's too thick to see it," one of his men called back.

"Up above…" Wash said. "There's nothin' up there but mountain and elevator landings. And that's way too close to be someone dockin' up at the top."

"I don't know what to tell you, boss," the grunt outside said.

"Morons…" he grumbled, slamming down his pen and stomping to the door.

He pulled it open and marched out onto the catwalk. The wind was cold and fairly constant, and now that it didn't have to filter through the walls of the shack, he could tell the sound of the unseen airship was most certainly coming from somewhere directly above them. If he squinted through the lenses of his mask, he could convince himself that he could see the vague outline of the ship in the purple haze above.

"There's no place to moor a ship up there," he repeated to himself, as though reality simply needed a reminder.

"You ain't never had to take cover in a storm real quick," shouted a voice from above.

Dr. Wash and his men turned to the source of the voice. A lanky figure slid down the elevator cable and dropped onto the roof of the shack.

"Cooper?" Dr. Wash said. "I'd've figured you'd at least keep your distance until the swelling went down, ya nut."

Coop hopped down onto the catwalk, where he was immediately menaced by the bodyguards. He had something gleaming and metallic in each hand, but after the initial flare of fear that he might be armed, the baffling truth became apparent.

"Get him against the railing, boys," Dr. Wash said.

His grunts did as they were told. Though it probably would have only taken one of them to wrangle Coop, their assorted injuries from the previous clash persuaded them to present a united front.

"These boys must *really* have scrambled what little brains are rollin' around in that head of yours. I thought sure you'd bring a gun next time. Or at least a knife. What're you gonna do with... what do you even have?"

"Carabiners. Six of 'em," Coop said simply.

"What exactly do you think you're going to do with those?"

"Back yourselves up and act proper or you're fixin' to find out," Coop said. "I got questions and I reckon you're the fella to ask."

"Oh, I'm the answer man, but you come to *my* turf, drop in unannounced, and expect *me* to—"

Coop didn't bother waiting for the end of Wash's attempted intimidation. In a blur of motion, he snapped three carabiners onto the railing behind him. The grunts jockeyed for position to be the one to get their mitts around Coop and extract some payback for the prior clash. It was enough confusion for Coop to click a pair of carabiners to two of their belts and, with an impressive bit of manipulated leverage, send both of the beastly guards over the side. They reached the ends of the ropes suddenly enough to bend the metal railing. At seeing two of his coworkers seemingly fall to certain death, the third grunt gave Coop a more-than-sufficient chance to clip the last two carabiners in place. A few angry kicks and a well-placed knee sent the remaining guard pitching over to dangle with the others from a now badly damaged railing. The whole clash took a few seconds, and had left Coop and Dr. Wash alone on the catwalk.

"Listen up," Coop said, grabbing a handful of Dr. Wash's shirt and marching him into the office. "You got your feet set on the ground, maybe then you're on your turf. But you start hoistin' yourself up into the sky, and you're doin' business where *my* bread is buttered. Now I could've just left your boys smeared on the ground, but I'm a decent fella and them's just workin' men tryin' to earn a livin'. But you're the boss, and I'm fresh out of patience for bosses."

He pulled Wash a little closer. "More important, leastways as far as you're concerned, is I'm fresh out of carabiners, too."

"Here's the problem with you tryin' to intimidate me, hotshot. It doesn't matter what you want to know, chances are, if I don't already know it, I'm the guy who knows how to find out. You can't scare me, because you're not dumb enough to kill me."

Coop pivoted, turning Dr. Wash toward the doorway and rushing him up to the sagging railing. He leaned him *far* over the rail, such that his feet were scrabbling to stay on the catwalk.

"Don't ever tell a Cooper what he ain't dumb enough to do. Ain't nothin' in this world I ain't dumb enough to do. I'm the fella what pulled the trigger on Tusk."

The statement was far more intimidating than it had any right to be.

"You can't kill me! You'll never get the answers if you kill me."

"Then start talkin', because if you decide you ain't gonna answer, you bein' a stain on the ground is a better reason than just you bein' stubborn."

"*You haven't even asked me yet!*" Wash yelped.

"… Fair enough." Coop pulled him back to his feet. "I'll make it short because I got a feelin' them boys ain't too happy about danglin' down there. My sister Lil's sick. Got too much fug in her. I got it on good authority there might be away around it, but we're going to need somethin' called… somethin' called…"

A rattling tap came from inside his jacket.

"Con-tam-in-ant Six. And everything worth knowin' about it, so's we can cook up some medicine. Now, I ain't never heard of the stuff, and since we grabbed plenty of books and medicine and whatnot out of the warehouse in Fugtown, it's gotta be hard to find."

"I see… I see… Do we know anything about it?"

"Just that it probably's got somethin' to do with South Pyre."

"That'd be a good reason for no one to know about it. Ain't much that goes on in that place that makes it past the walls."

"So you gonna be of any use, or am I gonna go lookin' for answers on my own and leave you to see to your boys?"

"It'll take some time. And it won't be cheap."

"Money ain't no issue. And I'm meetin' the rest of the crew in Lock just as soon as I can get there. We ain't waitin' long, and if we don't hear from you one way or the other, I'm liable to be awful sore about it."

"If you want my help, you gotta be more specific than 'we ain't waitin' long.'"

"I ain't the one holdin' the stopwatch on this one. Lil's sick, and she ain't got much time. The time runs out on her, and I can blame it on you, I ain't gonna need no more carabiners for my next visit. So you better get what you need and be waitin' for us with it. We clear?"

"Yeah, yeah. I got it," Wash muttered.

"Good. Let's get your boys back up here, then," Coop said.

He reached back and pulled a coil of rope from across his back. With a few deft twists he put a loop on each end. One found its way to a solid anchor point inside the shack. The other flopped over the edge.

As the rope grew taut, Coop hauled himself back onto the roof of the shack.

"Where are you going?" Wash called.

"I ain't stickin' around long enough to be outnumbered again. And I left the ship runnin' up there with no one at the wheel."

"You... but... a strong breeze could have sent it smashin' into the wall! And what did you even moor it to?"

"I only needed to stick around long enough for a yes or a no. No sense moorin' it."

He climbed up the elevator cable. Shortly after, a long, grating grind signaled a graceless turn away from the cliffside as Coop departed. Wash tightened his fists in fury as he listened to the idiot who had managed to get the better of him departing. The first of his men finally tumbled to the safe side of the railing and started to hoist up the others.

"Fat lot of good you idiots did me," Wash barked. He looked back to the sky. "My mom always told me that drunks, children, and fools had their own personal angels keeping an eye on them. Cooper and that whole damn crew pretty much prove Mom knew what she was talkin' about."

He turned back to them and clapped. "Come on, come on. Up, up. I gotta dig up some info on whatever Contaminant Six is before that nut comes back and finds some way to take my whole operation down with climbing gear. And get word out to what's his face. The mining guy. Tell him I don't care if it's all set up. We're movin' this whole operation inside. It ain't just a warehouse no more. It'll be a pain gettin' in and out, but it seems folks havin' a hard time gettin' in is gonna be more important for a while."

#

Nita and Lil made their way along a plank street in Lock ahead of the rest of the crew. Their visit to Keystone had been a good idea, but beyond

Joseph R. Lallo

contacting a handful of potentially useful people all at once, it hadn't done them much good. The speed and scope of the *Wind Breaker*'s exploits meant that in any given crowd of people, there were half a dozen different attitudes toward the crew. Some people treated them with an air of celebrity and awe. Others were beginning to buy into the claims that they were somehow in the pocket of the fug folk and little more than spies and traitors. Nita, despite having been a part of the crew for quite some time now, continued to draw a fair bit of attention simply for existing, as she remained the only Calderan most of these people had ever met in person. They got as much information as they were able to get and moved on to the friendlier harbor of Lock. There, at least, the general opinion of the group was *much* more positive. So much so that they chose to convene at the lesser of the town's two pubs, the better to have a chance at some privacy.

Nita and Lil pushed through the door of the pub.

"Back in town, are you?" said the bartender. He peered out the door behind them and asked, "You're not... expecting any trouble, are you?"

"We're never expecting trouble. It just sort of follows us around," Lil said, a splash of pride in her voice.

"We're going to need a table for five," Gunner said, holding the door for Prist.

"I'll see if I can find you a spot," the bartender said, eyeing up the otherwise empty establishment. "Listen, money's been tight this month and I *really* can't afford there to be a gunfight or a brawl or anything."

"Do we appear as though we are on the cusp of fisticuffs, sir?" Prist said, daintily taking a seat.

"Last time Mack and Butch came through, they shut me down for a couple days, and when I came back, I found half the place shot up and two different shades of blood on the floor. There comes a point when enough patched-up bullet holes will keep even the most desperate drunk from coming here for a drink."

"We're just here to meet up with Coop and have a chat," Nita said. "However, if Lil has a flare-up, you're liable to have the stink of fug coming out of your bathroom for a bit."

The bartender gave her a long, defeated look. "Unless that's some sort of slang I haven't heard before, you're going to have to explain that."

"What a lady does in the head is her own business," Lil said. "Now you got the customers, so ain't no sense mopin' about money. Set me and my friends up with some ale and a couple of shots of that good stuff we stocked you up with. And a bowl of nuts for the little fella."

"Little fella?" he said.

On cue, Wink bounded through the still-open door and clambered up

44

to the center of the round table they had selected. The bartender gave him an overtly hostile stare. Wink returned the glare with remarkable effectiveness.

"You know what those things have been doing, don't you? You've heard what they're for, right?" the bartender said.

"They're for inspectin'," Lil said. "Seein' how that's what they're called, that shouldn't be too much of a surprise."

"They've been *spying* on us. For the fuggers," the bartender said.

"Word's gettin' around on that, is it?" Lil said.

"If it is any consolation, it wasn't strictly obvious to most of us beneath the fug," Prist said. "At least, not to all of us."

The bartender shot her a glance. His expression flickered with the complex combination of shame, embarrassment, and concern that comes from thinking bad thoughts about a group that you've just recalled has a representative in earshot. As he grappled with the internal struggle of determining if he'd said anything out of turn, and whether or not he should care, he directed his attention more solidly toward Lil.

"Point is, what those little ears hear, the folks at the base of this mountain talk about."

"You're in Lock. This entire city is on the bad side of the fug folk," Gunner said. "And Wink is hardly the filthiest vermin you've poured a drink for over the years."

"Not to mention, there ain't but two aye-ayes in the whole world that can keep a secret, and we got 'em both. Now make with the nuts," Lil demanded. She scooped her hand into her pocket and threw down pair of silver coins. "That ought to cover it all. This one's on me. No sense savin' my money."

They all took their places at the table. Wink cocked his ears and listened intently to the tapping and rattling of other inspectors in the ships flying overhead, silent to all but him. The bartender fetched a glass and began wiping it out with an old rag, eyes fixed on the aye-aye.

"It's rather unfortunate that people are becoming more aware of the inspectors," Gunner said. "True as it may be that they helped the fug folk keep the leash nice and tight on people like us, they also serve some very important purposes."

"Rapid communication, for instance," Prist agreed.

"And actual inspection," Nita added.

"Plus they're cute as all get-out," Lil said. "Even if the one we got spends most of his time lookin' at ya like he caught ya with one of his daughters."

"I've heard ships are beginning to abandon their inspectors or trying to outright kill them," Prist said. "Horrid."

45

Wink rattled the table with his opinion on the subject. *Inspectors did what they were told. Crews that hurt inspectors deserved to crash.*

When spirited, Wink tended to forget the more nuanced grasp of the language he'd been picking up.

"Hah! That's tellin' 'em, Wink."

"Most of them *will* crash, too. It isn't as though people up here have gotten any better at maintaining their own ships. Outside of this town, anyway. Trying to get rid of inspectors is going to do more harm than good in the long run."

"I reckon it'd do folks a lot more good to strike a deal with their inspectors like we did. It don't take much to get one to come to his senses. Just some macaroons and a scratch between the ears," Lil said.

"Lil? Is that Lil Cooper?" shouted a voice from outside.

The door swung open, and a fat, well-dressed man with a waxed mustache and worn-but-fancy clothes stepped inside. "I thought I heard you talking in here. My lord, it's been forever, hasn't it? Forever and a half, even. Where you been?" the man said, slapping her heavily on the back.

"Hey, you ol' rascal you!" Lil said, hopping to her feet. "What you been up to?"

"Oh, this and that, this and that. I tell you what, that brother of yours is raising royal hell down there in the fug. Since you left I've been hearing about him getting in fights so much it's hard to tell if it's a new one or just the last one with a couple more lies mixed in for color." He slapped her back again. "He needs his sister to keep him in line, I tell you what. His sister or his captain. Where *is* ol' Mack anyway? I didn't see the *Wind Breaker* in dock, or I'd have come looking for you."

"He's doin' secret cap'n stuff, and it ain't none of your never mind."

"Sure, sure. It's a captain's prerogative to keep to himself. The only door on a ship that locks, half the time. But listen, in case you haven't heard, Coop's pretty well got half the fug buttoned up as far as who they're buying phlogiston and burn-slow from. Coal too, though heaven knows where he's getting the stuff. Feels kind of good to be getting some money back out of the fug after all we've tossed into it. Even if it isn't *me* who's getting it."

The man delivered a final back-slap to Lil. "I should be running along. You folks have your own business and I've got mine. Tell Coop I said hi, will you?"

"Ha! Will do, will do."

The man hustled out the door and shut it behind him. Lil waved vigorously as he left, then leaned aside. "Do we know that fella?" she asked.

"Lil, he's our main buyer here in Lock," Nita said quietly. "You've been doing business with him since before I joined the crew."

Lil blinked and stared at the door. "He felt familiar, but I couldn't place him. May as well have been a fella I saw in a dream." She shut her eyes. "It's gettin' worse."

"We'll figure it out, Lil."

"We better light a fire under us, or the figurin' is only liable to help out the next girl." She raised her voice. "Hey, barkeep! Set us up with a mess of them meat pies, would you? And boil up some coffee. We got plannin' to do."

Wink's ears flicked a few times. He turned to Nita and drummed on the table. *Nine p.m. at Old West Magisterberg City Hall. Coop found help.*

"I knew Coop wouldn't let us down!" Nita said.

Coop said to bring lots of guns, Wink added.

"Ooh!" Lil said eagerly, snatching up the ale that was set on the table. "Must've found somebody good. Been a while since we had to make a deal with our guns out."

Joseph R. Lallo

Chapter 5

Coop marched back and forth in the abandoned town hall of a city in the fug. It had been called West Magisterberg. These days people called it Old West Magisterberg, if only because the surface folk had written off anything under the fug once the Calamity happened. It was a misnomer for any number of reasons. For one, there was no *New* West Magisterberg, so it was hardly fitting to call this one old. It really wasn't suitable to give it any name at all, as the fug folk had found little worth using in the place, so it had fallen into over a century of disrepair as the landscape slowly reclaimed it. Most of the buildings were decrepit and overgrown with the strange pale moss that tended to accumulate in the fug, given enough time. The city hall was in slightly better condition, if only because its stone walls meant the only thing left to rot away were the doors and rafters. During his time running about in the fug, making deals and unloading goods, Coop had made it something of a home base. The place was unremarkable enough to keep anything he kept here safe out of simple obscurity, but distinctive enough that he could spot the sturdy stone bell tower of city hall from as far away as the fug would allow him to see. It even served as a decent mooring point.

Of course, now that he'd invited Dr. Wash here, that was over. But there was no shortage of other forgotten towns to use for the same purpose, and there were far more pressing concerns than where he could stash his spare booze, ammo, and books of "fashion."

Coop stopped where the bell had shattered the floor when, however many decades ago, its supports had given way. He leaned back on the heavy hunk of brass and gazed up along the shaft. Nikita clambered out of his jacket and perched upon the broken yolk of the bell. Coop adjusted his filter mask to burn off some nervous energy.

"What do we think, Nikita? We been stood up?"

The little inspector shook her head. She tapped her finger against the bell, producing a satisfying tinkle as she spelled out her message. *Four ships moved. Two came close. One closer. Close enough for you to heard soon.*

"Nikita, we been through this. If somethin's fixin' to happen, you gotta use a different word. Ain't no one gonna take you serious if you ain't speakin' good and proper." He tipped his head, angling his ear up along the shaft. "But

49

I reckon you were right. I hear a ship comin'."

That was… that is the man with the bird face, she said.

"Figures Wash'd show up first," Coop muttered. "Why don't you get yourself up someplace high and keep an eye on him? When you've gotta pitch a fella's boys over a railing to get him to listen, he's liable to be sore the next time you talk to him."

Nikita bounded from the bell and up along the wall, where her pale brown fur blended nicely with the moss in the dim corner of the shaft.

Coop stepped to the doorway. Wash's ship suited a man who made his fortune selling things he shouldn't in a place that wanted him dead. The thing looked like it was designed by someone completely unwilling to make compromises. A huge gondola, the better to store cargo, and the oversized envelope it needed to stay aloft had the dense, stiff look of something layered with two or three too many bolts of canvas in a vain attempt to shrug off attacks. Every spare section of railing had a fléchette gun bolted to it, and slung under the belly of the ship was a strange-looking cannon with an abnormally long barrel. It was the ship-mounted equivalent of a sniper rifle, likely enough to one-shot anything not built specifically for combat at well beyond the range of visibility one could expect below the fug.

All that capacity and armor came at a price. The thing was *ponderous.* Even now, rather than attempting to moor at the tower as Coop's speedy craft had, this thing was using anchors to drag four deep furrows into the field to the east of the city. It had probably been trying to stop itself for the last two minutes. It didn't finish until its front left anchor splintered through the mushy wood of what had once been a schoolhouse.

Rope ladders slapped to the ground. Six grunts climbed down.

"We're up to a half dozen. Fella's startin' to take me serious," Coop observed. He cracked his knuckles and waited for the significantly smaller figure of Dr. Wash to slide down the ladder. "Ain't too neighborly of you to bring all this muscle to a friendly chat," Coop said.

"You and me got two very different ideas of what's friendly, Cooper," Dr. Wash called. "Besides, last I counted, your crew was you, your sister, that Calderan broad, your senile old captain, your four-fingered gunner, and the bulldog who cooks your meals. I figured one grunt per, plus me to make sure I got the numbers on my side."

"You better check your figures," Coop said. "For starters, Gunner's got seven fingers, and if you think your fellas are worth half of what the *Wind Breaker* crew is worth, you ain't got your scales set right."

"Considering they ain't *here* right now, I think my numbers stack up just fine. We gettin' started with the chat now, or are we waitin' until someone with half a brain shows up?"

Contaminant Six

"Why, you got someone else comin' on your end?"

Dr. Wash's black lenses stared blankly at Coop. "Don't try to be clever, Cooper. You'll hurt yourself."

A new set of turbines churned up the fug to the west. Coop and Wash turned to watch the *Rattletrap* carrying the rest of his crew slide into view. He smiled as he saw his sister on the deck grab the mooring rope and eye up a likely tree to wrap it around. She hopped up onto the railing, but a moment before she could dive over the edge in the acrobatic display that had become commonplace for the Coopers and suicide for most others who attempted it, Nita grabbed her and pulled her back.

Coop frowned behind his filter mask. If Nita wasn't letting Lil do her thing, this was as serious as they'd implied in their message.

"That ain't the *Wind Breaker*," Wash said. "Guess it's true that the crew's starting to come apart, huh?"

"Where'd you hear a dang-fool thing like that?" Coop snapped, eagerly latching on to the statement to direct his uncertainty and anger rather than dwelling upon what he'd just seen.

He took a step forward. Wash took a step back, and all six of his men advanced, closing ranks in front of him.

"Easy there, tiger," Dr. Wash said. "Where I hear this or that is my business, literally. It don't matter who says what to me, what matters is if it can be trusted. That borrowed bucket of a ship up there says I had a good source, so you'd better be wearing a smile under that mask, because good info is what you're after."

The *Rattletrap* was moored between two trees in a decidedly more mundane manner, and the crew climbed down the ladder. Dr. Wash stepped up to Coop.

"Well, well, well. Since you're so good at figures, maybe you could check my math on this one. That's one, two, three, four people stepping off that ship. And one's a fugger lady who you *know* isn't going to put up her dukes if things get messy, so that leaves three. Plus you leaves four. And there's seven of us. You like those numbers now?"

"Yeah," Coop said. "I reckon that just about makes us even."

He turned his back to Wash and his men and trotted toward the approaching crew. As he got closer, his pace quickened to a sprint. Lil dashed toward him, and the two collided in a hug that lifted her into a spin.

"Now what's this I hear about you gettin' sick? I head off for one little trip and you come down with a case of the fugs?" Coop said.

"Don't act like you don't know that if this'd happened to you, you'd've been dead already. You get a cold and you act like you're liable to keel over. One good lungful of the fug and you'd be toes-up."

The joviality left his expression as he dropped her to the ground and looked her over. "You're lookin' off, Lil."

"Feelin' off. Pert near half my life is startin' to feel like it was durin' a bender. All blurry and spotty." She huffed and coughed. "Can't seem to get a good clean breath either."

"She isn't in any danger of dying," Prist assured him. "But the swifter we look into a treatment, the more likely she'll be able to safely recover, both physically and mentally."

Coop turned to Wash. "You and your boys inside, then. And none of this banterin' and sizin' each other up. Clock's tickin' and I ain't havin' my sister forget her favorite meal because you wanted to make a point of how tough you are."

#

The group gathered inside a room that had likely last been used over a hundred years ago for city council meetings. Most of the furniture had been spared the worst of the rot, so they had gathered on either side of a conference table. Coop pulled a small vial from his jacket and set it down in the center. A twist of the cap revealed ichor, which pushed the fug back enough to leave the group free of the fug. One by one they removed their masks. Everyone but Dr. Wash, that is.

"Well?" Coop said. "No sense talkin' through that silly costume you got."

"The mask stays on," Dr. Wash said.

"You don't need it. There's good air now," Nita said.

"The mask stays on. Who's to say the minute I take it off you don't just cap that thing and here I am choking on fug?"

"Because we all got our masks off too, ya dope!" Coop said.

"Listen. You lightweights *visit* the fug. You breathe free all the time. Take trips up above in between jobs. Pop a cork on your secret sauce to get a nice whiff. So you have easy-on, easy-off masks. I *live* down here. This thing is bolted on. It stays."

"It *is* a rather distinctive design," Prist said. "I don't think I've seen its like in ages. How do you eat, I wonder?"

"In private. Now you gonna start talking business or are we going to yap until Lil's head finishes emptying out?"

"Oh, you better hope it finishes, because you better believe if I only end up with two memories left, one of 'em is going to be that your smart mouth deserves a fat lip."

"Another reason the mask stays on. Now let's get down to it. The way I figure it, the *Wind Breaker* crew, if I can even call you that anymore, should be my enemies."

"You better believe we're still the *Wind Breaker* crew!" Lil said. "Just because Cap'n Mack and Butch are babysittin' the ship don't mean we ain't still a crew."

"Fine. The point is, you're competition, and you're competition with supply lines I don't have. That said, you're *also* the ones runnin' around pokin' hornet's nests and stirrin' things up. You guys cause chaos, and chaos helps my bottom line ten times out of ten. You're the golden goose. I could cut you open now and get what's inside, or I can help you out and keep collecting them eggs, plus you'd owe me besides."

"Seems like this is the sort of figurin' you should be doin' inside your head," Coop said.

"A little truth never hurt nobody, especially when it works out so well for you."

Dr. Wash dug into his coat and retrieved some papers. He spread them on the table. They didn't appear to have writing on them. Instead they were dotted with strange sequences of lines and loops. It was all handwritten, and upon closer inspection it seemed to be nothing but line after line of dashes, dots, underscores, and hash marks.

"What do you call that chicken scratch?" Coop said.

"To me, it's shorthand. To you, it's meaningless. Ever since we got hit by Alabaster, it seemed like a good idea to start keeping notes in a way that fancy-pants idiots couldn't just snatch. Now, unless Coop here got it wrong, you wanted to know about somethin' called Contaminant Six. Where to get it, what's to know about it, all that stuff. I got some good news. It ain't hard to find."

"This a good-news, bad-news thing?" Coop said. "Seems like every time someone's got good news for us, they pair it up with bad."

"Then this ought to feel familiar. It's easy to *find* but it ain't easy to *get*. I talked to some of my guys, and it turns out C-6 all comes from South Pyre. But the stuff is hazardous waste or somethin'. So they keep it for processin', whatever that's supposed to mean."

Lil and the others turned to Prist.

"It certainly has the ring of truth. The substance, as far as I've been able to determine, *is* an irritant. If it was deemed to have more serious deleterious effects with prolonged exposure, it would be kept safe."

"Yeah. Kept safe in South Pyre. Like I said," Wash said.

"The place in the fug where the fug comes from," Lil said.

"The place in the fug where most of the fug folk's supply of phlogiston, pyrum, and burn-slow is produced," Prist added.

"And thus the most financially crucial place in the fug," Gunner said.

"I presume this makes it the best *guarded* place in the fug," Nita said.

"It is quite impenetrable," Prist said.

"We done impenetrable before. A couple times. Pert near our specialty. We can do it again," Coop said, no sign of concern or doubt in his voice. "What about the learnin' we were after?"

"No good news on that," Wash said.

"You are supposed to be one of the best information merchants in the fug. That's why Coop went for you," Nita said.

"I am, but merchants do business in merchandise that's *worth* something. Believe it or not, there ain't too many people beatin' down my door demandin' the ins and outs of hazardous waste treatment." He hiked a thumb in Coop's direction. "Except that idiot. But there's no such thing as information that can't be got. You just gotta know three things to learn anythin' else out there. Who knows it, where they are, and what they want. That much was easy to dig up."

"Spill it," Lil said.

"You're lookin' for academic stuff, but you got Dr. Prist here, and she barely knows anything about it. She's, what, number two or three in the fug when it comes to chemical stuff?" He leaned closer. "Speaking of, I'd be willin' to make a pretty generous offer for some of your insight on—"

"You get what you get when we get what we get," Coop snapped.

"Fine. Point is, if she doesn't know it, it means it isn't somethin' they teach *important* people. So who *do* they teach about it?" Now he jabbed his thumb toward his bodyguards. "These poor saps. They're the ones who'll be doin' the dirty work of hauling it around. So what we're looking for is one of the rarest things in the fug. A couple smart grunts. And there's only one place to find them."

"Of course... Solderwick Vocational Academy," Prist said.

"If anyone's got it written down, it's written down there," Wash said.

"I've never heard of the place," Gunner said. "Not that I was terribly familiar with most of what's beneath the fug until recently."

"It is where most of the skilled labor is taught," Prist said. "I'd never even *considered* it as a place to look for the information we need, but I was thinking from the point of view of people who were seeking to use the information in the same way that I intend to. To most of the people who have ever heard of Contaminant Six, the question has only ever been how to store it and extract it. The extraction part found its way to me. The storage is all that's left, and that is entirely the purview of laborers. Vocad is most certainly the best chance we'll have at finding the information."

"That's my thinkin' too, Doc," Wash said.

Lil coughed lightly. Nita quickly donned her mask as Lil pounded the desk with her fist.

"Dang it!" she snapped, wheezing a bit as Nita pulled her away from the table. They retreated to the thick purple mist at the edge of the ichor's influence. Lil took a few deep breaths of the stuff while Nita kept her steady.

"Wow… You weren't kiddin' about her. That's a hell of a thing to see. A human breathing that stuff. … Well, human-ish. For now," Wash said.

"Keep talkin' to me like that, and I ain't liable to be the only one breathin' the stuff," Lil said, stalking back into the clearing. She furiously exhaled a cloud of the stuff through her nostril, sending violet tendrils curling away as though she were a particularly flamboyant dragon.

"Look, this is what you wanted from me, right?" Wash said. "We're square. I told you where to get the goop and where to learn what to do with it."

"It's about the best I figured we'd get out of you," Coop said.

"Fine. Then there's the issue of my fee."

"Your fee is we let you go on bein' the rascal you are while we go work out what needs doin' and get it done," Coop said.

Gunner shook his head. "No sense making this more complicated than it needs to be, Coop. We pay the man and avoid having another front to fight this thing on. What's your price, Wash?"

"I want what you're after," Wash said. "And I want to help you get it."

"It's for Lil," Coop said.

"The *recipe*, dope," Wash said. "You might have your blinders on, focused on usin' that concoction to keep the last few marbles from spilling out of your sister's head, but I'm still lookin' at the bottom line. A treatment for fug poisoning? That's worth a mint. Even if it'll only work if you get it to someone in time. Even if it'll only do any good for one in every thousand people who fall in the fug. A treatment and proof it works is enough to put this stuff in the emergency kit of every ship in the air. That's real money."

"It ain't like you're liable to make any of the stuff," Coop said.

"We aren't even certain it will work. This is all terribly theoretical," Prist said.

"You're certain enough to come down here and rough up my guys, make threats, make deals. Seein' as how it seems like you always come out on top, I'm throwin' in with you this time. My payment is you gettin' what you want and me getting a piece. It's a good deal. I don't get paid unless you succeed. And Dr. Wash *always* gets paid."

Coop blinked. "We ever work out who's callin' the shots on this one? Did the cap'n pick one of us to be in charge?"

"I think he trusts us to run this one ourselves," Nita said.

"I reckon we should ditch Wash and get it done ourselves," Coop said.

"I trust him about as far as I can throw him, so long as I'm throwin' him off something high enough."

"I think we should take him up on his offer," Prist said. "Fug folk take information security very seriously, and his skills may come in handy."

"If we can spring the girls from Skykeep, we can steal a book," Coop said.

"It won't be a matter of stealing a book. I'll need to go through several volumes just to locate what we need, and it would be best if copies were made rather than stealing them. If Dr. Wash has the means to help us access Vocad without raising concern, that would make the entire enterprise far more likely to succeed. My vote remains. We should take him along."

Nita shook her head. "We don't know enough about him. We keep this small and nimble. Leave him out."

"I say he stays. I want him where I can see him until this thing's sorted," Lil said.

Gunner drummed his fingers. "More information, more resources. Better than less. We keep him aboard," Gunner said.

"So it's settled," Dr. Wash said.

Coop shook his head. "Two more votes to go."

"What are you talkin' about? That's the whole crew."

Tapping sounds rang out from above.

"Another one for and another against," Gunner said. "The ayes have it."

Dr. Wash glanced up into the darkness, then back to the *Wind Breaker* crew. "The rats get votes?!" he said.

"They're part of the crew. Now let's get to plannin'. Who's doin' what?" Lil said.

"We should split up. Tasks in parallel will help collapse the timeline. I'll need to be among those who go to Vocad to find the research, such as it may be. And presumably Dr. Wash should accompany us as well," Prist said.

"I got the fastest ship among us. Two-seater. How much of that stuff we liable to need? If we need a whole mess of it, I'll have to go solo," Coop said.

"We shouldn't need much. A few gallons," Prist said. "It will probably be stored in a highly distilled state to reduce storage requirements."

"So I can take someone else," Coop said.

"I'll go," Gunner said.

"That leaves me and Lil heading to this Vocad place with the rest of you," Nita said.

"Fine, then that's the plan," Lil said. "Let's get movin'."

"That's not a plan, folks. That's a set of directions," Dr. Wash said.

"Me and Gunner go get the goop," Coop said. "The rest of you figure out what to do with it. I reckon that's enough."

"But you haven't decided *how* you're going to do any of it."

"Plenty of time for figurin' when we're on the way," Coop stated.

"Well, maybe *you* don't need time to prepare, but I do. I'll take my own ship and—"

Lil slapped her hand on her hip, just shy of the grip of her pistol. "I thought I was the one who was losin' my memory. I wanted you with us so I could keep an eye on you. You're with us."

"You don't trust me to take my own *ship*? And you expect *me* to trust you enough to head all the way up to Vocad without my guys?"

"Call it a compromise," Nita said. "Besides, you aren't afraid of riding on a ship full of nothing but women, are you?"

"Don't try playin' that card against me. I done enough business with ladies to know they kick just as hard as men and ain't half as nice about where they do the kickin'."

Lil narrowed her eyes and slid her hand a shade closer to her pistol's grip. "Maybe you ain't pickin' up what I'm layin' down, Wash. This ain't a pair of boots I'm fiddlin' with."

Dr. Wash's men adopted considerably more hostile positions. Lil and Nita didn't flinch.

"Have you ever done something like this, Wash?" Nita asked.

"Stolen a treatment for somethin' no one knew could be treated? *No one* has."

"We'll, we'll be the first," Lil said.

Nita placed a hand on her shoulder. "That's what got me on the crew to begin with."

"… And the second," Lil amended.

"The point is, if you want this to succeed, you're helping us, but we're in charge," Nita said.

An angry breath hissed through Dr. Wash's mask. "Fine. I'll need to get some things and send some messages."

"Don't drag your feet!" Lil called after him as his men formed a wall to follow him out.

#

A few minutes later, Lil was crammed into the hold of the *Rattletrap* again, rummaging for fasteners as Nita attempted to squeeze in some last-minute tune-ups before pushing the ship to its limits on another journey.

"I forgot why we did the heist," Lil muttered. "The whole reason you're here."

"Do you remember it now?" Nita asked, holding out a hand.

Lil dumped some nuts into her palm. "A bit. It's like… it's like a hole in my memory. I knew the shape of it. I knew that's what was missin' just as soon as you said it. It fit right in. And once it was in, it got a little fuzzy around the edges. I get these little flickers and glimpses of what we did that day."

"Then this is excellent news. It means your memory isn't *going*, it's just fading. Once you've been treated, we can freshen it up and you'll be right as rain."

"I don't know why folks always say rain is so right. Rain comes along and wrecks a nice day half the time. All gloomy like."

"You know what I mean." Nita leaned on the handle of her wrench, giving it a bit extra torque. "We've had some leakage here. I can see where it discolored the wood. This should keep it tight and get a little more pressure to the turbines."

"Uh-huh," Lil said. "I don't like the idea of someone havin' to remind me of my life. It don't feel real. It don't feel solid. Like it goes from something that happened to me to something that happened to someone else."

"The treatment will work. It'll bring back everything you lost," Nita said.

"There ain't no way you could know that." Lil paused. "…Unless we already went and got it and Prist said as much, and I just forgot."

Nita shook her head and couldn't help but crack a smile. "No, Lil. That didn't happen."

"Good! Regardless of why we're doin' it, this here mission sounds like a fun one, and I ain't keen on missin' it. But how do you know it'll fix me up?"

"Sometimes you've just got to believe, even without knowing."

"… I reckon so. But all the same, next time I forget if it'll work or not, just tell me Prist gave it the thumbs-up. No sense pretendin' when I don't have to."

The telltale scratch of claws signaled the approach of one of the inspectors. Wink appeared in the hatch and tapped out a message. *The bird-faced one sent a message.*

"What did he say?"

Wink answered, but it was just an unintelligible sequence of random punctuations. Nita shook her head.

"Stop, stop. No sense in continuing. It's his code," Nita said.

"You know… I reckon it's just good sense for him to be usin' codes and such for sendin' messages. We're doin' it, after all. Shame it went from only folks in on the secret bein' able to send messages to everybody knowin' in such a hurry. Would've made eavesdroppin' way easier. But somehow, when *he* sends out a message and it's all coded up, it feels sneakier than most."

Contaminant Six

"Lil, your memory might be failing you, but your instincts are still needle sharp. He's up to something. I only hope it's the sort of thing that has to wait until we get you fixed up before he springs it. If he gets in the way of making that medicine, I am not going to be proud of what I end up doing to him…"

Chapter 6

The sun had set, affording Gunner and Coop the luxury of traveling above the fug rather than below it. The top layer of the toxic mist was always the thickest. During the day a skilled navigator could travel quite safely regardless of who was after them. From above, an airship was little more than a hard-to-place whir of turbines or props. The two-seater Coop had been using during his extended trade mission was quieter than most. From below, the ship was an indistinct dark blob in a sky of indistinct dark blobs. But it was a wretched way to travel. The thicker fug had a sharp chemical sting against the skin and burned the eyes terribly. A few hours high above the stuff, with the fresh crisp high-altitude air to fill their lungs, was a welcome change.

Coop adjusted the heading. "You done goin' over them sketches Prist gave you?"

"There really isn't much to go on," he said. "South Pyre is quite secretive. The whole of her assessment boils down to 'You'll probably need to break into the auxiliary complex to the west of the main facility.' That and a spot on the map with the note 'South Pyre will be rather difficult to miss.'"

"If she don't think we need to know more, that means she thinks it'll be easy," Coop said.

"I don't think it's a matter of her not feeling we need more information, so much as a lack of information to give. She was only the backup chemist, you'll recall. Most of her time was spent at the academy, not South Pyre. I can't imagine they give just-in-case substitutes a full security briefing before sending them out on their way."

"What's it liable to have? Big walls. Fellas with guns. Airships all about? Fughounds? Nothin' we ain't seen. Show me that label again."

Gunner slipped a page from the sheaf he'd been flipping through. It was diamond shaped, with a *C* and a *6* aligned vertically in a squarish type in its center. Notes indicated the text was black and the diamond was yellow.

"Just gotta get inside the first thing that looks like a warehouse, grab a couple gallons of the goo, and get out. I got a gun, you got a gun. Ain't no big thing," Coop said.

"We still need a plan."

"I just said it."

Gunner shook his head. "At this rate, we'll be seeing it before much longer. Or at least evidence of it. There will be constant shipments in and out, but there's not much to the south of that position, so all the cargo haulers should be heading north, east, and west..."

"Mmm-hmm," Coop muttered, adjusting the heading again.

"Am I boring you?"

"Look, just work it out in your head and let me know. It'll all fall apart anyway once someone sees us, and then it's a mess of runnin' and shootin', and I'm ready for that bit already. All this yammerin' is givin' me a right powerful headache."

Gunner put the notes away. "Coop, I think you and I need to have a word about the current situation."

"You got somethin' in your ears? I just said we *ain't* gotta talk."

"I need you clearheaded for this mission. At least, as clearheaded as you *get*. And I don't think we're there yet. This might be the first time I've ever seen you with a lot on your mind, and you're not handling it well."

"I'm handlin' just fine. Who says I ain't?"

"Coop, you've been fiddling with the ship's heading completely arbitrarily. You're fidgeting. Flying a ship, it just means a bit more sway for the rest of the crew. Holding a rifle, it means missing your target. I'd ask what's bothering you, but we both already know it."

"Ain't nothin' botherin' me, and if you keep claimin' there is, I'll feed you your boots to shut you up."

"Obviously the calm and reasoned disposition of the mentally serene." Gunner scratched his chin. "Fine, let's change the subject. The captain has been ensuring we all learn a bit about the ship's upkeep from Nita. Have you been keeping up with your lessons?"

"Been away a bit, but I know what I been taught."

"Having known you for as long as I have, I'm a bit slow to believe you've grasped some of the more complex aspects of boiler repair."

"Then how about you quit talkin' about it?"

"I think a test is more useful. What happens when you close all the valves on a boiler with a fully stocked firebox?"

"Pressure goes up," Coop said. "I knew that even before Nita started givin' us the ins and outs."

"And what happens if the pressure keeps going up?"

"The boiler blows."

"Let's say we're back on the *Wind Breaker*. About... fifteen hours out from Caldera. Right where the trade winds start bearing down on us. If the captain sent you down, and the firebox was overstocked and the pressure was redlined across the board, what would you do?"

Contaminant Six

Coop drummed his fingers on the ship's wheel.

"Well?" Gunner said.

"I'm thinkin'... There's a... whatchacallit. One of them big valves that heads out the side. ... Relief valve. That's what ya call 'er. I'd open that up."

"Why?"

"Because I don't want the boiler to blow."

"Why not?"

"Because the boiler blows right in the middle of a trip, best case, we're dead in the air, gettin' pushed all willy-nilly by the wind. Worst case, we're straight up dead. Can't let a boiler get too built up. When you got someplace to go, and there ain't no land in sight, you keep an eye on that boiler good and hard, because if it pops its cork, it'll..." Coop turned and glared at Gunner. "I got me the sneakin' suspicion you didn't change the subject at all."

"Coop, I am genuinely impressed you caught on as fast as you did. You don't often have a mind for metaphor."

"Maybe not, but I'm fair at pickin' out when folks're sayin' one thing as a flowery-like way of sayin' another."

"That's precisely what—" Gunner shut his eyes tight. "Look, never mind. Do you understand what I'm getting at?"

"You reckon me talkin' about what you reckon is eatin' me but you reckoned wrong about because ain't nothin' eatin' me is liable to clear out my head that ain't filled up because you reckoned that wrong too and then I won't get all weepy when we're fixin' to do something important."

Gunner had to take a moment to untie the sentence in his mind. "Yes, that's what I'm thinking. And when this is said and done, we've really got to work on your vocabulary. There is entirely too much reckoning going on."

"Ain't nothin' goin' on that yappin'll fix."

Coop's coat rustled. Nikita crawled out enough to be seen and reached up to tap at one of his buttons. *Talk out the bad thoughts. Better than letting them be worse thoughts.*

Coop glanced down at her. "Fine."

"Fine?!" Gunner said. "I reason with you and nothing, but one little nudge from her and it's 'fine'?"

"You're always thinking things through too much. Nikita ain't like that. She don't say nothin' unless something needs sayin'."

"But I'm—but you—" Gunner took a breath. "Fine. I don't care why you wised up. But talk."

"There ain't nothin' goin' on in here that you don't know about. I'm scared. I'm ornery. And I don't know what's goin' on. The last part I'm used to. Most times I don't know what's goin' on. I used to have to pretend, just so's

Lil'd feel better when the wind was blowin' too hard or the goats were gettin' sick back when we had 'em. But she wised up fast. Once we got on the *Wind Breaker*, didn't much matter that I didn't know what was goin' on. The cap'n did. You did. Butch did. Later on, Nita did. All I had to do was do what I was told. Maybe *they* didn't know half the time, but they were a darn sight better at makin' like they did than I ever was, so I reckon even if they *were* feelin' lost, someone that good at not seemin' it was worth followin' regardless. But don't nobody know for sure if anything we're fixin' to do will do a lick of good. So that's got me scared. And that's got me ornery. And most times if I'm scared or ornery about something, I can slug it in the chin or fill it full of holes. But this ain't that kinda thing. And if it was me who the fug got, I wouldn't be scared, on account of the whole crew and Lil would be fightin' to make things right. But it's Lil who got it. That means there's one less good head puzzlin' it out, and just me to replace it."

He squeezed the wheel tight. "Ain't never been a Cooper who was half as sharp as most folk. We're slow. I know it. Even if sometimes I make like it ain't true. But Lil's sharper than I'll ever be, and I got a couple years on her. She was on her way to bein' the best dang Cooper the world ever seen."

"It's a little early to be using the word 'was,' Coop."

"I'm her big brother. Ain't but one thing in the world I was ever supposed to do. One thing that matters. And that was keep her safe. I can't do one dang thing right. Not one dang thing."

"She isn't going to die. Even if everything fails, she'll still be alive."

"There'll be someone walkin' around wearin' my old boots. But it won't be Lil."

"It will still be Lil, Coop."

"She'll look different on the outside. And she'll be all emptied out on the inside. What's left of her after them things're gone, Gunner? Memories, I reckon. And not hers. Only mine. You don't gotta have college learnin' like you to know they already got a word for that."

"This isn't the first time we've been in a situation where one of us could have died. 'Risking death' is the default state of being for an airship crew."

"It's the first time the one who'd be dyin' would still be walkin' around after. Wearin' my old boots. The first time there'd be a hole in the shape of my sister that I'd have to look at and see someone who don't see her brother lookin' at her." He gritted his teeth and punched the side of the cabin. Tears ran down his cheeks. "Dang it, Gunner, you said it'd make me feel better to dig all this up."

"I made no such claim. All I said was it would let the pressure out so you didn't blow when things got heated."

Contaminant Six

"Fat lot of good that does me now! All I managed to do is say out loud what I been tryin' to tell myself wasn't true. That I feel it in my bones that I'm gonna lose Lil before we're through here. What good does it do me to have that floatin' around in my head?"

"It was already floating around in your head. The goal was to let it out."

"I ain't lookin' to let things out if all they'll do is buzz around on the outside doin' just the same damage as they did on the inside."

"Fine, then look at it this way. You're *sure* we're going to lose Lil, right?"

"Deep down. Deep, deep down I'm sure."

"And when's the last time you were right about anything?"

Coop stared at him. "I reckon you got a point about that, Gunner."

Gunner gave him a level look. He was still quivering like a freshly picked guitar string, but the weight seemed to have been lifted from his shoulders.

"You've got an admirable nimbleness of disposition, Coop," he said. "I suppose when something is that unencumbered, it doesn't take much for it to turn on a dime."

"Hey, you callin' me dumb is all well and good when I need it, but quit rubbin' it in. Point is, the pressure's been blown. But the firebox is still stocked and burnin'."

He glared at the sea of purple ahead. The wind had whipped it up a bit, but even in the darkness, it was clear that *something* was different about the stretch ahead. It had mounded higher than the rest, like the curving final flourish of a geyser. Hints of phlo-lights flickered below the surface. It was South Pyre.

Coop grinned. "I mean to put this steam to good use."

#

It was Nita's turn at the wheel. Between the not entirely unlikely event that they'd need to hide to avoid raiders or patrols and the certainty of Lil needing a quick breath of the fug to keep herself steady, Nita had decided to navigate by the instruments and stay beneath the fug.

"You really ought to sleep," Nita said. "Prist isn't the steadiest of pilots, you're sick, and there's no way we're trusting Dr. Wash alone at the helm, so I'm the only one who can handle the ship alone."

"I don't know how many hours I got left. I don't want to waste my time sleepin'," Lil said.

She had been sitting on the deck, leaning against the front of the helm while Nita navigated. The same small phlo-light that kept the instruments visible also served as light enough for her to scratch away at a pad for hours

65

on end.

"I ever tell you about that uncle of mine that taught Coop how to open a can with a knife?" Lil asked.

"Plenty of times," Nita assured.

"Do you remember his name?" she asked.

"I… I don't think you ever told me his name. You just called him 'Uncle Stubby.'"

Lil nodded. "Good enough. I got a story about me and him that I don't know if I ever told Coop and I don't want it to go away." She scratched out a few more lines. "I tell you what. If you told me that learnin' to write quick would be the difference between me forgettin' what little family I had or not, I'd've worked harder when they were teachin' me."

"Everything's going to be fine, Lil."

"You can keep tellin' me them sweet lies, but even if they're true, a nice big book of memories is worth havin' regardless."

"I can't argue with that."

Dr. Wash stepped onto the deck and paced to the front of the ship. "How close are we?" he asked.

"A few more hours," Nita said.

"You know, I had it in my head that you *Wind Breaker* folks got to where you were by bein' faster than the rest of us, but you're taking your sweet time on this one."

"We got to where we got by actually gettin' to where we were gettin'," Lil snapped. "The quickest way to get from here to there is to not get caught in the middle. Goes double for his ol' ship."

Dr. Wash pulled a rag from a pocket in his coat and wiped the dark lenses of his mask. "Anybody figure out what we're doin' once we get to Vocad?"

"Dr. Prist gave us some names of people back at Ichor Well who went to Vocad. Some of them worked here not so long ago. She might be able to use their names to get in."

"And who are they?" Dr. Wash said.

"Wouldn't *you* like to know?" Lil said.

"What are you afraid of? Tellin' me somethin' that'd help me work out where you been hidin' Ichor Well? You think I don't already know right where it is?"

"We'll still be keeping information to a minimum, if you don't mind," Nita said.

"Fine, fine. Shows you've at least got a couple bits of good sense knocking around in your collective skulls." Wash pocketed his rag. "Just so happens you won't need to use any names."

"Why not? They just gonna open the door for us?" Lil asked.

"They will once you grease a couple palms. Prist'll tell ya, that place isn't the la-dee-da university she came from. It's a down-in-the-dirt workin'-man sort of place. Always short of money. Drop a couple coins in the right place, and they'll let you land this ship right in their courtyard and swear up and down it was a pigeon."

"They still got pigeons down here?" Lil asked.

"It's a turn of phrase," Dr. Wash muttered.

"Ain't never heard that one. And you didn't answer my question. They got pigeons down here or not?"

"Is she always this stupid, or is this the final stages of brain rot?" Dr. Wash said.

"Tell me about the dang pigeons!" Lil said.

"There are no fug pigeons!" he said.

"Oh... Well that's too bad. I'd love to see what the fug'd make of them critters."

"The point is, a bribe will get you as much time as you need to do whatever you want. I gotta believe you been doing most of your business in Ichor Well with grunts. You know as well as I do they ain't got no love for the skinny fuggers who call the shots. You guys got any Calderan sea salt or trith?"

"We've been cutting down on trith and salt ever since we found out Tusk was using them to make abrasives that could cripple turbines," Nita said.

"So, what? Victors then? Or do you have some other Calderan goodies? Fine cloth is usually good. Not-so-fine cloth would probably be fine, what with you havin' an actual Calderan to hand it over."

"When we sell Calderan goods, we sell *real* Calderan goods," Lil said.

"Must be nice to have a supplier... I been in the business for *years*, and I ain't never had a good solid supply of island wares until I started getting *your* stuff secondhand."

"Am I crazy, or did we start off talkin' about the actual mission we're on?" Lil said.

"Right, right. You give me a couple minutes to go through the goods you've got to trade, and I'll put together a list that'll get you in and out with their heads turned the other way the whole time," Dr. Wash said.

"What's so special about you that you can work out a price better than we can?"

"I been doing business down here longer than you'd believe. Maybe you worked with grunts and such for a while, but when you been down here day in, day out for *years*, you start to get a handle on the little things. Like in a good game of cards, fuggers got tells. Maybe it just lets you shave a couple victors or a jug of hooch off the top of a deal, but that ain't nothin'. And you stretch that sort of thing over a couple, three decades? You got the difference between the skin of your teeth and a tidy livin'. Or for the here and now, it's the difference between havin' enough left over to trade for whatever other ingredients you might need to cook up this treatment without havin' to waste time restocking."

"I don't believe him," Lil said. "I think he's just curious what sorts of goodies we got."

Wash shrugged. "Believe me or don't," he said. "It ain't *my* brain that's leakin' out."

Nita glanced to Lil. Lil glanced back. Nita leaned forward and tapped the speaking tube. "Dr. Prist, Dr. Wash will be heading down in a moment. I'd like you to give him a list of everything we can spare for trade, specifically for the purposes of a bribe."

"Smart lady," Wash said, brushing his hands on his shirt and heading for the hatch below decks.

"Hey!" Lil said. "Just what kind of doctor are you, anyways?"

"Dentist," Wash said. "Half this business is pulling teeth."

#

Gunner leaned low, his eye level with the scope of his rifle. Colored glass sights of his own design gave him a bit more visibility through the fug. What he saw was the very model of an operation intended to be kept as secure and as secret as possible. The buildings stretched out in the cardinal directions, with the longest leg reaching far to the north. Rails exited the far end of each of the narrow complexes. There was virtually no outdoor lighting. Ships were constantly coming and going, but they activated their phlo-lights only briefly, just long enough to give them a fighting chance to moor or avoid collision. Vast walls ringed the place, with heavy mechanical gates spanning the rails. And then there was the pyre itself.

"I always figured it was just this big flamin' hole in the ground," Coop said, voicing the same thoughts that were drifting through Gunner's mind.

"Considering how important this is to them, I can't imagine that would be a wise thing to allow," Gunner said.

They'd completely enclosed the ichor well with an angular structure of black iron. The center of each triangular panel in the massive dome was a vent, and each was spewing fug with impressive intensity. Like the head of a watering can, it turned a singular column of the stuff into a spread. Without it, the gentle bulge of the fug would have been a towering burst, visible to all around. Under this umbrella of particularly dense fug, which would render them wholly invisible from all but the nearest or lowest of observers, some limited illumination indicated where small patrol craft and ground security were making their rounds.

"They haven't noticed us yet, but I don't think we can venture much closer without the risk of being spotted," Gunner said.

"We're miles out. That's a long way to go on foot," Coop said.

"It's better than having to dodge fléchettes for the full flight in. We don't even know how hard it will be to find some C-6. And then we'll need to have a ship to get it home in."

"So we're gonna run in, find the stuff, and haul it out here, all secret-like, and all the while trust no one's gonna find the ship? Here I was thinkin' you were the fella who said 'hope real hard' wasn't a part of a good plan."

"No, you're right. We need a way to speed it up. And we need a reliable way inside."

He scanned the countryside. With the help of instinct and training, he made mental notes of potential targets one by one. He tracked their positions in the back of his mind. Finally his sights fell upon the rails. They ran in perfectly straight lines leading out of their respective complexes. The one to the south seemed to drive itself into the mountains for mining. The rest just vanished into the distance.

"Yes... That'll be our way in. And if we're lucky, our way out."

"What?"

"The rails. They probably bring in the raw materials they need via steam carts. I can't imagine the steam carts are all that different from the ones we use. Except unlike the ones we use, they'll be working the way they were intended."

Coop scratched his head. "We ain't usin' the carts right?"

"Nita has converted them into something far, far from their intended purpose. Most of the time a single steam cart will be hauling dozens of unpowered ones. And the way fuggers run things, it'll be minimal manpower."

"Just point me in a direction so we can get to gettin'," Coop said.

Gunner swept the sights about. "Nothing to the north... Nothing to the west... Nothing to the east, that would be far too easy. ... There. It looks like the mechanisms for the south gate are pressurized. They must be getting ready to open the gates. Take us down south. Get us as close to where the rails enter the mining tunnel as you can without risking being seen."

"And then what?"

"Oh, you'll like this plan. It involves hurling ourselves onto a speeding vehicle..."

#

The rails were already rattling when Gunner and Coop reached them.

From where they'd moored the ship, it had been a long sprint to reach the mouth of the mine to the south. Carrying his usual arsenal of weapons, probably three guns too many and a heavy pack besides, hadn't made it any easier on Gunner. They were granted only a minute or so of respite before the first steam cart emerged from the tunnel. A single fug man, a grunt, was at the controls of the cart. From the look of his face in the dim light of fug-shrouded night, his was not a terribly exciting position. He spun some knobs as he swept past. The steam venting out the side of the cart tapered off a bit, and the speed started to increase.

Cart after cart slid out of the tunnel, linked together into a train behind a single powered one. Each was heaped with unprocessed ore. There were ladders on the side of each cart to give workers access to the top of the hopper. Gunner and Coop silently acknowledged each other with a quick look. Coop held back. Gunner made the first move. The veritable armory of weapons that he'd brought along were strapped tightly to his body so that their rattling and jangling wouldn't alert onlookers, though the rumble of the cart train probably would have been enough to drown out a rifle shot. He dove for a ladder as it swept by. Having lost some fingers to his overzealous experimentation, Gunner's grip strength wasn't what he would have liked it to be, but one should never doubt what the body can achieve if the alternative is being dashed to a pulp on the gravel beside the tracks. He held firm long enough to get his feet onto the rungs.

Once steady, he turned to face the tail end of the train of carts. Coop was already making his dash. The deckhand's long limbs made short work of the distance and matched the speed of the train even as it continued to accelerate. He made the leap from the ballast to the ladder so smoothly one would think it was simply the proper way to board a train. Gunner swung himself aside and tucked himself onto the coupler between the carts, the only part of the train that offered any reasonable sort of cover.

The train rattled along the tracks. From between the carts he had no way to know how far they'd gone or how much farther there was to go. He considered digging out the mirror he used for a periscope when the situation required it, but it didn't truly matter. It would buy him perhaps another thirty seconds to craft a plan, and that was assuming he would have a clear view past the open gates of the walls. If this was going to be improvisation, he may as well focus on keeping himself properly hidden. The risk of them seeing his mirror was greater than the value of a few scraps of new information.

"Hey-ya, Gunner."

The jolt of hearing a voice nearly knocked Gunner off the coupler he was crouching on. He looked up to find Coop peering down at him from the top of the hopper cart.

"What are you doing up there? Get down here!" Gunner hissed.

"What's that? Can't hear ya. It's noisy as heck."

"Get out of sight, you idiot! They'll see you!"

"Not yet they won't. It's real dark, and there ain't no lookouts on the wall up ahead. Ain't nobody but us and the fella drivin' the cart, and he looks like he's about ready to nod off."

"That could change at any second. They could flick on a phlo-light and our cover is blown."

"Yeah... Yeah I reckon so," Coop said.

He hopped down beside Gunner and casually propped himself with a boot against the leading cart and his back against the trailing one. A moment later the huge walls of the complex whipped past.

"I figured gettin' past them would've been the hard part of this whole thing."

"I doubt they predicted someone would jump onto a moving train."

"So what's our plan once we get in the place?" Coop asked.

"I don't know yet. We don't know what is waiting for us in there."

"We're still at 'sneak our way to the east hunk and find some of the goop all secret-like,' huh? Hang on. This'll help." He tugged his coat open. Nikita crawled out and onto his arm. "You got better eyes for the dark than we do. And you're little, so folk won't see you as easy. Take a look and see if there's anything worth seein'."

The aye-aye nodded and clung tightly to his hand as he raised her up. As her nicked tail curled around his arm and she shrugged off the anxiety that was a hallmark of her species, she drummed out a message on his hand.

"She says there's a big door. Dim lights. One of 'em's flashin' real slow," Coop translated. "And now the door's openin'. It's brighter inside. Loads of phlo-lights. Three guys. Grunts."

"Where are they? What's their vantage?" Gunner asked.

"Up on catwalks."

"That's our chance, then. Let's just hope those are the only ones, because there is no way we're getting inside without *some* sort of security sweep."

Coop pulled Nikita down and let her crawl back under his coat. Once again, the pair of crewmembers didn't need to collaborate. If the eyes in the room were up high, the best place to hide was down low. Missions like this were all about comparing risks and picking the lesser of them. Rare was the situation that clinging to the bottom of a multiton piece of machinery speeding along a track was the safest option available, but when the alternative was being spotted by people with orders to kill intruders on sight, it was a no-brainer. Coop and Gunner slipped under the cart. There was no shortage of struts and cables to hold on to. Though Coop was a fair bit better at navigating upside down, Gunner found the possibility of being tumbled along the ground or sheared in half by steel wheels to be a powerful motivator to keep a firm grip.

The train began to slow. Brakes engaged. The air filled with the choking scent of overheated metal, an odor that uncannily made it through the filter masks to burn their lungs. They screeched to a stop. A moment later, the grunt at the head of the train dropped down.

"This is it. Last load for the night. I'm done with my shift." He shouted, "Take 'em up!"

Gunner didn't like the sound of that last order. Nor did he like the sound of jingling chains and mechanical interlocks. A rattling clank echoed off the walls, and a few carts ahead of them, light shone down on the tracks. He gazed up and realized the preponderance of struts that had made it so simple to hold to the bottom of the cart was there because the cart was little more than a removable metal crate sitting on a wheeled base. More chains, more clanking. Another crate lifted away from its wheels and shined light down through the framework left behind. They had perhaps a minute before the cart providing their cover was suddenly about as useful for hiding under as a fishing net.

He glanced down to Coop, who had taken a hand from holding himself up to ready his pistol. Gunner couldn't risk reprimanding him, and in all honesty, he didn't have a better idea. He swept his gaze around the room. He couldn't see the catwalks where the workers or guards were. Nor could he see the machinery that would in just a few seconds reveal them. But he did spot a stout steam pipe that had the telltale tremble of being in use. He lowered himself quietly to the tracks and pulled one of his pistols. The aim was important, but more important was the timing. Chains jingled. Latches engaged. The chains pulled taut, and the crate of the cart ahead of them screeched free of its base. Under the cover of the ear-splitting din, he fired his pistol. It struck the pipe, and instantly the loading bay filled with a horrifying, high-pitched wail of escaping steam. The chain hoist sputtered and sagged, and the cart dropped back to the base.

Profanity and thumping footsteps fought to be heard over the escaping steam. Workers were rushing to the source of the rupture. Gunner and Coop took advantage of the chaos and rolled into the open. Gunner sprang to his feet and once again called upon his training and instincts. One quick sweep with his eyes assured him that there were a total of five fug folk in the whole of the bay, typical of the sort of efficiency the low-population fug folk required of their operations. They were far too distracted by the scalding steam belching from the pipe to notice Gunner and Coop dashing for the opposite side of the room. They ducked into the first open door they could reach and found themselves in a strangely spacious and horribly underlit corridor.

"That was some real good thinkin'," Coop said, slapping Gunner on the back.

"Let's save the congratulations for after we get out of here with our skin. We're still in the south complex. This place is city-sized, and while I doubt there's more than two hundred people working here, that's still plenty of chances to run into someone who can make our lives much more complicated than we would like."

#

"You wanna hurry up with that?" Coop said, leaning against a slightly ajar door to keep watch through the crack.

"Give me a moment," Gunner said. "These people may be incredibly efficient with their physical labor, but they more than make up for that with the amount of paperwork they generate."

They'd found their way to what looked to be some sort of an accountant's office at the point where the South Complex joined the main hub of South Pyre. It was the sort of place where the daily itineraries were processed, duplicated, and distributed. In theory it would hold all the information they required. It was just a matter of finding it in the endless piles of memos and filing cabinets of reference material.

The closer they got to the center of the facility, the more activity there was. Right now they must have been very close indeed, because they could hear the hiss of the constantly burning ichor pit. It added a degree of tension and anxiety to the situation that didn't help Gunner's concentration at all. The lighting was a problem, too. Fug folk had better eyes for darkness, so they tended to work with less light than Gunner would have liked, but in South Pyre it was a whole new level of lighting economy. Notices were posted everywhere reminding workers to keep lighting to the bare minimum. The notices were terribly wordy, codifying seven different reasons for the darkness, but they boiled down to the twin threat of high fug concentrations making phlo-lights burn unreasonably bright and said brightness drawing attention to the facility.

Sifting through reams of paperwork in search of information was frustrating enough. Doing it through squinted eyes while in constant threat of discovery was another thing entirely. Gunner's patience had run out several minutes ago.

"It's all indexed, which would be terribly helpful if I knew what their indexes *meant*. They're horribly opaque."

"What's 'opaque' mean?"

"It means they aren't clear at all."

"Why didn't you say they aren't clear at all?"

"Because it's *faster* to say opaque."

73

"All this explainin' is faster than just talkin' plain?"

"*Just keep watch!*" Gunner growled. "I've exhausted the storage list. Nothing about Contaminant Six. Maybe there's information about transporting it from wherever it's collected to where it's stored." He pulled open a new drawer and slid out a folder.

"I hear footsteps," Coop said. "Nikita says they're headin' away, not toward."

"Keep those ears good and open, Nikita," Gunner said. "What do we have... Impurities... Contaminants! Three... Eight... Six, here we are. The transportation orders are... wait. They're for off-site."

"Makes sense to me. If that stuff was the sort of stuff to make me all itchy or whatever it does to fuggers, I'd want to get rid of it too."

"The whole point of us coming *here* was because it was supposed to be locked up here, remember?"

"So he got it wrong or we been lied to. Ain't the first time, won't be the last. Where do we get the stuff?"

"It's in the East Complex, in an internal mooring bay, loaded up in a cart like the one that brought us in, due to be picked up and dropped off somewhere once the cart's full. I guess the travel orders will be on the ship itself."

"Then let's get movin'," Coop said. He gave the hallway a final quick look, then motioned for Gunner to follow.

"I have to put the paperwork back. If I don't, they'll know we were here."

"What're the odds they ain't gonna work that out?" Coop said.

"Very good, if we continue to take care."

A strange, piercing whistle split the air. Gunner and Coop turned to the source, which was the output of a speaking tube not unlike those in the ship.

"Attention. An equipment failure in the southern complex appears to have been the result of sabotage. Be on the lookout for intruders in the compound. This is not a drill. Intruders may have infiltrated South Pyre," the voice warned.

Gunner threw the pages over his shoulder. "I suppose that will speed things up a bit," he said, drawing his pistol from his belt.

#

One of the lean, stooped fug folk gripped his gun tightly. His expression was sour as he stood at his post beside the door.

"I don't understand why *I* am in the high-alert rotation," he grumbled to the empty foyer around him. "Seven years at Fadewell Academy. A doctorate in chemistry. And when an engineer refuses to admit his poor installation is at fault for a rupture, I have to hold a pistol and stand watch like a common grunt."

He cocked the hammer and eased it back. "This is a job that could be done by a fughound. I've increased our pyrum yield by six percent in the last two years alone. And I have a gun, and I'm standing guard at the door of a *waste* facility. As though someone would come and steal our *garbage*. It is beneath me. It is a horrific misuse of my skills."

He turned his back to the door and glared out at the activity visible at the end of the hall. A soft click from the door caught his attention. Before he could turn to investigate, the door whipped open. The temporary guard managed a startled inhale before Coop grabbed ahold of his shirt and pulled him into a dizzying headbutt. The deckhand pulled the dazed chemist into the dim area beside the door while Gunner slipped in behind.

"Little piece of advice," Coop said, tearing the arms from the man's crisp white dress shirt. "If you're gonna complain about a job bein' too easy for you, I reckon you should make sure you're *good* at it first."

Coop gagged the man and hogtied him with the sort of silent efficiency that illustrated far too much practice in such a bizarre activity. He tucked the pistol in his belt.

"This is it," Gunner said. "We've reached the East Complex. If those reports were accurate, there should be a small, secure stockpile of C-6 in something called Hazard Containment C."

The pair stalked toward the main open area of the complex, keeping tight to the north wall where the already-dim light was dimmest. It was a good deal more active in this complex than in the southern one, and considerably more cramped. This was due, in large part, to the airship moored in the center.

Gunner scanned the complex. It was something of a mechanical marvel. Rails not unlike the ones that they'd used to sneak into the facility ran along the floor. But rather than simply continuing forward, there was a branching network of switches, curving tracks, and turntables leading off to side tracks and storage bays. A gantry with a cart hoist was directly overhead as they entered the facility proper, but it was fully retracted. Chains matching those of the hoist were dangling down from the cargo bay of the airship. Clearly they were loading it up for export.

More impressive than the rest of the operation combined, however, was the roof. Massive rails and complex linkages ran along the front and back.

"The whole roof must open up when the airship has to leave," Gunner whispered.

"Ain't I the one who's supposed to be easy to distract? Keep lookin' and keep quiet," Coop said.

They crept as far along the wall of the foyer as they could without risking revealing themselves. Eight workers were busy maneuvering carts and steadying chains. Assuming at least another four in the cargo ship, that meant they had a dozen sets of eyes they would have to avoid, all while attempting to steal some hazardous waste.

"There," Coop said. "That's the thing we're lookin' for, right?"

Tucked into the far corner of the complex was a half-empty cargo cart. The loading door was open and it was loaded with thirty or forty casks, each emblazoned with the C-6 marker. Though the search was over, their troubles were just beginning. Each of the casks was the size of a beer keg. There would be no sneaking around with one. They would be lucky if the two of them would be able to lift it.

"What're we supposed to do now?" Coop said.

"Give me a moment," Gunner said.

He scanned the room again, this time with a different aim in mind. This was most certainly the complex used to handle potential hazards. Fortified compartments with small loading hatches lined the walls. They were like the fire cabinets in Dr. Prist's lab, designed to keep their contents contained, both to protect the chemicals and to protect the personnel *from* the chemicals. One full wall was made up of compartments holding burn-slow. One or two held pyrum. The rest were scattered among things like coal and oil.

"Look at this place. It's a bomb waiting to happen," Gunner said with a grin.

"Why am I gettin' the notion it ain't liable to be waitin' too long?" Coop asked.

Gunner looked to him. "Two questions, Coop. How confident are you that you can work one of those hoists, and how attached are you to the ship we rode in on?"

"Not very."

"For which question."

"Both."

"Good enough for me. Here's what we need to do…"

#

Nikita huffed and puffed, scrambling as quietly as she could along the thick struts that ran along the complex roof. A few thick threads affixed a load to her back that was a good deal heavier than she was accustomed to hauling. But she'd been given her instructions, and she'd been with Coop and the others long enough to know that the only way any of them were likely to get out of the messes they seemed to constantly get into was by everyone playing their part.

She grabbed tight to a complicated-looking bit of mechanical equipment. She'd not spent much time as an inspector, but the training was rooted deep in her little mind, so despite not knowing what it meant, she knew that what she was looking at was a piston-actuated latching hook, currently coupled with a retention loop. This was the fourth and final such mechanism she'd had to access, not counting the two big, thick chains she'd had to find her way to beforehand. It was with no small amount of relief that she lashed the mass of claylike gunk Gunner had given her to the retention loop and scurried away. The stuff smelled horrible and looked like a chunky white-and-black-marbled lump. Gunner had cobbled it together out of things Coop had scooped from various bins around the room while the workers had their attention focused on the ship in the center.

Her sharp eyes scanned the walls and came to rest on Gunner. He was huddled in the darkest corner he could find, one of his guns held high so he could peer through its sight. She waved. He waved back and slipped along the wall for the entrance. Next she sought out Coop. While she'd spent little time in her namesake role, in her more common role as a point of communication, Nikita *had* spent a fair amount of time watching fug folk work. That was the job she'd been doing when the *Wind Breaker* crew had rescued her and introduced her to a far more harrowing yet far, *far* preferable life among them. When the fug folk were working, particularly those in a position to be reprimanded for goofing off, they could be admirably focused. The grunts working in and around the ship, which was being prepped and fueled, seldom cast a glance toward anything but their task. Coupled with the poor lighting, it allowed Coop a surprising amount of latitude to sneak around behind bins and raid their contents. His job done, presently Coop was crouched like a stalking animal, eyes trained on the soon-to-be pummeled grunt at the switchboard for the rails.

She turned back to Gunner and waved again. He lowered his weapon and hurried to the foyer. A moment later, a whistle split the air and Gunner's voice rang out over the speaking tubes.

"Attention. All staff to battle stations. A two-man craft has been spotted to the southeast. Ships are instructed to intercept, all workers take up arms and guard exits," he instructed.

The effect on the crew was neither immediate nor pronounced. The grunts looked about in confusion. One of the scrawnier fuggers on the ship shouted something down to them. Outside, sirens rang out, fughounds howled, and turbines spun up. The workers, for the most part, stayed put.

"I told you it wouldn't work!" Coop bellowed from his hiding place.

The fug folk turned to the source of the voice, just in time to see Coop barrel full speed into the back of the man at the switchboard. He fell over the railing of his station, and Coop threw some switches. One by one, the various tracks moved into position between the C-6 cart and the loading

77

station beneath the ship. The grunt he'd dislodged rallied to stop him, but the ricochet of gunshots convinced him to take cover instead.

Gunner burst onto the floor of the complex armed with two guns that looked to be the result of insane tinkering. With said weapons akimbo, he was able to put an astounding number of bullets in the air. Rounds hissed past grunts like angry hornets, missing by mere inches. Coop dashed to the C-6 cart and spun the valves to disengage the brakes. The luck, and more importantly the slope of the facility, was with him as it rumbled into motion. He hopped on top of it. Even those grunts lucky enough to be spared the covering fire Gunner was providing dared not take a shot at Coop while he was standing atop a heavy load of toxic waste.

He rode the half-empty uncontrolled cart all the way to the loading station. It smashed into the cart waiting there, knocking both from the tracks and spilling the contents of the fully loaded cart to the ground.

Nikita didn't quite recognize the stuff, but it smelled nearly as bad as the gunk she'd attached to the retention loops and seemed to make the grunts *very* upset. That was her cue. She scrambled across the overhead struts and dropped down onto the envelope of the airship.

#

Coop climbed to his feet and brushed himself off. "Dang it. I should've known it'd take more than that to get this sucker where it needed gettin'."

The collision hadn't *quite* been enough to push the cart entirely out of the way, and now that both of them were off the rails, it wasn't a simple matter of firing up steam engines and shifting them. He was going to have to hope there was enough slack in the loading chains.

"It's one of those *Wind Breaker* guys, I'm sure of it!" called a voice from inside the cargo hatch above.

"Dang right it is! You reckon one of you boys'd be willin' to lower them chains a bit?" he called.

"What are you, crazy?!" the man shouted down to him.

"That's what folk keep tellin' me," Coop said.

He jumped from the cart to one of the dangling chains and started to pull himself up. As he drew closer, he noticed only one of them was armed, and the weapon was at his side. One of the other grunts tried to boot him from the chain when he was close enough, but he swung to the edge of the cargo bay and pulled himself up. In a flash, he had his own gun out.

"Awful kind of you to not take potshots at me when I was on my way up," Coop said. "We got a truce or somethin' I don't know about?"

"No, you idiot!" shouted the man with the gun at his side as his partner circled around to try to flank Coop. "That stuff you just broke open is pure pyrum. You can't be firing guns around that stuff. The whole place will go up in flames!"

Coop backpedaled, eyes fixed on the man nearest to him. Outside, Gunner's own shots had notably died away.

"Huh. If all it takes to keep things civil is to dump a load of that stuff on the ground, I reckon I ought to start carryin' it around with me." He holstered his gun and raised his fists. "Hope you don't mind if I make this one quick. Got a job what needs doin', and it ain't gonna wait."

#

Gunner dashed across the tracks to the loading station. He tried to ignore the fact that he was wading through enough pyrum to immolate him in a flash. Fortunately, a ready distraction came in the form of a hulking grunt plummeting down from the cargo hatch to thump painfully onto the ground. A moment later a second one fell into the C-6 cart. Gunner hopped the side of the cart and dumped the man out, then looked up to find the chains lowering. He grabbed the hooks and pulled them over to the mounting points on the cart. Additional angry voices were filling the air now, and a muffled voice was shouting something over the talking tube. For better or worse, the pool of accelerant around him was enough to keep all but the most foolhardy of grunts and fug folk at bay. The moment the pair of men willing to brave the flammable stuff drew near enough, Gunner pulled a pistol out again.

"You wouldn't dare," barked the scrawnier of the fug folk. "One wrong shot and the whole place goes up, you included."

"You forget two very important things," Gunner said. "I don't make wrong shots, and I really don't think whatever you'd have in store for me if you caught me would be superior to a short, fiery death. I really suggest you take your boys here and get clear, because you do *not* want to know what I've got planned next."

The two fuggers tested him, each taking a step forward. Gunner cocked his weapon. The motion was enough to drain the last bit of resolve from his foes. They held their ground as the chains drew tight and the cart started to rise into the cargo hold.

Gunner looked up. "Coop! Did you clear the ship out?"

"Been a little busy workin' the machinery, Gunner. We ain't all been runnin' around makin' a fuss. Some of us've been workin'."

"Then head out and secure the ship. I'll handle the rest."

Coop nodded and dashed into the bowels of the ship. Gunner scraped the pyrum from the bottom of his shoes as best he could and waited until the cart was far enough inside for him to hop the side and dash to the controls. He finished the bare minimum of precautions to secure the payload and shut the cargo hatch, then dashed off to help Coop.

When he reached the deck, he found the remainder of the crew was clustered about the helm. The captain, a diminutive aristocratic fug man, was supported by two grunts. One had a knife. The other had improvised a club out of a belaying pin.

"The roof is closed and locked. It can't be opened from the ship. It can't even be opened from the complex. That's operated via a control room half a compound away, for precisely this reason!" the captain shouted. "You've trapped yourselves, you idiots."

"Captain, I do so hate to disagree with a man on the vessel he commands, but just how much do you know about me and my fellow crew?"

"More than I care to believe," the captain said. "No one could do the things people claim you've done. No one insane or foolish enough to attempt them would be intelligent enough to succeed."

"Then you're wrong on a number of levels. First, my friend Coop here is more than foolish enough to try anything. And I fancy myself intelligent enough to succeed. And as for insanity? More than enough of that to go around. But the biggest mistake you're making is the assumption that it's possible to trap a man with access to coal, pyrum, and burn-slow."

He heaved the pack from his back. It struck the deck with a dull thud. The flap fell open to reveal a few more pounds of the chunky clay mixture.

"What the hell is that?"

"We just call it burn-fast. I reckon you'd call it a bomb," Coop said. "Wanna know where we smeared it?"

"You wouldn't... you wouldn't *dare*," the captain said.

"Why do people keep saying things like that?" Gunner muttered.

He turned and raised his pistol, taking aim at the retaining hook farthest from the more energetic of components being stored in the complex. He fired. The bullet struck. With a thunderous burst, the clay exploded, taking the retaining hook with it.

"You'll kill us all!" the captain said.

"Nonsense. Only the people in the complex. I'd suggest you all retreat. The next few explosions are likely to be a good deal more exciting. My friend will help you to the ground."

Coop took the hint and grabbed one of the still-startled grunts. He heaved him over the side, where he landed on a stack of emptied sacks from the loading process. Quick work from Gunner and Coop sent the other men swiftly after him.

Gunner said, "You take the controls. I'll take the mooring lines out and get the door open."

"One second," Coop said.

He whistled sharply. After a few moments, a scrabbling form rounded the edge of the envelope and dropped down onto his shoulder to nestle herself back into his coat.

"All right. Make with the noisemakers," Coop said.

A few rifle rounds were all it took to sever the pair of mooring ropes keeping the airship anchored. Next came the shots for the booby-trapped retention loops. One by one they were shattered by the explosions. A few errant fragments started to smolder, encouraging the crew of the facility to choose discretion over valor and remove themselves and their injured brethren.

Orange flames started licking up from below as crates, sacks, and pyrum lit.

"Is this place going to stay in one piece long enough for us to get out?" Coop asked.

"That depends upon how quickly you can get us out," Gunner said. "I would err on the side of speed in this case."

Gunner aimed for the sabotaged chain next and took his shot. A counterweight fell to the ground with an earthshaking thud, and half the roof screeched open with two apocalyptic crashes. The freshly opened roof revealed three heavily armed patrol ships moving into position overhead.

"I've got good news and bad news," Gunner said as he peered through the smoke in his search for the glob of explosive that would blow the final chain.

"Still comin' in pairs, I see," Coop said.

"It looks like only about half of the patrol ships took the bait and went to check out where we left our ship."

"Is that the good news or the bad news?"

"It's the bad news," Gunner said. "The good news is they seem to be similarly concerned about opening fire with all of this pyrum and burn-slow about."

"Ain't gonna help us once we get clear though," Coop said.

Gunner spotted his target and raised his weapon. "Then I suppose we'd best be ready for Plan C."

"I ain't much a fan of plans that get that deep in the alphabet," Coop said.

"Just be glad that one of us isn't allergic to contingencies."

He fired his weapon. The second counterweight fell. The roof screeched fully open, and Coop hammered the throttle to start easing the ship up and out.

"Remember the plan. Keep us over the complex. They can't shoot us down if we'd come down over the complex," Gunner said.

"You just get that doodad mocked up so I can get busy," Coop called back.

Gunner tried to ignore the slowly increasing group of ships clustering around them. He also tried to ignore the downright evil fumes beginning to rise up from the burning complex below. Heavy iron fire doors had already slammed down, separating the place from the hub. If nothing else, the fug folk knew proper fire safety. They *also* knew how to equip a ship. A small first aid station near the door to the lower deck held everything Gunner needed to prepare the key part to the most unreasonable and ill-advised part of an already completely absurd plan. He rolled out some bandage and doubled it over. The size was important.

Grapplers lofted over the railing and dragged across the deck. Gunner finished his crafting and ran to Coop.

"Here! You'd better be as good as you said you were," Gunner barked.

"Hah! You bet I am," Coop said, rather casually accepting the improvised sling and scooping out a handful of the explosive gunk that Gunner had whipped up. "You herd goats for more than a couple days, and pretty soon you're workin' out how to get their attention without climbin' up the side of a mountain to knock 'em in the head. That's when you get good with a sling."

He loaded it up, ignoring the splintering of wood as the sailors on the patrol ships took potshots at him. A few test swings gave him the feel for the weight of his projectile. He spun it up to speed and launched a glob at the envelope. With a soft splatter, it stuck firm to the fabric.

"At this range it ain't even a matter of aimin'. It's just a matter of hittin' hard enough," Coop said.

Gunner kept low and feathered the throttle. He didn't want to keep them from dragging him away from the complex—not that he could have. He just wanted to slow them down, so that Coop's work could be done before they felt comfortable opening fire in earnest.

Splat after splat after splat, Coop delivered healthy dollops of explosive onto each of the ships. The last one—the only ship wise enough to keep its distance—proved the hardest. After three tries, he got a fist-sized glob to hold firm.

"That's just about it. I hope you been watchin'," Coop called.

"I assure you, you've had my rapt attention. Trade places and be ready to push this thing for all its worth. I didn't spot a single weapon, and this plainly doesn't have much in the way of armor, so if we don't pull this off, we'll be trusting the nimbleness of a cargo hauler to save our skins."

Right next to the first aid kit, and in many ways far more crucial to the health of a vessel in the fug, was the emergency ax. He fetched it and put it to work, severing grappling lines. When the ship was cut free, the revving turbines pulled it away and off over the open field surrounding the complex. Gunner raised his pistol and fired, detonating the glob of explosive. As before, it wasn't a colossal blast, but with little more than a few layers of canvas and sealant to punch through, it didn't need to be. The explosion blasted a ragged hole in the envelope, and brilliant green gas streamed skyward. The ship began its slow, inevitable descent to the ground, where the crew would have no choice but to watch helplessly as the same happened to the rest of their patrol.

Seeing one of their own taken down by a single pistol round was enough to persuade the other patrol ships to open fire. Gunner ran low to the deck. An ax swing and a squeezed-off shot were all it took to free them of each new ship. By the time his pistol was ready for a reload, they had only one patrol ship to worry about, and it was the one without a grappler attached to them.

"You know, Gunner," Coop said, barely flinching as a fléchette sent shards of decking in his direction. "That stuff works so good, maybe we should start usin' it against wailers."

Gunner holstered his pistol and pulled his rifle from his back. "Let me get this straight, Coop. You think having a quantity of explosive so volatile a hot bullet is all it takes to detonate it is a good idea, specifically so that we can wait until ships get close enough to stick it to their envelopes and blow holes in them."

"Yeah. Works good, and I forgot how fun a sling is."

Gunner squeezed off a shot, striking the final glob of explosive and sending the trailing patrol ship gradually to the ground.

"I'll take it under advisement," he said. "You know what to do. Straight up until we're out of fléchette range. There are bound to be mounted guns on those walls. I'll search this thing for anything that might be useful to us and relieve you in two hours. It'll be twelve-hour shifts until we get this thing up north, and that only gets longer if we need to shake someone before we can set down at the rendezvous."

Joseph R. Lallo

Chapter 7

The first few hours after their less-than-elegant operation at South Pyre had been harrowing, but Gunner and Coop seemed to have lost the handful of vessels that were after them. Years of experience of avoiding pursuit in the fug, combined with Nikita's polite insistence that the ship's inspector depart, made it unlikely that they would be spotted again. That was good news, because the glorified garbage scow wasn't going to fare well in ship-to-ship combat. It lacked anything in the way of armor, and they were fresh out of improvised explosives. Granted, Gunner still had the rifles and ammunition to make things unpleasant for anyone who might try to tangle with them, but one way or another, their next encounter would almost certainly be their last. They would have to be careful and alert—which was why it was terribly frustrating that Coop had made himself scarce.

"Coop," Gunner barked through the speaking tubes. "Answer, Coop."

A knocking sound echoed back through the speaking tube, followed by Coop's voice. "We got trouble?" he asked.

"If we did, we would have been leaking phlogiston through six new holes by the time you answered," Gunner said.

"I been in fights enough times to know that folks pokin' holes in the envelope sounds a whole lot worse than you gettin' all ornery on the tube."

"I hear a scout ship approaching from the south."

"I hear it too. We're too low for them to see us."

"I would feel more comfortable with a lookout on deck. Either get up here or send Nikita up."

"In a minute."

"What are you doing and where are you doing it?" Gunner barked.

"I found the cap'n's quarters and jimmied the lock. Already been through the cargo hold, and there ain't nothin' worth stealin' outside of spare parts, so I reckon the cap'n might at least have some booze or cigars."

"… Did you find anything?"

"Nothin' to smoke or drink, just loads of paperwork. Workin' for Cap'n Mack all this time, a fella starts to forget how much regular navy types have to cross their *I*s and dot their *T*s."

85

Gunner groaned. "Linguistic shortcomings notwithstanding, if you're through pillaging, I want you on deck."

"In a minute, I said," Coop snapped. "There's a puzzler down here I'm tryin' to work out."

"I really don't have the time to wait for you to unravel a mental knot. You haven't got the intellectual dexterity for it."

"You been really showin' off them long fancy words of yours ever since you started writin' letters to Prist on the regular."

"Just tell me what you're trying to work out so we can get focused on the task of running a four-man ship with two men."

"You remember how we had to load this barge full of that condiment stuff?"

"Contaminant."

"Right. Well I got the manifest here, and we didn't need to bother. That was next up to be loaded."

Gunner's jaw tightened. "Where was it going?"

"Taxton Yards."

"Taxton Yards..." Gunner's voice was simmering with anger. "The waste station west of Ford's Peak."

"That's the one."

"The waste station the Well Diggers routinely scavenge goods from. The one that's not a *tenth* as difficult to break into as South Pyre."

"Yeah. Says here this is the fourth shipment of six. I reckon we'd've had a quicker, easier time of it if we'd just gone there in the first place. Which is why I'm tryin' to work out why Dr. Wash'd send us to South Pyre to begin with. Ain't but two ways I could figure that a man would do what he done. Either he didn't know about the easy pickin's, or he was itchin' to get a fat lip and a busted rib from us after we worked out he sent us the long way round."

"Dr. Wash hasn't earned himself the benefit of any doubts." Gunner spun some valves. The ship started to pitch upward.

"What's your plan?"

"We're going to get in tapping distance of that scout ship. It's a good deal faster than us, and it's heading in the right direction. Get Nikita in position. We're going to try to get a message to the others to let them know they need to keep a closer watch on our new collaborator."

"They better watch out for Dr. Wash, too."

"...Yes, Coop. Yes they should."

#

Out of a combination of habit and common sense, Nita put the ship down just beyond the point she reasoned it would be visible to the academy. As strange as it was to have visitors arrive on foot, it was worth the questioning glances of the locals if it meant they wouldn't be able to find and disable the ship and keep the group from leaving.

Dr. Wash and Dr. Prist were leading the way, the latter with a bag over her shoulder containing the bulk of what they'd earmarked for trade. Lil and Nita were a few dozen paces back.

"I don't like it one bit," Lil said. "I don't like this guy doin' the talkin'."

"We agreed that Wash and Prist would have the best chance of working out a deal. Wash has bribed more than his share of guards over the years, and Prist is a fug woman. The alternative is a Calderan, who may as well be a visitor from another world as far as most locals are concerned, and Lil Cooper, who may as well be a boogeyman."

"All I'm sayin' is I never signed off on this," Lil said.

"... You did, Lil. Just before we left, we were unanimous in this decision."

Lil squinted at her. She wheezed a bit and loosened the mask to let a whiff of fug in. "You sure about that?"

"They wouldn't be ahead of us if you hadn't given your blessing. This whole mission is about you."

"This whole mess is speedin' up, then," she muttered. "We ain't gonna make it."

"We'll make it."

Lil unbuckled the mask and pulled it off to take a few deep breaths before restoring it. "I ain't had a proper breath through this thing in a day. Look at me, I'm breathin' this stuff pert near exclusive now. Even the fuggers don't do that. I'm some sort of super fugger in the makin'," she said.

"Dr. Prist says that's just until the change is complete."

"Dr. Prist's just guessin'. She never went through this. She was born the way she is. For all we know, I'm liable to need a backward mask to give me fug when I'm up top from now on."

"That won't happen."

"It won't unless it does. We ain't had this argument before, have we? It's one thing for me to be losin' it. You don't need me chewin' your ear off about it every few minutes."

"Until now you've been a bit more optimistic."

"Well, I ain't no more. Give it to me straight, Nita. How am I lookin'? How fugged-out am I? I been avoidin' mirrors 'cause I ain't in the mood for bad news. You can at least break it to me easy."

"Do you want me to give it to you straight or break it easy?"

"Straight. In an easy sort of way."

Nita peered at her. "It's hard to tell in this darkness and with the fug painting its haze over everything, but you're looking a little pale. And your hair is lightening up a bit at the roots."

"I ain't gettin' all long and bent up, am I? Dr. Prist ain't too twisty. You reckon maybe ladies get it easy, don't end up stooped over like half of the other skinny fuggers?"

"You look just like the deckhand I met back in Caldera. The one who helped me get through my first voyage and did me the kindness of not laughing at me when I couldn't keep my lunch down past the first turn. I just wish you didn't look so tired and worried."

Lil snickered. "You made an offering on the *first turn*?" She pulled out her pad and hastily scribbled it down.

"Okay, then. You did me the kindness of waiting until we were friends for a while before laughing at me."

"Was it at least the big swing on the first turn or were we just tiltin' a bit?" Lil asked. "I wanna know how you stacked up against Coop. I remember *he* was feedin' the fish for pert near the whole first trip…"

#

Dr. Prist marched beside Dr. Wash, eyes fixed firmly ahead. She wasn't accustomed to being on the front line of the *Wind Breaker* crew's shadier dealings, but it would have been a lie to suggest there wasn't something of a thrill to it. Not only was she about to get access to a trove of new information, she was doing it to expand the horizons of known science and potentially remedy a woman who had been a very good friend to her. Rare did a situation arise that allowed a career academic to feel like a revolutionary.

Wash looked up to her. "You just let me do the talkin'. Inside, you'll be callin' the shots and tellin' these guys what you need to know, but until we get through those doors, I'm the one with all the know-how."

"I have no problem leaving the specialty work to the specialists, Dr. Wash. You need not remind me."

"Yeah, well, most of the smart fuggers I deal with have a way of takin' charge on things they don't know squat about. You ain't seen things go haywire until a bean counter shows up and tells a whole workshop how they should be doing their jobs."

"You speak as though you have experience in such things."

"I seen a few things turn sour. All right. Here's our guy. Watch how it's done," Wash said.

The pair stepped up to the main gate in the fence surrounding the academy. It was a far cry from the institution to which Prist owed her training. It was downright dilapidated. Long buildings that looked like truncated versions of assorted workshops barely stood. Pieces of heavy equipment were scattered here and there, training versions of the machines the workers in training would use in their future careers. The sign, which at some point in the past had brightly proclaimed the place *Solderwick Vocational Academy* had faded over time, with only strategic letters repainted. It now read *So d Vo cad.*

"I'd wondered where they came up with that name," she said. "It seemed an awkward portmanteau."

"Who you callin' a awkward port-mont-oh?" barked the hefty grunt at the gate.

A stubby cigar as thick as his thumb dangled from his mouth. Its end smoldered with an inch or so of ash that had yet to be flicked away. He wore a black and gray guard's uniform that was more patch than fabric, and had a rifle over his shoulder decorated with assorted scratched-in patterns and marks.

"The doc's just workin' through some figures that she needs to settle," Dr. Wash said. "You look beat. How long they had you out here?"

The guard turned to peer at a clock tower at the peak of the only building in the academy that looked like it was properly maintained. "Only seven hours. I'm on for another five, and that's assumin' Bazza gets out here when he's supposed to. He never does. The slob."

"Cryin' shame, friend. Cryin' shame." Wash dug into his pocket and revealed a much finer-looking cigar, along with a rather flashy lighter. "Maybe this'll help pass the time."

The hulking fellow looked at the cigar like a bear being offered a salmon. "That... that a Fugtown Mahogany?"

"It is. I'm a trader by profession. I always keep a couple of these on me. You ain't smoked nothin' so smooth."

"... You're that Wash guy, right?" the guard said.

"My reputation precedes me," Wash said slyly to Prist.

The guard stubbed his own cigar out in his palm, pocketed it, and took the fine replacement. He clamped it in his jaws and leaned low until Dr. Wash had obligingly lit it.

"Not too many people down here wearin' masks as old as those. They got better ones now, you know."

"Call me a sucker, I like the classics. Listen, we gotta get in there and look through your records and research and such. The doc here is a chemist. Rumor has it there's somethin' worth findin' in that records building of yours."

"Obliged for the cigar, but I can't be lettin' surface folk in here, even if they're going to poke around in a pile of worthless papers."

"If you know my name, you know I ain't spent more than a weekend up top in years. I got a whole staff of grunts. I'm about as fug as you can get."

"You need a mask to breathe. You ain't comin' in."

"What about the doc? No mask on her."

The guard tapped his chin. "I don't know. Seems like I could lose some wages if she got caught."

He scratched his elbow with his free hand and turned his head away from them. In what the grunt likely thought was a perfectly subtle and casual gesture, he turned the free hand palm up and waggled his fingers. Wash motioned for Dr. Prist to lean down.

"Give 'em thirty victors," he said, moderating his mask-muffled voice to keep the grunt from overhearing.

Prist fetched the proper bribe from the bag and dropped the coins into the grunt's hand. He jangled the bribe and shoved it into his pocket.

"I could let the pretty lady in, so long as she's gone by the end of my shift."

"I won't be able to do this in five hours if I'm working alone," Dr. Prist said.

Dr. Wash scratched his head, more an act of theater than relief, considering the mask covered his entire scalp. He turned and peered back at the others. Though there was no way to see his expression, from the way he straightened up and delivered a slap to Dr. Prist's back, he was clearly beaming with a devious smile.

"That's why you brought your assistant along, remember? I'll go get her." He trotted back along the path until he reached Lil and Nita. "Hey. Mask off, you're going to be helping Prist," Wash said quickly.

"What? I ain't gonna be of no help to nobody the way I am," Lil said.

"He won't let anyone with a mask come in. I can't hold my breath for five hours, and I don't think the Calderan can either. So that leaves you."

"I'm Lil Cooper! If somethin' like a mask is liable to make 'em skittish, ain't no way they're lettin' a member of the *Wind Breaker* crew in."

"Believe it or not, you guys got fans down here. But more to the point, the guy they got on guard detail ain't the sharpest knife in the drawer, and the grunts don't get up to the surface too much. He ain't never seen you without the mask, guaranteed. If you think this guy is good enough at his job to recognize a pair of eyes and some blonde hair from rumors and assume that they belong to an enemy of the fug who just so happens to be able to breathe down here without a mask now, I think you're givin' fuggers more credit than they deserve."

"… I don't know…" Lil said.

Wash snapped. "Quick, quick. The best time to take advantage of a bribe is when the coins are still cold in the hand. Once he gets comfortable with the idea of havin' earned the money, he'll start thinkin' twice about doin' what it takes to earn it."

Contaminant Six

"What do you think, Nita? My brain ain't what it oughta be right now, so I reckon I'd best lean on yours for stuff like this one."

Nita gave Wash a measuring look, then gazed at the walls of Vocad. "I think it's the quickest way. And if something goes wrong, those are number-ten bolts, and I've got just the right wrench. I'll dismantle this whole place to get you."

Lil smiled. "That settles it." She unfastened the buckles and slid her mask off. "Oof... Never thought this stuff'd feel like fresh air to me," she said, handing the mask to Nita.

"Stay back here," Wash instructed Nita. "This guy might be thick, but it don't take a detective to figure out the lady with the dark skin might be that Calderan everyone's always talkin' about."

"Understood," Nita said.

Dr. Wash grabbed Lil by the arm to lead her forward. Lil shook off his grip.

"Hands off me," she said. "Just because you're helpin' don't mean I trust you."

"Fine, fine. Just hurry up." He led her back to the gate. "Here! Here she is. Dr. Prist's research assistant. Just let them in and—" Wash began.

"Whoa. That don't look like no fugger to me," the guard said.

"What are you talkin' about? Who else can breathe down here without a mask?" Wash said.

The guard leaned low. "Lookin' a little dark..." he said.

"Maybe *you're* lookin' a little pale. You ever think of that?" Lil said.

"She don't talk like one of them fancy fuggers either."

"I assure you, decorum does not come part and parcel with the leaner and less formidable physique," Dr. Prist said.

The guard gave Prist a look. "You're fancy enough for the two of you, I guess. But more of you means more chance I'll get caught so—"

Wash thrust his hand into the bag Prist was carrying and fished out a bottle of gin. "That cover it?"

The guard flashed an impressively pearly set of teeth and grabbed the bottle. "Pleasure doin' business with you."

#

Dr. Prist opened the door of a disused room and peered inside. It was lined with floor-to-ceiling filing cabinets, with a long narrow table running along its center.

"This should be the place," she said. "Come on. We'll try to do this quickly."

She slipped inside and found a phlo-light to illuminate. Lil stepped in after her.

91

"I can't believe they allowed us to walk freely through the academy. In Fadewell, access to a room with this much irreplaceable material would require a key and a personal escort."

"I reckon folks in these parts don't think books're near as valuable as you do," Lil said.

"I suppose not. Now, if we are going to find what we need, we will need to divide and conquer. Remember, we are looking for Contaminant Six. You're likely to find reference to it in books about material handling, safety procedures, accident reports…"

"See, you started all that off with the word 'remember,' and that ain't a thing I can just *do* anymore," Lil said.

"Right, right. One moment. I'll make a note of it."

Prist paced along the table until she found a sheaf of blank pages and some pens. She blew the dust off the pile and fought with an inkpot until she was able to fill a fountain pen.

"Uh… Doc?" Lil said.

"I'll be through with your notes in a moment."

"No, it's not that. I was just… what's it like?"

"What is what like?"

"Bein' a fugger."

"I'm afraid I don't have any points of comparison, Lil. It is not wholly unlike being a surface person, I suspect."

"It sure seems different. The grunts seem pretty okay. But you and Digger are pert near the only skinny fuggers… Sorry, is there a name for what you folk are? As opposed to the grunts?"

"We simply refer to ourselves as fug folk, while referring to the labor class as grunts. In retrospect, it *is* rather classist and dismissive."

"Point is, you two are the only ones that didn't seem like your whole deal was lookin' down on folk and figurin' out how to keep 'em in their place. Am I gonna be like the rest of those fuggers when I come out the other end of this? Or am I gonna be like you?"

"Our society is… I am not certain I can justify it, but there are reasons for it. There are so few of us, the position from which we look down upon others is far more precarious than you might perceive it to be. Living as a fug person is a bit like living like a circus performer. Taming wild creatures with whip and chair, always knowing that given half a chance they would rip your throat out."

"You ain't paintin' a picture that's makin' me feel like I got you folk wrong, Doc."

"As I said, it may not be justifiable, but it is reality. People like me? The second-generation fug folk? We inherited a world where faltering in our established ways for even a moment puts us at risk of bringing it all crashing down on all of us. If things had been different from the beginning, perhaps the world would be a more equitable place now. But it is what it is, and all of the well-deserved animosity developed over years of executing what it now turns out was primarily the plan of a single man, the late Mr. Tusk, has served to reinforce the widely believed fact that rigid superiority is the only alternative to oblivion."

She handed over the first sheet. "This is what you're looking for. I'll write down some other possibilities as well."

"Gotcha, Doc. But… tell me, what was it I asked?"

"You asked if you would become the ruthless sort of fug person, or if you would be like me."

"I thought so, but with what you were goin' on about, I wasn't sure maybe I asked another question and forgot."

"No, no. Forgive me. I seek to establish context for my answers, as so often context is everything. And that, I believe, is the answer to your question. I don't think there is anything different in a fug person's heart than in a surface person's. In the metaphorical sense, at least. Physiologically, fug folk tend to have a slower heart rate and—"

"I ain't got the wits left for you to be wanderin', Doc."

"Right. Our minds may be sharper or duller—and even that is supposition and conjecture—but you will no more be afflicted by Tusk's sensibility from the start than a child might be born with hatred in their soul. Perhaps it is wishful thinking on my part, but I cannot believe that my people are implicitly evil." She handed over the second sheet. "This should be enough for you to do your search."

"Got it," she said, snatching the pages and trotting over to the first filing cabinet. "Hey, so long as we're on the subject. You folks got favorite foods and such? Seems like you don't get near as into a meal as we do."

"I have noticed that surface folk and grunts seem to more enthusiastically partake in some of the more basic aspects of life. I suppose it is possible that sense of taste and similar aspects are muted somewhat."

"No offense, but here's hopin' I'm a grunt, then. Losin' my memory and gettin' all twisty is one thing, but you tell me I ain't gonna enjoy a plate of biscuits and gravy no more and I'm liable to wonder if life is worth livin'."

#

"I think I got somethin', Doc!" Lil said.

She trotted over to Dr. Prist, holding a folder. So far the search had been largely fruitless. Dr. Prist had found a Material Safety Sheet, a match for what she likely had in her library in Ichor Well. She'd copied it on the off chance it was more detailed or up-to-date than her own. That was the entirety of their findings.

"It says here 'Incident Report' and 'Contaminant Six' like you jotted down for me."

"Splendid. Let us hope we can find something worthwhile within."

"Should I keep lookin' while you go over it?" Lil asked.

"You absolutely should. We've been at this for hours and I don't know how much longer we can risk remaining here."

"Hours? Feels like we just got here…" Lil said. She paced back to the open cabinet. "Doc?" she called. "Was I searchin' up or down?"

"Left to right, top to bottom, front to back," Prist replied quickly.

She gave the instructions with a practiced efficiency, because she'd had to remind Lil of them three times since they'd arrived. The poor girl was getting worse.

Prist opened the folder and began to digest the contents.

Subject: Winston Albus

Cause of Death: Acute Respiratory Failure due to toxic exposure.

Description of Incident: Three hours into a ten-hour shift, subject was deployed to the central reaction chamber to assist in the transportation of casks of Contaminant Six. Subject was a plumbing specialist in the midst of a full system repair of a water supply issue. His lack of specific materials-handling training led to an exposure, the result of a small leak in a larger cask. After experiencing the skin irritation indicative of C-6 exposure, the subject followed available sanitation protocols. Standard procedures were utilized to cleanse and sanitize the exposed portion of the facility and the exposed flesh of the subject. Shortly after the sanitation procedure, subject complained of shortness of breath and a burning sensation in his hands and face. Excessive coughing produced indigo discharge.

Thus far it had roughly matched the incident in her own reference material. There were a few inconsequential additional details, but nothing enlightening. Unlike in her book, however, the event remained detailed rather than lapsing into vagueness.

Safety officers on duty responded to the complaints of discomfort according to established safety procedures. The subject was taken to the nearest first aid station. En route, the subject appeared to recover. Ragged coughing eased. Complaints of burning sensations on exposed areas decreased. After topical treatment, he was transferred to the infirmary. En route the symptoms returned and escalated. The subject expired seven minutes later.

That was where the record ended, though it was not where it *should* have ended.

"You got this from that third drawer, yes?" Prist said, hurrying to Lil as the deckhand moved to another drawer and checked her notes against the contents.

"Beats me," Lil said.

"Never mind, there is a reference number on the folder. It matches."

"Why, found somethin' good?"

"It is part of what we were looking for, but proper accident reports, particularly of this type, include the postmortem. This man died, but there is nothing about the confirmation of his cause of death. I am hoping it is in another folder. If we are *tremendously* lucky, the whole of the next folder will be dedicated to it, and it will include everything we need."

She sifted through the file drawer. A gap in the numbering showed where the folder had been. Having copied the useful information, she stowed it again. But the next folder was unrelated. Nowhere else in the entire drawer was there anything indexed with C-6 or any variation of it.

"The files here have been redacted as well."

"Huh?"

"Someone removed information. ... I don't understand it. Why would they *do* that? A man's life was lost due to an unknown chemical interaction, and rather than investigating, identifying, and distributing the underlying threat, someone has gone to extreme lengths to conceal it."

"Maybe folks weren't too keen on other folks knowin' there was a way out of bein' a fugger," Lil said.

"Admittedly, my sample set is not comprehensive, but I've yet to meet a fug person who had any desire to *cease* being one." She shut the drawer and paused. "We have been focusing on C-6 events that end in death, and to our knowledge there has been just one. If they've stripped away the parts of the file that were of interest to me, then we need to find out what made this one different. Give me your reference sheets."

Prist took the pages from Lil. "Go back to the beginning. Ignore this line here about fatality. I'll cross it out. I want to know about *all* C-6 events. While you're at that, I'll start looking into safety procedures."

"If you say so."

#

With four hours gone and time running out, Prist was left with little more than a dozen or so hand-copied pages.

"What time were we supposed to be out of here?" Lil asked.

"We have forty minutes," Prist said.

"You sure you ain't got nothin' more for me to do? I swear I can feel my marbles clackin' around, waitin' to slip away. Sittin' in a dust-smellin' room waitin' and watchin' a lady pull her hair out over some scribbles ain't how I was hopin' my last memories would go."

"I'm sorry, Lil, but we need to be certain there is nothing else we need from this place. All we've found that separates the fatal C-6 event from the nonfatal ones is that there was a plumbing problem at the time. That implies the absence of water, and perhaps the absence of drainage. I don't see how either of those could have caused this reaction. I would suggest it was genuinely something as simple as an allergic reaction, but if it *was*, why would so much information around it be redacted?"

"You actually askin' me? Or you just thinkin' out loud?"

"It was a rhetorical question."

"Sure, but are you actually askin' it, or just thinkin' out loud?"

Prist sighed. "I wasn't actually asking you, but if you have any insight, I would dearly love to hear it."

"Uh... You said there was a plumbing problem, yeah?"

"Yes."

"And this fella was cleanin' up?"

"He was."

"With what? If there wasn't any water, how'd he clean up?"

"Procedures call for sawdust to absorb C-6 spills, even when plumbing *is* available. Such was the case in every other spill."

"Oh. Well, that's all I got."

Dr. Prist gazed over the walls of information. "... Death..." she murmured, pacing to the end of the records room.

"What's that again?" Lil said.

"The postmortem was missing from the accident report. Presumably they were seeking to conceal something. But it's just possible one hand didn't know what the other was doing. Separate from the investigations are simply the raw death records. Here."

She pulled out a drawer and consulted a file. It was the work of moments to find the month the incident took place. Deaths were quite rare in the fug facilities. For what it was worth, they took their own safety very seriously. The fatal accidents were so rare that there wasn't an individual file for the month. Rather there was one for the full year. Only seven deaths. For six, there was the full report: Name, date of birth, date of death, cause of death, next of kin, and various physical measurements. But for the final one...

"There is an entry here for an unnamed surface person. Cause of death is asphyxiation. He was the same weight and height as the man who had the accident, and the date of death is the same with just a seven-hour separation."

"What's that mean?"

"It means this was a fug man who died a surface man."

"So the stuff works?" Lil said excitedly.

"The stuff was able to, in the space of several hours, render a living fug man into a dead surface man. I wouldn't call that evidence of an effective treatment, but it is very strong indication that a physiological change is possible. The questions are how, and if it can be done safely."

"Good enough for me!"

"Well, there we have it. We could spend days sifting through this and not find another morsel that is useful to us," she said. "We've copied incident reports, safety protocols, and what little specific information there is to C-6. If there *is* something of use here beyond that, I doubt we'll find it in forty minutes. Come on. Let us head back."

They gathered their notes and ensured every book and file was as it had been when they arrived. This place looked like it hadn't been used in months, so there was very little chance that their research would be noticed, but given the history of chaos that followed the *Wind Breaker* crew, a few ounces of precaution were advisable.

Dr. Prist and Lil left the records room and hurried to the courtyard. Though this was ostensibly the precise sort of place the good doctor should have felt at home, something in the expressions of the students and trainees made her uncomfortable. Female fug folk were a rare sight, but something told her the novelty of spotting two of them in once place wasn't the only reason for the lingering stares she was getting.

"Stay close," Dr. Prist whispered. "I've suggested that baser appetites are less subdued in grunts. I would further suggest we not test that hypothesis." She turned. "I... Lil?"

The deckhand wasn't beside her. A brief, panicked look revealed her to be standing a few strides behind, eyes turned skyward.

"Come on. Don't dawdle," Dr. Prist said, hurrying back to her. "You don't want to stand out right now."

"Why ain't... why ain't we up top?" Lil said, eyes squinted and gaze distant. "Ain't we supposed to be up top?" She turned to Prist. "When'd we get off the ship?"

Dr. Prist stooped a bit to look Lil in the eye. "You are disoriented. We've been in this academy doing research, but it is time to get back to the ship. Quickly."

"Academy? No. No, I ain't had the time or notion to go to no academy. Nothin' for a Cooper at the academy except for a mess of snooty eggheads who ain't got nothin' better to do than look down their noses at us and give us figures that don't need figurin'."

"Quickly," Prist said, wary of the intensifying interest of the grunts milling about in the courtyard.

She grabbed Lil's arm. Lil pulled away.

"You get your hands off. We ain't even been introduced yet. Lady or not, I ain't lettin' somebody paw at me while I'm down in the fug. Bad place for a tussle, on account of I might lose my…" Lil attempted to adjust her mask and found it missing. "What the…" She gasped. "I lost it! I lost my dang mask!"

"Lil, please. I'll explain everything. You just need to calm down."

"Like heck I need to calm down." She started to gasp and wheeze. "I can't—I can't breathe this stuff. I'll choke. I can't—"

"You've been breathing it for hours," Dr. Prist said.

"Something wrong with the little lady?" asked the guard they had bribed.

He was pacing in from the entrance and had the look of a man who was beginning to regret giving these two the benefit of a doubt, bribe or no.

"You gotta get me up top! Quick!" Lil squealed.

"I apologize for my assistant's behavior," Dr. Prist said quickly. "She didn't quite have the attention span for research and she, er…"

The creeping fingers of panic started to grip Prist's mind, but she wrestled one last bit of subterfuge from her wits before they abandoned her. She grabbed hold of the bag over Lil's shoulder and fished out a bottle of whiskey that had been earmarked as a possible bribe if needed. She held it up.

"She had a bit to drink to steady her nerves, but it's had quite the opposite effect."

"You two don't just stand there. Maybe it don't matter to you, but if I don't get some fresh air, I'm liable to keel over, and then you'll have to answer to Cap'n—"

Dr. Prist clasped a palm across Lil's mouth and thrust the whiskey bottle into the guard's hands. "I think you'd better take this away from her, and if you wouldn't mind, lead us to the exit," Prist insisted.

"Gladly," the guard said, slipping the whiskey into a jacket pocket and reaching for Lil's arm.

Visions of flailing fists and boots flitted through Prist's mind. She wisely pulled Lil away from the guard's grasp. "I'll calm her down. Just lead the way."

"Fine, fine. Just get moving. You act up any more and people will ask questions I don't want to answer."

The guard quickened his pace. Prist pulled Lil along.

"You better—" Lil wheezed. "You better have a dang good explanation for what's goin' on…"

Chapter 8

Lil took long, slow breaths through her mask. She'd been wearing it since she'd returned to the ship, fiddling with the straps and holding them like a security blanket. Nita sat beside her, clasping her hand.

"And that fug lady, how long she been with us?" Lil said.

"Quite a while."

"Long enough to get over me bitin' her finger to get her to let me go."

Nita laughed. "If she was willing to go on this mission, I think a sore thumb isn't going to break her."

The skin around Lil's eyes wrinkled, suggesting a smile beneath the mask.

"Another reason to keep this thing on me. Turns out it's a muzzle too." The mirth left her expression. "It was bad, darlin'. It still is. This ain't like the little ones. It ain't like I'm just graspin' for a word I can't quite remember. This was... this was like all of a sudden everything was new. Like I just woke up standin' in the middle of that courtyard. And everything was gone. The whole plan. The whole trip. It ain't little bits I can't remember. Just me. Out in the open. Under the fug. Surrounded by strangers. Alone."

"You're not alone, Lil," Nita said, holding her hand a bit tighter. "I'm here. We're all here."

"I don't even remember how long ago it was. There's bits missin' from when I got on the ship. It's... it's been a while, hasn't it?"

"We've been on our way for a while, yes."

"Where we headed?"

"We've got to figure out what we're going to do with Dr. Wash so Dr. Prist can finish working on the treatment. There's a small water-filling station that's been receptive to visits from the *Wind Breaker* in the past. We're coming in for a landing soon, and we'll drop Wash there, then go straight to Ichor Well to get your mind back where it ought to be."

"Dr. Wash. Dr. Prist. We got two doctors?" Lil paused. "Wait. Wash is the bird-faced fella."

"That's right. See. You're still holding on to some things."

"Holdin' on by my fingernails. I ain't got but one anchor in all this.

One thing that's keepin' me from driftin' away. And that's you." She shuddered. "When you're out of my head, I don't know what I'll do."

"Then we'll get to meet again. Maybe this time I'll make a better first impression."

"Don't you dare. If we gotta do this thing over, you do it just the same, you hear me? I want us like we are now. Bumpy bits, smooth bits, and all. I like where we are and who I am. Ain't no one gonna mess with the recipe."

"It might be a little difficult recreating the Skykeep incident, but I'll see what I can do."

A soft clink rang throughout the room. Someone was tapping on the speaking tube.

"Listen, Lil. I need to go. With me down here, it's Dr. Prist at the helm, and she's not terribly comfortable with landings. Do you want to come or—"

"No. If I get all turned around again, probably best I ain't wanderin' around on the deck while it's happenin'. I'm liable to pitch over the edge."

Nita stood. Lil held her hand just a bit tighter for just a bit longer before letting her go.

The engineer climbed up out of the belly of the *Rattletrap*. Wash was at the head of the ship, the vacant lenses of his mask gleaming with the faint fug twilight.

"I'll take over," she said.

Dr. Prist gratefully stepped aside. Nita took the helm.

"You know, it's really saying something that I'm the one who can be best trusted to moor this ship. It wasn't so long ago I'd never set foot on an airship."

"I could land it just fine," Dr. Wash said without looking back.

"Maybe so, but I did say *trusted*."

"How is she?" Prist said.

Nita checked the status of the assorted gauges and started to, rather mechanically, work her way through the procedures. When the readings were heading in the proper direction, she glanced over her shoulder. The rattling of the ship would be more than enough to keep Lil from overhearing.

"She's scared. I wouldn't say she's come to accept what's happening to her, but she's become resigned to it. I don't think she believes we're going to be able to help her before it's too late."

"That's good. Best to be prepared," Dr. Prist said.

"We're going to stop this," Nita said sharply.

"I can't work miracles. I still don't know if the information exists to reproduce the effects in the accident report. It could be anything from a rare impurity in the C-6 to something present in the hallway where it spilled to some combination of temperature and humidity. It could just be a fluke. I'll try. Science is about finding the answers. But sometimes the answer is no. As important as it is to be prepared to treat her before the change is completed, it would be wise to start planning how we intend to treat her *after* it's completed if there's no way back."

"We'll treat her like Lil, because she'll still be Lil," Nita said.

"You believe that, do you?" Wash said.

"I believe it because it's true."

Wash turned and leaned on the railing, his back to the looming mooring towers ahead of the ship. "Think about the world," he said. "There's the surface and there's the fug. The light and the dark. Above and below. What you're sayin' is you're gonna find a way to mix them. Can't be done. You can't mix black and white without losin' 'em both. You can't mix top and bottom. Life ain't a couple of magnets. When it comes to people, opposites don't attract, they repel."

"Dr. Prist has become a valued member of the crew, and we have an exceptional partnership with the Well Diggers. This crew can have a fug person. There is no doubting it."

"Dr. Prist? The Well Diggers? We're talkin' about people who, as far as they're concerned, have always been what they've been. Most of 'em either were born fuggers or may as well have been. No one alive remembers them any way but the way they are. And Lil? She won't remember, but—"

"You don't know that she won't remember. You don't know that for sure."

"Why would she be special? Hmm? She already won the jackpot by not droppin' dead from the stuff. You think she's *so* lucky she's gonna be one of the ones who gets to remember who they were? First off, you're kiddin' yourself. Second, I thought she was your *friend*. I wouldn't wish that sort of thing on my worst enemy. Wakin' up one day and seein' a different face in the mirror. Feelin' your brain start workin' different. Squirmin' just a little bit every time fresh air hits you because it feels *wrong* now. Clean slate's the best she can hope for. But you? And that whole crew of yours? You'll remember. And you'll treat her like someone she ain't. Like someone she don't even remember. And it'll grind and grind and grind at her. It'll push her away, push her into the arms of people who don't expect her to be anything but what she is."

"Do you have some special insight into this?" Dr. Prist said.

"I work with fuggers. I work with surface folk. And believe me, walkin' the line between them gets me some lousy looks. You go up and do some business in Keystone with the stink of the fug on you and you might as well have started the deal by spitting in their face. And you come down here and let them know you ain't one of them and the rules change just like that.

Now you're stupid. One of the folks from up top. Gotta pay more. Gotta be kept in the dark. Trust me. I been doing business clinging to that cliff, splittin' the difference between top and bottom just the way I said *you* couldn't. And it ain't no kind of life. I live on the scraps of people like the fuggers, people like the surface folk. People like you. It's a crack big enough for me and no one else. So don't go shoving her into it. She ain't got the constitution for it now, and she sure won't once she's wiped clean."

He shrugged. "Or ignore me. Believe the tale you're tellin' yourself. So long as we get that yes or no that Prist is workin' on, I'll have what I need."

"I think it's time for you to shut your mouth and get the lines lowered to the ground crew," Nita fumed. "Dr. Prist, if you would lower the opposite side."

"Yes. Yes, certainly." She hurried to the reel and started to unwind it. With each revolution she winced. "I tell you, it will be good to be on solid ground. That bite Lil gave me is beginning to itch terribly. One can only wash a wound so well without a proper sink and…"

Nita turned. "Something wrong?"

"Without a proper sink it is difficult to clean properly… The incident report said that there was a plumbing problem on the day of the fatal C-6 incident. I'd focused on the cleanup of the contaminant itself, which does not require water, but if the worker got any of the substance on his exposed skin, he would have had to wash it off. Without water, either it would have remained in contact with him longer, or he would have had to use some sort of solvent to clean it."

She cranked more vigorously to lower the line. "It narrows things down *considerably*. And more importantly, it gives me an experimental range to operate within. There are only so many reasonable combinations of substances that a worker would have had access to in order to clean up."

"Great!" Nita said. "That's excellent. We'll stop long enough to draw some fresh water and food, find something to do with Dr. Wash, and be back in the air as soon as possible."

#

It would be charitable to call the place they'd stopped a town. Even calling it a station was more than it deserved. The unlabeled spot on the map was home to a storehouse, a huge vat of water, a beat-up steam cart, and a shack to house the workers. The only halfway notable thing about the place was the haunting view of the southern end of The Thicket it had. The workers, well aware that anyone stopping here wasn't expecting world-class service, moved at their own pace, which was frustratingly slow, given the circumstances. Things got worse when a second ship showed up halfway through, splitting their attentions further. Rather than extending what should have been a twenty-minute stop into two hours, Nita and the others had disembarked to help with the resupply. The only one still on the ship was Wink, who was watching from the edge of the envelope while Nita directed the workers.

"No, no. We're good on burn-slow. Just coal. Thank you. And you can get the pressure up on that boiler, or the water tank will take forever to fill," she said, hefting a box into the basket of the *Rattletrap*'s hoist.

"You want to know somethin' funny?" Lil said, hefting a box of her own into the basket. "I remember this place."

"Do you?"

"Yeah. For the life of me, I can't remember the name of my neighbor who I lived next to for years before I got on the crew. But this place? I remember. This guy here still owes me for the game of cards he lost when Cap'n Mack, Coop and... what's-his-face were loading up to make a run to... wherever it was we were headed."

"At least that's something," Nita said.

"Not a memory I would've chosen," Lil said.

"Dr. Wash, if you wouldn't mind lending a hand," Nita called.

"You're ditchin' me in this jerkwater and you want me to tote cargo? Nothin' doin'," Wash said. "You want any more help, you take me along."

"The next stop is Ichor Well, and you're not going there," Nita said.

"I gotta say. This lack of trust ain't a good look for you. If this is how you treat people who help you get what you need, I don't know how you haven't been starved out of this business."

Lil adjusted her mask and tapped the filter. "Somethin' ain't right."

Nita signaled Wink. He hopped down and tugged at the controls until they began to reel in the hoist.

"What's wrong?" Nita said.

"Can't. I can't..." Lil wheezed. "I can't get a good breath through this thing. The filter works, but—"

"Take it off. You need a breath of fug."

"I don't *want* a breath of fug. I just *had* a breath of fug."

"Don't fight it. If you need the fug, you need the fug," Nita said, tugging Lil's mask off for her.

The deckhand took a deep breath of the swirling toxic mist and quickly cinched the mask back on.

"You're trying to dig a hole in the ocean," Wash said. "You can't just *will* your body to do what you want it to."

Lil was already wheezing with just the first few breaths through the mask. "Dang it... *Dang it...*" She pulled it off. "Ain't no use..."

Dr. Prist walked up to her and looked her in the eye. "I'm afraid you've reached the second stage," she said. "You are fully dependent on the fug now. I'd theorized such would be the case. Until your physical transition is complete, you can't leave the fug."

"That ain't even how it works with *you* folk," Lil snapped.

"It must be limited to the transition itself. I should be making a note of this. It is genuinely expanding our knowledge of the early stages of surface-to-fug transition."

"I don't wanna expand nobody's knowledge of nothin'!" Lil barked. "I just wanna get back to bein' me, the way I always *been* me, while I can still remember some of what it was to *be* that way! I'm sick of bein' the sort of thing folks take notes on."

The low hum of a distant scout ship passed overhead. The hoist with their equipment squealed for a moment. Wink suddenly appeared on the line, sliding down and startling the already-agitated Lil.

"Wink! What are you doing?" Nita said. "Be careful!"

Rather than the reproachful look Wink tended to give when reprimanded in any way, the aye-aye looked intense and focused. He climbed up to Nita's shoulder and drummed something out on her arm. *Coop and Gunner are close. Coop and Gunner said they had C-6. Coop and Gunner said there was a manifest. It said there was C-6 in Taxton Yards.*

Nita gave Wash a slow, suspicious look.

"What'd the little rat say?" he said, taking a step back.

"Where did you say the contaminant was?" Nita asked, fingers tightening on the handle of one of her heftier wrenches.

"South Pyre. Where else would it be?"

"Apparently, according to the shipping manifest Gunner and Coop found, Taxton Yards."

"Look, I don't know *every little thing*. You should just be happy I knew *one* place you could find it."

"It seems rather unlikely that you would know about something in South Pyre, one of the more secretive places in the whole of the fug, but not something elsewhere," Dr. Prist said.

"You tryin' to double-cross us?" Lil said.

"What possible reason would I have for double-crossin' you?" Dr. Wash said. "I want you to *succeed*. I don't get what I want unless you figure this out," Wash said.

"Could be you wanted Coop and this Gunner guy dead," Lil said. "Could be that's why you sent 'em someplace where they were liable to get killed."

"Talk sense. Then you wouldn't have any C-6 to do your monkeyin' around with," Dr. Wash said.

Contaminant Six

"If I were an untrustworthy person trying to gain the trust of people who were savvy to my deceitful nature, I'd try to make myself just that much more indispensable. Swooping in with a new source of C-6 would certainly do the trick," Nita said.

Wash glanced back and forth at Lil, Prist, and Nita. He slowly reached a hand into his coat.

"You'd best keep your hands where I can see 'em. I ain't so far gone that I can't spot a fella reachin' for his gun," Lil said.

"You think I'm gonna try *fightin'*? I'm a businessman. I work with numbers. There's one of me and three of you. Three and a half if you count the rat. Those figures just don't work out in my favor." He backed against the equipment shed, where the last of the supplies were waiting to be loaded.

"You're actin' awful jittery for a fella who ain't got nothin' to hide," Lil said.

"What do you expect? The *Wind Breaker* crew is famous for two things. Stealin' and killin'. And there ain't nothin' to steal."

"Then why aren't you running right now?" Nita said.

"Because if I'm going to get shot, I'd rather get shot in the front than the back. Call me crazy, but I like to see it coming."

"If I was him, I'd be runnin'," Lil said. "Not gettin' shot beats a bullet in either side."

The group stared each other down for a tense moment. The moment was broken by a distinctive mechanical click somewhere in the dim mist around them.

Lil glared at Wash. "You got guys with guns out there, ain't you? I bet that other ship that came in was one of yours. I bet it's been followin' us since we picked you up, but this dang rattlin' bucket made it so we couldn't hear it."

Wash tilted his head to the side. When he spoke, one could almost hear the smug smile in his voice.

"Sometimes fate just smiles on you, you know? I couldn't't've risked havin' my boys on your tail if you were in the *Wind Breaker* or up above the fug. But down here, and in that thing? I ain't one to turn my nose up at a nice meaty hunk of good luck."

"What do you want?" Dr. Prist said.

"What do you think I want? I want the notes on the cure. And you, Dr. Prist, while I'm at it. You can finish up your work on my watch. I'll take the soon-to-be-former Lil Cooper as collateral. The way I figure it, havin' her aboard will keep that idiot brother of hers and your trigger-happy armory officer from openin' fire if they catch up."

"What makes you think we'll go along with that?" Lil asked.

"Figures. Now I got six guys out there in the dark and you got three and a half. The scale's tipped my way."

"Yeah, well, you forgot two big things. First, I ain't never been good at figures. And second, I ain't got nothin' to lose."

Lil snatched her pistol from its holster. Dr. Prist released a rather undignified squeal and dashed for the ship. Shots rang out. Nita dove aside as bits of gravel and stone pelted her from an off-target blast from the darkness. Lil fired three quick shots in the direction the attack had come from, then turned to take a shot at Dr. Wash. He'd ducked into the supply shed.

"You think I ain't willin' to come in there and hand you your liver, Wash?" Lil barked, dashing toward it.

"Lil, don't!" Nita called. "If he had this planned, who knows what else he's set up!"

"You just get someplace safe!" Lil shouted as she dashed for the shed's door. "This here is the sort of thing I'd've hoped would be the last thing I remember."

A fresh shot came from the darkness, biting into the dirt just behind Nita. She ignored the danger. Wrench in hand, she dashed after Lil. Wink bounded to the ground and scampered toward the foolhardy deckhand as well.

Before either of her fellow crewmates could reach her, Lil kicked open the shed door. She dodged aside as a canister came hurtling out from inside. It struck the ground. The valve on the canister ruptured. It was a canister of phlogiston. The moment the lighter-than-air gas came into contact with the fug, it took on a brilliant, blinding gleam that swallowed the whole of the station.

"Lil! *Lil!*" Nita called.

She could hear the sounds of punches and kicks being thrown. Nita pulled her goggles down, but in the fug the concern was always too little light, not too much. They did little good to restore visibility. What she *could* see in the brief breaks in the swirling green glow were a half-dozen fug folk rushing the shack. All wore lenses just as dark as Dr. Wash's. She charged toward them and through sheer luck managed to drive her shoulder into the midsection of a grunt twice her size. The pair went sprawling to the ground. Nita's wrench met its mark again and again. She bashed the gun out of his hand, then thumped his temple and bashed his ribs. She might well have beaten the man to a pulp if not for the knobbly fingers that found their way to her throat from behind.

A panicked struggle tore her free of the grip, but not before the buckles of her mask gave way. The protective apparatus spun away into the blinding green haze. She held what was left of her last breath and scrambled to her feet. Blinded as she was, there was no hope of her finding it again before her breath gave out. But she still had one chance.

Nita dove clear of the tangle of men and reached into a pouch on her tool sash. Inside was her vial of ichor. She loosened the cap, and the wall of fug pushed back, providing her with a small void in the fug. Pushing back the fug also meant pushing back the glow. For the moment she was left gasping for breath while utterly surrounded by a radiant glow marking the edge of her breathable air.

"Lil! Dr. Prist!" she called.

She wanted to dash toward Lil, to find some way to help her, but she'd lost her bearings. Even if she hadn't, with nothing but the influence of the ichor to provide her with air to breathe, she couldn't afford to move faster than a walk. Any more speed and she would move into the fug faster than the ichor could move it away. She was in a life raft in the middle of the ocean. Worse, she was a sitting duck surrounded by hunters. The only bit of luck she had was that the thicker fug at the edge of the ichor's influence served as something of a smoke screen. At least she wouldn't be an easy target.

#

Dr. Prist reached the rope ladder. She may have been an honorary member of the *Wind Breaker* crew, but she most certainly did not share their zeal for armed conflict without a ship to protect her. She'd scarcely gotten a boot onto a rung when two fresh shots in her direction convinced her that this would be a terrible time to be slowly ascending a ladder. She chose instead to dash for the base of the mooring tower, the sturdiest bit of cover she could spot. This far from the rapidly exhausting canister of phlogiston, the slightly weaker glow made it *just* possible to navigate. She slid to a stop and huddled against the stout support column.

"This is no place for an academic," she muttered, crouching to pull up the hem of her dress and fumble at her boot.

"I see you over there!" barked one of Wash's grunts. The hulk of a fug man thundered toward her from the far side of the mooring tower. "You're in luck. The boss wants you alive. And thinking straight," he said as he got closer. "So I can't even thump you upside the head."

"You do realize you can't force me to perform acts of science under duress, don't you?"

"You think you got any say in it?"

"Perhaps not." Finally she found what she was digging for. "But my gift from Guy may have something relevant to offer the discussion."

She pulled a pearl-handled revolver from her boot and stepped out to face the man. The weapon was downright dainty. He rumbled with derisive laughter.

"What'd'ya think you'll do with that peashooter?"

"I'll have you know, something that Guy made *quite* clear is that, despite his predilection for large equipment, size is quite secondary to its precise utilization."

She lowered the weapon and fired. The pistol made a pathetic little bark. It had but one round, and a very small caliber one at that. But given her choice of target, it was more than sufficient to collapse him into a cross-legged, gibbering heap. A second grunt rushed to the aid of his stricken companion. From the look on his face, and the cudgel in his hand, he lacked the same dedication to keeping Dr. Prist's mind and body intact. She took a step back and silently cursed herself for turning down the far larger weapon Gunner had offered her.

"Now see here, just what do you hope to accomplish?" Dr. Prist said.

"Following orders. And getting even for what you did to my buddy here," the man said as he stalked forward.

Dr. Prist took shaky steps backward, gun in hand. That he wasn't pouncing upon her suggested he wasn't aware it was a single-shot pistol, but the bluff wouldn't last for long. She glanced past him. The phlogiston tank had all but exhausted itself. As such, she could now much more clearly see what had become of the station in the chaos. Dr. Wash and the rest of his men were gone, probably already aboard the second ship. The station workers were nowhere to be seen. Now it was just herself, the stricken man, his partner, and a conspicuously thick cloud of fug creeping toward them.

"Just lower the gun and maybe I'll go easy on you," the man said, stepping over his fallen comrade.

"I have very little reason to believe that your offer is genuine," Prist said.

"You ain't got no choice."

The dense fug-bank caught the grunt's attention just a moment before it enveloped him. A sharp metallic clank sent him stumbling back out to trip over his fallen associate.

"Nita? Is that you?" Prist asked.

"I need a spare mask! Quickly! They have Lil."

"We don't even know where they are! What if they shoot at us?"

"They *will*. The question is whether we'll be able to do anything about it, and I can't like this. Please!"

"Right. Yes of course. I'll return as quickly as I can."

Dr. Prist rushed up the ladder, carefully ignoring the sounds of rattling turbines and barked orders lest she lose her nerve.

#

Nita stood at the base of the ladder. The pistols from both the clobbered grunts had found places in her tool sashes. The blinding glow was gone, but the thick wall of fug at the edge of her personal life raft of fresh air allowed little visibility. All she could do was watch the curling tendrils of toxin fight to get close to her, every breath of wind nudging the poison briefly closer to her. She could hear a great deal of commotion near the other ship.

"Here! Here, I'm here!" Prist called from above.

"Drop it! And come down after it!" Nita called.

"Shouldn't we be getting on the ship? It sounds like they're getting ready to leave. Surely that means they have Lil and—"

"If they have Lil, then we're getting on *their* ship, not ours. Besides, if they brought that many men, they probably have more firepower on their ship than we can manage with just the two of us."

"Y-yes, of course," Prist called.

The mask plopped down in front of Nita. The moment it was cinched in place, she tightened the lid to the vial of ichor. The fug washed over with its chemical chill. That she wasn't currently dodging bullets suggested Dr. Wash and his crew were all busy getting their ship airborne. As the ground crew had made itself scarce once the bullets started flying, that meant unmooring was going to be tricky. There might still be time.

She dashed across the courtyard to the second berth. One mooring rope was dangling free. A grunt was busy unfastening the second one. A surgical strike with a wrench sent him crumpling to the ground. The airship was far more formidable than the *Rattletrap*. Twin cannons emerged from the hull, fore and aft. More worrisome was the line of fléchette guns along the railings of the main deck. Two of the three remaining grunts were hastily taking aim with them.

"Prist! Under the ship, quickly!" Nita called. "They can't target us if we're beneath the gondola."

The breathless chemist slid into the shadow of the ship a moment before the buzz of rapid-fire metal spikes traced twin lines along the ground behind her. They didn't linger, instead tipping up to pepper the deck and envelope of the *Rattletrap* until it was belching steam and phlogiston in equal measure. The ship twisted and strained at the single rope anchoring it to the ground. Nita and Prist dove for the dragging ladder. Rung by rung they hauled themselves up. A face appeared in the hatch above. Nita drew a pistol and took a few shots, but she lacked Lil's gift for accuracy while dangling from a rope. All she managed to do was take a bite out of the wood around the hatch and convince the grunt to slam it shut on the ladder.

Fléchettes continued to blast the *Rattletrap*. It was already slumping to the ground, beyond repair. The mooring rope snapped free, severed at the deck level, and the ship lurched skyward. Through the hatch, the rope ladder began to twitch and sag.

"They're cutting us free!" Nita shouted.

Prist looked down. "We've got to be thirty feet high, and climbing. We're going to die."

Nita squinted in the distance. The ship was struggling to right itself after its battle with its own mooring line. Ahead, the desiccated trees of the lower fringe of The Thicket were emerging from the mist.

"Listen to me. When I say the word, let go."

"Let *go*?!" Prist squealed.

"If we land in the trees, we have a chance."

One of the ropes of the ladder snapped. Prist and Nita slipped a bit. The trees rustled beneath them.

"Ready…" Nita said. "Now!"

Nita let go first, plummeting past Prist. She curled into a ball, hands clasped over her mask to keep it in place. The wind whistled in her ears. Her aim was true. Her body smashed against dry twigs. A sturdy limb struck her in the side and splintered. A short, savage trip through the tree brought her to a brutal but survivable stop. She blinked stars and tears from her vision and caught her breath. The world was still spinning.

Above, the pale green glow of a phlo-light flooded the area. She peered through the remaining branches of the tree she was dangling from and saw the airship making a ponderous turn. Wash didn't trust the fall to kill them.

Hands still shaking from the fall, Nita lowered herself to the next solid branch, then slid to the ground. In this soup, even eyes accustomed to living in the fug wouldn't be able to spot her through the trees, but she'd pushed her luck as far as she was willing to. Her aching, bruised legs pumped madly. She sprinted toward the denser trees and took cover. Above, the fléchette guns buzzed again. Steam-propelled spikes perforated the tree she'd landed in, reducing it and two of the surrounding ones to splinters. A few more blasts peppered the forest around her before the ship turned its attention to the station.

Three deck guns focused their fire on the storage and equipment sheds. Fléchettes couldn't ignite coal and burn-slow, but they didn't need to. Once a few scattered shots struck the boiler for the pump, the main tank failed in a thunderous, deafening boom that swallowed Nita's hearing even at this distance. Pieces of shredded boiler and splinters of what had once been a shed rained down around her like hail.

Nita remained in the cover of the trees until her hearing had turned from a useless hiss to a dull whistle. Wash was gone. Lil was gone. The question was, what was *left*?

She hobbled into the open. "Prist?" She coughed. "Dr. Prist!"

There was no sign of the scientist. Nita tried to scrape together enough of her wits to recall which direction the ship had been heading when she let go. She took her best guess and paced along the ground. Tiny craters from fléchette impacts covered the ground. After a few minutes, she found the rope ladder.

"Prist!" she called again.

"H-here!"

She turned. The fug woman was huddled against the base of a tree. Her rather more elegant outfit hadn't been as useful as Nita's leather and canvas. The skirt and sleeves were torn to ribbons. One arm was held to her abdomen. Her face and arms were slashed by her landing in a far less forgiving tree.

"Are you all right?" Nita asked.

"Nothing... critical. But the arm is broken, I'm sure of it," Prist said.

"Here. Let me help you." She crouched beside Prist and tore away a bit of her ruined skirt to begin fashioning a sling.

"We've lost her, haven't we?" Prist said.

"We haven't lost her. They have her. There's a difference."

"Nita, she had precious little time to be treated as it was."

"We'll get her back." She turned away and raised her voice. "Wink? Wink! Have you seen Wink?"

"Not since the chaos began. You don't suppose..."

"He's alive. He's a scrapper. I'm not sure anything can kill him. He's probably better off than we are. We'll find him and we'll get Lil."

"She was in the final stages of the change. We don't know that—"

"We'll get her back!" Nita snapped. "You know the things we've made it through as a crew. This is no different. We will find her, we will treat her."

"Yes... Yes, optimism. Hope is important. But how shall we find her? How shall we find *anyone*? We are in the middle of nowhere. We have no ship. And the chances are very much against anyone who might come to investigate what happened here being friendly to our cause. We'll likely be blamed."

Nita paced toward the remains of the station. Prist hurried after her.

"What is our *plan*?" the chemist asked.

"I've only been with the *Wind Breaker* crew a bit longer than you have, but one thing has rubbed off on me quite thoroughly. When you don't know what to do next, you point yourself toward where you need to go and keep moving, no matter what that means. I've got my tools. We've got what's left of the station. That's more than I've usually got to work with. If I can't figure out how to get something moving, I don't deserve to call myself a free-wrench. Now let's go."

"But where *will* we go?"

Nita took a breath through the mask. "That's The Thicket, yes?"

"Yes."

She dug a compass out of her tool sash. "Then *that* way is Ichor Well."

"Quite a long way."

"Yes." She gazed at the compass as though it could reveal secrets if she only looked hard enough. "But I know of a place that's closer. And if we're lucky, they'll be able to get us moving faster."

"Who?"

Nita stowed the compass. "I'm not sure you want to know."

Chapter 9

Heavy footsteps echoed down a long, dark shaft. This place had been carved from the very stone of the mountains, a square corridor vanishing into the darkness in both directions. Here and there, a crude sign had been affixed to the timbers that shored up the ceiling. The marks were strange and seemingly without meaning, the same curling shorthand that Dr. Wash relied upon to keep his secrets. He and his remaining crew emerged from a cross-tunnel and tromped onward. The largest of his men had Lil over his shoulder. She'd been trussed up like a pig being brought to market.

Dr. Wash himself held a phlo-lantern in one hand and a stack of scribbled notes in the other. "Should have figured a way to get the notes. My guy ain't exactly a high-class chemist like Prist."

Lil, though gagged, did a remarkable job of making specific threats and handpicked profanities clear.

"Who taught you to tie a gag?" he snapped at his henchman. "I shouldn't be able to tell which bit of anatomy she's threatenin' to yank out of me."

"Eye uhvur ill *ill* oo," Lil mumbled.

"Your brother will *try* to kill me. Should've known I couldn't trust the fuggers down south to take you suckers out." He kicked open a door that seemed far too fine to be in a mineshaft. "Tie her up. Get the lights on. And I want two men on her until she's good and secure. Who's got the rat!"

"Here," rumbled one of the men.

"Put it in the supply room. I want it alive for now. Those things have good memories and bad loyalties. Should be able to get some secrets out of it."

All but the final grunt entered the room that would be Lil's cell. There wasn't much inside. A single chair, which the grunts swiftly set about tying Lil to, and a long table pushed against one wall. Dr. Wash slapped down the notes he had and cast glances at his men and their prisoner every few seconds.

"We know it's going to be C-6. Probably we won't need much of it. Did we hear back from the boys down at Taxton?"

"Not yet."

"Get me as soon as we hear from them. This whole thing gets a lot harder once whatever's left of the *Wind Breaker* crew gets wise to what happened. I want us well on our way by then."

His men finished binding Lil to the chair.

"Good, good. Leave me with her. One of you stay by the door. I'll handle this. I know if I leave it to one of you dopes, she'll be free and swinging one of your guns around before I could pour myself a shot."

His men sullenly obeyed their orders. Dr. Wash turned to Lil.

"Now... Let's just get this over with, huh?" he said. He tugged at the knots and pulled the gag from her mouth.

"When I'm done with you, you're gonna be breathing out your ears! Your own momma ain't gonna recognize you! You pile of—"

"Enough!" Wash snapped. "You and I both know by this time tomorrow you won't remember why you're here or who did this to you." He paced to the table and started to rummage through the bundled-up coat and other things his men had stripped from her when they first grabbed her.

"I got a bet with the boys on how many weapons you've got hidden on you. The over-under is five," he said. "I've got the over." He pulled the pistol from her confiscated gun belt. "Fug made. You remember where you got it?" he asked, clicking the cylinder.

"You shut your face! Or better yet. Get over here so I can shut it for ya!"

"That's a no." He set it down and a moment later pulled a knife from a sheath and set it beside it. "That's two so far. You know, I ain't thrilled to be puttin' your crew outta commission. I been doin' pretty good followin' you around, exploitin' this and that. The stuff you stirred up made for high times around here." He shook her jacket. A pair of brass knuckles tumbled down.

"Three. See, a lot of the dust you guys kicked up, I already knew, more or less. The inspectors sendin' messages. Didn't need to chat one up to know that. Just have to hang around down here long enough and you'll work it out. I'm a little jealous you figured out the tap-codes as fast as you did. Took me forever. But then, I also didn't know they were smart enough to do their own talkin'." He clicked open a switchblade from one of her inside pockets.

"Four already." He continued to rummage through her coat. "A guy I knew told me, until you know better, always underestimate the common man. You'll hit the target nine times outta ten aimin' for the bottom of the barrel. Of course, that guy ended up gettin' shot in the back by a guy he thought wasn't smart enough to keep a spare gun. That's a good way to know if someone's worth listenin' to, wait and see how they get killed. Point is, I give people the benefit of the doubt. Those ladies you were with? I bet they survived. Gotta plan for it either way. But even I didn't think those bug-eyed rats crawlin' all over the ships could hold a conversation if you gave 'em a chance. I guess there's no accountin' for what the fug can do to somebody."

He walked over to her and knelt to start frisking her legs. She squirmed in the chair, but the rope was too strong and the knots too tight.

"Oh. Boot knife. That's five. One more and the boys owe me a bottle. Like I said, though. Mack's ship has hacked quite a reputation out of the fug, and I been there to gather up the spare parts that came clattering down. Skykeep went down and all of a sudden there were all these people runnin' loose, willin' to break the rules for the right price. Alabaster started bein' a pain and you got rid of him. And then you took down Tusk, which stirred things up like nobody's business."

"You plannin' to talk me to death?" Lil growled.

"No. No. You're worth keepin' as collateral." He slid her belt free and tossed it with the pile of searched clothing. "Besides. Pretty soon you won't know to struggle anymore."

"The rest of the crew is going to get you."

"Yeah, yeah. The rest of the crew. Like who?"

"Ain't nothin' in the world gonna keep Nita from findin' me."

"Mmm-hmm. And?"

"And you just know Coop's already on his way."

"Sure. Sure. Family's like that. Who else you got?"

She blinked at him, a look of growing panic in her eyes.

"And then there were two. It won't be long now."

"The *cap'n!*" she blurted. "He'll come."

"Sure. Sure he will. The captain. And his wife. Without a crew. Without a ship. Alone on Laylow Island." He stood and folded the clothes into a neater pile and laid the weapons out. "Only five. It figures you'd find a way to make the whole bet a wash."

"The cap'n's probably got a plan already. He's probably—"

"Oh please. Give me *some* credit," he said. "I may not have an army to call the shots on. Hell, you made me sacrifice three of my best guys back at that jerkwater. But I got the money for mercenaries. And I sent out three of the best crews I could afford to blast Laylow Island to pieces just as soon as I found out you'd left the boss helpless back there. If the wind was with them, they'll be showin' up any minute now. And as for the rest of the crew, I got plans."

"Yeah? Like what."

He turned to her, blank lenses staring into her defiant eyes. "You're tied up. Your head's half-empty. You're in a mine it'd take you hours to find your way out of. And I *still* don't trust you to know my business. Not the stuff you might be able to do somethin' about. You should be honored. That's a hell of a lot more respect than I ever gave anyone else I tangled with." He called to the man at the door. "Get in here. Bets off, she had five. Get the gear into the supply room, get the weapons into the armory. And get me the aye-aye wrangler. I'll have somethin' for him in a minute."

As her things were gathered up and carried out, Dr. Wash glared at Lil with those empty black lenses one last time.

"I'll be seein' you again real soon, Lil. And you'll be seein' me again. Maybe for the first time."

#

The wind tousled Captain Mack's hair and rustled his beard. It was just past dawn, but he'd been pacing the planks of his freshly installed deck for more than an hour. A full career largely defined by the tendency for other ships to show up with guns blazing had made him a light sleeper, but that wasn't the reason he was awake. The problem was, in part, the island itself. He swayed a bit. An airship was never truly stationary. Even when it was moored, it bobbed in the breeze. The same went for the cities of Rim. Built onto the sides of the mountain, most of them creaked and shifted with the breeze just as surely as a ship did. Better they should bend and shift than splinter and break. Thus, a truly solid, motionless bit of land left him uneasy and swaying.

Like his ship, a captain is never truly stationary either. There was always something to do. Someone to oversee. Some plan to make and some mission to complete. All of that had gone away with the bob of the breeze. He was still now. And he didn't like it. If Butch were awake, she would have had a thousand jobs for him to do. Shutters to install. Walls to paint. They would get done. But they didn't feel like real work. They felt like the sort of thing a man did to keep busy while he was waiting for the sand to run out in his hourglass. It felt like there was something important to do, and someone else was out there doing it instead of him. All he could do was watch and wait to see if his crew handled things without him.

Thus, when three dark blots appeared in the glare of the rising sun, he spotted them immediately. Well-honed instincts shouted their warnings loud and clear. Even while they were specks on the horizon, he was measuring them. Judging them. He was a captain. He knew the ship was an extension of the one at the helm. Just as a man might betray his intentions with body language, so too could a ship betray its intentions with subtle elements of speed and angle. What he saw was raw hostility. They were well outside the maximum range for any reasonable cannon, but they were already setting their sights.

"Mercenaries..." he muttered. He reached inside the door and pulled on his long coat, then fished a tin from the pocket. "Glinda! Battle stations. We've got three visitors, buzzin' like wasps."

He could hear her less-than-eloquent grumblings from within as he clenched a thin cigar between his teeth and struck a match. "Gunner talk to you

116

about his little project?" he asked.

Butch replied in the affirmative, punctuated with her own particular brand of colorful vocabulary. Mack cupped his hands around the end of the cigar to ward against the wind until it was lit. Sickly sweet smoke rolled from his nostrils. He shook the match out.

"We'd better hope it was him bein' a perfectionist that kept him from callin' it done, because there ain't nothin' else that's liable to help us out."

Butch emerged, tying a kerchief around her head with all the intensity of a warrior suiting up for battle. She glared at the ships on the horizon, angry not just that they were threatening her home but that they had spoiled her sleep. Mack took a deep puff on his cigar and blew it out.

"Let's see just how bad this can get."

#

Dr. Wash gritted his teeth as he marched into one of the dozens of hollowed-out chambers that he'd had separated into storage rooms. It was almost comical. A small cage had been set on a table. Inside was a very unhappy inspector glaring with a single good eye. Despite his size, he was guarded by two of Wash's men.

"The things I have to do to get what I want done," Dr. Wash muttered. He pointed to the larger of the two grunts. "You, grab the cage. We're goin' up top." He nodded at the other man. "Stay close and keep your eyes open. This rat-monkey comes from the *Wind Breaker*, so it's just as likely to blow up in your face as any of crew."

He turned and marched toward the elevator. As he walked, he spoke. "They call you Wink. Huh? Namin' the equipment. Numbers ain't good enough for the *Wind Breaker* inspector."

Wink remained silent as they stepped onto the elevator. Wash tugged a small stack of notes from his pocket. He slapped it against the cage.

"Know what this is?" he said. "This is that code you been usin'. Supposed to keep what you been tappin' back and forth secret. That crew of yours can do an awful lot of stuff they ain't got no business bein' able to do, but they came up with a piece of trash code. I got it cracked weeks ago."

The elevator reached its highest level. One of the grunts opened the door. The trio and their prisoner paced toward the wind-rattled wooden hatch ahead.

"Right now I bet that little brain of yours is all poppin' and cracklin'. You're a rat, and you're just itchin' to rat me out and tell your bosses about how they been found out. Only you ain't gonna do that. And I'll tell you why. For one, I know the code, and I'll know you said it. You even *start* sayin' it, and you're dead. Number two, you ain't gonna say that, because I got a message here that you *are* gonna say. And you're gonna say it because if you

117

don't, you're dead. Got it?"

He opened the door. They were above the fug. The unique skyline of Keystone was a short distance to the north. Directly in front of them was a long pole with a flag. Precisely the sort of thing an inspector would drum on to send its messages.

"Line him up. Close enough so he can tap through the feed slot there." Wash leaned low. "You listen up, rat. You do anything but what I tell you, and it's over for you. Now I could've had my aye-aye guy send the message, but this code is so worthless, I'm bettin' you've got extra stuff. Little twists and pleasantries and whatnot. Little quirks. Stuff that lets them know who said what. You probably ain't even sure you been doin' it. But I ain't takin' no chances. You send this message the way you'd send a message from your crew."

Wink crossed his arms and turned his back.

"Oh… I see. Brave little critter ain't gonna turn on his crew. Fine. That's fine. Here's the deal. Your buddy down there? The soon-to-be-former Lil? Once she's all emptied out, there ain't more than a fifty-fifty chance the crew'll still want her. So she ain't *that* much good to me. I want her alive, but it wouldn't break my heart if I had to kill her. And I *will* have to kill her if you don't do what I tell you to. I'll kill you too, naturally. Or you could send the message, and the two of you keep on livin'. Got it?"

Wink turned over his shoulder, then sullenly faced Wash. *Give message.*

#

"Do we have a solution on the cannons?" shouted the captain of the lead mercenary ship.

"Still outside of range."

"Wash was pretty clear, we should start firing as soon as we can and don't stop until there's nowhere left to hide.

"It's an *island*, sir. Plenty of places to hide."

"Then we'll be doing an awful lot of firing, won't we? He's paid good money, and he'll be paying better money once we bring him proof. So I don't want anyone taking any chances. I'm piping steam to the deck guns. Man the forward guns. Who knows? Maybe he's got something up his sleeve he's going to send this way. In fact, Number One! Get on the helm. I'm taking over the spotting position."

The second in command rushed to the rugged and poorly maintained helm while the captain marched forward. There were only a few classes of ships that were any good in a genuine battle. Circa had a few. Westrim had a few more. The fuggers had theirs. This wasn't any one of them. Like most mercenary vessels, this was a patchwork mess. Every few months they would dip down into the fug with a barely functional ship and a pile of equipment scavenged from what few of their victims weren't completely swallowed by the sea, and a week later a lumbering monstrosity would emerge, the new parts bolted on and the fuggers well-paid for their service. This ship was unwieldy, it was slow, but it could take a punch and give it back twice as hard. He raised his telescope and surveyed the island.

"Well I'll be... And here I was thinking those stories about taking down dreadnoughts were lies. He's got the carcass of one floating over his harbor like a trophy." He lowered the telescope for a moment. "Wash was right about taking this seriously."

He scanned the island again. "The dreadnought looks to be of little concern. See if you can punch a hole in some envelopes, but don't waste too much ammunition there. Looks like his house is just south of those mooring towers with the red flags. Southwest of the harbor." He swept the scope to the north. "Looks like we've got a two-man long-distance runner moored up. Let's take that down. No other ships in the air, except for the decommissioned dreadnought, and the half-finished something-or-other in dry dock. Don't waste the ammunition. Ah... Munitions shed and fuel shed. Midway between the dry dock and the harbor."

He collapsed the telescope. "Get on the signal flags. Primary target, munitions and fuel depot. Switch to grapeshot once we are within range. After munitions and fuel, focus all fire on the cabins. Fléchette guns, train yourselves on anything that moves. As far as we know, there are only two living people on the island. Let's make sure there are none before we land to investigate."

Subordinates pulled flags from their cases and set about signaling the ships to the port and starboard. The mercenary captain smiled. There were very few mercs in the sky with three ships to their name, and he knew it was all due to professionalism. He was no raider, no pirate. He was the commander of a navy without a flag. He didn't discriminate when it came to targets, certainly. If a man like him started asking questions about who they were shooting at or why, sooner or later they wouldn't have the stomach for the battle any longer. But he was still precise, still disciplined. And that's what separated him from the dozens of ships cluttering up the seafloor.

The three ships under his command started to carry out his orders. One or two salvos smashed into the remains of the dreadnought. The damage was superficial, but a subtle streamer of green suggested they'd perforated the envelope. His own ship fired its main cannons. Puffs of soil and splintered trees rose up from the land behind the fuel depot.

"Reload. Fast, fast. The sooner that gunpowder is gone, the sooner we can move in with confidence and finish the job."

A stationary target is a rare luxury for a gunship. It took just two

Joseph R. Lallo

more shots to find their target, and another two to reduce the supply sheds to crackling and bursting masses of fire and smoke.

"Good, good. Now let's get on top of them. Get those bombs ready to drop."

The three ships split up to widen their swath of destruction. The captain raised his telescope and started calling out specific targets. An unfinished cottage collapsed into jagged splinters. A small fishing boat and the dock it was tied to were chopped to ribbons. The one airworthy ship was blasted to bits. It took mere minutes to flatten anything that might serve as a hiding place or an escape vehicle. Before long, the guns went silent. There was simply nothing left for them to fire upon.

"Nothing..." the captain muttered, eyes trained on the ruined little settlement. "Not a shot fired in defense. I suppose it could be we took them in their sleep. Seems an ignoble way to go for a captain with such a legendary pedigree. Men! I want a crew of six from each ship ready to deploy. Heavily armed. We scour the island in six-hour shifts until we find proof of death. Signal the other ships. Those two trees on the southern tip of the island look to be workable mooring points. Prepare to—"

"Captain! Movement!" called one of the deck gunners.

He turned and followed the man's gesture. It took several seconds for him to spot what the man had referred to. What at first seemed to be a particularly moss-covered bit of stone was fluttering a bit more than seemed appropriate. As he gazed at it, it shifted almost imperceptibly.

"They've camouflaged something. Open fire on it. No sense taking chances."

The gunner angled his weapon. There was a distant, chest-shaking thump. A moment later, they heard a horrid screech and splinter to their port side. He turned to find one of the other ships had been utterly shredded. Half of the decking had been reduced to a cloud of debris, and a ragged hole was venting phlogiston out the top *and* bottom of the envelope. It plunged into the sea like a stone.

He turned back to see that the covering of moss had been partially torn away, revealing the source of the attack.

"Evasive maneuvers! Hard to starboard. They've got defenses! Get bombs ready and keep them harried with fléchette fire, damn it!"

#

"Fine shooting, Glinda," the captain said.

Butch didn't answer, as her ears were packed to avoid being deafened. She was seated at the controls of Gunner's pet project. A steady supply of trith, a good source of high-grade explosives, and the rare benefit of a close look at Caldera's cannons had given him the itch to work with Nita to build one of

120

his own. It was scaled down, significantly, which meant that it was *merely* five times the size of a ship-mounted cannon. It could still punch a hole through anything light enough to stay airborne, just at a somewhat diminished range. That was just as well. Butch had a great many talents, but aiming an anti-airship cannon wasn't among them. Point-blank was the only way she was going to make a hit.

The ship's medic pulled levers. Steam-powered gears whirred and turned. The barrel shifted, drawing a bead on the next of the ungainly warships. In its rush to get free of the cannon's targeting range, it had turned broadside. Cap'n Mack pulled at a chain winch to load the next shell into firing position. That, it turned out, was the bit that Gunner had yet to complete. The device had to be loaded manually, and the sort of ordnance that could take down an airship with a single shot wasn't precisely a walk in the park to load.

Butch barked for Mack to hurry, her words falling on ears just as deaf as hers. Spikes chewed up the stone around them and sparked off the heavy metal of the cannon. It was only a matter of time before a lucky shot put the two-person gunnery crew out of commission. Mack finally finished raising the shell into position. It tumbled into the chamber with a clang that Butch felt rather than heard.

She pulled the firing lever. The gun lurched back. A shell whistled through the air. The timing of the shot was off. It wasn't nearly the killing blow of the first shot. It tore clean through the gondola, venting steam and tumbling planking and equipment into the sea, but the envelope held fast and the ship remained aloft. From the way it pitched aside, chances were good it wouldn't be aloft for very long, but there were still men aboard, and they still had weapons.

Mack huffed and puffed, levering the next round into place. There was only one shell left. They were going to have to make it count. The chain hoist rattled and clinked. Slowly it rose into position. Spikes peppered across the ground around them with increasing accuracy. The whole platform pivoted as Butch took aim. Lighter, sharper claps of rifle fire joined the din. Just as the round clattered into place, their luck finally gave out. A line of blindly fired fléchettes found the well-hidden boiler that powered the cannon. A jet of high-pressure steam whistled from a ruptured pipe, and the workings of the cannon rattled to a stop.

"Dang it," Mack growled. "Glinda! Get down from there. No sense havin' a gunner if we can't move the gun."

He managed to get her attention and signal her to do what she'd failed to hear him say. She slipped from the seat and pulled a rifle from her back. From the way she held it, she wasn't a stranger to the weapon, but was clearly not comfortable with it. They both tugged the wadding from one of their ears.

"Two of us, each with a rifle, against one and a half merc ships. Ain't the odds I was hopin' for when I woke up this mornin'." He took his own weapon from his back. "Remember to lead your shots. Gotta let 'em move into where you're aimin', so…"

He trailed off. Wheels started turning in his head. He removed his glasses and gazed up at the fully functional ship, then looked up through the targeting apparatus of the cannon.

"If we can't move the cannon…"

The captain took a small spyglass from his pocket and scanned across the island. There were precious few places intact, but a small shed at sea level had been missed. It was built low and far from everything else for a reason. It was Gunner's laboratory. It wasn't far from the mounting point of a support wire that ran the speaking tube up to the cannon. They'd yet to install the tube itself, so it was just a narrow cable that had been spared any direct fire.

"New plan. You stay put, hunker down, and keep an eye on that ship. When they give you a shot, take it."

Butch didn't argue with him or question him. In matters domestic, the pair would argue until they were blue in the face, but in combat, they each had their jobs, and his was to know what to do. The rest of the crew's job was to do it. And for now, she was the rest of the crew.

Captain Mack put his glasses back on and stepped out to the edge of the gun platform. He licked his finger to test the wind, then raised the rifle. He took aim and fired at the ship. A cloud of debris burst from somewhere just left of the ship's helm. He'd missed his target but got their attention. The fléchette guns traced their lines of fire toward him. He hooked the rifle over the wire and took a breath.

"If the dang Coopers can do it…"

He stepped off the edge and began to slide along the cable. Fléchettes streaked through the air, steadily tracking closer to him even as he picked up speed. He could hear them getting closer. He was moving fast, dangerously fast. But not fast enough. The ground rushed by beneath him. He risked a look over his shoulder. The airship was beginning to pivot, twisting and lumbering in his direction to put more of its deck guns into play.

The branches of trees started to whip and slash against him as he neared the end of the wire's run. It was now or never. He released the rifle and struck the ground in a chaotic roll. His heart was hammering in his ears, and limbs unused to this sort of exertion screamed for relief. But relief would have to wait. The fléchettes sheared through branches and dug into tree trunks. He could hear the turbines of the ship revving up. The ship was getting closer. He took cover behind the thickest tree he could find. It was all up to Butch now.

#

122

Contaminant Six

Butch stood at the base of the gun and watched. The angle was less than ideal. At this range, the shot would arc high. But she just needed to catch a piece of the envelope and the job would be done. For better or worse, Mack's very visible escape had drawn all the attention of the airship. Four gunners focused their fire on the stand of trees that hid him. She wanted to fire now, to do anything to keep the gunners from grinding up his cover, but she'd been given a job. Her eyes were glued to the range finder. With agonizing slowness, the very top of the envelope brushed the reticule. It would have to do.

She tried the firing lever, but it was as dead as the rest of the mechanism. A crowbar hung on one of the rungs leading up to the gear box, left over from the most recent "adjustments" that Gunner had made. She grabbed it and hooked it over the diabolical device's massive equivalent to the hammer on a pistol. She heaved. It ground back inch by inch, tensioning a huge leaf spring. Finally, it clicked into place. She tried to trip the release, but it was too solid. Like a duelist drawing her pistol, she pulled a large meat tenderizer from her apron and brought it down hard on the release. A second blow. A third. Finally the release tripped and the mechanism sprang. A thunderous blast sent the shell ripping through the air. It was just a glancing blow, but it shattered one of the airship's turbines and ripped a jagged hole through the envelope. A short, spiraling drop sent the airship plunging into the waves.

Butch turned to the partially disabled airship remaining. It continued to shed bits of apparatus and chunks of decking. The turbines had sputtered to a stop. The ship was at the mercy of the wind. It would be a miracle if it made it ashore, and it was already at the extreme end of rifle range. She could set the danger aside for now. There were more important things to do.

She trudged down the steep path. Her heart urged her to run as fast as her legs could carry her, but her brain overruled it. The path was treacherous even before a trio of ships had turned it to jagged gravel with their sustained fire. She wouldn't be any good to Mack if she tripped and fell while trying to find him. When she reached the bottom of the slope, she picked up the pace. She wasn't any more accustomed to sprinting across uneven ground than Mack, but desperate times called for desperate measures. Finding Mack wouldn't be difficult. She just had to wade through the greatest concentration of damaged forest until…

She sniffed. The sharp scent of his cigar hung heavy in the air. It led her to the base of what was now barely recognizable as a tree. Mack was reclined against it, puffing on his cigar.

"You're a hell of a shot, Glinda. If I ain't never tasted your gravy or seen you set a bone, I'd've supposed you missed your calling."

He leaned hard against the tree to climb to his feet. She helped him. This heavy canvas coat was sliced and perforated. Here and there the faded blue

123

was stained with fresh blood. Splinters of tree and shards of shattered spikes had given him hundreds of cuts and gouges of assorted sizes. But the stubborn old man seemed to have been spared anything that a few stitches couldn't cure. Butch suggested as much and grabbed his arm to pull him toward the remnants of their cabin. He tugged his hand away.

"Time for that later," he said. "We had three ships go down. Chances are we'll be havin' company in the form of whatever mercs were lucky enough to survive the plunge. We need to be ready for 'em. I ain't takin' down three warships with a crew of two only to get picked off by a waterlogged gunsel with more duty than sense."

He drew deep on the cigar and exhaled with a pained wince. "Besides, ain't like we got a proper place to patch me up regardless. You all right?"

Butch's only answer was a forceful point toward the dug-in little bunker of a laboratory Gunner kept not far from the shore.

"He got equipment in there? Bandages and such?" He puffed thoughtfully. "I reckon he would. Fair enough. Let's get some of these holes sewed up."

#

The once-proud mercenary captain dragged himself ashore and coughed up a healthy dose of seawater. He rolled to his back and took a grateful breath. The shore was cluttered with the remnants of the three ships he had unwittingly sent to their doom. One envelope was still in the air, but it was drifting ever higher as the last few bits of the gondola fell into the sea.

"Gone... All of them... I'll get them. I swear if it's the last thing I do, I'll get them for what they did to me!"

He rolled to his stomach and tried to climb to his feet. Before he could get his shaky legs beneath him, he felt a rough grip on his waterlogged collar. Someone dragged him to his feet. Next came the cool pressure of a pistol muzzle on his temple and the choking scent of cheap cigars soaked in cheaper brandy.

"Took you long enough, boy," Captain Mack muttered. "For a fella who makes his livin' over the sea, you'd think you'd be better at treadin' water."

The captain raised his eyes to meet his foe's. Cap'n Mack had fresh stitches in his cheek and stained bandages visible through his shredded coat.

"How dare you..." the mercenary captain said. "How *dare* you make light of me? You killed my men."

"Your men came gunnin' for me and my medic. Me takin' you down before you can get my hide ain't called murder, it's called defendin' myself. Or, the way I see it, it's called givin' some folks what they had comin' to 'em."

Mack grabbed the back of his neck and turned him toward the center of the island. "See that, there? That pile of posts and splinters? This mornin' that was the place I was fixin' to spend my golden years. What's left of 'em, anyhow. If you wanted me out of the skies, all you and yours would've had to do was sit and wait. Father time was takin' care of that for you. But you had to come and knock on my door with a cannon. That sort of thing is liable to make a fella ornery. And curious. Now, you might be the one who got to the shore first, but I see a couple other of the folks unlucky enough to fall under your command splashin' this way. First one to answer my questions gets spared. The rest of you are takin' the long way home. First question, who sent you?"

"What good does an answer do you? You have no ships. You have no fuel. You have no weapons."

"I got about half a ship, I got about as much fuel as half a ship'll need, and I got a pistol to your head. So you're off on all three counts. Startin' to see how you came to be in this predicament, if that's the level your brain's workin' at. If you were listenin' close, you'd know that you answerin' me ain't about doin' *me* any good, it's about the good it'll do you, on account of a proper answer's the only difference between a long swim or a hot bullet."

The mercenary tried to muster himself for a defiant glare, but trying to stare down Captain Mack was like trying to stare down a stone carving. When the bearded brute clicked back the hammer of the pistol, he felt his resolve break.

"It was Dr. Wash. Dr. Wash hired us to demolish the island."

"Wash? The fella who runs the hoist network near Lock? Now what would he do a damn-fool thing like that for?"

"He doesn't tell us *why* he wants things done."

"Fair. What were you supposed to do once the deed was done?"

"We were supposed to deliver some evidence of your death."

"Head on a silver platter sort of thing?"

"He supplied a camera. A photograph would have sufficed."

Mack puffed his cigar. "I don't like that one bit. The last few fellas we tangled with have been the dramatic type. Flowery threats and whatnot. If this fella is reasonable, I reckon we'll have a harder time with him. Where were you supposed to meet him?"

"He gave us a rendezvous point in Keystone."

"Where and when?"

"As soon as possible. The surveyor's office. He said it wouldn't draw any attention, someone handing over a big payment there."

Mack eased the hammer of the pistol down and holstered the weapon. "There. You see? You act all reasonable-like, use your brains, and you don't end up with 'em clutterin' up my beach."

"So what are you going to do with me now? And what about my

men?"

"First, we wait for the stragglers to show up. Then you get to see just how obligin' a proper cap'n can be."

#

Within an hour, the rest of the survivors reached the shore. There were seven in total, some worse off than others. Butch treated the most dire of the wounds. When everyone was properly dealt with, she and Mack led the crew at gunpoint to the dry dock.

"Look at her, boys," Mack said when they reached the carcass of his ship. "This here's the *Wind Breaker*. You heard of her. Most everyone has. If you were the philosophical sort, you might say there ain't no sense callin' her such anymore."

He knocked on the skeletal hull. The sound was solid and sturdy. The envelope was deflated, sagging against its supports and shriveled like a raisin. The ship was less a vehicle and more an anatomical model of one. The steam system, the basic framework, and a few strategic bits of decking around and behind the aft cannon and the helm were all that were left.

"This keel is new. The whole dang thing is new. Got repaired and replaced, bit by bit. But philosophers? They just ask themselves questions, tyin' themselves up in knots over things that're clear as day to the common folk. Of course it's the *Wind Breaker*. Because I'm still the cap'n, and this here's still my ship. And lucky you, just about the only piece of this thing that's ready for proper service is the one part you need."

He gestured with the pistol. "If one of you fellas would be so kind as to pull that chain there? All that runnin' and tumblin's left me a bit sore."

The defeated captain stepped forward and started hauling at the chain hoist. Slowly a small but sturdy skiff lowered from the underside of the ship. The captain's gig. It touched down on the slope of the dry dock.

"Climb in, boys," he said.

"Just what are you planning to do?" the mercenary captain asked.

"I'm gettin' you outta my hair. Get yourself in the gig, get yourself in the water, and head due east."

"Seven men in that little boat? We'll be dead in a day!" the captain said.

"Plenty of oars, plenty of fresh water. Put your backs into it, and you can get to the fishing shoals inside of a day, easy. Somebody'll pick you up. It's a fightin' chance. Better than you gave me and a damn sight better than you deserve. Now get movin'. And don't try anything funny like tryin' to turn around, or I'll pick you off like another man would've done while you were fightin' your way to the shore."

Again the survivors attempted to signal their defiance. Again the

126

stone-faced captain stared them down. One by one, the men took hold of the boat and started to slide it toward the shore. True to his word, Mack kept his rifle at the ready and watched them go. Butch lumbered up to him and dropped a sack on the ground beside him. He gave it a glance.

"Fine work diggin' up some proper provisions. Good to know it ain't all scattered and charred. Once these boys are far enough for me to trust they ain't comin' back, you and me gotta work out what's to be done. If Wash is sendin' folks after us, I reckon he's got plans for the rest of the crew. I mean to have a word with him. You find any more weapons worth usin'?"

She shook her head.

"A couple rifles and a couple butcher knives ain't liable to make it easy to get taken serious. Might have to get creative. Ain't no two ways about it, though. Dr. Wash is gonna wish he left me be. Dang fool knocked down my hammock." He smiled around his cigar. "Ain't nothin' for it but to find some other way to keep busy."

Joseph R. Lallo

Chapter 10

Coop leaned heavily on the wheel of the garbage scow. The deckhand's expression seldom changed. On the average day it resided somewhere between dim contentment and idle boredom, with brief spikes into manic glee when the more energetic aspects of his job came to bear. Today, his expression was complex. A mix of impatience, anxiety, and frustration twisting him into something almost unrecognizable to Gunner as he climbed to the main deck to relieve him.

"That's your shift," he said.

"I'm stayin' on the helm," Coop said.

"You've been up here for twelve hours. Take your relief and eat something."

"Ain't nothin' down there but fugger food. Ain't worth eatin'. I'm stayin' on the helm."

"I outrank you, you know."

"So you gonna order me?"

"I already did. Twice. A third comes with a reprimand."

"You ain't never reprim… you ain't never punished no one. That's the cap'n's job."

"The captain isn't here, and *you've* never disobeyed a direct order. Not on purpose, anyway. Now sit your narrow behind down and get some sleep."

Coop reluctantly relinquished the helm. He trudged below decks. Gunner checked the gauges and made a slight adjustment. A few seconds later, Coop returned with a can. He pulled the knife from his belt and deftly opened it.

"I said head below decks to—" Gunner began.

"You said I oughta take my relief, and you don't get no say in where I take it," Coop snapped.

He flopped down on a crate, leaned against one of the envelope supports, and twisted the cap for his vial of ichor. The fug was pushed back, and he was hidden in the thick cloud of toxin surrounding the clean air the ichor provided.

"What sense is there in wearing yourself out, Coop? You being on deck isn't going to make this ship move any faster."

"Ain't nothin' that'll get this ship movin' any faster. In all my life, I ain't been on a ship this slow. That time we had to limp back to Keystone on one turbine wasn't as slow as this."

"It's a hauler. It's not meant to be fast."

"I don't care what it ain't supposed to do. We'd've been better off figurin' out how to get the goop we stole back to that two-seater."

"If you recall, it was the distraction that allowed us to get the 'goop' to begin with."

"Didn't do a whole lot of good. We still had to chuck some of that nasty stuff you rigged up and blow holes in a couple ships to get this far."

"What's done is done. We'll be in Ichor Well in another two days."

"I don't care if—hang on. Nikita's got somethin'."

Gunner turned to see the little aye-aye with the notched tail scamper from within the thick haze around Coop and scramble up the rigging to the envelope. Her enormous eyes were wide, and her ears were twitching and angling to a point in the horizon. Gunner turned his head and cupped his ear in the same direction. He could just barely hear the whine of distant turbines. A passing ship, and thus, a chance for a message.

Nikita drummed at the railing a bit, sending a short message back, then twitched her head at the reply. She crawled back down and hopped onto the helm. Coop had capped his ichor and now stood with his mask in place, focused on what the little inspector had to say.

Someone sent a message from Wink, she tapped.

"What'd he say?" Coop asked.

Nikita slowly drummed out a message. *From Wink. Dr. Prist, Nita, and Lil have the cure. Meet at Caer Wilcot. Need additional ingredients. Merchant has been arranged. Meet with them. Payment has been made. Run up red flag over white to identify yourself.*

"I knew we could count on them! I'll get the charts. Ain't never heard of Caer Wilcot," Coop said, dashing below decks.

"Is that the whole message?" Gunner asked.

That was the whole message someone sent from Wink, Nikita said.

"That's an awfully awkward phrasing you keep using," Gunner said.

Someone sent it from Wink, she tapped, urgency in her expression.

"Got 'em here. Caer Wilcot ain't more than six hours north. Pert near dead on the course we're already takin'. Maybe a touch north-northwest."

Nikita hopped to Coop and drummed out her message on his button, chattering anxiously as she did. *Someone sent it from Wink.*

Gunner narrowed his eyes. "Just how is 'someone sent a message from Wink' different from 'Wink sent a message'?"

Wink didn't send the message.

Contaminant Six
"You ain't makin' sense, darlin'," Coop said.

When inspector sends message from inspector to inspector, inspector says message the way inspector says message. When inspector sends message from crew to crew, inspector says message the way crew says message. When Wink says message to Nikita, Wink says "had." Someone not Wink sent message to Coop. That one said "have."

The aye-aye was clearly frazzled, anxiety and linguistic shortcomings making it difficult to understand her.

"One moment," Gunner said, when he was able to work through the overly simplified language. "I think I understand. You and Wink, and presumably *all* inspectors, have that quirk where you mostly speak in past tense. I take it you speak *properly* when you have to deliver a message meant for human ears."

The way the crew says, Nikita tapped.

"And the message came through with present tense."

Have. Not had.

"Surely that's how it should be, though. Wink was sending the message from someone else. Samantha, presumably. Or Nita."

Nikita shook her head and quickly tapped again. *From Wink. From Wink. Said from Wink. Not from Samantha. Not from Nita.*

"Are you suggesting the syntax was wrong?"

"Ain't you listenin'? She's sayin' the message wasn't put together right."

"That's what—" Gunner released a pained sigh. "The point is, this clearly concerns you."

Not from Wink. From someone from Wink.

"Was it using our code?"

Yes.

"Then it had to have been sent by Wink."

Someone used Wink. Someone forced Wink.

"And you got that all from a few awkward words?"

I know Wink.

"I trust her. She ain't never been wrong before," Coop said.

"Just how often are you relying upon Nikita's advice?"

He scratched his head. "Can't say I can think of any time, but that don't make a difference. She still ain't never been wrong before."

"In order for what she's suggesting to be true, someone would have had to break our code. They would have to have Wink. They would have had to coerce him into sending a message…"

"I bet Wash could've done all that. And had good reason to, if he was willin' to send us down to bounce off South Pyre instead of hittin' the easy

131

spot."

Gunner's hand dropped to his belt, where he anxiously fiddled with one of his holsters. "Open up those charts again, double-check the path and how far off the proposed rendezvous is."

Coop obliged. "Like I said. Maybe a touch north-northwest."

"Now plot a course that goes to the center of The Thicket instead of directly to Ichor Well."

Coop ran his finger along the chart. "Goes right through Caer Wilcot."

"If I was setting up an ambush, that's right where I'd put it. Put some ships somewhere in the rough path, then see if we can guarantee a run-in with a message like this. Which presents a problem."

"I reckon so."

"If they are savvy enough to manage this, they'll have a proper patrol. One way or another, we're likely to have a run-in. We just don't have a fast enough ship to be certain we can escape someone who knows roughly where we're going and roughly where we're coming from. Not without taking a detour that might cost us a day or more."

"We ain't got a day or more. We ain't got the time we spent already."

"Agreed. Thus the problem."

"Let me know if I got this figured right. We ain't goin' out of our way, so we got the choice of headin' in for a meetup where we're pretty sure we'll get dog-piled. We could skip the meetup and near as certain get dog-piled anyway. Or we can hope Wink wasn't thinkin' straight when he tipped us off."

"That would seem to be the current situation."

"I say we meet 'em head-on. At least if they think they got one over on us, but we know it's comin', we sorta got one over on them. That's better'n nothin'." He stroked his chin. "Matter of fact... I reckon I got a plan."

Gunner shut his eyes tight. "Ichabod Cooper has a plan. That is perhaps the most frightening thing I've heard on this entire mission."

#

The next few hours had passed with aching slowness. It was telling that, after hearing Coop's plan, Gunner couldn't counter with a better one. It wasn't that the plan was good. It was about as well thought out as any of Coop's plans. The problem was, when there is no good idea, the only option is to go with the least bad idea, and Coop's was as good, or bad, as any.

Caer Wilcot was a husk of a city, one of thousands that dotted old maps. If they hadn't been on a fug folk vessel, it might not have even been on their charts. Even before the Calamity, it couldn't have been home to more than a thousand people. A factory town, with a handful of homes and a handful of great towering industrial buildings.

"Looks like it was a mill," Gunner said.

He was lying prone on the deck, his longest-range rifle trained on the approaching rendezvous point.

"What sort?" Coop asked, unnervingly relaxed considering what even the best-case scenario held in store.

"Lumber. Does it matter?"

"Just wonderin' how good it'll burn if it gets hit." He scratched his head. "I reckon there ain't much that'd come out of any sort of mill that wouldn't burn real good, though."

"I see our contact," Gunner said.

"What sort of ship?"

"Lightweight patrol craft. Looks like a stolen fug vessel. Recent, too. Hasn't had all of the insignias patched out."

"It sure would be nice havin' one of them. All gussied up so the fuggers'll think it's one of theirs. And fast, too."

Gunner nodded. "It probably has a top speed five times what we can manage."

"We sure it ain't just fuggers?"

Gunner adjusted his sights. "I see surface crewmen."

"Well that settles it. Ain't nobody been up to no kind of good that's doin' it in a fugger ship that ain't theirs."

"Need I remind you what sort of ship we are presently piloting?"

"You implyin' we ain't up to no good?"

"… Fair point." He adjusted the sights again. "There are two armed men on deck. Both are at the fléchette guns. They've spotted us. Weapons trained on us."

"Reckon I ought to run the flags we were told to run? Just to be sure?"

"It can't hurt," Gunner said.

Coop stepped away from the helm and hoisted a red flag, then a white one.

"They're still at the deck guns," Gunner said. "Those two mills are just about big enough to hide a like-sized ship each. The question is, are we up against two of these ships or three?"

"I hope it's three. If they were only hidin' one other ship, we'd have to flip a coin to guess which side the ambush is comin' from. This way we can figure on it bein' both."

"You have a curious view of the world." Gunner stiffened a bit and flipped down a colored lens in front of the sight. "Turbines are spinning up. They're getting ready to target us with their cannons."

"It's now or never then. Don't miss."

"I don't intend to." He leaned low, eye leveled with the sight. He fired once, worked the bolt, and fired again. "Helmsman is down."

"Took you two shots."

"Shut up and get ready for the next part," Gunner said, hopping to his feet and dashing for the hatch to the lower decks.

"It's my plan! I *been* ready!" Coop called after him.

Gunner slipped down into the belly of the hulking ship as he heard the patter of the first few fléchettes start to pepper the hull of the huge, sluggish vessel. He burst into the cargo hold and kicked the emergency release to the loading bay. The heavy hatches fell open. One of them buckled its hinges and dropped away. Now the heavy steamcart filled with casks was dangling by its loading chains over the countryside sliding by below them. Gunner pulled the lever for the hoist. The cart began to lower, and Gunner dropped down onto it.

It would have been normal, even *sane* to be terrified in this moment. There wasn't room left in Gunner's head for fear. A battle like this, quite often, came down to numbers and timing. To have a shot at knowing where to point his gun and what to do with it at any given moment, he had to have a dozen moment-to-moment timers ticking down. To keep track, he counted out the most pressing portions aloud.

"Three-person crew. Helmsman down. Takes time to notice, shout out a replacement, get on the wheel, and get control. Leaves the ship with one less gunner. Rifle shot at this range, likely wasn't heard by the flanking ships. Next target, new helmsman, first ship."

He flattened against the top of the dangling cart and did his best to target while compensating for wind, the motion of both ships, and the swing of the cart. They had the mixed blessing of having killed the man at the helm just as he was beginning to accelerate forward, so the entirety of the time spent replacing the original navigator had been spent accelerating directly toward Coop and Gunner's ship. It made for a much easier shot for Gunner and a much more difficult maneuver for Coop when the time came.

Gunner squeezed off two more shots. Both came close, but the angle and speed just didn't make for a clean bead on his target. He spat a profanity. Four shots and three misses. It was enough to shake his confidence, but it still served a purpose. The new man on the helm crouched for cover. It more or less guaranteed he wouldn't have the presence of mind to fire any of the main cannons with any accuracy. He shifted his view to the other ships. They were creeping out of cover, having worked out for themselves that something had gone wrong. Each was angled away from the one ship they'd already opened fire on. It would have been the proper position if the ambush had gone to plan, as it would have allowed them to flank and have their deck guns on target while the third ship took aim with its cannons. Now all it meant was that one or both of them would have to try to target with cannons.

"No discipline," Gunner muttered. "Didn't plan for this. They deserve what they get."

Even an untrained eye could see that neither of the flanking ships knew what to do. They both were angling inward, each taking the initiative to start targeting with their cannons and assuming the other would handle cover fire. It was a windfall that might only last a few seconds, but seconds were a lifetime in a situation like this. Gunner squeezed off one last shot, this time targeting the man on the fléchette gun. This one missed as well. Gunner cursed at his accuracy and slung the gun over his back. Above, the winch was producing a worrying noise. It had reached the end of its travel and, without someone up there to shut it down, continued to grind itself to oblivion.

Coop wrenched the ungainly ship, pitching it hard and angling up. Gunner held tight to the chains supporting it as he tipped farther and farther aside with the dangling load. This next piece was the most "Coop" part of a very Coop plan. They were gaining altitude and getting closer to the ship that, without Gunner's harrying, was finally beginning to slow and reassess. If they weren't ready for the ship they were planning to ambush to go on the offensive, they certainly weren't ready for what Coop had come up with. Gunner wasn't certain he was either.

The chains creaked and complained. The arc of the swing ended and started its return. Coop's aim wasn't quite where it needed to be, but it was too late to do anything about it.

"He should have done this part," Gunner said through clenched teeth, bracing himself as he approached the rigging of the ship. "*He should have done this part.*"

The dangling steam cart smashed into the rigging of the ship, snapping two thick supports and sending Gunner tumbling across the decking. He struck the railing on the far side. Sparks filled his vision. Such a dazed arrival would have cost him his life if not for the fact that several tons of steel suddenly asserting itself onto the deck of an airship had a way of distracting its crew. The whole ship was rolling aside as Coop continued to push the engines of the hauler, which was now dragging the scout ship from above using the cart as a grappler.

The crew shouted in confusion and dismay. The man on the deck gun was the first one with the presence of mind to draw his pistol and take a shot at Gunner. This, unfortunately for him, made him the first person Gunner drew his own weapon on. Of the pair, only Gunner was accustomed to firing his weapon while the entire ship he was on was busy being torn to pieces. The

135

hapless mercenary was struck in the chest and stumbled over the side. Gunner turned and rushed the remaining crewman. He tackled him to the ground.

"Who sent you!" he growled, pistol to the man's chin.

"You're a maniac!"

"The maniac is the one at the controls of our ship right now. I'm the *reasonable* one. Now who sent you?"

"I don't know who it was! I just took the job. Mercenaries can't be choosy."

"You're telling me you took a job to hunt down members of the *Wind Breaker* crew, and you didn't ask who was paying the bills?"

"You're the *Wind Breaker crew*?! I was just hired to take down the first ship to fly through here that wasn't on an official manifest."

The ship creaked threateningly.

"What are you *doing* to us?" he shouted.

"Dragging this ship into that one. There are only so many options available to you when you don't have any ship-to-ship weaponry. Where did you get the job?"

The next of the ships loomed closer. Its helmsman had committed to turning the ship to bring the cannons to bear and now didn't have the time or space for evasive maneuvers. A collision was imminent.

"Answer my question," Gunner barked.

"In Lock! I do my business out of Lock! It was a standard job!"

"Could it have come from Dr. Wash?" Gunner demanded.

"It could have come from anyone! Let me go or we're both going to die!"

Gunner glanced over his shoulder at the ship they were being dragged toward. With a frustrated growl, he holstered his weapon and grabbed the man by the collar. He climbed to his feet, hauling the man up and dragging him toward the rigging. They were a few steps away when the man struggled free. He snatched the gun from Gunner's belt and brandished it.

"Ha! The shoe's on the other foot now! Call off your cohort!" the maddened crewman demanded.

Gunner held tight to the rigging and stared him down. "Just how do you expect me to do that?"

"You must have had a plan! You wouldn't have boarded a ship you were planning to scuttle!"

"If you knew the man who made this plan, you'd know better than to say a thing like that." He gripped the rigging with both hands and hooked a leg around it. "And if you'd ever been on a ship on the verge of collision, you'd know better than to waste one of your hands on a gun."

"And leave myself unarmed?" the man grabbed ahold of the rigging as well. "You must think I am—"

The rest of the man's retort was swallowed by the cacophonous smash of two ships colliding. The impact nearly wrenched Gunner's arm out of joint. The crewman holding him at gunpoint was torn from the rigging and pitched over the edge.

Gunner snarled. "Idiot had to take my favorite small caliber with him…"

His ears were ringing from the clash, but he could still make out the metallic clank of chains failing. The steam cart sagged to the deck and strained the damaged rigging further. Meanwhile the ship they'd struck still had its three-crewmember compliment intact, and they were recovering enough to raise their weapons. Gunner dashed along the pitched deck to the cover of one of the stouter envelope mounts as bullets started to chew up the wood around him. He retrieved a larger caliber weapon from his belt and clicked it open to check the chamber. Fully loaded. He waited for a lull in the shots, then leaned out to fire a few shots. He didn't score any hits, but he didn't expect to. The purpose of that little barrage was to catch a glimpse of where the mercenaries were and to give them a reason to take cover. He reloaded the pistol. Five more shots rang out, then a strange silence.

"You can get out of cover there, Gunner. They're dead," Coop called.

"Coop?" Gunner stood up from the cover. "What are you doing on that ship?!"

"Savin' your skin," he shouted from the other ship's deck.

"The *plan* was for you to cut the cargo free, then stay in the air as a decoy for the third ship."

"It's my plan. I can change it if I want."

"Not without telling the other person involved." Gunner angrily pulled the rifle from his back and sighted on the third ship, which was pivoting to pick its new target. "They're gaining altitude. I can't get a shot at them. What do you think is going to happen when they realize that ship is abandoned and just going in a straight line?"

"Don't make no difference, on account of how that ain't gonna happen." Coop pointed at the hauler. "That there ship's gonna turn and start headin' down right about… now."

On cue, the ship gradually started to turn and pitch downward.

"How…" Gunner narrowed his eyes. "Did you leave *Nikita* at the helm?"

"She was climbin' all over the wheel durin' my last shift. She could just about get it movin', so I figured, why not let her have a part in the plan? Now quit jawin' and get ready for pickin' off those other guys before they blow her up. I showed her how to turn left, go down, and throttle down. Once she does them three things, she's about done with the fancy moves and they're liable to blow her out of the air."

"How are we going to get her back?" Gunner asked, taking position.

"She'll figure it out. She's pretty clever."

#

On the hauler, Nikita held tight to the wheel as it slowly rotated under her weight. The sparkling feeling of pride and duty at being given an important job besides sending and receiving messages had carried her for a time, but she was already longing for the warmth and safety of the inside of Coop's jacket. A distant thump of cannon fire caused her to shudder. She scrambled up a little higher, and the wheel continued to sag. All the valves she'd been told to turn had been turned. With an audible click, the wheel reached the end of its travel.

The very moment she had no more instructions to follow, she chattered anxiously and scampered up into the rigging to watch the nearby ships. Two of them were smashed together but airworthy. The other was turning and pitching upward, bringing its cannons to bear for a second salvo. She heard the quieter, sharper crack of rifles, then the distant shouts of sailors. Her huge eyes watched and waited as the chaos started to spread among the three remaining sailors. Sensitive ears trained from birth to pick out every little bit of information available sifted through the maddened shouts on the pursuing ship. The captain insisted the hauler was the primary threat. Two rifle shots later the captain's opinion no longer mattered, as he'd been replaced by his first mate. The field promotion lasted for one more shot. In the confusion, the remaining crewmember failed to notice he'd become the de facto captain, as he was below decks loading up a fresh cannonball. He emerged, discovered what had transpired, and promptly befell the same fate as his fellow sailors. Just like that, the ambush had been defeated.

Unfortunately, there was still the matter of reaching the badly needed comfort of Coop's jacket.

Nikita turned her gaze to the direction the ship was headed. It was near enough to the ground now that the chimney of one of the abandoned houses scratched across the ship's belly. Her little inspector mind ticked through its training. After a collision like that, she'd been taught that she would need to crawl across the belly of the ship to inspect. There were likely buckled or splintered boards. A moment later, the thatched roof and stone walls of another house crumbled under the ship, adding to the tally of things that would need to be inspected under normal circumstances. She looked ahead to see one of the two mills that had hid the other ships as they were arriving. The long, slow turn and decline in altitude meant that the ship was now lumbering toward a head-on collision with one. Again, her training popped up. She rapidly determined that it would utterly destroy the hauler. Alas, she'd not been trained what to do in circumstances such as this. She was likely expected to do what came naturally, which in this case meant she should die horribly.

The frightened little creature turned madly about. The sparse rooftops of the deserted city were sliding by at eye level. The belly of the ship was grinding on the ground. A single, desperate idea fought through the icy terror gripping her. She coiled her little body and sprang.

#

"Get it closer," Coop called out.

He was hanging off the outer curve of the envelope of one of the former ambush ships.

"I'm trying. As you might imagine, a scout ship with a steam cart lodged in its deck doesn't handle very reliably," Gunner called back.

"That's why I'm tryin' to hop over to the one that ain't had nothin' done to it yet. So get closer." Coop crouched a bit, ready to leap. "Dang fools couldn't've had the decency to throttle her down before they went and got themselves shot."

Gunner was able to cut the distance between the two ships in half without gouging a slice into the envelope of the one healthy ship. Coop heaved himself across and grabbed hold of the strapping that secured the envelope.

"I'm on! I'll have her wrangled in two shakes. Get the grapplers ready so we can dock up proper and get that goop over. And keep your eyes peeled for the hauler so we can fetch up—"

A crash of buckling stone and splintering wood filled the air. A surge of brilliant green flooded the whole of the city as an envelope spilled its load. Gunner and Coop turned to see the hauler bashing itself to pieces as it collided with the husk of a mill.

"Nikita. *Nikita!*" Coop hollered. He slid down the outside of the envelope and flung himself from the rigging to the deck. "Dang it, Nikita, if I got you killed, I ain't never gonna forgive myself," he growled, heaving the former captain aside and spinning the wheel.

After splitting his time between a ponderous cargo hauler and a crippled scout, this ship felt positively sprightly in its motion. It pivoted to face the lingering green streamers emitting from the wreckage and closed the distance in no time. Once he was as near as he dared get without smashing his own ship up, he slowed it to a stop, throttling just enough to keep the wind from pushing him about.

"Coop, you dang fool," he whispered. "Ain't like a critter's got too many options to handle a ship…"

Gunner eased his own ship closer.

"Cut them turbines!" At this distance, there was no chance Gunner could hear him. He jumped up and down and signaled. "Cut them turbines! I gotta *hear*."

Gunner got the message and silenced his ship. Coop put just enough distance between himself and the wreckage to be sure an errant gust wouldn't push him into it, then shut off the turbines completely.

An airship was seldom silent. The moment felt eerie and heavy. The ropes and planks creaked as the ship swayed. Masonry and timbers clattered down as the ruined mill continued to settle in on itself. Somewhere deep beneath it, though, there was something more. Something out of place. It was distant, soft. A rapid tinkling sound. He realized it wasn't just the creak of a cooling boiler. It was a desperately tapped message.

Get me get me get me get me get me, Nikita tapped from somewhere below.

Coop patted his pockets, then spotted a spyglass around the neck of the fallen captain. He pulled it free and scanned the city below. There, in the church tower, he could just make out Nikita clinging to the bottom of the bell and rattling her claws against it. It was the work of minutes to guide the ship close enough to dangle a mooring line down to her. She rocketed up the line and hurled herself at Coop with enough speed to force a breath out of him. She buried herself into his coat, her little heart rattling in her chest. After a full minute, she reached her claw out to one of his buttons.

No more plans, she tapped.

"I reckon between you and Gunner, ain't no chance of me workin' out what's to be done again anytime soon." He spun up the turbines again and headed for Gunner. "Worked out, though. Once we get the goop over here, this ship'll get us back to Ichor Well a whole heck of a lot faster than that hauler you crashed."

He grinned. "Hey! You reckon you're the first inspector what ever got promoted to skipper?"

No skipper. No plans. Sleep now, she tapped.

Chapter 11

The fug is a terrible place for anyone accustomed to the surface. It is dim on the brightest days and pitch-black on most others. Without a mask, the air is lethal to surface folk. Much of it is empty, and what isn't has been either converted into a fug city or reclaimed by what the fug had made of the local flora and fauna. The cities were livable, though rare was the city that actually tolerated surface folk. But as much as the fug folk had made themselves enemies of the surface, they had nothing on the wildlife. Thus, while the fug was wretched, The Thicket was infinitely worse.

Between the fug itself and the jagged branches overhead, Nita couldn't see much more than a few paces ahead. Dr. Prist, more at home in the fug than she, could see a bit better, but not sufficiently to make navigation more than guesswork. The handheld phlo-light Nita kept in her tool sash had long ago run dry, so this was as good as things would get until they found help.

"How is the arm?" Nita asked, helping Prist over a fallen tree that had more thorns than bark.

"I think my body has reached the limit of how much pain it can communicate. It's all fallen away to a general ache. I'd be fascinated if I weren't the one experiencing it."

"That is a small mercy, at least."

Between Nita's handiness and Prist's greater-than-average knowledge of medical care, they'd been able to splint the chemist's injured arm and patch up the worst of the gashes they'd endured during their landing. There simply wasn't enough intact machinery in the ruined station to make a vehicle of any sort, but they were able to scavenge some food and water. Walking through the thorny thicket had steadily replaced the patched-up cuts and scrapes and burned through many of their supplies with no end in sight.

"It has been ages. Are you certain you know where you are going?" Prist asked, eyeing the darkness around them with distrust.

"I am not even certain there *is* a precise destination. We've only ever done business with these people a few times, and they've been in a different place each time."

"Then why did we come this way?"

"Because it will take us a week to get somewhere friendly on foot. Our best chance is getting to Ichor Well, and that means going through The Thicket anyway. If luck is with us, we'll find help and shave a few days off that."

"Nita, I think it is fair to say that present evidence suggests luck is most certainly not with us." She stumbled. "If I'd known I would be hiking, I would have chosen different shoes…"

"You don't think we're lucky? We each fell out of the sky and survived. And we've been hiking through The Thicket and haven't had to fend off anything nightmarish. That's better luck than I'd expected."

"Mmm… I suppose luck is relative. We are marginally closer to the best case than the worst." Prist glanced into the darkness. "I wish the phlo-light had lasted a bit longer. I hate not knowing what the darkness holds."

"It would only draw attention to us." Nita paused. "And I'm not sure I want to know what the darkness holds."

Prist shut her eyes. "A bit of ignorance would be nice, right now. I'm haunted by the images in my biology books. What sort of fug beasts have you seen?"

"Aye-ayes, squarrels, fughounds, and one or two shadowy things in cages. Now and then while I was helping to set up Ichor Well, I saw eyeshine that I had to look up to spot. I'm hoping they were squarrels in trees."

"There are mice. Smaller than you'd think. You wouldn't have seen them, they stay out of the light and never leave the fug. You should feel fortunate you haven't encountered any of the lizards. They are mostly to the south. Drier climates." She shuddered. "Some of them have wings. And the bears. I've only seen the bones, but—"

"Dr. Prist, what were you just saying about ignorance?"

"Right, right. I apologize. I lecture when I'm nervous." She trudged a few more steps. "I wonder what… I should keep quiet."

"What were you going to say?"

"I don't think it will be conducive to a placid mindset."

"Nothing is conducive to a placid mindset right now. What were you going to say?"

"I was wondering what Dr. Wash is doing with Lil right now."

Nita squeezed her fist tight, her leather glove creaking at the pressure. "He is taking *very* good care of her."

"What makes you so sure?"

"Because he doesn't know that we're dead. And if he doesn't know that we're dead, he has to assume we're alive. And if he has to assume we're alive, he's has to assume we're coming for him. Either he's hoping to use her as a hostage to keep us at bay, or he's hoping that by sparing her life, he'll earn our mercy. I am absolutely certain that he's got her safe and sound."

"And what about after she loses her memory? What about after she

142

isn't Lil anymore?"

"She is Lil. She will always *be* Lil."

They trudged farther. Nita looked at Prist. She looked to be considering something very carefully.

"If you're worried something you're going to say is going to come across the wrong way, speak. Right now we've just got each other. No sense one of us pussyfooting around the other."

"Every minute that passes, Lil is more thoroughly a fug person. The more thorough, the more *complete* the transition, the more dangerous the treatment will be. Even if it works precisely as I predict it to, it will be a match for the danger of the initial change from surface folk to fug folk. While she is mostly human, it should have little risk at all and happen quite quickly. If this takes even a few days longer, it could easily turn her survival to a flip of a coin. Much longer than that and she would have little hope of survival."

"How will we know the risk?"

"We won't. This is unprecedented. Uncharted territory. I could easily spend the rest of my career carefully studying the effects of this substance without having a solid answer to that question. And there is the matter of the memories. I don't even know enough to hazard a guess, what will—"

"I don't care about the memories," Nita said. "If she loses what memories we had, we'll make new ones. We have more of our life together ahead of us than behind. I just want her safe, and I just want her back."

"It is an easy thing to say, but when she looks at you and doesn't know you..."

"We do what we can. What happens happens. One way or another, we're getting Lil back."

The pair continued, leaden silence hanging over them for a few minutes. The thorny trees gradually became sparser. Not so sparse that they had left The Thicket. Indeed, by now they were likely entering the depths of the rugged place. This was either a rare clearing or simply a place where the smaller trees had been choked out by the larger ones. Still, the change gave each of the women pause.

"I don't like this," Nita said. "Something about it seems... wrong."

"I agree. This place seems perfectly suited for—"

"A trap?"

"Precisely."

Nita crouched and felt around the ground. Dr. Prist did the same.

"Here," Dr. Prist said, after a bit of search. "Come look. And stay to my left."

The free-wrench approached. Sure enough, Prist had found a stout bit of simple rope. It had been laid out along the ground and led to a tree, where it continued upward.

"It's a net trap. I can just see where the leaves have been spread over it."

"It's an *enormous* trap," Prist said.

"Big enough to haul up one of those things from your biology books?" Nita said.

"Some of them. I suppose we'd best take this route around the outside. I'll lead the way."

Dr. Prist crept forward. Nita considered the trap a bit longer.

"Wait," she said. "I think we can use this."

She looked around until she found a sizable piece of half-rotten log. She heaved it onto the netting. Somewhere, a thread snapped. A weight came plunging down from above, dragging behind it a rope, which, through a sequence of pulleys, drew the net up and away. Most importantly, whatever mechanism was hidden in the trees above produced an ear-piercing siren-wail. Dr. Prist and Nita covered their ears as the sound grew to a climax, then gradually died away.

"What was that?" Dr. Prist said.

"Hopefully it was an alarm to let the trappers know they've caught something. If nothing else, this gives us a good reason to stop for a rest."

"I shan't argue with that."

Nita helped her to sit, then flopped down beside her.

"Is there any food or water left?" Dr. Prist asked.

The engineer rattled the canteen they'd taken from the station. "All out. Oh! But I do have this." She unfastened one of the larger pouches and revealed a small tin. Inside, wrapped in waxed paper, were two macaroons. "Wink has grown quite fond of them," she said. "You should see the look he gives me when he comes tapping and I don't have any for him."

"Wink... what's become of him, I wonder?" Dr. Prist said. "It's odd how such a disagreeable creature can come to be so beloved a part of the crew."

"That's the nature of a crew. At least, the sort of crew the *Wind Breaker* has... or even the steamworks back home. When the work is hard, when it's dangerous, you have kinship, whatever your differences. You know that you're in it together. When the worst happens, you know that any one of the crew could be the one to save your life. And you could find yourself having to save the life of any one of them. It's a special sort of family."

Prist slowly shook her head. "And to think, I was *pleased* to have had such a sheltered life. But if it cost me that sort of kinship, perhaps all of this madness is worth it."

She held the macaroon for a moment, then handed it back. "Save it for

Wink. I would hate to be the one responsible for getting on his bad side."

#

Forty-five minutes had passed since Nita had triggered the trap. There had been nothing. Not a buzz of airships overhead. Not a crackle of boots tromping through the forest. Just the rustle of windswept leaves and their own anxiety to keep them company. The silence and anticipation combined to make both Nita and Dr. Prist keenly aware of the motion approaching from the northwest. Nita instinctively put her hand to the grip of a spud wrench she favored for self-defense. Dr. Prist held her unloaded boot pistol, ready to bluff if the newcomers turned out to be unfriendly.

"There!" Prist said.

High in the trees, eye-gleam flashed. Nita and Prist stared back, each on their feet, ready for whatever might come next. The unseen head jerked a bit, and a far-too-deep chatter chilled their spines. Then came two short whistles. The eye-gleam vanished and the tree rattled with sudden commotion. Then came the crunch of footsteps from the base of the same tree. A strange gentleman emerged from the darkness, marching slowly but confidently toward them. As fug folk went, he was rather diminutive, a match for Nita's height. He was dressed in the very finest that found and patched clothing had to offer. That included a derby that had been repaired so often it was almost quilted, and a suit jacket with whole sections replaced with ratty fur pelt instead of the usual wool. He had a gun over his shoulder that would have made Gunner's mouth water. It looked like the sort intended for bird shot, if someone expected the bird to be the size of a horse.

"Ladies?" he said, with something between chivalry and swagger. "Fancy meeting you in The Thicket."

"Do you represent the…" Nita paused. Their dealings with these people were limited. So limited that the precise *name* for their little band was something of a mystery. The grunts called them savages, but that hardly seemed a diplomatic bit of terminology.

"Traders," he helpfully supplied. "I'd say 'who else would you find in this part of The Thicket?' but, well, here *you* are. … You're that Calderan girl. From the *Wind Breaker* crew."

"That's right. And this is Dr. Prist of the Well Diggers."

"Right, right. Over at that Ichor Well place. We've been selling your boys meat and skins on the regular." He gestured at the empty net hanging overhead. "You set this off?"

"Yes. We are in a terrible hurry and we hoped it would get someone's attention," Prist said.

"You got mine, but I'm not happy about it. These things are a pain to set." He tipped his head. "That arm looks rather painful."

"It is. Thank you for your concern," Prist said.

"Well, I'm here now. What'd you want?"

"We want a ride to Ichor Well," Nita said.

"We aren't a ferry service."

"Sir, my crew is scattered across the fug, my dear friend is in dire trouble, and we are in need of help. If you provide it, you will be owed a significant favor from the *Wind Breaker* crew. I think you and your associates can appreciate how useful that might be."

The man whistled. An enormous, vicious-looking creature emerged from the darkness. If it had been a few pounds, it would have been called a squirrel. But this beast looked like someone had put a baggier, fluffier pelt on a tiger, puffed up its tail, and given it chisels for teeth. It was a squarrel, and the saddle and bridle didn't serve to take an ounce of the madness from its twisted, grinning expression.

The man climbed onto its back quite casually, talking all the while. "You're talking to the wrong fellow, I'm afraid. We don't make any decisions about outsiders without talking to the man in charge. And I've got a job to do right now. I've got to reset this trap, then there's two more to check."

Nita sighed. She reached into one of the pouches on her tool sash. "You may have noticed there hasn't been very much trith floating around lately," she said.

"There's never much trith in these parts. If you think a bag of sea salt is going to change my mind..."

She pulled out a small sack and rattled it. Trith had a fairly distinctive sound, and judging by how quickly he coaxed the squarrel back down the tree to investigate, it was clear this was a man who'd heard the sound of trith washers rattling against one another before. His steed surged up to Nita with startling speed and he hopped off. Before he could snatch it from her, she pulled it back.

"This sack now, and two of them when we are safely delivered to Ichor Well."

"Let me see the goods," he said.

She opened the sack and dumped it in her palm. The man's eyes sparkled with avarice. He mounted the squarrel.

"Short one in front, tall one in back. Three's a pretty heavy load for a mount this size, but we'll make do."

"It is rather disheartening how much more persuasive lucre is than righteousness," Dr. Prist said.

"You can't buy gin with righteousness, madam," he said.

Nita and Prist mounted the beast, each holding tight to whatever was available to them. The beast released a buzzing, irritable chatter.

"Heads down, by the way. These branches are vicious."

He gave two quick whistles with his teeth, and the squarrel bounded off into the forest.

#

A short, harrowing ride later, both women were seated in the cramped interior of the boss's wagon. He was a man named Lusk, and the sack of trith washers had been emptied onto the plank of a desk beside where his name had been carved. Lusk was somewhat taller, scrawnier, and better dressed than the man who had fetched them. He adjusted small, round spectacles and stacked the washers.

"The *Wind Breaker* crew…" he muttered in a smoke-roughened voice. He pulled open a small drawer mounted to the wall and placed the washers inside. "You are Nita Graus. And you are Dr. Samantha Prist. Correct?" he said.

"That's right," she said. "And we very much need—"

Lusk waved her off. "I'm familiar with the situation. You do much gambling, Miss Graus?"

"Only with my life, it seems."

He huffed something that wasn't quite a laugh. "I like cards, myself. Gives a man a notion of just what the odds are. A bit of skill and intuition and you'll know if a bet's worth making. The *Wind Breaker* is *not* a hand of cards. The *Wind Breaker* is a lottery with a very expensive ticket. You paid off nice with that Cipher Hill job. We're still selling off the goods we grabbed. But I like to quit while I'm ahead with that sort of thing. I stick to cards. And you know who is a good hand at cards?" He leaned forward. "Dr. Wash."

Nita's face became stern. "You're working with him?"

"Have been for years. Tries to swindle us from time to time, but I know how he works. I call his bluffs when I can and fold a deal when I can't. Risks I can calculate. And once Tusk went away, all the strings he was pulling became loose ends. Working with Dr. Wash has been a very good investment. The man is an expert at tying up loose ends. It's the sort of thing he pays well for."

Nita glanced toward the door.

"He's not here," Lusk said. "Nor are his men. But we've gotten word that we're to keep our eyes open for members of the *Wind Breaker* crew and report on what we find."

Nita shuddered with anger, but the moment passed. "Mr. Lusk, let's talk gambling. You seem comfortable taking calculated risks with Wash because you are confident you can see his treachery coming. And you say you're not comfortable with the *Wind Breaker* crew because we're not the sort of gambling you enjoy."

147

"Correct."

"That's because we aren't a gamble. You don't need to bet on when someone is going to stab you in the back with us. We make deals, we make promises, and we protect our own. You're a decent man, or at least a reasonable one. I know this because your people have crossed paths with the Well Diggers at Ichor Well and we haven't had to fend off a flood of attackers ever since, so you can keep a secret when you know it won't do you any harm to do it. I'm not asking you to risk anything for us. I'm not asking you to place a wager or up the ante. Because your trust and your help is an investment, and it'll pay off."

"So I've been told. Two more packets of trith washers." He knocked on the drawer where he'd stowed them. "Funny thing about trith washers, Ms. Graus. Everyone knows where they come from. I can't invest in both the *Wind Breaker* and Wash. Once I throw in with you, after he made his position clear, that'll be the end of our association with the masked man, and he might not take it well."

"I'm not going to issue an ultimatum. I'm not going to tell you it is us or him. Because, and I say this without an ounce of bravado or rancor, when this is through, that's not a decision you'll have to make. We took the gamble with Wash. He turned on us. Or more accurately, he was against us since the beginning. So this doesn't end until either we're gone or he is. Because the *Wind Breaker* crew is endlessly loyal, but that leaves no room for mercy."

"And what about those of us who worked with him? Where do we shake out in this little exchange of vendettas?"

"I wouldn't worry about us coming after you. But everything you invested in Wash will go down with him. And it would be *awfully* useful to have a little something invested in the *Wind Breaker*."

Lusk drummed his fingers on the plank. "Lil Cooper is in trouble?"

"Dire trouble. Wash has her, and as you might imagine, he hasn't got her best interests at heart."

"To date, you and Lil are the only surface folk to ever ride one of our beasts. And the critters made it back alive. Albeit on their own."

"I recall. It was a memorable experience."

He drew in a long, slow breath through his nostrils. "Step outside with me for a moment."

Nita and Prist stood. The boss flipped his plank desk up and sidled past them to lead them through the door.

"You would be surprised how many of these beasts roam the forest. You wouldn't think there was enough to eat in the whole of The Thicket to keep them fed. But then, I suppose when a beast will eat just about anything, it doesn't take much."

Contaminant Six

He paced slowly through the nomadic village he and the other traders had set up. The nearest thing to a permanent component to the village was a light but sturdy bit of fencing that enclosed a particularly strange squarrel. It was hanging from the top of the cage, bowing the long rods that made up the bars. Its eyes were rather odd as well, seeming to dart about independently of one another. When they came near, it focused on them and released a hoarse chatter that sounded more like a honk than the usual vocalization.

"They come in all shapes and sizes. Some are fighters. Some are climbers. Some are too clever to hang on to, breaking our locks and unraveling our lashing. And then there's this one." He thumped the cage. "Thick as last week's porridge. Fast though. And strong. If it was brighter, it'd be one of my better beasts. As it is, I don't even have to put a lock on the cage. The thing can't work a latch. I'm frankly amazed it can remember its commands."

He turned and raised his voice. "Boys! How many do we have in camp right now?"

A motley crew of a dozen or so hunters and trappers assembled before him like troops awaiting review.

"Tell you what, boys. I've got a good feeling about the traps to the northwest. How about all of you head out and give them a check. Stay close. That's where that fug bear was, last time we encountered it. If you bring that in, I've got a buyer who'll make our season."

The group acknowledged the orders. Within a minute they'd all grabbed their gear and ventured off, leaving Lusk and the girls alone in the camp.

"I've got some figures to work on. I'll be inside for about fifteen minutes. After that, I'll be out to lock you girls up. Don't go doing anything foolish. If you do, I'll have to spread the word that you've been through here."

"Understood," Nita said.

He nodded and added gruffly. "Say hello to Lil for me."

He slipped back into his wagon. Dr. Prist and Nita were alone. Nita stepped up to the crude gate of the enclosure. She gave a short, sharp whistle, somewhat muted by the mask. The creature tilted its head to look down at her, both eyes slowly focusing. She whistled again. It simply released its grip on the roof and plopped onto its back, then rolled over to right itself.

"Are we... planning on riding that thing?" Dr. Prist said.

"He may as well have offered it to us," Nita said.

"He said he would send word if we escaped."

"Hedging his bets," Nita said.

She whistled what she was reasonably certain was the command to lower himself to be mounted. He honked twice, then plopped down with his legs splayed. Dr. Prist looked at the creature doubtfully.

"I am not entirely convinced Lusk isn't trying to get us killed."

Nita climbed to the creature's back. Dr. Prist, somewhat more cautiously, climbed on behind her. She held tight as best she could with her one good arm. Nita briefly grappled with the need to recall how to ride one of these creatures and the desire to forget just how chaotic it had been. She raised the reins.

"Wait!" Prist said. "Don't we have to name it? Isn't it some sort of superstition for sailors if they sail a ship with no name?"

"I don't think that applies to squarrels. And I wouldn't think you'd be the superstitious type."

"At this moment, I will take any opportunity to improve our chances, scientific or otherwise."

"Fine. Then we'll name him..."

Nita looked down. The squarrel twisted his head sideways and swiveled one eye to stare at her. He honked.

"Goose," she decide. "Onward, Goose!"

Chapter 12

It was cold and dark. She didn't know how long she'd been here, or why her arms and legs were tied to the chair. She squinted in the dim light. There was a man beside the door.

"Hello?" she called. "Hello! What am I doin' here? Why are you holdin' me ?"

He turned a long face to her, then plodded away. A few moments later a new figure appeared, smaller than the other man. He was dressed in black and wore a strange bird-like mask. She didn't recognize him, but seeing his face sent a spark of anger rushing through her. He signaled for the door to be opened.

"So. How much is left?" he said, sliding a second chair into the room and taking a seat.

"Why are you holdin' me here!" she snapped. "I ain't done nothin' wrong!"

He nodded. "Oh, we're gettin' nice and close. You! By the door! It's time. Get lost."

"Answer me..." she demanded.

"It feels like it's empty, doesn't it? Feels like you're all hollowed out. But those eyes aren't lost yet. You sorta know who you're lookin' at. So it ain't over. Not quite. But any minute now." He turned again to see if the man by the door was gone, then slowly tugged at his gloves. "You probably don't even remember your name anymore, do you?"

"I... I... what's going on..." she said.

"You'd think that'd be the last thing to go. Right now it probably feels like the last. But there's lots more in there, let me tell you. It's just all floatin' around now. Little chunks of who you used to be, waitin' for somethin' to tie 'em together. It don't feel like it, but there's almost as much 'you' left in there as there was this morning."

He folded the gloves on his lap, revealing pale hands untouched by sun or dirt in ages. "I bet it felt slow so far, losin' what you had in that head. These last few hours? It probably felt so slow it wasn't even the sort of thing you could put your finger on. But that's not how it works. Not at the end. At the end it's about as slow as walkin' off a cliff. Those first few steps are fine.

151

But that last one…"

He reached back and worked at the straps for his mask. "I envy you. Pretty soon, you'll be fresh and clean. When you're the one whose head clears out, it's everyone else who feels the pain. You're even lucky enough to not have any friends or family around. Imagine, gettin' the gift of a completely clean mind. All of the wisdom and none of the baggage. And then the first face you see is twisted up in agony and tears because they just lost someone you never met. I tell you, did you a favor, keepin' you here."

"I have… I have friends… I have a brother. They're lookin' for me."

"See? What did I tell you? Plenty of bits of you still floatin' around in there. For a few more minutes anyway. That's the strange thing about the change. I'll know about it, and you never will. All I need to do is look you in those eyes and wait for the light to go out."

He finished working at the straps and pulled the mask away. The face it revealed was paper-white and covered with a wispy black beard. To call it youthful would be a gross misclassification. The skin was uncreased by wrinkles. At a glance, she might have thought him to be in his thirties at the most. But the eyes… they had a horrible wisdom to them. They had seen a lifetime of hardship.

"You'd think I'd have forgotten," he said, running his fingers through matted-down hair. "After all. I only ever seen it twice. But that was two times too many. I thought I was lucky. I thought *we* were lucky. A whole family, together, touched by the fug but somehow spared the death that the Calamity brought pretty much everyone else. But their minds started to go. And then they went. And there I was, lookin' into the eyes of my wife and my daughter and seein' them turn into strangers right in front of me. Havin' them see *me* as a stranger."

He looked into the lenses of the mask in his hand. "There were people who called me lucky. One of the miracles. One of the ones who stayed alive, went fugger, and kept his memories." He squeezed the mask. "I'm just about the unluckiest man alive. A fugger with the mind of a man… There's maybe five of us. Your captain killed one of 'em. Small mercies."

"My… captain…" she said.

"Oh, it's happenin' now. I know that look," he said.

A chilling grin came to his face. She couldn't focus on it. She couldn't focus on anything. The whole of her mind felt like she was waking from a dream. With each passing moment, any notion of what she'd been experiencing was slipping away. She couldn't hold on to it. Before long, she wasn't even sure why she wanted to.

…

A man with a curious smile gazed into her eyes. He seemed pleased.

"Oh good, you're awake," he said.

She tried to move her arms. They were tied.

"Quit squirmin'. You'll hurt yourself. You're tied up. We had to do it. You were shakin' so bad. Sick with somethin'. You could have tore yourself up. I'll get you loose."

He disappeared behind her. A moment later her wrists were free.

"What's happened?" she asked. "I can't remember nothin'."

"You can't remember *anything*," he corrected. "It's one thing for me to be all sloppy, but you're a high-class lady. Diction."

She tipped her head. "Right… high class. But what's happened?"

"You're in the fug. You remember the fug, right?"

"A bit. It's… it's what we're breathing, right?"

"Yes." He stood up. "You're free. I ain't got time to explain everything that needs explainin', sorry to say. You just got through a rough patch. Bad condition. Kills most of the people who get it. I been watchin' over you to make sure you got through it okay. I'm a friend. People around here call me Dr. Wash. I call the shots in this place. I gotta get back to it, but there's some stuff you need to know. There are people after you right now. To keep them from gettin' you, I've got you here in this mine. It ain't much, but it's safe."

"Why are people after me?"

"Circumstance. You were in the wrong place at the wrong time. I was gettin' together the ingredients to make some medicine so people with your condition won't lose their memories. Didn't get it done in time, but there's a vicious group of nuts who want it for themselves. Until we get them locked up or knocked off, I'm all you got if you want to stay safe."

"I… I don't understand."

He shook his head. "It'll be a long time before you understand much of anything. Your noodle's cooked. But we'll get you through it." He grabbed a mask from the floor. "Don't be scared of this, by the way. Those people who want you? They want me too. The mask is cheap protection."

Dr. Wash slipped the bird-like mask on and began tightening straps and buckles. "Here's some stuff you need to get straight. First, once we get outta here, you're gonna meet some of my guys. They'll be… I'll give it to you straight, they'll be jerks. They're grunts. Most of 'em are jerks. Gotta stay hard if you're gonna do the jobs them guys do. Don't talk to 'em. They ain't allowed to answer anyway. But if they tell you to stop what you're doin', stop. There's a lot of dangerous stuff in this mine, and the *last* thing we need is you wanderin' around outside where the nuts can get at you. So stay where they tell you to stay and you'll be fine. But most important, if you hear the name Lil, run. That's what the nutjobs call you."

"That ain't…" She shook her head. "That *isn't* my name?"

"No," he said. "Your name is Blanche." He pulled the last strap into place. "I've got loads to do, but I'll be back to try to untie the knots in your head."

She stood and rubbed her wrists. Her gaze lingered on him.

"Somethin' wrong?" he asked.

"Nothing. The mask... something about it rubs me the wrong way."

"That's the plan. Intimidation." He turned and hurried to the door.

"Dr. Wash?" she said.

"Yes?"

"... Thank you."

#

In a cold pitch-black room elsewhere in the mines, a small cage rattled and rocked. The tiny prison was weighed down quite deliberately with almost every other sack and crate in the store room, evidently because the shaking and jostling of the cage was hardly a new problem. Wire mesh covered the front and back of the cage, far too thick for even chisel-like teeth to gnaw through, though the shiny gashes covering them suggested there'd been no shortage of attempts. Similar scratches covered the steel-clad lining of the rest of the cage. It had been built with precisely this sort of prisoner in mind.

Wink heaved himself against the mesh and chattered angrily. He didn't have a plan, but so much fury in so small and focused a mind needed an outlet, and there was little else he could do. So he scrambled back and bounded at the mesh, bashing his little body against it again and again. He ached with bumps and bruises. Some had been from when he'd been persuaded to send a message to the *Wind Breaker* crew. Most were from his own escape attempts.

After a particularly energetic thump, a sack slapped down on the floor, dislodged from the top of the mound. He stopped and glared at it. He couldn't see. Even his remaining eye, perfectly made for the darkness, needed *some* light. But his ears were a product of the darkness, too. They told him a great deal more than a human's hearing might. And his nose, hardly his most powerful sense, was sharp enough to detect a waft of Lil's scent. He flattened against the floor and reached his little arm through the small feeding slot beneath the mesh door. His spidery claw found its way to the fabric of the sack. It was too heavy to drag with his delicate finger, but lots of anxious tugging and teasing caused the top of the sack to flop toward him. He thrust his hand inside and found the leathery texture of a belt. He chattered eagerly and pulled the belt through the slot.

Bred and trained for memory, Wink keenly recalled this particular belt. It was one of Lil's favorites, and with good reason. It wasn't just that it was a gift from Nita. And it wasn't just that it was quite fancy. His cunning fingers found a small slit that blended perfectly with its complex pattern. From within, he drew a small, exceptionally sharp, and very tough blade. Even this little blade was a bit ungainly in his grip, but that wasn't the important part. The important part was the purple tinge to the metal, the telltale luster of trith. Nita had upgraded the belt with a knife of her own make, and thus it was guaranteed to be a great deal harder than anything this cage might be fashioned from.

He jabbed and wedged at the wire, working the blade between the loops and hammering it forward. One by one, he was treated to a sharp metallic snap as the wires failed. When there was enough damage for him to peel the mesh back, he burst through, knife tight in his grip.

There was still the wooden door between him and freedom. It was far too thick for him to hack or gnaw through without a week of work, but he knew he wouldn't have to. He screeched and wailed, bounding about the room and knocking over crates and sacks. In no time at all, the heavy thumping footsteps of one of Dr. Wash's lackeys arrived. Faint green light from a phlo-lantern filtered beneath the door. Jingling keys worked at the lock.

"I swear, if that thing has made another mess, I'm going to personally crush its skull under my boot," the lackey muttered.

The door creaked open. In a gray and brown blur, Wink streaked through the gap and scampered through the corridor. Behind him, he could hear the grunt dully realize what had occurred and hastily dash in the opposite direction.

"Dr. Wash! Dr. Wash!" the man bellowed.

Wink stopped, far enough that he knew he wouldn't be seen in the darkness. The aye-aye could tell by the echo of this place that it was massive. He had no doubt he could find his way out, but he wasn't the only one here. There was still Lil. And Lil was one of the good ones. He could probably find her too, but that wouldn't be enough. She was big and clumsy, like other humans. Less clumsy than most, but still too big to squeeze through this gap or that to find her way out. She'd need to use the doors, which meant she would need to use the keys. He had to have them before he could find her, and to have them, he'd have to find them.

The inspector crept along after the running grunt. Wink had only worked on one ship, but it had taught him plenty. The person in charge always had the most important things. And in this place, Dr. Wash was in charge. Wink followed the lackey.

It was a very educational journey. The man hurried first down a long hallway, then into an elevator running along vertical rails in a shaft that echoed like it went up and down forever. Wink rode on the cable that hauled the elevator along the rails, just outside the edge of the lantern's light as it sank lower and lower into the mountain. Finally it stopped on a level that sounded and smelled much more alive than any of the other tunnels or shafts. Soft squeaks and scratches filtered through the thick walls. And shortly after, angry shouts.

"What do you mean the rat got out?!" Dr. Wash shouted.

"It was in there making noise. I thought it knocked over the pile. But when I opened the door, something darted out, and the cage was all torn up."

"It was an *aye-aye* cage. That's how they *deliver 'em*. How did that thing get out if not by you bein' an idiot?"

"Point is, it's out. What do we do now?"

Dr. Wash growled. "We sit and wait. If we're lucky, that thing just ran away. We ain't lucky. It'll be sendin' word. The *Wind Breaker* crew is spread out, and we're dug in. Get the aye-aye guy to tell us when his rats pick up what *that* rat sends out. That oughta tell us where it is, and we can grab 'em. Maybe we can't keep the message from goin' out, but we can make sure a *second* one don't go out." He punched the wall.

"But it means I can't take my time on what I've been workin' on."

"I just told you! You forget how them ears work?"

"After I talk to the aye-aye guy."

"I want you to look for it. Kill it if you find it. It outlived its usefulness anyway. And keep a closer eye on our other guest. She's the more important one."

"Yes, sir."

The lackey hurried away. Wink huddled a little closer into the shadow of one of the support timbers until he was past. Dr. Wash was the new focus. He walked with purpose, stomping along and muttering to himself. Wink kept his distance. As they moved along the tunnels, the smell of vermin became stronger, and the sound of their scratching and clawing was constant. One of the more intellectual sort of fug folk appeared at the edge of the light cast by Dr. Wash's lantern. He was dressed head to toe in an outfit quite similar to Wash's, though the mask and coat were white instead of black. The other man held vials in each gloved hand and walked with the slow care of someone who feared the consequences of even a single drop spilling.

"Hey!" Dr. Wash shouted. "The timer's tickin' faster now! What've we got!"

The other doctor flinched, nearly dropping one of the vials. "Dr. Wash, please! This is delicate work."

"Like hell it is. The delicate work is for later. I ain't askin' for a scalpel from you. I'm askin' for an ax. Now have you got it for me or not?"

"I am about to administer a test. But this is well beyond my expertise. I took this job under the expectation I would be working on intoxicants and narcotics. I wasn't *fond* of—"

"Just tell me if we've got what I'm after! What're you testin'?"

"Vial A has C-6 in equal concentration with antiseptic. Vial B has C-6 in equal concentration with detergent. There was no visible reaction in either case. I am doing the dosage test now."

"Good. I want to see it."

The pair marched to a large, stinking chamber carved out of the mountain. Dim lights were scattered around the edge of the chamber at regular intervals. In the center, a huge grid of wooden slats divided the floor into small, mesh-covered cells. The cacophony of squeaking and scratching suggested they were each swarming with fug mice. The white-suited doctor approached the nearest of the cubbies and carefully upended the second vial.

There was a brief swell of squeals and scratches.

"The same as the others. Signs of irritant reaction. No further signs of distress," he said.

"Fine, fine. Do the other one."

He dumped the first vial into a cubby. This time the sound was far more chilling. The mice screeched horribly.

"Signs of obvious distress. Visible convulsions. Panic reactions."

"That's more like it. You think this is as good as we're going to get?"

"Unlikely. Based on the reaction, I suspect it isn't the antiseptic itself, but a component of the antiseptic that has produced this. I should start testing in different concentrations."

"Good. Good. Shouldn't take too long, right?"

"To do it thoroughly, I would—"

Wash repeated, far more forcefully. "It shouldn't take too long, right?"

"I should have results for you by tomorrow evening."

"Good. Remember. Scale. I want this to be *big*."

"I'll need access to the fire cabinet."

Dr. Wash dug into his jacket and revealed a large ring of keys. He removed one from the ring. "Here. You know where to find me to return it."

He turned and marched back toward the entrance of the chamber. Wink darted up a timber and huddled in the darkness, his ears attuned to the soft jingle of keys within Wash's coat. The little inspector viewed him with reproach. There was no way he would be able to snatch them from him.

There was nothing for it but to find Lil. Regardless of what he had to do, he would have to do it with her. Perhaps there were other keys. Perhaps there was another way. He'd soon find out.

He waited until Dr. Wash was out of earshot, then dashed for the elevator.

#

Blanche paced through the tunnels. She was a bit lost, and not just thanks to the network of tunnels. She scoured her mind for something, anything

157

to use as an anchor, but all she found was the vague feeling of absence. She felt that something was wrong, but she had no point of reference. Even the fact that her name was Blanche felt like something floating on the surface. It didn't have any roots.

One thing was for certain, though. She may have been free to move about, but she was most certainly not free. Whenever she was in the tunnels, there was always a pair of grunts keeping an eye on her. Whenever she went into a room, they remained at the door. Whether it was for her protection or not, she was being watched, and there was never any need to ask which doors she wasn't allowed through. Most were locked, and the grunts silently slid into position to block any others that might be off-limits. The most frustrating part wasn't the aimless wandering, it was the lack of conversation. For someone who was adrift in a brand-new world with only scattered echoes of familiarity, it was frustrating to the point of torture.

"I'm a bit hungry, sir," she said, attempting politeness as a means to get through. "Would either of you know where I could find something to eat? Maybe you could join me for a bit?"

The broader of her two guards pointed down a tunnel.

"So I'll be eating alone, then," she said.

"First left, then the third right," he replied.

"Thanks."

She trudged to what her mind insisted upon labeling the galley and sat on one of the crates that served as both storage and furniture. The food was plentiful, but not terribly appetizing. All of it was in cans, and most of it was labeled with red-ink stamps proclaiming it to be "surplus." She found a tin of sardines and a key to unroll the top.

"This isn't half-bad," she said. "You boys want any?"

They didn't reply. They just slowly turned their backs to her in a decidedly prison guard fashion.

"Well, let me know if you change your mind."

She dangled her legs, enjoyed another sardine, and tried to ignore the odd little sensations her mind threw at her when things were still. Things like the way she had to swing her legs, rather than them swinging on their own. Why *would* they? Things like her bone-deep desire to have something to go with this sardine. Something small and fluffy and buttery and delicious that she couldn't seem to recall the name of. Things like how she perpetually had to stop and correct herself before speaking. Somehow her reflex was to say things in a horribly muddled manner, despite the fact she *knew* how to say them properly. She didn't like it. She didn't like that she was beholden to mannerism without context, to notions without insight. She didn't like the way the odd tapping noise she was hearing seemed to *mean* something.

158

Blanche paused and set down the can.

Tap-tap-tap. Tap. *Don't talk. Just tap back.*

"Boys?" she said, keeping her eyes on the crate that seemed to be producing the sound.

Didn't told them. Didn't told them, the taps continued urgently.

"What do you want?" asked one of her "protectors."

"Is there anyone else lurking about?" she asked.

"No."

Didn't. Didn't told.

"Must have been hearing something," she said. She picked up the tin and took another fish.

Need to be alone, the taps continued, somewhat less stressfully.

Blanche casually dropped a hand down to quietly tap in response. *Why?*

To talk. To not get caught, came the reply.

Who are you? she tapped.

Wink.

What are you?

Crew. Family.

The final word rang in her mind.

"Boys!" she called. "Where could a girl find the head... er, the restroom?"

#

The restroom, such as it was, turned out to be a set of planks built into a seat that hung rather precariously over a vertical shaft. She dearly hoped it was the *only* such feature in this particular shaft, or there was likely to be an unpleasant surprise somewhere along the line. The door was the only one she'd been allowed through that didn't have at least a slot through which her protectors could keep an eye on her. They'd provided her with one of the phlo-lanterns to light the way.

"Now what..." she muttered. "It isn't as though whoever that was told me how it would meet me or—"

We need to go.

She jumped and looked up. An absolutely hideous little beast dropped down from the ceiling of the carved-out alcove. Though she was startled by his sudden arrival, once the initial jolt passed, she found herself more intrigued than concerned. Even the fact that he seemed to be clutching a knife in his teeth didn't stir any real concerns.

"Who are you, little fellow?"

Wink. Don't talk. Tap.

She nodded and crouched down. *What are you?*

Joseph R. Lallo

Inspector. We need key. We need to go.

Easier said than done. Do you know what's going on here?

Wash kidnapped you. Wash needed you to keep crew from killing him.
What crew?

Wind Breaker *crew.*

I'm a sailor?

Deckhand. Good deckhand. Fast. Need keys. Need to escape.

Why don't I remember?

Fug. You were surface folk. Fug folk now. Lost memory. We need to get keys. Need to leave.

What was my name?

Lil.

She straightened up. "Dr. Wash said people who wanted me dead would call me that."

Tap. Don't talk.

She looked at him uncertainly. On one hand, he was a bizarre little creature with long, disturbing fingers, a surly disposition, and an eye patch. On the other hand... even at first glance, he didn't give her the same feeling of anxiety as Wash did once he'd put the mask on.

How do I know I can trust you?

Wash is bad. Wind Breaker *crew is good.*

You'll need to do better than that.

Need key. Need to escape, Wink tapped emphatically.

He seems to be keeping me prisoner, but at least he has an excuse that makes sense. You're just telling me a bunch of names I've never heard of. And you're a creature. He's like me.

Wears mask. Mask bad.

You wear an eye patch.

Wink slammed the ground in a frustrated tantrum. *Trusted Wink,* the creature tapped.

Give me a reason.

Wink glared at her. Slowly, his expression changed. He looked more certain. He removed the knife from his mouth. *Lil not trust Wink. Wink trust Lil.*

He crept forward and placed the blade at her feet, then turned and sat with his back to her. Blanche was at first confused, but she made sense of it soon enough. Dr. Wash, whatever his intentions, absolutely did not trust her. He assigned armed guards and didn't allow her to go where she pleased. This thing, already small enough that she could easily dispatch it, wasn't just willing to turn its back to her, it was willing to *arm* her before it did so. That said something. It spoke volumes.

160

She kicked the blade back toward him. *So we get the keys. Then what?* she tapped.

Wink turned and snatched it up. *Get keys. Get to elevator shaft. Get out.*

Then what? What's the plan?

Out first. Plan after.

"What's taking you so long?" called one of the grunts.

"Just a minute," she called. She crouched down to tap. *I guess you should hide, and I'll see what I can do about the keys.*

Wink scampered up the timber and concealed himself in the shadows above the door. Blanche tugged open the door.

"Say, boys. I know I'm not allowed to go through any of the locked doors," she said, pacing out. "But what if something happens? What if there's a fire? Surely there must be a way for all of us to leave quickly."

"Never mind that. Move along," he said.

"You *are* here for my protection, right? I know these lanterns don't have any fire, and I know we're eating cold canned food, but fires happen. How do we get out? What happens to me if something happens to you? Here I am, locked behind a door with no one to let me out."

"Just get moving," the grunt instructed.

"Really, now. Surely you have keys to these doors and gates. And you naturally spend every waking moment watching me. Again, for my own safety. So what is the harm in letting me have a key of my own? I won't be able to leave without you knowing, and then if the worst happens—"

"You're not getting a key!" he barked.

Blanche put her hands on her hips. She was feeling the urge to punch this man square in the chin, but she was able to overrule that instinct. "I think you should bring this up to Dr. Wash. I think he will see my side of the argument."

The larger grunt turned to the smaller one. "Go get the boss. Tell him our 'guest' is being a pest."

The second protector gave a sullen nod and plodded away.

"Thank you. That's all I ask. I don't mean to be a pest, by the way. But I really think if my safety *is* what you're after, there should be a plan for me to make myself safe when you're not here. I'm not a child, so I've obviously handled myself well enough without supervision until whatever happened happened."

She continued talking, filling the air with empty words to fill the time until she was able to come up with a plan to get the man's keys. No cleverness was forthcoming, however. She was beginning to suspect that—prior to her losing her memories—she might not have been terribly bright. The only real

161

"plan" that asserted itself, with increasing insistence, involved giving him a boot between his legs and a head-butt to the nose once he'd doubled over. Given the size difference, it seemed unwise, but the deeper impulses in her slowly recovering brain didn't assess risks in quite the same way. By the time the distant clank of the departing elevator signaled the other guard's departure, her opponent in the aimless debate had lost any shreds of patience he had.

"Look! You do what *we* say!" the guard shouted. "You don't get a key, because then you might get out, and I'm here to *keep* you from getting out. So you just shut your mouth and be happy that I haven't shut it for you. I can tell you right now, you've earned the back of my hand, and if it wasn't for—"

Blanche could feel her muscles tensing for a blow to his groin that she would probably regret. A half second before she could deliver it, a screeching, flailing ball of fur and flashing metal burst from the open door to the restroom. She took a startled step back as Wink scampered over to him. He moved like a tornado, dodging the grunt's desperate attempts to swat him away. The little creature couldn't wield its knife with much force, but a dozen shallow cuts and untold vicious bites were just as bad as one big one. The man bellowed and clawed at Wink until a bite in a particularly tender spot caused him to double over. Blanche, partly to satisfy the vicious little voice in the back of her head and partly as an act of mercy to prevent a death of a thousand cuts, finally delivered a blow. She grabbed him by the shoulders, yanked him in, and bashed her forehead against his nose.

He crumpled like a poorly starched suit. The crazed and blood-spattered Wink grabbed hold of the keychain and tore it free. For the first time since the debate began, there was silence. A brute of a man lay dazed on the ground, bleeding. The inspector stood on his chest like a conquering hero, knife in his teeth and keys in his hand. Blanche stood, heart pumping and flushed with exhilaration.

"That felt… far too good to be proper. Just what sort of people *are* this *Wind Breaker* crew?"

The best, Wink tapped on the blade of the knife. *Elevator. Now.*

She nodded and rushed down the tunnel. Wink dashed to her and scrambled up to her shoulder. Their target was quite near, but when they reached it and unlocked the door, they were faced with a new issue.

"Dang it!" she blurted. "Of course the elevator isn't here. It's down getting Dr. Wash! What do we do now?"

Wink didn't answer. He was already in the air when she'd asked the question. He deftly caught the thick cable of the elevator and hung from it.

Climb! he tapped on the blade.

Blanche looked down. The light of the phlo-lantern didn't cut very far into the inky blackness of the shaft, but from the echoes of Wink's taps, it was a long, long way down, and the cables didn't look like they'd be very easy to hold on to, and the rails even less so. All in all, it seemed very likely that any attempt to imitate the inspector's escape plan was quite likely to end in a messy splatter at the bottom of the shaft. This made it all the more worrisome that the same rush of exhilaration and excitement she'd gotten from assaulting the guard was tingling in her brain once more.

"I'm not so sure that is a good idea," she said.

Lil climb. Best climber.

"Says you! All I have to prove that is the word of a surly, one-eyed creature that I probably should be running from."

Climb climb climb climb climb, Wink tapped impatiently.

"Fine!"

She held tight to the elevator door and leaned out into the shaft to try to reach the cable, but it was just beyond her reach. She shakily took a step back, eyes on the cable, and jumped.

The very moment her feet left the ground, she felt something rush over her. It wasn't the fear and panic she'd expected. It was blissful, almost a feeling of relief. Far from the feeling of defying death over a bottomless pit, she felt like she was stepping into a warm, familiar, beloved activity. She deftly caught the cable, curled one leg around the stout cord, and curled the other to lock the first more tightly. The whole maneuver felt as though someone else had taken over for a moment. When the instant passed, she was firmly hanging from the cable with no hint of struggle or difficulty.

"... *Wow!*" she said. "That was more fun than I—*eek!*"

Her revelation was interrupted by the cable jerking into motion. The section she was clinging to started to rise upward. The one Wink held began to descend. She tried to scramble downward to keep pace, but it was too fast for her, and getting faster. Sliding wasn't an option either, as a brief attempt tore a long gash in her pants leg when a barb of frayed cable zipped by. She hesitated to think what would have become of her hands if the cable had reached them first.

In just the short time that she'd been in motion, she'd been dragged well beyond the pool of light from the phlo-light. She was now soaring upward in darkness, unable to see even the other cable that was zooming downward at the same rate she was rising. After a few seconds the cable started to slow. It did her little good. She was still dangling in the darkness.

"Why the hell is this door open? What did I tell you about makin' sure *every* door was locked?" echoed the familiar voice of Dr. Wash.

"I did lock the door," his lackey insisted.

"Well it's open now!" He slammed his fist against something in anger. "Go get your partner. Somethin' happened. I'm stayin' here, just in case she shows up."

Footsteps clicked down the tunnel below. Dr. Wash continued to mutter, his words barely discernible at this distance, garbled as they were from the echoes.

"… Couldn't have faked it. … Those eyes…" he murmured.

Moving with the utmost of care, Blanche started to climb down the cable. Holding tight to it was one thing, but constantly having to adjust her grip, and having to do so *silently*, was another thing entirely. There was a glaze of grease on the cable that was steadily caking her hands, making each subsequent grip more tenuous than the last. She hadn't closed half the distance between herself and the elevator car when she heard more footsteps stomping up.

"Now what the hell happened to you?" Dr. Wash barked.

"There was… it was a… *thing*. An inspector, I think," slurred the man they'd grabbed the keys from.

"An inspector. You're tellin' me a single rat-monkey did this to you? What am I payin' you for?"

"He had a knife!"

There was a telling silence.

"You been drinkin'?" Dr. Wash said.

"Does this look like a bite to you? I'm telling you, he had a knife! And then the prisoner head-butted me right in the nose."

"Old habits die hard, I guess," Dr. Wash rumbled. "Morons! The whole *idea* was to put some slack on the leash so she wouldn't pull. This place was still locked up tight, and I had her under double guard! It should have…" Again, there was an angry slam. "Fine. This is fine. Doesn't change a thing. I got guys on the door down below. She ain't gettin' out."

"How do you know she went down?" asked one of his men.

"Because she *has* to go down. The top of the shaft will dump her just outside Keystone, and she can't breathe outside the fug right now, so even if she *did* go up, she'd be comin' right back down. So she's gonna be headin' out into the back fields of the Fugtown Iron Yards. Just make sure the boys down there ain't as useless as you. I gotta light a fire under the guy I got cookin' up the soup. On the off chance word gets out, it's gotta be ready to drop and do its damage or this whole mess ain't gonna go our way."

Another, far more vicious blow of frustration sent a tremble up along the elevator cable. "You know what? I don't trust you. I'm tellin' the guys down there myself. You just get this jerk patched up. I'm scrapin' the bottom of the barrel when it comes to employees. Even *with* this screwup, I can't afford to lose you."

The door slid shut and the elevator rattled into motion, this time dragging her downward along with it. She slipped past the dim light filtering through the cracks of the elevator door just in time to see Wink, still clinging to the other cable, rise up past her. He hopped from his cable to hers and held tight to her back.

"I'm not sure I wasn't better off as a prisoner..." she whispered to him.

Joseph R. Lallo

Chapter 13

"We there yet?" Coop griped, poking his head up from inside the stolen scout ship.

"Does it look like we're there?" Gunner said. "Do you think I would keep it a secret?"

"What's the point of stealin' a faster ship if you're gonna creep your way there all sneaky-like?"

"This is *precisely* the sort of ship that the wall-gunners at Ichor Well would be well advised to shoot down if it came anywhere near them. We've got to make sure they know who we are. That means keeping our speed down enough to give Nikita a chance to warn them off."

"So we're close, then."

"Of course we're close! I wouldn't have slowed down if we weren't close!"

"Easy, Gunner. No sense yellin'."

The fug was thicker here, a sure sign that Ichor Well was near. Just as the smaller vials of the stuff pushed back the edge of the fug into a thick wall, the well itself provided a veritable dome of purple mist that kept the whole operation quite thoroughly hidden from any who didn't already know where to find it. As the churning tendrils of fug curled around the prow of the ship, Nikita started softly drumming on the envelope's main support, subtly delivering the assurance to those below that a friendly ship was incoming. It was almost startling when they finally broke through the dense wall of mist and found themselves above the bustling operation.

While it was smaller than South Pyre, Ichor Well had quickly become its equal in all ways that mattered. In the time since it had been established, temporary structures and defenses had one by one been replaced by permanent ones. The whole place still had a fairly slapdash, hastily assembled look, but it was sturdy and it was buzzing with activity.

The sort of heavy spike guns that would normally be mounted to the deck of an airship stood at the tops of scattered pillars. Mesh fences stretched between the pillars, and intense phlo-lights cast their green glow down onto the courtyard below. The grunts manning the guns pivoted and took aim. They'd likely gotten the message that this was just Gunner and Coop on their way back. Given the way the *Wind Breaker* crew did business, it wasn't unusual for a "borrowed" ship to be their means of arrival, but one could never be too careful. Particularly not these days and with a ship that still bore the insignias of an in-operation scout vessel.

"There's no ships moored up," Gunner observed.

"Yeah. They been real busy since Tusk went down. Before you got word to me about Lil, they was runnin' me ragged gettin' goods out. Just gettin' burn-slow and phlogiston to folks who need it was stretchin' us thin. We didn't even start tryin' to get it to folks who want it."

"It is disturbing to know that a manipulative, would-be genocidal puppet master was so crucial to the logistics necessary to keep the fug functional."

"Yeah, and Tusk was pretty good at gettin' stuff to folks, too."

Gunner shut his eyes and sighed. "Yes, Coop. That too."

They pulled in over the courtyard. A pair of workers took a break from pushing carts to dash over and catch the mooring lines to secure the ship.

"Bruce! Kent! Did Lil show up with Nita and the doctor yet?" Coop called down.

"No one yet. But we been hearing some rough stuff coming down from the ships that pass over, and coming in from the cargo boys."

"What sort of bad stuff?"

"*Wind Breaker* sort of stuff. Mercs getting sent every which way. Ships going down. A jerkwater got blasted off the map. Rumor has it South Pyre got hit."

"It will never cease to amaze me how easily gossip outpaces the people responsible for it," Gunner said.

Coop threw a rope ladder over the edge. "I need some strong fellas up here. We got a whole load of this goop the doc's gonna need, and this ain't a cargo ship, so there ain't no easy way to get it down."

"I'll get Donald and we'll get a winch bolted down. How much of the stuff is there?"

"Enough, I hope. Because there ain't no time to be gettin' more of it."

#

"Left, left, *turn left!*" Nita urged, hauling at Goose's reins.

Shortly after departing from the trader's camp, it became clear why they were willing to part with this particular steed. He was fast, *incredibly* fast, and seemed completely indefatigable, but he lacked basic understanding about how to navigate with riders. He had precisely two modes of travel. The first and most favored method was to continue in a straight line, heedless of the obstacles ahead. He would happily run headlong into a tree or plow through a bush rather than adjust his path to avoid it. The second method, which tended to assert itself at the least opportune times, involved taking the most indirect path imaginable. At odd intervals Goose would lose interest in following her directions and simply dash up the trunk of a tree and bound between branches in the canopy for a while.

It was a harrowing experience to say the least. Nita's goggles had never been more essential. Even with them firmly in place and the mask covering the rest of her face, stray branches and thorns had left their mark on every bit of exposed flesh.

Goose dug his claws into the soil and skidded to a stop, then dashed to the left. He barreled through the thick fug that marked the boundary of Ichor Well and, three leaping strides later, ran headlong into the mesh fence of the place. He bounced back, shook his head, and sprinted up the fence. A wave of shouts calling for the beast to be shot, followed swiftly by a fresh wave of shouts calling to hold their fire once they recognized the riders, caused a stir of chaos that didn't end until Goose skidded to a stop in the center of the airship courtyard. He released a panting honk, then helpfully plopped to the ground with legs splayed.

Nita shakily dismounted and helped Prist to do the same. Well Diggers assembled around them, shouting questions. A half-second later, Coop burst through the crowd.

"Where's my sister!" he cried.

"Dr. Prist needs help. She was hurt." Nita said to one of the Well Diggers before turning to him. "Dr. Wash has her. He turned on us."

"Where's he got her! I'll tear that mask off and feed it to him."

"I don't know. He attacked us and took her. We were separated from Wink as well. Kent! Get Donald. We need to feed Goose."

"Who's Goose?" Kent called from the assembling crowd.

"This squarrel here."

"What'd you name it Goose for? It don't look like—"

Goose honked loudly and dashed to a nearby rain barrel to slake his thirst.

"Never mind," Kent said.

"Did you get the contaminant?" Nita asked.

"Barrels of it. How we gonna find Lil?" Coop said.

"I don't know, but we'll find her. Dr. Wash has been doing business for a long time, he *must* have some known hideouts. Ones he thinks we don't know about. It'll be something he can defend. But we've come this far in search of a way to treat Lil. We owe it to her to get things moving."

All eyes turned to Prist. She dragged her good hand across her hair to gather its tousled mess into something resembling order.

"Painkillers," she said. "The small blue pills in the white cabinet in my office. Bring the entire jar. And some water. If the contaminant isn't already in my laboratory, get a reasonable quantity of it there. I'll draw up a list of materials that will be required for testing. In addition, I shall require a blood sample from every fug person in the facility."

"What do you need blood for?" Kent asked.

"I cannot very well test the treatment on anyone. It is likely to be extremely toxic. Combining it with blood and observing the effects will have to suffice."

"And you need blood from *everyone*?" Donald asked. "I ain't much fer needles."

"Everyone, I am already tasked with creating a treatment in the research and development equivalent of the blink of an eye. If nothing else, I intend to be as comprehensive as possible."

The crowd, now mostly with tasks to perform, scattered to get to work. Nita hurried toward the supply shed.

"Where you goin'?" Coop said.

"I have to take care of Goose. If it wasn't for him, you'd still be waiting for us."

"When we headin' out for Lil?"

"We'll find her as *soon* as we know where to look."

"We can at least get movin'! Wash is bound to be down near Lock, ain't he? That's where he does all his business."

"Coop, if it's where you think he is, then he isn't there. He's wily. Wily enough to pull the wool over our eyes."

"I ain't just sittin' here waitin' while Lil's locked up somewhere," Coop barked. "She's my li'l sister and I'm her big brother. Ain't nothin' in the world more important than keepin' her safe, and I can't do it here waitin' for this and that. These folk I can understand if they don't want to risk their necks for her. She's just someone they know. But if there was one person who I thought'd be as rarin' as me to go bust a hole in a mountain if that's what it'd take to find her, it'd be you."

"Coop, we can't afford to make a mistake. We need to know where to go, how to get there, and what we'll do before we even start."

"I'm a Cooper. What needs doin' is the only thing I ever needed to know. How to do it'll come when it comes."

"Dr. Wash has been setting traps. We've taken more hits than we can bear already. If we spring another trap, we can't be sure we'll all come back."

"We already ain't all comin' back. Lil's somewhere out there." He stomped his foot. "If you ain't fixin' to do somethin', then I am." He thundered toward the mooring towers.

"What are you going to do?" Nita said, hurrying to keep pace with him.

"I got a scout ship fueled up and armed. Me and Nikita are gonna head out. We're gonna find someone to grab ahold of. If they don't talk, we'll knock enough teeth out to loosen their tongue. If that don't work, I'll grab the next fella and keep at it."

Nita looked him hard in the eye and took a breath. "Give me a moment to get some food."

"And then what?"

"And then I'm coming with you."

"You got a plan?"

"No. But whatever ends up happening, we'll be better off if we're together than apart. And once Prist is busy with the treatment, I'll officially be useless around here." She adjusted her tool sash. "I'm a free-wrench. I'm not accustomed to being useless."

#

Gunner pulled the ties of his smock tight and stepped into Dr. Prist's laboratory. "Samantha," he said. "I'm ready."

She turned to him. In the green light of the phlo-lights and the yellow light of a pyrum burner, she looked wan and weary. The hastily constructed splint had been replaced with a proper cast, though it still had the telltale sheen of plaster that had yet to fully cure. Her good hand clutched a cup of tea with the urgency of someone clinging to a lifeline in rough seas.

"Fine, fine," she tried to blink the sleepiness from her eyes. "You'll need to be my hands for this. I've read a great deal about Contaminant Six, and while it is merely unpleasant to handle in its raw form, we will very shortly be rendering something particularly hazardous to fug folk."

"Do we know if it is similarly hazardous to surface folk?"

"If you follow proper safety precautions, we won't need to find out."

"When have you ever known me to forgo proper safety precautions?"

"Would you like a precise tally? Or will an estimate do? I personally can recall over a dozen times you've left my laboratory smelling of burnt hair. And that's neglecting the issue of how many fingers you are missing."

He glared at her but decided not to push the point any further. "How are you feeling?"

"Like something that's been thrown from an airship and dragged through the forest by a crazed beast." She sipped her tea. "The regularity with which the reality of today has begun to sound like the hyperbole of yesterday is beginning to make me fear for what the future holds. For now, though, I shall heal." She sipped her tea again.

"Is drinking tea in a chemistry lab proper safety?"

"As it is entirely necessary for my sanity, I consider it a safety measure, not a violation. At least until we begin mixing C-6 with potential reactants. Now, I have already tested the contaminant itself in its raw state. It causes mild discomfort and inflammation, equivalent to a minor rash. That shall be considered our datum for this experiment. Have a look at the slide under the microscope to see what that looks like on a blood sample."

He gazed into the device. "I see."

"Now, if you would, look at slide number two. That is your blood sample. Our hope is to see treatments that cause the former to resemble the latter."

He slipped the slides back and forth.

"Fascinating, isn't it, how visually different our blood is," she said.

"I've seen my fair share of both fug and surface blood," Gunner said. "Albeit not so close."

"Ah... Yes, I imagine you would have, wouldn't you?" She set down her tea and flipped up her notes. "For most would-be assistants, working with blood would have made them squeamish. Fortunate that for you, this is a refreshingly small sample. There is little time to waste. I've laid out the apparatus. Extreme precision is important, and I shall be keeping my distance. To speed the process, we will be batch testing. First, a twenty-to-one ratio of test material to C-6. We will first identify the reaction, then decrease concentration until we find the minimally effective dose."

He set out the beakers and began measuring fluid. "May I ask, what do you intend to do when this testing is complete?"

"Send as safe a dose as I can create to be administered to Lil. Hopefully she will be in a position to administer it personally."

"No, I mean longer term than that. Supposing you end this process with a treatment that cures..." He paused as though he could feel the glare she was giving the back of his head. "That is to say, a treatment that *reverses* the change from surface folk to fug folk. What do you do with it?"

"I hadn't given it any thought. I imagine I would properly document and file it away for academic knowledge."

"I've got to imagine it was Wash's plan to sell it."

"A foolish endeavor. Who would purchase it? It isn't as though there are terribly many people becoming fug folk these days."

"I think there are quite a few people who would jump at the chance to change if an opportunity presented itself."

"Shall I repeat my prior statement about the relative lack of surface folk turning to fug folk these days? Your people aren't eager enough for change to hurl yourselves into a near certain death. Why should my people feel any differently?"

"Because we were born the way we are. Fug folk are just altered versions of us. In the case of this treatment, it is *undoing* a change."

"I was born as I am. What of me, then?" she asked.

"… It is possible I am not articulating myself elegantly."

"It is possible you have a backward, stubborn misconception of the world and its people."

"Perhaps we should focus on creating the treatment and set its implications aside for now."

She finished her tea and selected a breathing apparatus from a hook on the wall. "I would consider that wise."

He dosed out the different measurements, and the pair waited in silence for the solutions to combine.

#

Coop stood anxiously with one boot on the rope ladder dangling from the bottom of the airship. He wanted to be in the air. He wanted to be doing something, *anything*. But as much as his instincts told him to leap first and look second, he'd learned a thing or two under Captain Mack's command. These last few months he'd also learned what happened when he was left to his own devices. Primarily, without the captain, he got about half as much done and earned twice as many lumps for doing it. He still didn't have the patience to look before he leaped, but with someone else to do the looking, he tended to have a softer landing.

"Stop it! No! Stay!" came Nita's voice as she emerged from behind one of the buildings.

Coop grinned as she appeared. At least having her along wouldn't make things boring.

The squarrel she had ridden into the compound was padding along behind her. Every time she turned to reprimand him, through either shouted commands or whistled ones, the creature flopped on his belly. The moment she turned away from him, the creature hopped back to his feet and followed. Two grunts were doing their very best to hold him back, but the beast's brutish strength was such that they were simply dragged along behind.

"What's with you and critters?" Coop called.

"I don't know, and I am not entirely fond of it. The blasted thing ate three sacks of grain, and now it won't stop following me." She turned. "You can't come on the ship with me!"

Goose honked, no glimmer of comprehension in his eyes. She whistled the command to stay. He paused for a moment, then continued to plod along behind her.

"Bring it along," Coop said.

Nita started climbing the ladder. "We can't bring it along!"

"It's quicker than beatin' a simple command into a thick head. We're

173

topped off on water, and with just the two of us, a critter won't slow us none."

"You can't be serious."

"I ain't in a jokin' mood."

He hopped into position and started working the various dials and levers that would get the ship moving. Nita followed, and a few moments later, Goose scrambled along one of the mooring lines to join them on the deck.

"You boys get me loose," Coop shouted down to the men who had failed to keep Goose under control.

Nita looked uncertainly at the creature as he calmly plopped down and wobbled his eyes back and forth between her and Coop.

"Where you reckon we oughta be headin'?" Coop asked.

Nita did the best she could to rub the bridge of her nose without dislodging her mask "You've got Nikita with you?" she asked.

"She's about as willin' to stay behind as your critter."

"I suppose our best bet is to get ourselves somewhere near a lot of airship traffic. As much as I'm sure you'd enjoy putting your knuckles to someone's jaw to get the information we're after, we're more likely to learn something by having Nikita overhear a message from the ships' inspectors."

"Yeah, I reckon so." Coop made no attempt to mask his disappointment at the reasonable suggestion. "The Well Diggers got a place they like to spend their money. Gets all sorts of deliveries and whatnot. Should have a lot of traffic for Nikita to snoop on. If we get movin', shouldn't take us more than half a day to get there in this ship. Speedy little thing."

The mooring ropes went slack. Coop took the controls and guided the ship up and away. The moment it shifted, Goose's wayward eyes widened and darted. He dug his claws into the decking and produced a long, half-panicked honk.

"Whoa! Easy. It is all right," Nita shouted, taking a step back.

"Get in there and put a hand on him," Coop said.

"I'm afraid of what he'll do with my hand if he gets ahold of it," Nita said. "I'm awfully small compared to him."

"Critters only act like you're smaller than them if *you* act like you're smaller than them. Get a hand on him before he starts to flip," Coop said.

Nita gathered her not-terribly-formidable frame up and marched in. "Calm down," she commanded, placing a hand on Goose's neck.

The creature went rigid. His head turned aside to lock one eye on Nita. He twitched once, as if ready to spring.

"What did I say? Be calm," she reinforced, patting him on the neck.

Goose gave an inquisitive, uncertain honk, but eased his posture a bit. After a few more pats, the ship's more vigorous motions eased down into a smoother, speedier ride. The squarrel's anxiety slipped away, and he resumed his "normal" position of belly down, legs splayed, and head awkwardly perked up to observe the world.

Nita stepped forward. "How did you know that would work?"

"I used to herd goats, back before Cap'n Mack picked us up. They get all jumpy sometimes. It can be a real handful if the whole herd starts to do it. So you get good at keepin' it from gettin' bad."

"But those were *goats*," Nita said. "This is a squarrel. I can't imagine they can be trusted to behave in the same fashion."

Coop shrugged. "Critters are critters."

Nita looked at the calmed creature. "You must have been a very good goatherd, then."

"Couldn't't've been too good. The whole herd died the day cap'n picked me up. Found a good bit of grazin' down on a low level piece over to the east. Turns out it was good grazin' because when the wind kicked up, it'd get covered over in the fug, so no one else grazed there. Wouldn't you know it, we was down there when the wind did its thing. Darn near caught a few too many lungfuls of the fug that day, but Mack scooped us up."

Nita nodded and wiped her eyes. "Do you ever wonder what things would have been like if that hadn't happened? If you hadn't decided to graze there and the captain never picked you up?"

"Nope."

"Things would have been very different."

"I reckon they'd have to be, on account of we'd probably still be runnin' goats up and down the cliffs lookin' for grass."

"If you had it to do over, would you have preferred that?"

"I don't reckon so. Things've been mighty fine with the cap'n. Best food I ever ate. Seen most of what there is to see. Found somethin' I'm good at."

"You've risked your life quite a bit more."

"Not by my figurin'. It ain't like crawlin' all over them cliffs tryin' to keep goats in line is the safest sort of thing to do. And out there, there was just the two of us. Somethin' happened to Lil and I couldn't get her, she didn't get got. Likewise for me."

"I just..." Nita shook her head. "I just think about what's happening right now, and I can't help but feel there's something that we could have done to stop it. I'm an engineer by training, and we're all artists by birth. I'm accustomed to actions having meaning, intent."

She tipped her head, angling her ear toward the envelope. "Right now I hear a rattle. And I know that it's because the retainer strap for the steam lines headed to the port-side turbine is loose. If I leave it, the rattling will get worse, the steam line will wear, and eventually the port turbine will fail. If I tighten it, it'll quiet down, hold firm, and the ship continues better than I left it. Everything has a way that it works. There's always a correct thing to do. Art is less well-defined, but there is still always meaning behind everything."

She slipped a wrench from her sash and hauled herself up to reach the culprit of the rattling. "It just feels like life should be the same. But here we are. We did our best. I thought we made all the right decisions as far as we could determine, but it's all gone wrong." Nita tightened down the bracket, and the rattle died away.

"Back in the steamworks in Caldera, any time something went wrong, every one of the engineers, and *especially* every free-wrench, would gather together and trace things back until we found what went wrong. It was always something tiny. Something that could have been fixed early to prevent all of this. It's just in my nature to look back upon things that fail and try to prevent them from failing again. And I can't bear the thought that if Lil doesn't come out of this, it'll be because of something I did. Or something I didn't do. There may have been a world where she'd have lived a longer, happier life if I'd never weaseled my way onto the ship to get that medicine for my mother."

"Longer, maybe. But long lives ain't so special. Look at the fuggers. They live longer than us, and most've 'em are pert near as miserable as a body could get. Spend all their time tryin' to spread the misery out nice and thin so their bit of it don't look so bad. And then there's them big tortoise critters on the islands way down south of Caldera. Them things live forever. Back when we were tryin' to find a good place to moor up near you folks, we kept comin' up on this same island, and we kept seein' this same tortoise that had this spear head stickin' out of its shell. Gunner said it was from way back, pre-Calamity. So that sucker was even older than the fuggers. Nice long life on it. But near as I can figure, it ain't never done nothin' but wandered around lookin' for grass to eat. Or whatever them critters eat. You give me a chance to chew on grass and live for a long time or swing from some rigging and live a little time, I ain't gonna waste my time thinkin' it over. Riggin' runnin' is fun, and grass ain't half as tasty as it looks.

"Lil would feel the same. Ask her to choose between livin' like a tortoise forever or flyin' the skies with you for a couple years? Won't find no grass in her teeth." He twisted some knobs. "I'm takin' her up above the fug. Ain't no one liable to hassle a fug scout ship in these parts, and I got a hankerin' for a breath of fresh air that ain't been filtered through a mask, and it shouldn't hurt the squarrel none."

The ship angled upward. Nita held tight to the rigging and gazed at the sky as it slowly revealed itself through the fug.

"I tell you something, Coop. I admire how clear and certain you are sometimes."

"Gunner says it's easy for a fella to be clearheaded when there ain't too much in there to get in the way. I reckon he's probably right." He waited until they were fully clear of the fug, then pulled a flask from his pocket to take a nip. "I only hope him and the doc can get that goop to fix what's ailin' Lil, because one way or another, I'm bringin' her back, and if they ain't got somethin' for her, we're both gonna be awful sore."

#

After an extremely long climb, Blanche reached the bottom of the elevator shaft. The boiler and gearing that ran the mechanism, as well as an assortment of other devices here at the ground level, were noisy enough to cover any incidental sounds she might have made. There was little fear of her immediate discovery unless someone spotted her in the darkness. This was fortunate, because the revelations brought about by the climb were too significant not to give voice to.

"What... what kind of person *was* I?" she muttered, looking at her grease-soaked hands. "Was I part ape? My arms are barely tired, and I've been dangling from a greased cable for *so long*."

Deckhand. Good climber, Wink tapped on the knife.

"That was the sort of thing I would do? Climb cables all day?"

No. Rigging, in airship. This way. Fast. Low.

"The rigging of an airship. On the *ground* I hope."

No.

"In the sky? I was expected to climb like that while soaring over the ground?"

Wanted to. Liked it. Fast. Low. Out.

She crouched. "I wouldn't be expected to do that anymore, would I?"

Yes. Inspector inspects. Gunner guns. Engineer engineers. Deckhand does everything else. All like it.

"No more, thank you," she said moving in a crouched run along the roughly carved machinery section of the old mine. "I don't think I'll be returning to that."

Lil liked climb.

"Maybe so, but I'm not Lil, regardless of what you call me. I agreed to escape because it was clear I was a prisoner, and it doesn't take much thought to work out that a prisoner should try to get free. But freeing myself to return to a life of danger isn't much of an improvement."

Was-Lil liked climb.

"Don't call me Was-Lil. That guy called me Blanche. You may as well call me that."

Whatever name. Liked climb. Liked this climb.

177

"I wouldn't say I *liked* it. It felt normal. It felt good to be doing something I was good at." She huddled a little lower and watched the doorway to the main section of the mine entrance. "It *might* have felt a bit fun. But a drunk likes his bottle, and eventually it'll kill him. Maybe I'm just smart enough to see that and Lil wasn't. The point is, my memory only goes back a few hours. My whole *life* has only been a few hours. I don't want to waste any more time locked away, and I don't want to cut what I've got ahead of me short by doing something foolish, even if it *is* fun."

Wink hopped down and looked her deep in the eyes. He seemed to be measuring her. *Not climb. Not risk. Not Lil,* he decreed.

"That's what I'm trying to tell *you*."

They'd reached the more heavily trafficked part of the mine, which in this case meant that there was a pair of grunts on patrol.

Some leaders earn the respect of their workers. Most merely buy the time of their workers. The differences in those two types of leaders are many, but at this moment the most glaring of them was a simple one. A respected leader's people can be trusted to go to the end of the world to achieve the goals set out for them. For the rest of the leaders out there, the enthusiasm of their workers is directly proportional to the proximity of their boss. Wash was deep in the mine, working on something that would require his full attention. That meant that guard duty was more of an opportunity to smoke a cigarette and nip from a flask than an actual assignment. It meant that a well-timed scurry was all that was necessary to get clear of the mine's mouth and into the ratty shrubs on either side of its opening.

Blanche and Wink moved as quickly and silently as they could until they were out of view. When they were in the clear, Blanche finally took the moment to view the world around her for what was technically the first time.

They were at the midpoint of a slope that became ever steeper behind them and ever shallower ahead. The cliffs were almost sheer above them, and the ground had an uneven, gravely texture here, the remnants of an eternity of shrugged-off stone and debris. The sky was a rich purple mist that gave the landscape before her the look of perpetual twilight. A footpath—which they were avoiding for fear of being spotted—wove back and forth until the slope leveled off, then headed toward the one feature of the tableau that pushed all the rest from Blanche's mind. It was a sprawling city. Phlo-lights lit the streets in dazzling stripes. Smoke rose from chimneys, airships crisscrossed overhead. In the distance, a large car glided along a stout cable that vanished into the mist above, leading presumably to the very top of the cliffs behind her.

"Is that... is that the fug town they were talking about?" Blanche said.

Yes, Wink said. *This way. Fast.*

"Is there someone there who can help us?"

No. Was-Lil was from Wind Breaker. *Fug folk hated* Wind Breaker.

"Then why are we hurrying?"

Send message to Wind Breaker. Wind Breaker *come to get us.*

"They'll come? Even if these people hate them?"

They will come for you.

"Do they know what's happened. Do they know that I'm not who they think I am?"

Maybe.

"And still they'll come?"

Yes.

"It doesn't sound like a smart idea."

Wind Breaker *crew not do smart things.* Wind Breaker *crew does right things for* Wind Breaker *crew.*

"If they come and get me... what then?"

Wind Breaker *things. Fast. Sooner, better.* Wink bounded along the roadside, stopping periodically to ensure she was keeping pace.

"*Wink Breaker* things. The sort of things that would make someone comfortable with sliding down cables in dark shafts and sneaking past guards and following one-eyed creatures?"

Yes.

"The sort of things that are liable to get me killed?"

Yes.

"... I'm not sure I'm keen on meeting them. I don't *know* them. They seem dangerous and foolhardy. It sounds like their hearts are in the right place, but when it comes down to it, the only person I *know* I can trust is me. I don't think anyone who would risk my life to save me is someone I should be trusting with it in the first place. That's just sense."

Wink flicked an ear and turned his head to an unassuming little spire a short distance away, at the very edge of the fug town. He pointed. *Wink send message. Was-Lil wait.*

"No, wait!" she called. "If you send a message, what's to stop Wash from getting it?"

Still send message.

"And what? Tell them where to find us? Tell him we got out of the mine? If you send a message, you'll be telling *Wash* where to find us."

Wink glared at her. *Wink wait for better time. Wink listen for messages. Wait here.*

The inspector didn't linger long enough for a reply. He simply dashed toward the spire, leaving her behind. She paused for a moment, less out of obedience and more to give herself a moment to think. Her skin crawled and her knees felt twitchy as she stood and considered her options. Slowly she realized, just as dangling in the elevator shaft had felt strangely comfortable to her, a moment of silent contemplation felt oddly uncomfortable. Everything inside her demanded she be in constant motion. Given the hints of her other proclivities, she wasn't certain how she'd survived this long, but even a single moment of clear thinking made one thing extremely and inarguably apparent.

If she wanted this new life of hers to last, she had a feeling she should *not* wait around for these *Wind Breaker* people to arrive. For now, she'd stick with Wink. She wasn't ready to be alone. But as soon as she felt she could manage it, she'd find out what this life had in store for her.

Chapter 14

Gunner tried to blink sweat from his eyes. Every scar and missing body part represented a lesson learned. Some were learned more thoroughly than others, but each of them taught him something. All it took was one poorly timed wipe of his face with a hand covered in potent chemicals to convince him not to touch any sensitive bits of anatomy with his hands while doing an experiment.

"Let me," Prist said.

The chemist who had been calling the shots since they'd gotten their hands on the key ingredient to the would-be cure mopped his brow with a dry cloth. Once they'd begun performing the actual experiments, Prist had made the ultimate sacrifice and forgone tea in favor of a face mask, a glass face shield, a heavy apron, and rubber gloves.

"Do you need me to take over on the observation for now?" she asked.

"Don't risk yourself," he said.

"I am confident we've learned enough to be confident of the adequacy of our safety measures," she said. "The substance is, if nothing else, exceedingly nonvolatile. Fumes are not a concern. That should make limiting exposure a simple matter."

"Even so. Keep your distance. There are several dozen reasons why it would be a terrible loss if you were to fall ill, but right now chief among them is the likelihood we wouldn't find the proper dosage and all of this would have been for naught."

"Science is never for naught, Guy. We have learned so much already. We've learned that the necessary catalyst for the transition of Contaminant Six into its fug-antagonistic form is high-purity alcohol. It explains a great deal about how we have come this far without learning about it. Alcohol in the proper concentrations would almost never come into contact with it. We probably never would have learned about it if the hapless worker hadn't— if the evidence we've discovered is indeed accurate—decided to clean his hands with the pure stuff rather than a dilution. We've also learned that the substance acts *very* quickly, and that even in its most potent form, the fug-antagonistic solution has little to no effect on surface folk. What's more, the fug-antagonistic—"

"Samantha, for the sake of brevity and sanity, I suggest we find a more manageable name for the treatment."

"… Antifug seems suitable," she suggested.

"Agreed." He stifled a yawn. "How long have we been at this?"

"I've ceased to keep track of such things," she said. "We work until the work is done. After which I look forward to sleeping for as long as my body will allow."

"And when is the work done?"

"When we find the safest form with the desired effects. It is all a matter of iteration with increasingly precise measurements." She picked up a clipboard. "We already know that concentration greater than one part C-6 to five hundred parts alcohol will produce lethal toxicity for fug folk. Naturally I cannot be certain from simple blood tests, but I would suggest a few drops on unprotected skin, if untreated, would be enough to produce death in a matter of days. More exposure than that, death in as few as a couple of minutes."

"And yet you claim to feel safe dealing with it?" Gunner said.

"I didn't say I felt safe. I said I felt confident."

"Well, *I* feel confident that you keeping your distance will serve us all much better."

She took a breath of relief and stepped back a few paces. "I shan't argue with you." She flipped through the pages. "I wish there was more time to study this in detail. I suppose there will be, afterward. But this substance is *fascinating*. The effects are astonishingly swift. Based on what we've seen, a few ounces of a properly formulated treatment, taken orally, would be enough to reach suitable exposure across the entire body in hours. More sensitive body parts like the eyes and lungs could see results in *minutes*. That is the chief concern with a proper treatment. We need to moderate the effects so as to not completely overwhelm the person receiving the treatment. And even then…"

"It may not work," Gunner said.

"I just… I can't be sure. We have blood samples from born fug folk like me. We have samples from those who were created during the Calamity. None of them have suggested, in even the smallest and gentlest exposures, a reaction I would deem consistently survivable. Lil is midtransition, or at the very most, extremely freshly fugified. We can't know how she will react. The blood from the youngest donors has shown the more promising results, but none would have survived. This isn't… I can't condone…" She paused.

"What? What can't you condone?"

"Just how do you intend to administer this treatment? Because honestly, even if I had another two weeks to work on this, I couldn't be certain I wasn't providing you the medical equivalent of a half-loaded revolver. I don't know that I could live with myself if I sent you out there with the best treatment I could concoct, knowing that it was your intent to administer it to someone regardless of the danger it represents. Even if we could be *certain* it would restore her to just as she was before she was exposed to the fug, we still don't know Lil's state of mind right now. We could be asking her to kill the person she's become to save the person she once was. And the side effects! Even in the most promising test batches, the shift from fugified is not *complete*. All evidence suggests that a perfect cure doesn't exist. The *best* we can hope for at this point is some sort of neither fish nor fowl version of a surface person and a fug person. Perhaps it is ten percent of one and ninety percent of the other, or vice versa."

She leaned heavily on the wall behind her. "I've been dropped out of the sky. I've had my arm broken. I've been dragged through the woods on the back of a particularly mad member of an already utterly mad species, and I've worked for untold hours on this chemical riddle without sleep. But *this* part is what is most trying. I am not a philosopher, Guy. I am not a theologian. I am a *chemist*. My task has only ever been working out how to create a substance we need out of substances we have. It's never been any concern of mine if such a substance should exist or how it should be used."

He dosed out the next sample of the serum. "You call me Guy. Most everyone else calls me Gunner. My role in the crew is to prepare the weapons and point them in the direction where they will do the most good for our side and the most harm to the other side. I, too, am neither a philosopher nor a theologian. I have a far more direct and pragmatic view than those lofty positions do. Soldiers and doctors are the ones who develop a relationship with death. A partnership in the former case and an adversarial role in the other. The kindness that soldiers have is that, for the most part, we face other soldiers. When we pick up our weapon and we square off against our equals across the gulf of sky, land, or sea that separates us, we know the same thoughts are passing through our heads and theirs. We know we chose this role, or at the very least were prepared for it."

He finished stirring the solutions and began to prepare slides for analysis. "Choice and awareness," he continued. "The sense that each side knew what it was getting into. That's the only thing that can make something like this tolerable. You want an answer for how to set your conscience at ease when creating something that even when used correctly could be seen as taking a life? Delegate the decision. A soldier takes his orders from a commander. You shall pass the decision on to us."

"Then the blood is on *your* hands," she said.

"Our hands are stained with the stuff," Gunner said.

She shook her head. "I ask this not out of judgment but out of genuine curiosity. How do you sleep at night having had to make such choices?"

"Exhaustion helps," he said. "And I'm never short of that with this crew."

He stepped aside. She looked through the microscope at the samples.

"I don't suppose we'll be able to do much better than this. Not without more resources and more time than we have," she said, stepping back to mark her findings on the clipboard. "These utilized the stabilizing agent, correct?"

"Yes."

"We don't have much of it, but we should be able to produce a few doses. That just leaves what, from my very selfish view, is the more pressing concern."

"What is that? I thought the treatment was the goal."

"We've solved the riddle of how to make a medicine out of this stuff, to a minimally viable degree. There's still the question of how best to render it safe to those who might be accidentally exposed. The lack of volatility is an asset during preparation, but it also means that once the stuff has been rendered toxic, it shall remain so for ages. I have to work out what solvents can cleanse my laboratory, or a stray drop of the stuff could poison me weeks from now." She stifled a yawn. "A problem for another time. I don't suppose you could prepare the final dosage on you own?"

"I think I could manage."

"Excellent. I believe the time has come for me to see if exhaustion is indeed as effective as you imply."

#

Nita and Coop loitered outside the hangout that the grunts so often favored. It wasn't what Nita had expected. Rather than the dank little shack in the middle of nowhere that tended to be the haven for people on the fringes of society, the Well Diggers and their associates had taken advantage of one of the fug's greatest resources: pre-Calamity ghost towns. They'd resurrected what, before the fug had blanketed the land, was likely a performance hall. Most of its sign had broken away, and what remained had come to be its adopted name: The Grand.

The Grand had fallen into disrepair, as all things had. But the Well Diggers were more resourceful than most. Scavenged materials and copious amounts of elbow grease had metamorphosed the place into an oddly beautiful pastiche of a grand lost culture and the makeshift one that had replaced it. Cracked plaster had fresh patches. Faded murals had been "updated" with crude graffiti and doodles. The stage still served some semblance of its original purpose, though rather than concerts, operas, and plays, it was home to whatever member of the clientele felt like noodling around on one of the instruments they'd been able to clean up. Presently that was a rather inebriated fellow who seemed to think a guitar was mostly a percussion instrument. For better or worse, his performance was being largely ignored in favor of keeping a wary eye on Goose, whom they could not persuade to remain outside.

"I wish I'd learned about this place with a clearer mind," Nita said, gazing up at the cracked reliefs arching over the stage. "This is the first real evidence I've seen of something my culture reveres being given similar gravitas in your culture."

Coop looked up from the broken chair leg he'd been idly whittling since they'd failed to find anyone in The Grand who seemed to know anything about Dr. Wash.

"You been in the whatchacallit, the dancin' house up in Keystone. This ain't that much different. Just bigger, is all."

"Impressive though the cabaret is, its artistic intent is a bit more... *direct* than seems appropriate for a place like this."

"I like stuff that don't leave you guessin' what they were on about. Ladies with frilly underthings kickin' their legs up so you can see 'em don't take too much figurin' to get a kick out of." He glanced up. "You got anythin', Nikita?"

The inspector tapped out a reply that, thanks to the acoustics of the place, reached them with great clarity despite her being several stories above them on the arched ceiling.

Lots. Not from Wink or about Lil, she tapped.

Coop carved off a particularly large chunk of the chair leg. His lips curled in frustration. "Dang it!" he snapped, hopping up on stage. "You mean to tell me not one o' you fellas knows where Dr. Wash does his dirty doin's?"

The grunts milling about with their favored vices paused and looked at him. Nita tensed up a bit. The vast majority of The Grand's patrons were sporting bruises and split lips in some state of healing or another. Violence was something of a pastime for the coarser of the grunts. Coop had deftly managed to thrust the whole room into the middle of an argument they weren't aware they were a part of, and thus had issued an informal invitation for a therapeutic game of fisticuffs.

"Oi!" barked one of the smaller grunts. "What are you on about?"

"Dr. Wash. You know him. Got a mask makes him look like a bird. Did business between Lock and Keystone up until Tusk bought it, now he's tryin' for more. He got my sister tucked away somewhere, probably down that way, and that's more mountain than a fella can search on his lonesome. But I ain't never seen the man without a half dozen of you fellas followin' him around, and the way I figure it, you can't find a fella willin' to do a job like that without goin' through a couple who ain't. So either one of you fellas already works for him, or one of you's been asked. So quit actin' like you don't know nothin'."

Goose honked, eager to add his own voice to the escalating exchange of shouts.

"Look, we done *business* with him," offered one of the more reasonable grunts. "Besides the *Wind Breaker* crew, he's the only source for half of the stuff that's worth having up here, and you've been too busy spreading the phlogiston and coal and such around, so it's him or nothing for good booze that don't come out of a knocked-together still. But it's all through one of his fellas. They come, get the money, drop off some crates, and take back the old ones."

"Like hell," Coop said.

"You accusing us of being liars?" asked one grunt.

"I'm sayin' there ain't no way you *ain't*. On account of I know there's that whole batch of winches and such that Dr. Wash runs over on Kruger Mountain. Ain't no chance that's where he's got Lil, seein' as how there ain't no place to hide somebody, but pert near everybody knows about it and there ain't *one* of you who said a word about it when I asked."

"Coop, I think you should calm down," Nita said, already formulating a game plan when he inevitably failed to do so.

"What's the point of us telling you something we know you know?" a grunt asked.

"It ain't your job to work out what a fella wants to know. I got questions, and if you got answers, you cough up. Or you'll be coughin' up your own kidneys."

"You think you're man enough to call me a liar to my face?" rumbled one of the more brutish patrons.

Coop stowed his whittling knife and hopped down from the stage. He rolled up his sleeves as he paced toward the man. "I'm fixin' to find out. All this waitin' ain't doin' me no good regardless. May as well teach a couple lessons." He stood toe to toe, and eye to chest, with the hulk of a fug man. "You know where a fella can find Dr. Wash when he ain't in the mood to be found?" Coop asked.

"Nope," the man said.

"Well then you're a liar."

The grunt placed a hand on his shoulder. Coop delivered a kick to the knee. A heartbeat later, the room was a melee. Goose sat, eyes vacant, as though he was only dully aware that anything around him had changed. Coop and Nita were buried in a mound of workers with just enough stress and alcohol in them to be spoiling for a fight. There was no shortage of weapons that could end the fight in a few moments, but a combination of honor, discipline, and absentmindedness left them out of the fray. Fists, boots, elbows, and knees were the weapons of the day. That half of these grunts worked at Ichor Well and had probably shared a game of cards and a laugh with Coop as recently as the previous week didn't matter in the slightest. For Coop, the pressure had built to the point that a fight was the only thing that could vent it.

Nita, for her part, only took a few glancing blows. It wasn't chivalry. Two heavy tool sashes and a hefty monkey-toe wrench on the back were as good as a suit of armor when it came to a fist fight. Toss in the well-secured mask and there wasn't much of her anatomy left that wouldn't bloody any set of knuckles sent her way. She wasn't knocked from her feet until a particularly tipsy brawler was ejected from the scrum in the middle of the room and collided with her. She stumbled back and tumbled over a crate of empty bottles. As the thick glass bottles clattered about and Nita struggled to right herself, something caught her eye.

The crate was recently painted, but even through the thick layer of gray paint, she could see that the crate itself was a relic. She dragged it up onto the stage, where the lackluster lighting was brightest. There was the faintest evidence of a logo, the sort that would be burned in with a branding iron.

"Everyone stop!" she shouted.

The command was about as effective on the dogpile below her as one might expect. She pulled her two cheater bars from her belt and clashed them together.

"Enough!" she shouted.

This time the command got through. One by one the grunts peeled off the mound until a dazed but feisty Coop emerged.

"You boys said you get everything that you don't get from us from Dr. Wash, right?" she said.

"Yeah, that's right," said one of the larger grunts with a less complete set of teeth than he started the day with.

"Is this one of his crates?" she asked.

"Yeah."

"Are there any others?"

"Look, Nita, you got anythin' you're workin' toward? Because I been keepin' count, and that fella there's got two more lumps comin' to him."

"The crate is very old. And considering how much of the stuff in circulation down here is reused, I'm thinking it might give us a hint as to where he's been storing his stuff. Help me find one where we can make out the logo."

Most of the fug folk, their ears still ringing from Coop's remarkably effective flurries of punches, were slow to embrace the idea of helping out so quickly.

"Now! There's no time to waste! Move!" she barked.

A flinch rolled through the crowd, and they shuffled off to dig up other crates. Nita took a breath.

"They only act like you're smaller than them if *you* act like you're smaller than them…" she murmured.

Dr. Wash stomped through the tunnel at the base of his hideout. Ahead, he saw a pair of his guards. One tossed down a cigarette and stomped it out.

"Where is she, you dopes?" he shouted.

"What's that, boss?" replied the man unfortunate enough to be nearer to the angry employer.

"Now's not the time to play stupid. You're overqualified," he growled. "Your job is to make sure no one comes in or goes out without my say-so. Our prisoner is nowhere to be seen. My money's on you two not earning your money. We searched every place you can reach without prying open a fresh shaft."

"We didn't see anyone, boss."

"I know. That's the *problem*, morons." He adjusted his gloves and twisted a crick out of his neck. "She was half a numbskull to start with, and her worthless skull was emptied out, and she *still* got away. I got our inspector guy listenin' for messages from her little rat pal, but so far, nothin'. Without her, we got nothin' to keep the *Wind Breaker* crew from comin' in swingin'."

"Maybe they won't find us."

"*Of course they'll find us, you jerk!*" he fumed. "They found Tusk, for cryin' out loud, and he was a recluse. There's only two ways this goes down now. First, maybe there's not enough of the crew left to put up much of a fight. Considering the friggin' *rat* almost killed one of my guys, I don't think we're that lucky. The second is once they figure out we don't have the deckhand, they come in and start blowin' holes in everything they can find until there's nothing left but a bunch of stupid corpses and one smart one. So here's how it goes down now…"

"We gotta go find her in Fugtown?"

"Don't get ahead of yourself. I'll send somebody, not you. The best chance we got is makin' the *Wind Breaker* crew think we still got her. So I gotta send someone with tact to try to find her, and I gotta see if I can make it look like we got her back even if we didn't. It'll buy us time. I don't need much more of it."

"Why not? What's happening, boss? Got a plan to get rid of them?"

"I had *three* plans to get rid of them. Now we're on number four. The only guy in this whole organization with a good head on his shoulders besides *me* says all that's missing is a couple hundred gallons of pure alcohol, so I gotta go pull some strings and see if I can get some. Once I got it, I'll have what it takes to keep everyone nice and distracted. All I need you to do is stand here, make sure nobody comes in, and don't go runnin' your mouth about where the deckhand is or ain't. Just. Act. Dumb."

"But you just said we shouldn't—"

"Shut up and do what I told you to!" Wash stomped past them, grumbling. "How much you want to bet it was thickheaded lackeys that got Tusk killed? Why's it so hard to find someone smart enough to get things done but not so smart he'll try to take over? Friggin' worthless…"

#

Nita, Coop, and the assorted riffraff in The Grand turned up no fewer than seventeen of the crates. The slopped-on paint had been exceedingly thorough, clearly an intentional attempt to conceal their origin. Fortunately, they'd not expected someone with Nita's patience or perseverance, and one of them was in much better shape than the rest.

"Do we have any more of this stuff?" she asked, waggling an empty bottle.

"I always said this stuff was strong enough to strip paint," said one of the Well Diggers. "I kind of thought I was kidding."

He handed over a fresh bottle. She popped it open and dosed a rag. Careful blotting and scraping was steadily revealing an ancient burnt-in logo.

"Where's somebody learn to do somethin' like this?" Coop asked.

"Caldera wasn't always the place you've seen," Nita said. "Before the Calamity, we had our first exposure to the people of Rim, and it left a mark. Things changed. If you listen to my grandparents, your people 'infected' ours. A lot of our antiquity was knocked down, painted over, and rebuilt to be a bit more like what we'd seen of you. The backlash against it is one of the reasons we started to close ourselves off. Since then, we've been trying to strike a balance. Part of that involves uncovering the things we covered up." She wetted the rag again. "Spend a summer trying to restore a mural and something like this feels like child's play."

The last bit of the covering came up in a single large flake, revealing a brand that had been faded with time and a halfhearted bit of sanding before the paint job.

"Grummond Ironworks," she said, squinting at the words. "Does that ring a bell?"

One of the grunts shook his head. "There's only a few ironworks in the fug. I've worked for 'em all. That ain't one."

"Ain't no ironworks by that name up in Westrim neither," Coop said. "I don't think Circa's got one. Pre-Calamity then. Anybody got one of them old maps?"

"Or an atlas? Anything with a legend," Nita said.

"I might have one. I'll check the ship," said the scrawniest of the patrons.

"You two said you were in a hurry," said the swollen-faced fellow

189

Coop had chosen to initiate the fray with earlier. "Now you sit here peeling paint and looking through books?"

"It's either that or I figure out how to keep myself busy," Coop said, rubbing a blackening eye. "I don't think anybody wants no more of that."

"But you'll have to search the whole fug on old, faded maps to see if maybe this crate came from someplace Wash might be."

"Y'all got the crate from Wash. It for sure came from where he was," Coop said.

"But the *whole fug*."

"It won't be the whole fug," Nita said. "Coop said he does his work mostly between Lock and Keystone. It's not insignificant, but it's a good deal smaller than the whole fug. And we only need to find places that could have carried the logo of an ironworks."

"*And* the sort of place you'd hide a Coop from another Coop. Which I reckon means someplace that'd turn away a cannon shot or two, on account of I ain't comin' at him with anything smaller."

The helpful grunt returned with a stack of old pages. Nita spread them out on the edge of the stage. Sure enough, the map was a remnant of the old Rim. It had been heavily marked up with the new names for old towns, as well as anything that the fug folk had added. But faded text still labeled the major points of the pre-Calamity world. Coop and Nita picked sections of the map representing the mountains starting just north of Keystone and just south of Lock.

"What is it? Grainger Ironworks?" Coop said.

"Grummond," Nita corrected.

"Got a Grainger down near Lock and a little ways east. You reckon maybe they spelled it wrong?"

"Not unless it was one of your ancestors that did the spelling," remarked a grunt.

"I've got a copper mine here. Tin here. These mountains are incredibly bountiful," Nita said.

"Pert near the only way we kept on livin' after the fug," Coop said. "Mines so rich you could more or less core the mountain like an apple and still find stuff."

"Where is the light? I think I have something."

She scooped up a sheet of paper, one that was almost entirely red ink showing off assorted places of interest in Fugtown and Keystone. She overturned one of the crates and stood on top of it so that she could hold the page up to the nearest phlo-light.

"G... R... Yes! It's here! Grummond Iron and Steel. There was a steel mill, a coal mine, and an iron mine all in one complex. It looks like it's just south of Fugtown. I almost missed it because of all the markup."

"A mine… Yep, if I was afraid of what I'd do to me, I'd jump down a big hole and hide," Coop said.

"That's an awful little bit to go on," one of the fuggers said.

"It's loads more than nothin'," Coop said. "Even if it ain't the place, it'll get us movin' in the right direction to hear more news about what's goin' down." He raised his voice. "Nikita! Darlin, get down here, we're headin' out," he called.

"Goose! We're…" Nita placed a hand on her hip. "Goose, what are you eating?"

All eyes turned to the demented squarrel who had been disarmingly quiet until now. He was surrounded by wood shavings and had the remnants of a horsehair cushion sticking out of his mouth.

"I think… I think he ate one of them old rows of seats that fell apart," said a grunt.

"Well, that ought to tide him over for the flight back to Ichor Well. Let's go!"

They hurried out the door, Nikita bounding down the wall to take her rightful place in Coop's jacket. As soon as he noticed that Nita was on the move, Goose hopped up and followed.

"How fast do you think we can make it back to Ichor Well and then down to Grummond's mine?"

"That scout's pretty quick. Loaded up with all of us, plus the equipment we'll need… if we push her as hard as she'll go and push ourselves harder, maybe three days?"

Nita pulled a wrench from her sash. "I'll see if I can knock it down to two. We've been away from Lil too long already."

\#

Blanche breathed a sigh of relief as her boots finally clacked against the first cobblestone of a proper city street. Streets meant buildings, buildings meant alleys, and alleys meant places to hide. Wink had been riding her shoulder backward, eyes on the trail behind them and ears darting this way and that. He'd tapped out warnings when there was motion from the direction of the mine exit, but they'd been lucky enough to be in spitting distance of the city when the first genuine search party appeared.

"It feels as though I should be more worried," Blanche said, sliding into the shadow of the first building she passed.

Lil was always running and hiding. People always searching. Normal, Wink tapped.

"Hopefully we can put an end to that. That's no way to live."

Lil liked it.

"Well *I don't*," Blanche snapped. "The quicker I leave her behind, the better." She brushed at the filthy and ill-fitting outfit. "We'll start with the clothes."

She quickened her pace and slipped into the back alleys, splitting her attentions between staying ahead of anyone who might be on her tail and finding a source for the supplies she'd need. Wink made the first task simple enough. Between his hearing and his ability to scamper up to get a sharp lookout in a matter of seconds, any search party would have had to be particularly sneaky to get the drop on her.

The inspector was less obliging about telling her which way to go. As it so happened, that part was even simpler. Fugtown was a curious place. Most of the blocks were well-kept but utterly empty. The full activity of the city was focused into a handful of populated neighborhoods. In the eerie silence of the city, the slightest sound of voices or motion seemed to carry forever.

She found her way to what she at first thought was a market. As she crept closer, she realized it was actually some sort of distribution hub. A tall, scrawny, and terribly disinterested man with a gun was the only semblance of security, while two other fug folk worked a steam winch to load up steam carts from the contents of a warehouse. The crates were fastidiously marked. *Nonperishable Meat, Nonperishable Vegetable, Potable Water, Textile Goods.*

In this situation, there were probably a dozen different ways to go about procuring what she needed. She could try to negotiate with the fug folk. Perhaps try to trade something. She could wait until they were gone and steal the items she was interested in from the warehouse. None of those ideas occurred to her. The obvious answer, which didn't feel odd until the moment she started to enact it, was to jump into the cart while it was moving and take her pick of their stock while she was on the move.

When the row of steam carts was fully loaded and started moving, she waited until the guard was distracted and dashed up to the trailing cart. A smooth vault took her over the edge, and she was safely sheltered by the walls of the cart as she set about levering open the first of many crates with the emergency brake handle.

She paused after she'd managed to uncover the first crate and looked to Wink. "She did this sort of thing all the time, didn't she," Blanche asked.

Wind Breaker *crew got things however they got things,* Wink tapped.

"She was a thief…" Blanche sifted through the contents of the crate of clothing. "Hopefully this will be the last time I have to be reduced to this. Thieves probably don't live very long or happy lives."

She tugged a few items from inside. Things would go much more smoothly if she blended in. Most of the clothing she found was for men, but she had the vague memory that fug women wore dresses. She had to open a third crate before she finally found a dress and purse that might fit her. A nice heavy sack from a fourth crate was hastily filled with canned goods from a fifth, and before the cart train reached its first stop, she had vaulted over the side again.

"Look the other way," she instructed. "It's time to shed this filthy clothing and try for a fresh start."

Chapter 15

Nita watched the mountains. Before she'd joined the crew, the fastest vehicle she'd ever been on was a steamship. She still remembered how astounded she'd been by the raw speed of an airship. This ship was easily one of the fastest she'd ever been on. It still felt like the longest journey she'd ever been on. Even as familiar peaks started to appear on the horizon, she felt the weight of every second. Goose broke the monotony ever few minutes by honking at a random cloud or passing bird, but it wasn't nearly enough to pull Nita from her own mind.

Coop was at the wheel. Gunner was beside Nita. He must have felt the pressure from Nita, because he took it upon himself to break the silence.

"Not much longer now," he said.

Nita nodded distantly.

"Do you have your dose of the antifug?" he asked.

She patted a pouch. "Safe and sound. Do you have yours?"

"Mine and Coop's," he said. "He didn't trust himself not to break it."

"Go over it with me once more. What did Prist say?" Nita said.

"Nothing much to go over," Gunner said.

"Just once more."

"The full dose, orally. We should have a mask ready for her. The lungs will start to recover in minutes. The rest, if it comes, will come with time. And bad news comes fast. If it *is* toxic to her…"

"It won't be. If there is any justice in this world, this will work. We've come too far and fought too hard for anything less."

"She's gonna be fine," Coop called from the helm. "The doc's stuff'll fix her up, she'll be herself, and the two of us'll show Dr. Wash what his insides look like. Ain't no doubt. And it ain't about justice or fate or nothin'. I don't know the first thing about how or why any of this stuff'd work. May as well be magic for all I know or care. But the doc gets it, and you folk get it. So I don't need to. And you folk'll hem and haw about if you think it'll work because when you got brains enough to do thinkin', you can't rightly stop. So first you think, then you think twice, and you guess, and you second guess. But you all got it figured. Now all we got is to find Lil and dose her up. So quit your frettin' and get ready. This here's the fun bit."

#

Blanche marched down the street in Fugtown. The place was strangely comforting to her. A part of it was the odd balance of togetherness and solitude. The place was truly sprawling. Given the current status of her memory, it didn't mean much that this place was the largest town she'd ever been in, but even *she* could see that one would be hard-pressed to find a larger one beneath the fug. Streets of houses seemed to run forever in both directions, vanishing into the fug. Yet despite a place large and intact enough to be home to thousands upon thousands of people, most of the buildings were empty. Other people walked the streets, but they were rare and kept to themselves. If someone gave her a suspicious look, she was never far from a pitch-black alleyway to duck into and hide. It was an ideal place for someone on the run from captors. Indeed, even with the merest whisper of some very questionable instincts to keep her free and functional, she'd been able to spend several days in the place.

The sack of canned goods was holding up well. Her dress wasn't a perfect fit, but neither were Lil's clothes, which were now in a pile in an alley somewhere. Replacing them was a gray dress that was a shade too large for her but blended nicely with what few fug women seemed to be around. When the time came to sleep, she found a heavy can of beans was just as effective as a key. Bash a pane of glass, reach inside to unlock the door, and any building she chose of the hundreds of vacant ones could be her home for the night.

She walked past a storefront and paused to gaze into the window. It was vacant, but whole and well-kept. The only thing it was missing was a proprietor.

"I think I could get to liking it here," she said, shading the glass to see through the shine. "How hard would it be to set up shop? And then I could sit, safe and sound, and serve customers."

Deckhands don't serve customers, Wink tapped from one of the rooftops.

As Blanche became firmer in her insistence that she was not Lil, Wink had become less of a companion and more of a specter. He was never far, always watching, but she never knew precisely where he was. She could feel his reproach, like her very existence was an act of betrayal to him, but he was unwilling to abandon her.

"I'm not a deckhand anymore," she said. "I cannot believe I ever was. It just seems so... unreasonable."

Why didn't Was-Lil stop? Wink asked. *Why didn't Was-Lil stay here?*

She looked irritably in his direction, then back at the window. Her eyes focused on the reflection.

"I don't know... Part of it is this half-cooked mind of mine feeling like being on the run, or at least on the move, is proper. Like staying still is *wrong* somehow. I slept in a proper bed last night. The way everyone *should*, but I barely got any rest because my mind kept telling me I should be *swinging*. And then there's the other part..."

She reached out and ran her fingers down the window, as if to trace the shape of the face staring back at her. There had been other fug folk. Some echo of the woman she once was must have still held some sway, because she felt a flash of concern and distrust each time she saw one. But even during those brief glimpses they caught of her, she could feel that they didn't like her any more than Lil had liked them. She'd thought it was the torn-up deckhand's garb that had drawn their distasteful gazes, but even in the dress they looked at her with the same sort of vague disdain one would reserve for a mangy stray. Perhaps that was just how they were. She'd not felt an ounce of warmth from another fug person so far. But perhaps they felt the same way she did looking at her reflection.

"I just don't look like I belong. That's someone else's face. It doesn't match this place. But this place is the only place I can *be*." Blanche clenched her teeth. "Well I'm not leaving," she seethed. "I don't care how they look at me from across the street. They can just get used to this face. A person needs a place, and I'm carving this one out for myself. I'm not. Moving. From. This. *Spot!*"

"There she is!" came an angry shout from the next intersection.

She turned to see a pair of grunts, one of whom was still sporting bandages from his run-in with Wink.

"Dang it!" she snapped.

She turned on her heel and ran. The stiff skirt rustled against her, its hem constantly threatening to tangle in the boots that she'd yet to find a replacement for.

Anger welled up inside her. Fate couldn't see fit to give her a moment of righteous indignation without reality inflicting itself upon her. But what stirred the anger even more was the swell of almost giddy excitement she felt to be once again actively pursued. The same terrible, self-destructive instincts that had put her in Wash's clutches were again taking control. She may not have known how to find a place for herself here, but given the chance, she certainly knew how to make herself scarce. For the moment, she embraced it. The alternative was ending up locked away in a mine again, assuming Dr. Wash had *half* the compassion he'd seemed to have when he unmasked. She didn't waste any imagination on what the darker alternatives might be.

Between her new outfit fouling her gait and the far greater stride of the grunts on her tail, her lead was quickly dwindling. Her eyes darted toward the wall of a narrow alley up ahead. She could practically feel a shadow of her former self pulling her strings as she vaulted into the alley, planted a boot on the wall ahead, and sprang back to grab the ledge of the opposite wall. By the time the grunts had skidded into the alley in search of her, she'd shimmied up a drainpipe and pulled herself onto the roofs.

Like Lil, came an excited tap.

She turned to find Wink waiting for her on the roof across the alley. "Would you shut up!" she barked, neatly hopping the alley and continuing her flight.

Wink hopped to her back as she continued dashing from roof to roof. Increasingly hostile shouts echoed up behind her as the men chasing her reached the roof. Blanche could hear their hammering footsteps approaching as her hard-earned lead once again diminished. She could no longer afford to look back to see how close they were, because the rise and fall of rooftops and the questionable state of repair of the shingles made keeping her footing a difficult feat even while she was watching where she was going.

She hoped that whatever mindless reflexes were dictating her actions might perhaps have a destination in mind, but the only things she was feeling beneath her own panicked thoughts were manic glee and a desire to go farther and faster.

"Lil was wiped away, and she's still going to get me killed!" Blanche huffed.

The grunts continued to gain. It wouldn't be long before they overtook her. Ahead, the swirling fug revealed that their pursuit was at best the second most likely thing to put her flight to a sudden end. She was running out of rooftops. A narrow canal ran through Fugtown, a fact that Blanche was just now discovering. It was only a shade wider than one of the city streets, but that still made it considerably farther than she could hope to jump.

The hiss of a steam system and the glow of phlo-lights revealed that the strip of Fugtown near the canal was one of the stretches that was in active use. She hopped onto the long, shallow roof of what seemed to be some manner of trade house. It was in the act of unloading crates from a skiff on the canal. Her eyes locked on to the dangling line of the hoist in the courtyard. There was a brief tug-of-war in her mind. As tended to be the case, in a clash of madness and logic, madness won thanks to its disregard for the rules of the game. By the time Blanche had decided that aiming for the hoist's rope was more likely to break her neck than save it, she found she had already leaped from the roof. She caught hold of the rope and slid a few painful inches down it while swinging nearly horizontally.

The return swing revealed just how close the grunts had gotten. They were sliding to a stop on the edge of the roof. Even a moment's hesitation would have meant they'd have had her. A dash of satisfaction that felt uncannily like a "told you so" rippled through her. It lost its edge when she realized the cunning plan hadn't extended beyond the forward swing.

She slid down the rope a bit and released it on the return swing. Wink abandoned his perch on her back and continued onto the roof to dash between the grunt's legs. Blanche gracelessly crashed through a wood lattice window partition and rolled to a stop inside the trade house. An unsuspecting clerk softened her landing, and before she'd even come to terms with the fact that the acrobatic mishap hadn't killed her, she was already dashing out of the trade house and along the canal.

The flapping of the now-ragged skirt caused her to lose a step and nearly pitch into the water. She angrily grabbed a frayed edge and yanked at it, ripping away most of the ungainly garment. Her pursuers weren't willing to use the same tactic to dismount the roof and thus had yet to reach the ground. She felt her terrified expression gradually shifting to a gleeful, triumphant one. The cacophony of sounds all merged into one dull background din. Hissing boilers. Whirring turbines of airships overhead. The shouts of a dozen different voices. She half heard a chatter and the odd metallic clatter of claws on a flagpole somewhere behind her.

"I'm going to get away. I'm going to get away!" she crowed.

A burst of sound behind her briefly convinced her that the fug folk she'd left behind were cheering for her. A moment more gave her the comprehension to realize that the screams of anger had instead shifted to screams of fear and confusion. She wondered why. She didn't have to wonder for long.

A blur of gray fur filled her vision. She skidded to a stop and found herself face-to-face with some sort of chisel-toothed, wall-eyed monstrosity with a tool-strewn woman astride its back.

Blanche desperately reached back into her mind, hoping for fresh instructions from a seemingly savant-level escape prowess lurking within her. There was nothing. She was on her own. Instantly she found the flaws in her assumption that a sharper, more logical mind would do a better job at keeping her safe. There wasn't time for logic. All she could do was pick a new direction and wring as much speed as she could out of her burning limbs.

She barely got three strides away before the monstrous beast overtook her. Its rider snatched her by the back of the dress and hauled her up to flop down across the thing's neck. She struggled and tried to wrestle free of the grip that was holding her there until she felt the thing crouch and spring, then opened her eyes to discover she was soaring through the air and pivoting. The monster struck a wall, dashed up, and returned to the rooftops. It retraced her steps while she held desperately to the fluff beneath her. Then came a familiar chatter as something sank its claws into a grip on her back.

"I've got her, Wink. Let's get to the south end of town. The rest of the crew is meeting us there once they're through storming the mine."

"Y-you know these lunatics?" Blanche shrieked to the aye-aye on her back.

Nita yes, squarrel no. Friends. Family.

#

The scout ship, after being pushed so hard for so long, was whistling like a teakettle as its assorted connections struggled to contain the extra pressure. It ruled out stealth as an option. Gunner wasn't worried about that. He and Coop were the entirety of the crew at the moment. Stealth was never the plan.

"You reckon that's it? I reckon that's it. I'm gonna load up the cannon," Coop said, dashing for the hatch to the lower decks.

"Coop, we're not loading the cannon," Gunner said. "Stay on the deck. We're using rifles and deck guns if anything."

"What good's a deck gun going to do to a mine?" Coop said.

"About as much good as a cannon will. And besides, we have to be precise. Lil could be in there."

Coop stomped over to the deck gun and angrily wrenched it into position. "I'm gettin' pretty tired of you tellin' me we can't blow nothin' up. You used to be the fella who wanted to blow everything up, and as *soon* as I'm fer it, you're goin' on and on about how we can't be blowin' things up. Can I at least blow a couple holes in the first fellas I see?"

"We'll need information from them. Not only that, but the only thing that's kept us from being harassed by the Fugtown fleet is the fact that this is a fugger scout ship. If we fire cannons this close to Fugtown, we'll have six ships on us in a matter of minutes. Even the fléchette guns are a calculated risk at this range."

"You sure you're a gunner? You're soundin' an awful lot like one of them diplomat types. If it was your sister—"

"Coop, the whole crew has stretched itself to the limit to get her back. I would be doing you a disservice if I let you go off half-cocked."

"… I don't know what you heard, but I ain't—"

"Just keep the guns trained on the door and see if we can coax a surrender out of whoever is inside!" Gunner snapped. "If they're stubborn, once I've got the ship positioned, you can go down and pay them a visit."

"Now you're talkin' sense," he said.

Coop angled the fléchette gun and squinted across the iron sights. Sure enough, while the road heading up to the crew entrance of the mine wasn't nearly well enough trafficked to suggest something still in full operation, the door was in good repair and formidable enough to be more appropriate for something like a fortress than a mine. It was fairly good evidence they'd come to the right place. He dug out a small spyglass and looked over the doorway.

Contaminant Six

"Ain't no one down there, but there's a mess of cigarette butts. You reckon it'd be worth knockin' on the door?" Coop asked.

"Just don't be excessive," Gunner said.

"What sort of a fella do you take me for?" Coop said, angling the fléchette gun again.

He started delivering the carrot-sized iron spikes with a few intentional misses. Once anyone bracing the door had been given the chance to realize it was about to be a *very* poor decision to stand their ground, he shifted his aim and turned it into a pile of kindling.

"This ship got one of them loudspeaker deals?" Coop asked, once the fléchette gun had spun down.

"It does."

"Lemme try my diplomatic chops."

"I think I'd better handle the negotiation." Gunner fiddled with the controls. "I'll be brief."

Once he'd activated the loudspeaker, Gunner cleared his throat and leaned down to speak into it. There was no way to control the volume of the device, and every bit of noise was another chance to attract the attention of the not-so-distant Fugtown, so he tried to speak softly.

"Attention. We are here to recover a kidnapped member of our crew. Failing that, we're here to settle a debt with Dr. Wash. This is your one opportunity to do so in a civil manner. If you fail to do so, we'll be sending in a far less reasonable man to conduct the remainder of the negotiation."

He shut off the loudspeaker to silence the unpleasant compressed air sputter and pulled up his own spyglass to watch the door. A telltale gleam betrayed the intentions of the guard hidden in the darkness of the doorway. Gunner dropped to the ground just in time to avoid having a rifle shot tear through his shoulder.

"Coop, I think it's time to…"

He glanced to the deck gun formerly manned by Coop. Now Nikita was perched atop it and the rope ladder had been hurled over the side. Gunner shook his head.

"Tell me he didn't tell you to keep him covered," Gunner said, stalking over to the gun.

He did. How covered? Nikita tapped on the barrel, a desperate and confused look in her face.

"I'd be more concerned about his faith in your abilities if he wasn't right more often than not. That said, I'll take over."

#

Coop didn't bother taking much in the way of evasive action on the way to the shattered doorway. He was too angry and too set on delivering a

201

beating to trouble himself with petty things like self-preservation. The closest he came to discretion was picking a route that kept him out of line of sight from the doorway so they couldn't take a shot at him without stepping into the light to do it. Three short bursts of fléchettes kept the guards from getting too brave. Finally Coop reached the doorway and burst inside.

Beyond the entrance, the tunnel was pitch-black. He probably made a pretty attractive target for whoever was inside, just a silhouette against the light outside. That didn't matter much. The guards clearly didn't know him as well as they should, because they'd stuck far closer to the door than they should have. By the time they realized he'd arrived, he was practically on top of them. Two strides later, he was literally on top of them, as the lack of light meant the only reliable method to find one of them was to drop a shoulder and charge until he felt something fleshy.

Being unable to see his opponent only slightly altered Coop's chaotic combat technique. He guided his pinwheeling arms and flailing kicks by the volume of the meaty thumps and startled yelps they produced. When his knuckles struck the hot metal of a recently fired rifle, he latched on to it and wrenched it away until it clattered on the floor. At some point he heard the echoing boots of the guard who had been lucky enough not to be on the receiving end of his pugilistic tornado. He must have realized that the darkness wasn't an ally, because a phlo-light turned on and flooded the tunnel with green light. Coop took full advantage of the sudden discovery of where his closer foe's face was by delivering a savage elbow that sent the overwhelmed fugger slumping to the floor.

"It's *you*," barked the man by the light.

Coop looked up. "Yeah it's me. Who're you?"

"What's the matter?" the grunt asked. "Don't remember the face of the man you left dangling over the edge of a scaffold?"

"Seein' as how there's an awful lot of fellas I did that to, you're gonna have to narrow it for me," Coop said. "Except I'd rather you save your breath and just tell me where I can find my sister."

The grunt retreated a few steps to where the elevator let out and yanked at the cord. Somewhere far above in the shaft, there was a clanking sound.

"In a couple seconds, backup is going to come out of that elevator. And they're going to find you bloody and me laughing," he said.

"You got other fellas comin' in?" Coop said. "That's a relief. Means I ain't gotta go easy on ya. The next fellas can answer my questions."

"I'm twice your size. And you're not taking me by surprise this—" the grunt began.

He likely had a great deal more to say, but his taunt was cut short by Coop driving his shoulder full force into the man's abdomen. It was impressive just how much distance a man could cover while his opponent was foolishly anticipating a little verbal sparring as a preamble. The pair continued in an awkward stumble backward until the grunt struck the solid rock of the wall. He grasped at Coop. The deckhand planted one boot on the man's thigh, grabbed ahold of his shirt, and drove the top of his head into the bottom of the man's chin like some sort of inverted pile driver.

The attack left them both dizzied, but of the pair, Coop was far more accustomed to that state than the grunt. He blinked his eyes until the twin images of his foe became clear, then split the difference and aimed for the middle. Down the grunt went. Coop stood on his chest and crouched down to make sure the job was done.

A creaky grind drew his attention to the elevator door behind him. Another guard appeared. This one was the scrawny variety of fug man. He had a pistol in hand. The newcomer took a look at the blooded, mad-eyed Coop who was currently standing atop one of his fellow guards. A quick glance down the tunnel revealed a second moaning member of the security force. Coop hopped down and took a step toward him. The guard dropped his gun and raised his hands.

"He's at the top of the cable car in Keystone!" he yelped. "He saw the ship coming in and knew it belonged to one of the mercs he hired, and since it was alone and screeching he figured it was one of you. He took a bunch of that contaminant stuff with him and said he was going to pick up some alcohol or something and we were supposed to keep you busy and keep clear of the city!"

Coop blinked a bit and spat on the ground. "Who's this we're talkin' about?" he said.

"Dr. Wash! You're here for him, right? That's why you beat up these other guys, right? Because they wouldn't tell you about him?"

"... That depends. Where's my sister?"

"... The fug woman who came in here a little—"

Coop grabbed him by the shirt. "She ain't no fugger!"

"Fine, fine! It doesn't matter. She escaped days ago. We think she's still in Fugtown. Please! Don't beat me up. I'm just doing this for the money, and it's not worth a beating!"

Coop considered his words. "Well all right then. But do yourself a favor." He snatched the man's pistol and tucked it into his belt. "Get yourself a new job. Because your boss ain't makin' it to payday." He turned and stalked down the tunnel. "He ain't even makin' it to suppertime."

After hauling Blanche into a more dignified position astride Goose, Nita reached the edge of Fugtown in no time at all. But they'd yet to stop moving, something that clearly had Blanche a bit agitated.

"We're just riding in circles!" she shouted.

"Just a bit longer," Nita said. "Gunner and Coop are at a mine just past the edge of the city, looking for you or the man who kidnapped you. We've got to take the long way around to draw away some of the patrol ships. Chances are those two will attract their own attention. The least we can do is give them a little more breathing room."

Blanche looked over her shoulder to size up Nita, who was guiding Goose from behind her. "This madness seems old hat to you."

"I've picked up a thing or two while serving on the *Wind Breaker* crew. Lean forward. I think it's time to head for the meeting point."

Blanche leaned forward, as did Nita, pinning her down a bit to keep her in place while they picked up speed. They were sprinting through the city itself, dutifully keeping to unlit, abandoned streets. In what seemed like seconds, they burst from the south end of Fugtown while the three patrol ships they'd stirred up were still searching the northeast portion of the city.

They reached a small pond in the swampy fields to the south of the city. Nita whistled for Goose to stop, and he did so by digging his powerful claws into the moist earth so firmly that Nita, Blanche, and Wink were tumbled from his back. He honked wearily and plodded over to immerse his entire head in the pond to slake his thirst.

Nita got to her feet and helped Blanche up.

"Thank you," Blanche began. "That was a bit…"

"I'm so glad you're safe," Nita said, throwing her arms around her.

She held Blanche in the tight embrace as though she was afraid of what would happen if she ever let go. The hug ended slowly, and from the look in Nita's eyes when she pulled away, it had ended because Blanche had not hugged back.

Nita looked at her with a fearful, stricken look. "It's all gone, isn't it? You don't remember me at all."

"I'm sorry. I really don't," Blanche said.

"I should have realized. You weren't speaking like yourself."

Blanche nodded. "My first instinct is always to speak so sloppily. I have to constantly catch myself. I suppose she didn't care much for proper grammar."

"She?"

"Lil."

"Oh… You did have a distinctive turn of phrase now and again."

"I suppose you were very close to her."

"*We* are very close," Nita corrected.

"Nita, I am sorry, and I appreciate the rescue, but I'm not her anymore.

Lil is gone. He called me Blanche when I woke up, and as far as my memory goes, that's the only name I've ever had."

Much of Nita's face was hidden by her mask, but one only needed to see her eyes to see the pain such a simple statement could cause.

"Then... this is hello," Nita said. "Sweeping someone onto the back of a half-crazed squarrel isn't the first impression I would have chosen."

"Is this... *normal* for you?" Blanche asked.

"Normal has an entirely new meaning once you've joined the *Wind Breaker* crew. This isn't the first time I've ridden a squarrel. The last time, it was with you... with her. Lil had more of a knack for it than I do." Nita shut her eyes. "What was it like? What *is* it like? Having no memory at all of what came before?"

"It is... I was going to say that it is like waking up from a dream, but it isn't. It is like waking up *in* a dream. It feels like it has always been the way it is, but you know it can't possibly have been. You know things and feel things that you must have learned somewhere, but it's nothing. Gone. There's so much doubt and confusion. You learn pretty quickly you can't trust anyone."

Blanche tipped her head. "Come to think of it... even though I absolutely should not, given what's just happened, I *do* trust you."

Nita nodded. "That's not nothing. But listen. This, all of this, the mess we got into that led to you being kidnapped by Dr. Wash? It was all for something we were doing for Lil. When the fug got the better of her and when she started to lose herself, there was hope that perhaps she could be restored."

She reached into one of the pouches on her sash and retrieved a small corked beaker. The contents were clear and syrupy. "This is the treatment," Nita said. "This is what we all risked our lives for."

Blanche took the vial. "What does it do?"

"The plan was for it to stop Lil from losing everything, to reverse the change. Now, I suppose, the hope is that it will bring her back. We really have no way of knowing if it will work. And it isn't without risk. For most of the people in the fug, that vial would be a near certain death. Dr. Prist, the woman who created it, is confident it is much safer for someone so recently changed, but you would be the first person to try it. It would start working immediately. Right now you can't breathe fresh air. Prist says that if that stuff works, within minutes you'd be breathing as clear as you used to."

"But there's a chance I could die?"

"There is a chance."

"Then I won't take it," Blanche said. "It is just common sense. There is nothing *wrong* with me. Why would I take even the smallest risk to restore something that *I* don't even feel I've lost?"

"I could argue that the woman you were was willing to risk it all just for the *chance* that such a treatment might exist, but I suppose that would ring hollow." Nita tightened her fist. "Everything in me wants to beg you to take it, but to ask you to risk your life for something you don't believe in... it's just selfishness."

"I'm sorry. I—" Blanche began.

"Don't apologize." Nita blinked tears from her eyes. "Regardless of what happens in the future, right now there is no doubt that we need to keep you away from Dr. Wash. We'll get you to safety and deal with him."

The whistling wail of the overworked scout ship approached.

"That's the rest of the crew," Nita said. "Gunner and Coop. Coop is the tall one. He's your brother. He... he's going to have a harder time coming to terms with... I'm sorry, what is your name?"

"Blanche."

"He'll struggle with the concept that you're Blanche and not Lil. Be patient with him."

Blanche absentmindedly stowed the vial she'd been given in her purse as she watched the abused ship draw closer. She squinted at the deck. A man with features not so different from those she saw in her reflection whooped and hollered. He heaved a mooring rope down and dove over the railing. A long, artful swing brought him to the trunk of a withered tree. He secured the ship to it in a matter of seconds, as though he were performing a show-stopping stunt in some sort of circus.

"What'd I say?" he shouted, springing with long, gangling legs over the marshy ground. "What'd I say? You can't keep a Cooper down. Not even the *fug* can keep a Cooper down."

"Mr. Coop, I'm not—" Blanche began.

He practically tackled her, hoisting her up and spinning her around in a bear hug.

"Ain't nothin' strong enough to keep a Cooper down. Not when we've got a crew like this."

"I'm not who you think I am," Blanche objected.

He set her down and eyed her up. "You foolin'? You think I don't know my own sister? You're lookin' a little pale, but that's just the fug left in you. You take the stuff yet? That'll fix you right up."

"Coop, she's completely lost her memory," Nita said.

"That ain't no problem. Shouldn't take long to coach you back up on the important bits, Lil. I'm Coop. Ichabod Cooper, if you're bein' fancy. You're Chastity Cooper, folks call you Lil on account of you're just a little version of me, far as anyone can figure. Your favorite food's biscuits and gravy. You been sweet on Nita here pert near since you met her, but it took us all a fair bit to

206

work that out. You're a pretty good shot with a rifle and climb as good as Wink there. Your birthday's—"

"Coop, you don't understand. She doesn't know you. She doesn't know any of this."

"That's what I'm tryin' to fix. Now you keep interruptin' and it'll just take longer," Coop said. "And we ain't got much time for it. Seems like Dr. Wash's onto us and plannin' somethin'. We gotta get movin'. Come on, Lil. I'll let you know which uncles we ain't talkin' to no more, either on account of they died or they just ain't worth the time."

"If you are going to butt heads with Dr. Wash, I don't want any part of it," Blanche said.

Coop narrowed his eyes. "Did he hurt ya? How bad? You want me to get ahold of him so you can be the one who gives him what he's got comin'?" he said darkly.

"He had me locked up! Under guard! I don't know what plans he had for me, but I'm certainly not going to risk getting captured again to find out."

He cocked his head. "That ain't like you, Lil."

"I'm not Lil!" she snapped. "I wish I was! I wish I could remember all the things you seem to adore about me. I wish I could be the person who you all were willing to throw yourselves into chaos to help. But it's all gone. I'm empty, okay? It took her a lifetime to fill herself up, and I've only had a few days. And I'm not going to give up the chance to be whoever I am now just to get revenge on someone."

Coop stared at her silently, his face impassive. It was clear his mind was chewing on something that it couldn't quite swallow. His lip twitched. His shoulders tightened.

"Tell you what. We'll give Dr. Wash what fer, then come back and get you sorted out," Coop said. "I don't know how to fix what needs fixin' with you, but I can sure fix the fella who burned the last bit of time we needed to keep it from goin' wrong."

"What's happening with Wash?" Nita asked, equally eager to have a problem, even a dangerous one, for which the next steps were clear.

"A fella in his place said he saw us comin' and headed out to meet somebody up in Keystone to get his hands on some alcohol. Said he brought some of that goop with him."

Nita's eyes widened. "Contaminant and alcohol is a terribly dangerous combination, and he *must* know that," she said.

"For the life of me, I can't work out what he'd be doin' with it, is the thing," Coop said. "Gunner says it's a big deal that he told his boys to stay out of Fugtown."

"That does not bode well..." Nita turned to Blanche. "We've got to stop him. I understand that you don't want to join us. Things *will* get messy. But we're the only friends you've got right now. Find someplace safe. We'll be back to help you when this is through. Wink, stay with her."

Nita tugged open one of the pouches on her sash and pulled free two macaroons. "With Dr. Prist's compliments," she said.

Wink snatched them and eagerly devoured them. Nita turned to Coop.

"The two of you, head up to Keystone and see if anything is happening. I'll check the bottom of the funicular. If he has plans for the top, he may have plans for the bottom. If he has figured anything out about antifug, he'll know how dangerous it is. If we see the contaminant and alcohol in the same place, we've got to assume the danger is exactly what he's hoping to exploit."

She looked back to Blanche. "I'll see you after." She took a shaky breath. "I look forward to getting to know you, and helping you get to know yourself, whoever that might turn out to be."

Coop slapped Blanche on the back. "I'll bring you Dr. Wash's mask as a souvenir."

The deckhand hurried to the mooring rope. He untied it and hauled himself up along it until he was back on deck with Gunner. Nita hopped onto Goose's back and, with a bit of coaxing, bounded across the marsh toward the city.

Blanche stared after her, feeling strangely like she'd just been at the center of a storm that was now booming its way back toward the horizon. Wink climbed to her shoulder and matched her gaze.

Nita, he tapped. *Family.*

"I know I haven't had much of a life so far, but I have never wanted anything more than to be riding that beast with that woman." She gazed down into the pond Goose had been drinking from. "Was there something wrong with Lil for wanting to live a life like that? Or is there something wrong with me for wanting to play it safe…"

Chapter 16

Nita surged her way through the city. She wasn't familiar with Fugtown from ground level. Most humans weren't. She'd gotten some good looks at it from above, and she'd spent some rather notable time in the warehouse district, but that knowledge was doing her little good when it came to keeping Goose heading in something resembling the right direction.

"We're staying *down*. We're staying on the *streets*!" Nita scolded as Goose, for the twentieth time, leaped to a wall rather than navigate those pesky corners.

A compromise was found in that Goose was willing to run along the walls, bounding back and forth between them. Nita held tight and ducked low to keep from being bucked off. They were heading for the funicular, which as one might expect was in the busiest, densest part of the city. She wouldn't be able to avoid causing a stir for much longer, but the fact that she just minutes earlier had drawn the more worrisome of the patrols to a different part of the city would buy her a few minutes. With any luck that was all she'd need.

Goose dropped to the ground and galloped across the courtyard surrounding the funicular. The place was, by Fugtown standards, absolutely packed. Granted, this meant that there were merely a few dozen people milling about, whereas there would be a few hundred in a larger surface city or a few thousand in the biggest cities of Caldera. Goose didn't bother hopping over or dodging around the people in his way. A lowered head and a hoarse honk sent him plowing through the crowd lined up at the funicular's boarding platform. She wrestled him to a stop a few strides before he would have smashed into the two technicians scratching their heads at the empty platform. Each of them was the tall, scrawny academic sort of fug person. Prior to Nita's arrival, their biggest problem was the growing impatience of the crowd. It had driven them to such distraction that they didn't even notice Nita's chaotic arrival.

"What's happened here?" Nita asked, hopping from Goose.

The older of the two technicians spoke with weary impatience, not bothering to look at who had asked.

"Look, I've said it a hundred times already, the previous tech crew left the platform a mess and we need to..." He finally turned. "What in the world!"

"I am an engineer. What is the problem?" Nita said.

"You're a surface person and you're riding a beast an—"

"And I'll let it free to run amok in this city if you don't tell me what's happened here!" Nita snapped.

The younger technician hissed a warning to his partner. "She's that crazy Calderan from the *Wind Breaker* crew. Just do what she says. Who knows what they've got planned?"

He nervously turned to her. "A merchant came along and bought out every available slot for an emergency cargo delivery. Terrible waste. There wasn't nearly enough cargo to fill it. He brought a crew of technicians to do some maintenance to 'ensure the safety of the cargo.' They had the right uniforms and credentials, but I'm starting to wonder if they were genuine. When the car left, we found spare parts tossed off to the side. We've got the car held at the top while we work it out."

"Was the merchant dressed in black with what looked like a bird mask on?"

"It wasn't a bird mask, it was a first-generation filter mask. But yes," said the older man.

"Where are the parts?" Nita demanded.

"Look, we can't just let—"

"Let me see the parts now!" she barked, pulling one of the larger wrenches from her belt to slap against her palm.

Goose, obviously unwilling to let loud noises happen without making his own contribution, produced a loud, excited honk as punctuation.

"These are the people who took down Skykeep. Just do what they want until the patrols get here," the younger fugger urged. "The parts are right there. All of them. See for yourself."

Nita hurried over to a carefully laid out assortment of nuts, bolts, and mechanisms. There wasn't much there, but what *was* there told a very clear story. A scissor-like mechanism with a spring and two round weights was the most immediately worrisome item.

"That's a speed governor," she said. "And those look like brake calipers. They've disabled the emergency brake, haven't they?"

"Why does she know how our funicular works..." muttered the older man.

"*Because I'm a free-wrench!*" she snapped.

Goose honked excitedly and focused one eye on each of the two men.

"Are there any other safety measures?" she asked.

The young man pointed. "The funicular is still controlled by the technicians in the machine tower. And they absolutely will not let an unsafe

210

funicular move."

The platform rattled, steam hissed, and the cables started to move.

"No. No, no, no. I haven't received the all clear. They should *not* be moving," the older man said.

Nita hopped onto Goose and whistled a command.

He charged through the two technicians and streaked across the courtyard to the base of the machine tower. A few scrabbling leaps later, he crested the top of the tower and perched himself on the thin roof. Nita dismounted and jumped to the catwalk. It took far less time to work out what had happened here than with the pile of spare parts. Two technicians in similar garb to those below were hogtied in the machine room, which was secured with a chain from the outside. A quick twist and bash with her wrench busted the lock and she burst in.

"What happened?" she asked, untying them. "Who did this?"

"Two grunts. They sabotaged the controls," said one of the fuggers.

Nita turned. The complex control panel looked like it had been worked over with a mallet. The funicular seemed to have been locked into its maximum speed. An indicator displayed its increasing velocity. There wasn't enough of the mechanics of the control panel intact to make any changes.

"Is there a backup control room?" she asked.

"No."

"Are there controls at the *top* of the funicular?"

"Why would we let *surface folk* control *our* funicular?"

Nita pointed at the control panel. "For this exact reason!" She looked out the window of the control room and followed the steam pipes to the main equipment shed. "I am going to bring that car to a halt. If Dr. Wash wants it moving, I want it stopped."

"Who gave you the right to make that call? You're a surface person!"

"Things are moving too fast to ask permission, and you wouldn't give it to the likes of me anyway. You'll thank me when this is over." She took a few strides toward the door. "Who am I kidding? No you won't."

#

"You reckon she'll be okay down there?" Coop said, pacing on the deck of the ship as Gunner guided it.

"She made it for several days without us. She'll be fine," Gunner said.

"But her head ain't right. You heard her. She don't even know she's a Cooper."

"She's safe, Coop. Keep your mind on the mission."

"She was supposed to *be* the mission."

"And we found her. Now there's a new mission. We have to stop Dr.

Wash."

"We're gonna kill him too, ain't we? I ain't usually the bloody-minded type, but he needs killin'.'"

"You pulled the trigger on Tusk."

"He needed killin' too. Just 'cause I'm the fella with the gun when someone earns a bullet don't make me a killer."

"I'd love to debate the nuances of justice and impulse, but it's hard enough flying in this soup when we're just trying to moor up. Now we're trying to get to the top of something that the whole of Fugtown has a vested interest in defending. Keep your eyes open for the funicular wires. They're probably going to sneak up on us."

"If you ain't keen on smashin' into the cables, how come you're flyin' so close to them?" Coop asked, dashing to the railing to focus on the dense purple mist.

"Because, as I've said, Fugtown has a vested interest in defending them. If we stick close, at least they can't fire on us."

"Tower comin' up!" Coop shouted.

The steel structure of a support tower for the cables loomed out of the mist. Gunner spun the wheel and narrowly avoided peeling the envelope open on the struts.

"You sure this'll be safer than gettin' shot at? We been shot at before," Coop said.

"Listen close and you tell me."

Coop cupped an ear. What at first seemed to be the distant drone of the air traffic of the bustling airship port below slowly resolved into at least six separate sets of turbines that were steadily working their way closer. Soon the glow of ship-mounted phlo-lights started to approach from all sides. "I reckon stayin' close is the right idea," he said.

"I thought you'd feel that way."

The ships drew close enough to be visible as ghostly forms in the fug. This close to the surface, visibility was practically nil. One by one, voices started blaring out of each ship, making various demands that Gunner and Coop had no intention of heeding.

Gunner kept as close to the cables as possible without scraping the belly of the ship. They were far enough from the ground that there was no longer any concern for towers. They wouldn't show up again until they reached the cliff side. It seemed like it would be clear sailing until then. That apparent bit of mercy put both Gunner and Coop on edge. At times like this, if things felt like they were going smoothly, it usually meant they were heading into a trap. It thus came almost as a relief when a strange, reverberating sound split the air.

"What the heck is that, now?" Coop shouted.

"It's coming from the wires," Gunner said.

Coop leaned over the side and squinted down. "Tough to tell... Looks like that one little skinny loop there is hoppin' around like it stubbed its toe. What do you reckon that means?"

"I'd say it means someone's bringing that cable car to a stop."

"Who you reckon's doin' it?"

"Anyone with good sense would stop the cable car with this sort of madness going on. And with me on this ship, the only one with good sense left is Nita."

"How you reckon she pulled that off?"

"Something elegant and ingenious, no doubt."

#

Nita gritted her teeth and squinted through her goggles as the main drive gear of the cable car's winch sprayed sparks. A few quick turns of the vent valves had set the boiler to spraying its pressure, but the chamber was massive. Even with the dump valves open, the mechanism had plenty of oomph left to keep the car moving steadily. There was also the fact that if the cable car had gotten far enough along the wires, it would be on the slope and subject to gravity. If she wanted it stationary, she'd have to jam the mechanism. There were any number of ways to do it safely, but there was one surefire way to do it quickly.

"Almost... almost," she growled.

She held tight to the rattling end of the sturdy maintenance hatch that she'd popped free of its hinges and crammed between the gears. The potent mechanism had made a meal of most of it, but once it was pulled far enough into the works, it started binding in at least three places. For once she was grateful for the mask, as it reduced the metal-searing stench of sizzling grease and overheated iron to something merely unpleasant.

When the machine finally completely seized, she took a deep breath and climbed out of the compartment. Goose was there waiting for her, evidently completely unconcerned by the unholy screech of a powerful machine sputtering its last. His wayward eyes were darting back and forth between the two technicians who had followed Nita to the equipment shed but found themselves without the fortitude to both push past Goose and leap into the works of the winch while it was in operation. Now they had looks of utter distress on their faces.

"You've... you've *ruined it!*" said the older man.

"Nothing a new drive gear won't fix. Three days, tops," Nita said.

"But... you... I..." the younger tech babbled. "Where is security? Why didn't anyone stop you?"

"My guess, either Wash's men killed them, or they're still halfway across town trying to track down the lunatic riding the squarrel down by the canal." She gazed up. "Or they're distracted by that."

They turned and, now that the screech of the winch had died down, heard the cluster of ships jockeying for position over the city.

"What now?" the young man said.

"That'll be the rest of my crew. Gunner and Coop are the only ones I know who could hold the attention of that many patrol ships."

Nita climbed onto Goose's back. "Anything special I need to know about reinstalling the emergency brake on that cart?"

"How are you going to get there?" the young tech asked.

"That's my problem. Now is it a standard brake system or what?"

"The cart is *stopped*. The winch is *seized*. What does it matter? The cart isn't going anywhere."

"Why would they disable the brake if they didn't intend to cut the drive cable?" Nita asked. "Standard brake or not?"

"The emergency brakes are spring-applied wheel clamps with a backup cable clamp," the older tech said. "You'll need a spreader to get them reapplied. There's one in the kit there."

"Many thanks," Nita said, kicking open the tool kit beside the maintenance hatch.

"What are you *doing?*" asked the younger man.

"She's already ruined the drive system. If she's right, at least she can keep the car from breaking loose." The older fug person leaned closer, likely thinking he couldn't be heard. "And it'll get her and that crazy monster away from us."

Nita lashed the spreader to one of her sashes. "If you need a hand repairing this when it is all over, I happen to have a fair bit of experience," she assured them.

She climbed to Goose's back and gave a quick whistle. Goose charged forward and scampered to the platform, now deserted. Apparently the apocalyptic sound of failing machinery combined with the unexplained gathering of patrol ships overhead had persuaded the people of Fugtown to seek shelter. In that way, they were a good deal smarter than most of the innocent bystanders Nita had dealt with since joining the crew.

Nita gathered up as many of the parts of the brake system as she was comfortable Goose could carry. They were heavy bits of iron, and though Goose could probably tote the lot of them, there was still the issue of keeping them on his back. When she had the bare minimum lashed in place with the last of her rope, she looked up to the wires overhead that suspended the car. Images flashed in her head of the many, many times Goose had proved unable or unwilling to follow her directions. She forced them from her mind.

"If you're ever going to learn to stay focused, Goose, learn now. Let's go. Onto the wires."

She whistled a few commands through her mask. Goose tipped his head, turned to look her over with one wild eye, then launched toward the tower supporting the wires. He didn't lose a step as he moved from the sturdy supports to the narrow wire. Cunning claws gripped it tight. A swishing tail swept about to keep him upright, and he scampered onward and upward.

#

Dr. Wash drummed his fingers and waited. He was at the edge of the precarious overhanging platform where the Keystone locals boarded the funicular to Fugtown. On a normal day, the crowd at the top would be a match for the crowd at the bottom. A funicular was *mostly* a swift way to send shipments of assorted goods up and down. It wasn't unusual for a fug person to ride up with some crates, accept payment, and ride back down. Likewise for those delivering food, fish, and other supplies the surface folk were better equipped to send down. But the commotion in the fug below had attracted a press of people anxious to see what was happening. They were all gazing down into the stirring purple stew below. He was gazing up at the massive pulley of the drive wire.

"It stopped movin'," he muttered to the "supervisor" beside him.

The funicular, like all products of the fug, was under complete control of the fug folk. That meant that the handful of people in Keystone who were "in charge" had little to do beyond wear a uniform, open and close doors, and do whatever the tinny voice on the other side of a speaking tube told them. Dr. Wash gazed through the dark lenses of his mask at the bearded man, who was looking awfully small and lost as he glanced anxiously between the speaking tube and the churning fug.

"I said the car ain't movin'," Wash said more loudly.

"They're not saying anything," the supervisor said. "This has never happened before. As far as I know, it shouldn't have *started* moving. But it sure shouldn't have stopped before the bottom."

"You should make an announcement so these dopes don't start gettin' antsy," Wash said.

"They haven't told me what to announce!" the supervisor hissed.

Dr. Wash looked to the crowd. "Then you should start gettin' people off the overhang before it gives out, don't you think?"

The supervisor looked at the crowd. His relief at realizing that crowd control was within his authority and did not require authorization from the fug was palpable. He threw open the half-door separating him from Wash and the others and stepped out.

"All right, all right. Everyone back away. Everything will be back to normal in due course, but I can't have you all overloading the platform. Back, back, back..."

As he shouted, Wash caught the door with a gloved hand and slipped inside.

"Moron," he muttered.

He locked the door and shut the top half, giving him privacy and complete access to what little actual equipment was available on the Keystone side of the funicular. In addition to the speaking tube, which was mostly just echoing with the turbine sounds of ships that were far too close to it, there was a loudspeaker for addressing the public regarding schedules and delays.

Wash was no fool. He knew a hardware failure when he saw one. And though he wasn't sure if they'd figured out his precise plan, he knew that if he were in their place, he'd be doing everything in his power to stop whatever seemed to be going on. Thus, the halting of the funicular was almost certainly the doing of the *Wind Breaker* crew. Fortunately, because he wasn't an idiot, he'd planned for just such an occasion. He activated the loudspeaker.

"Attention, people of Keystone," he announced. "I'm the businessman who loaded up the car that's stuck out there right now. I was hopin' the *Wind Breaker* crew wouldn't figure it out, but I got some *very* dangerous chemicals in them crates. I was hopin' to use 'em to make medicine, but if they get their hands on 'em, they could just poison pretty much anybody with 'em. I don't know *why* they'd want to start slingin' poison. Maybe they just want to get even once and for all on Fugtown. Point is, if they get their hands on that stuff, it's curtains for Fugtown, and that means it's curtains for Keystone. Ain't gonna be no more trade. No more bein' buddy-buddy with the fug, and a *lot* of dead fuggers. So if you got a ship and you got a gun, get out there and take down them *Wind Breaker* guys. Either that or bust up the cart before they can get their hands on it."

The supervisor managed to tear the door open and pull him out just as he was finishing the message.

"What are you *doing*?" he said. "You can't just say a thing like that! Is it even true?"

Wash laughed. "It don't matter if it's true or not. I said it, and people who want to believe it will believe it. Now outta my way, I got some messages that need sendin'."

The supervisor began to object, but before he could get a word in, the now quite agitated crowd had turned to him for answers. That uniform meant he was the one responsible for announcements, so he naturally had to answer for what had just been said. Dr. Wash used the confusion to slip away. He found an out-of-the-way place tucked against the base of the primary support tower for the funicular's pulley system and discreetly fetched a folded bit of paper from his pocket.

With slow, deliberate taps, he rapped out a message in the inspector's language, reading from the page to ensure he did so correctly.

Open fire, boys.

#

"These fellas ain't makin' this easy on you, are they?" Coop said.

The cluster of patrol ships were getting bolder, attempting to force Gunner and Coop's ship away from the wires. It had slowed the progress terribly, and further underscored just how necessary the relative shelter of the wires was. There were six ships on them, with another two approaching.

"I ain't so sure we're gonna be able to find a place to set down and dig up Wash with all these folks on us," Coop said.

"We'll figure it out," Gunner said.

"Hang on. Nikita's actin' up. What is it, darlin'?"

The inspector tucked in Coop's coat madly tapped out a message. *They will shot. They will shot now,* she tapped in a grammar-destroying panic.

"How do you know that?" Coop asked.

"What did she say?" Gunner said.

A distant, familiar buzz of fléchette fire came from one of the latecomers of the cluster of hostile ships.

"She said that was gonna happen. I guess someone up there is callin' the shots."

They weren't quite near enough to fire with any accuracy, but they didn't need to. Once one ship started firing, the others did as well. With them uncertain of where the shots were coming from and already anxious about the proximity to their precious transit system, it didn't take much to set all weapons blazing.

"I'm shootin' back," Coop said.

"No you aren't! We're outgunned eight to one," Gunner said, spinning the wheel and preparing a retreat.

"So? Just means I ain't gotta be too accurate. Just sprayin' over that way'll be enough to hit *somebody.*"

"We're getting to a safe distance and picking a different approach."

Coop raised his head and squinted. "No we ain't."

"I'm the skipper of this ship, Coop. We do as I say."

"What'll we do about *that* then, Skipper?" He pointed to a half-seen figure darting along the cables.

"Tell me that isn't Nita," Gunner said.

"I'd be lyin' if I did."

He growled and spun the wheel again, angling back toward the fray as

217

spikes started to glance off the envelope and graze the hull.

"We'll keep to midrange. Harry them as much as you can. Our goal is to stay aloft and keep them focused on us. We can take a hell of a lot more shots than she can."

#

The trip along the cables had been surprisingly smooth so far. While Goose was easily distracted, having literally nothing else to jump to did an excellent job of keeping him on track. As they climbed high enough for the fug to thicken, there was nothing but the buzz of turbines, the wail of wind, and the lengths of cable stretching ahead and behind. Every gust of wind caused an extra swish and scramble to keep the beast on the cable, and she was becoming increasingly aware of the sway and slack, but as death-defying feats went, this was one of the least harrowing she'd had to endure.

Until the ships started to fire…

As impassive as Goose had been in the face of danger, something about the buzz of the guns and the hiss of spikes through the air finally broke past his dull view of the world and caused panic and fear to flare.

"No, no! Just a bit farther! We can't be far now!" Nita shouted.

Goose alternated between dashing unreasonably fast along the cable to screeching to a stop and huddling down as though he could hide from the crossfire. Nita whistled and shouted commands, but muffled by the mask as her commands were, the closer they got to the cluster of ships, the less often Goose even noticed he was being instructed. Finally, any semblance of following commands was abandoned and Goose charged forward, eyes shut and ears flat.

The wire shook and shuddered with the sort of motion that even a hefty squarrel like Goose couldn't cause. It must have been the car. The dark form of the passenger compartment loomed ahead. Nita whistled and shouted, trying to get Goose to slow down, but the beast continued his charge.

"This is a terrible idea," she muttered to herself as she shifted in the saddle.

They reached the car. Nita lunged aside to grab hold of the mechanism. Goose continued forward. She was dragged free of the saddle and hung precariously to the support mechanism of the car. Goose dashed onward until he became dully aware of the missing rider. He screeched to a stop, dashed back toward her, and simply continued on, bounding along the cable until he was out of sight.

"Goose! Goose!" she shouted. "I need you to get back here! And you've got most of the brake parts!"

He was already long gone, and certainly didn't understand what she'd said regardless.

Contaminant Six

"Okay... Okay... One problem at a time. Can I get inside the cart?"

She hauled at the roof hatch, but it didn't even rattle. It was either seized or braced from the inside, and the bolts were rounded off. She risked a look over the side to discover chains had been applied to the main door, and there wasn't anything to hold on to for her to try breaking them.

Nita turned her attention to the braking system. "Dr. Wash, you certainly know how to sabotage something."

The mechanism wasn't just disassembled, as she'd hoped. The mounting points had been beaten out of shape. None of the bolts still had their threads fully intact. Even if she had all of the parts and a full tool kit, it would take hours of work to get this thing back into safe condition. She leaned over the side again and gazed in through the windows. As she had feared, a cask of Contaminant Six and several sizable drums of alcohol were all packed into a cart that was set to be smashed into the heart of Fugtown. The collision would spray the chemicals everywhere. Thousands would die. Fugtown would be crippled.

A stray spike sparked off the side of the cart, snapping Nita back to reality. She called upon her engineering knowledge and took stock of what she had tucked into her tool sashes and what was left of the mechanisms. The hasty calculations were not encouraging. She wiped her forehead and selected a wrench.

"I've done more with less..."

#

Dr. Wash pushed open the door to a large cafe beside the funicular station. It was normally packed, but between the stalled funicular and the spectacle outside, he had it to himself save two members of the staff, who were anxiously looking out the windows.

"Relax," Wash said, tightening his mask a bit. "If things get outta hand, it'll be the people down there who'll get the worst of it. At first, anyway."

His words fell on deaf ears as the two waiters remained glued to the window, mouths agape. Wash propped up his feet and leaned back. He couldn't blame the waiters for refusing to tear themselves away. The cafe provided a fantastic vantage point. It was difficult to tell precisely what was happening, but every so often one or more of the ships would bob above the fug, or the wind would scoop out enough for the combat to be visible. Those brief glimpses were enough to establish what he'd hoped to see. The battle was still raging, and the vast majority of the fléchette fire was heading in one direction. The *Wind Breaker* crew, with their stolen ship, had not received any unexpected reinforcements.

Victory was virtually assured. If the battle raged on much longer, the funicular cab would be destroyed and the poison would rain over the city.

Failing that, the drive cable would be severed and it would crash into the city. Even if neither case occurred, two more members of the *Wind Breaker* crew would be killed. No matter what, the cart would be stuck in place for *more* than long enough for him to work out a way to send it crashing down and get the job done. He had won. No one would be coming. He simply had to sit and wait for sweet chaos to take its due. A permanent shift in the balance of power. Vast rifts separating people from the supply lines they relied upon. And who was the only one ready to fill the gap?

Dr. Wash.

He was so pleasantly lost in his own thoughts, he'd not noticed that one of the waiters had pulled himself from the fug-facing windows to gaze out toward the seaside portion of town. After a few seconds, he shouted for his partner. Their excited murmuring filtered through Dr. Wash's haze of victory when three very important words bubbled to the top of the conversation.

"The *Wind Breaker*."

"What's that?" Dr. Wash said, his head snapping around to glare at the staff.

"That looks like the *Wind Breaker* out there!" the waiter repeated.

"That's crazy," Wash grumbled, hopping from his seat to stalk toward them. "It's probably just another coast runner or smuggler. You'd be *sure* if it was the *Wind Breaker*. That Calderan worked to make it pretty damn distinctive what with the red…"

He trailed off as he reached the window.

For a moment he was still, his expression hidden by his mask. When he spoke, it was with a raw, chilling rage.

"Can *no* one do the job I pay them to do?!"

#

A ship cut sleekly through the air. Five gleaming turbines hummed in all their perfectly balanced glory. They were the only aspect of the ship that seemed to be as it should be. The magnificent red envelope had a slack and shriveled belly, internal supports showing through like the ribs of a starving dog. The once-magnificent gondola was a skeleton. Wind whistled through to the exposed decks within. A single cannon emerged from the starboard side. There were no deck guns. Few enclosed spaces. It was the absolute bare minimum necessary to keep a ship in the air. Turbines, an envelope, scraps of gondola, and, of course, a crew.

Cap'n Mack narrowed his eyes and tightened his clenched teeth around his cigar. He leaned low to shout into the speaking tube over the wind whipping by him.

"We got a big ruckus up ahead. I reckon we'll find our folks at the middle of it." He stubbed out his cigar and clicked it into its tin. "Mask on.

We're goin' into the fug for this one."

Butch replied in the affirmative, though a bit colorfully even for her.

"Just make sure you're loaded up, and treat them bits and pieces with kid gloves. I can't afford to lose you *or* the bits of this ship that'd get taken out if they went wrong."

He stood straight and danced his hands across the controls. For all the obvious issues of flying a ship that by rights ought to still be in dry dock, there were a handful of benefits. The *Wind Breaker* may have been missing most of its hull, most of its crew, and most of its equipment and gear, but it still had its full boiler and turbines. That meant the ship was faster and nimbler than anything else in the air. The ship roared across the sky like it was shot from a cannon, traversing the sprawling mountaintop city of Keystone in seconds. He barely had time to get his mask properly tightened before the *Wind Breaker* sliced into the fug fast enough to leave a wake.

Even with most of the ships little more than dark forms in the thick fug, he quickly determined that the ship he'd sent the rest of his crew to the mainland in was not present. They'd requisitioned themselves another one. The only question was, which one?

By process of elimination, the answer quickly revealed itself. Half the ships took potshots at the *Wind Breaker* as soon as it arrived. Those clearly were not his people. Fléchettes whistled through the air toward the *Wind Breaker*. Most passed right through the mostly hollow gondola. Still more of them missed the shriveled, undersized envelope. The handful that did strike it revealed another unexpected benefit of flying a barely airworthy airship. Without a properly inflated envelope, the surface was not nearly as taut, even on the upper edge. The thick, reinforced canvas flexed and dimpled with the blows, but few spikes achieved much more than a pathetic bounce and tumble.

Mack wove the stripped-down *Wind Breaker* between the various other ships, one by one drawing their fire. The most heavily damaged of them fell back, taking advantage of the momentary lapse in attacks to put some distance between itself and the others. That, Mack knew, would be his crew.

He continued to draw the other attackers away, using every ounce of the maneuverability to keep the bulk of the attacks from hitting their marks. He backed off on the speed to ensure he didn't get far enough ahead to convince the attackers to switch to cannons. In the visibility of this stretch of the fug, they wouldn't have much chance of hitting their target, but with the ship in its current state, even a handful of grapeshots would be all it would take to nick it out of the air.

Within minutes, he'd dragged the entire fleet of attackers far out over Fugtown. That job done, he doubled back and poured on the speed, returning to the limping but still mostly serviceable scout ship with his crew aboard. He pulled near enough to signal Gunner, then aligned the two ships. Coop cast grapplers across and pulled the gondolas close.

"Captain, I can't say I was expecting you to save our behinds, but I'm glad you did," Gunner called.

"Ain't got time for pleasantries. I take it you made a deal with Wash that went wrong?" Mack said.

"To put it very lightly."

"How's Lil?"

"We have a treatment, but she's completely lost her memory."

"Long as she's alive, that's enough for me. What needs doin'?"

"Nita's down on the funicular, working on the top of it."

"Why?"

"Haven't had the moment to ask, Captain, though we're pretty certain it's loaded up with enough poison to kill everyone in Fugtown. We've got to give her time to finish and then get her."

"Clear enough. Stand by. Best this ship can manage is to run interference and get one shot off, but we managed to snag some of your toys before we left."

"You didn't…"

Butch climbed onto the incomplete main deck with a duffle bag. She carried it like she was afraid it would bite her and showed visible relief when she was able to heft it across to the scout ship's deck.

"Most of these ships are patrols doing their jobs. I'd hate to kill them for it. Not to mention that everything we take down here lands on Fugtown."

"They're your guns and that's your ship. You use 'em how you reckon you ought to. I'll just keep 'em guessin' until you do."

"Aye, Captain. Coop, take the helm."

"Aye, Skipper," Coop said.

Butch dislodged the grapplers as Gunner hopped down to pull open the duffle bag with an almost childlike level of glee.

#

Blanche sat on a relatively dry stone in the marshy outskirts of Fugtown. She'd barely moved from the spot where Nita had dropped her off. Her eyes were locked on the sky, where the drifting lights traced out the battle overhead. As she watched, she clutched at Wink like a security blanket, her fingers anxiously stroking him between the ears. The little creature's expression was one of weary resignation as he tolerated the nervous affection.

Terrible, confusing thoughts swirled in her head. She felt so worried for these people. They were lunatics, every last one of them. And from her point of view they were strangers. By rights, she shouldn't feel any more worry for their well-being than she did for the people clashing with them. Their allegiance wasn't even to *her*, it was to the woman she had once been. But that didn't change the soul-deep fear she felt for what would become of them. It didn't change the instincts and notions shrieking at her to somehow join the fray and defend them. With every passing moment she became more certain that what they'd said to her was true. They *were* her crew. They *were* her family. Dr. Wash may have been trying to manipulate her, but everything about the *Wind Breaker* crew seemed genuine. And they were out there, fighting a battle they didn't even quite understand, while she was sitting here watching.

She felt for a pocket in her torn dress, forgetting that it had none. Instead she dug into her stolen purse and pulled out the vial she'd been given. They hadn't even forced it on her. They hadn't even really *asked* her to take it.

"It's no good," she mumbled. "I couldn't help them if I wanted to. The battle is taking place up in ships. Up on cliffs. I can't get to them. If they got this far, if they did all they claimed to do, then they'll get through this too. Won't they?"

They will try, Wink tapped on her arm.

"They'll do it. They'll do it," she whispered to herself.

She rocked back and forth, clutching Wink and watching the sky until a crunching sound in the darkness derailed her one-track mind. She nervously snapped her gaze to the source of the sound. About midway between her and the proper edge of Fugtown was the massive, wild-eyed squirrel creature Nita had been riding. He was pawing at the wet soil and pleasantly munching on whatever it was he'd dug up. He seemed to be looking for something, perhaps confused as to why his rider wasn't here waiting for him where she'd last climbed onto his back.

Blanche stood. Wink seized the opportunity to escape her arms and crawl instead to her shoulder.

"That's... Goose, isn't it?" she said quietly. "That's Nita's creature."

Yes, Wink tapped.

"Then where's Nita?" Blanche demanded, as though she was owed the answer.

Wink didn't reply. He had no answer to give.

Blanche dashed toward the squarrel, moving without thought or consideration. It turned its vacant gaze toward her and continued munching as she got closer. She put her fingers to her lips and, before she knew what she was doing, whistled out a command. Goose plopped to his belly, eyes blinking one at time, and honked.

"Okay..." she said, looking uncertainly at her fingers. "I remember the *commands* for these things. I didn't remember my own name, but I remember the dang commands."

She stepped closer and investigated the beast. Perhaps it had been sent back for her? Perhaps it was as bright as Wink was? She looked the thing in the eye. It honked again, sniffed at the ground, and took a big mouthful of dirt.

Clearly it was not all that bright. Still, it could have a message on the saddle or something. She inched closer and peered over the thing. A few pieces of mechanical equipment had been hastily tied to the saddle. She couldn't make heads nor tails of them. But in her search, she found a fresh gash in the squarrel's haunches. Nothing serious, at least for a creature this large, but she shuddered to think what a wound like that would do to a human. And she couldn't stop herself from imagining that it had happened to Nita.

Based upon the impulses left over from Lil, and the choices her past self had made, the diamond clarity of Blanche's thoughts were a gift from her transition to fug person. From the moment she'd awakened until now, it had been wholly devoted to self-preservation. Now that same logic turned its attention to a new problem. Saving Nita, wherever she was. She couldn't get onto one of those ships, and she had no reason to believe Nita was aboard one. She knew that the funicular was the focus of their attention. Nita had been riding the squarrel, which could easily scale otherwise precarious inclines and such. She probably had worked her way up to the top of the funicular, where Wash was almost certainly pulling the strings on what was happening now. If she wanted this madness to end and her new-slash-old friends to be safe, she had to find him and get him to stop it. That meant reaching the top of the cliff as soon as possible. That meant riding Goose.

She hopped onto the saddle and was immediately struck with a sense of familiarity. She grabbed the reins and hooked her feet into the stirrups. She'd done this before. She'd *enjoyed it*. Blanche whistled a command, and Goose sprang to his feet and into a dead run, honking excitedly as he went. She held tight and yanked at the reins to keep him vaguely on target, heading for the base of the cliff that the funicular serviced. Her eyes widened. A lunatic smile graced her face. It wasn't that she wasn't afraid. It was terrifying. And she still felt every ounce of anxiety for what might be happening to the old friends she'd only just been introduced to. But at the same time it was thrilling. It was action, motion. She wasn't fretting, she was *doing* something. And that thing was right. It was what she was supposed to do. They reached the steep slope she'd only days ago crept down in her escape from Wash's mine. An instant later they were bounding up a sheer cliff. She dared not look over her shoulder. Not yet. Until the ground was hidden in the purple haze, she didn't want to risk losing her nerve when she caught a glimpse of it retreating in the distance. The quiet voice of reason nagged her that she should have a plan beyond "find Dr. Wash and bring this to an end" but she set it aside. The whole of her mind, body, and soul was wrapped in the rush to the rescue. The rest could wait.

Until it couldn't…

Goose dragged her up the cliff in no time at all. The fug thickened to a dense pea-soup fog, and then it was gone. She burst out into the fresh air a few hundred yards away from the edge of Keystone. Immediately, she could feel that something was wrong. Deep, gasping breaths weren't enough. Whatever change had overtaken her, it wasn't through yet. She couldn't breathe without the fug around her. The panic finally overcame the exhilaration. She whistled a fresh command and hauled at the reins until Goose finally veered back down the cliff into the wispy upper reaches of the fug. She took a long, deep breath.

"Dang it…" She gasped. "Dang it!"

She squinted through the curling tendrils of kicked-up fug. More ships were arriving to take the plunge into the fray that she could hear even at this distance. The funicular cable was jerking and swaying. Things were getting worse, and there was nothing she could do. She was a prisoner of the fug.

Unless…

She risked taking one hand from the reins and felt for her purse.

#

"I thought you had me take the helm so you could do some fancy shootin', Gunner," Coop said, hunkering down as a stray smattering of fléchettes peppered the deck.

"It takes time. These weren't finished, you'll recall," Gunner said, screwing something onto an increasingly elaborate rifle-shaped object.

"I ain't so sure I want you pullin' the trigger on somethin' you ain't sure works. Laylow Island's got a lot of smoky holes from you doin' that."

"I assure you, this will be worth the risk. I haven't had the chance to fire a weapon of this type in *ages*. They only work in the fug."

He attached a final component and raised the weapon. He took aim at the edge of the envelope of the nearest enemy ship. When he pulled the trigger, first there was little more than a flash of light and heat in the body of the rifle, like someone had set off a lackluster firecracker. Then a puff of particularly thick fug curled from the top.

"Shield your eyes," Gunner said.

Coop squinted and turned away, not a moment too soon. The air sizzled and a needle-sharp shaft of piercing green light traced a line across the sky. Gunner swept it across the envelope, and it split like he'd pulled the thread on a seam. Still more bright green light spilled out as the phlogiston came spraying out of the slice in the envelope. The ship slowly began to descend. The eventual impact wouldn't be pleasant, but it would be survivable.

Gunner laughed dementedly. "It works! The raycaster works!"

He pulled a lever, and a smoking-hot canister ejected from the side. He slotted a fresh one in from the sack and took aim. Another lancing burst sent another ship to an unplanned hard landing.

"Ain't this that thing we stole from the warehouse?" Coop asked.

"It's *based* on it. That one used whole tanks of phlogiston. This one uses canisters of ichor and heats them to produce—"

"I don't care why it ain't the same thing. Why ain't we been *usin'* it?"

He pulled the trigger a third time. The weapon seared a thick black line across the envelope of another ship, but only the tiniest trickle of phlogiston came out.

"There's a lens inside," he said as he reloaded. "We can't figure out how to keep it from melting. As it is, we can get four or five shots before the entire focusing assembly—"

"Forget I asked. Just keep shootin' until it ain't worth shootin' no more. Looks like you just pullin' the trigger on that thing's sapped the nerve out of half these fellas. The newcomers are turnin' tail. This thing looks like it's pert near twisted around to go our way."

#

Sweat ran down Nita's face as she applied leverage to the strips of metal she'd bolted to what remained of the mounting points. It had been less an act of engineering and more an act of inflicting her will on a recalcitrant pile of machinery, but she'd managed to clamp something of a boot onto the wheels that ran along the cable. Now she was working on getting something attached to the cable itself. Between the two improvised safety mechanisms, the cart might just be able to remain locked where it was until help could come along.

She paused to catch her breath. Until now, the air had been thick with the hum of turbines and the buzz of deck guns. Now that they were thinning out, she became aware of a more subtle and far more concerning sound. A series of short, toothy raking sounds was reverberating along the drive cable. Every few seconds there was a sharp springing sound and a visible twitch. Someone was sawing through the cable.

"No, no, no," she muttered, hammering all the more vigorously to get the improvised braces tightened around the support cable.

Through her efforts, she managed to clamp one of them down on the broad wire before the thinner cable suddenly went slack. The moment the tension was gone, the whole cart started to grind slowly forward. The boots on the wheels scraped long furrows in their sides, clearly slowing them, but it wasn't enough. With each passing moment the cart was picking up more speed. Nita took a shaky breath and reached behind her.

"When all else fails, trust in the monkey-toe," she stated.

She pulled the massive wrench head from her back and hooked it over the wire. The wheels started sparking against it. She tightened the jaws until they were as tight as she could manage. A horrid metal-on-metal screech filled the air. Bits of scale and rust scraped from the wire and pelted her goggles. She pulled the cheater bars from her belt and slotted them into the nut of the wrench. Using all her weight and every ounce of leverage the bars could give her, she clamped the jaws down tighter and tighter. The teeth started to glow a dull red as the friction ground away at wire and wrench alike.

"Come on... Come *on*..." she begged.

Her boots started to slip, but one heel found is way to a fléchette that had been driven into the roof. She braced against it and pulled harder. The jaws of the wrench were almost white-hot. Two cherry-red streaks ran along the cable where it was gripped, and a brilliant ring wrapped the wheel that was grinding at the wrench. Now even the mask couldn't take enough of the edge off the stench of burning metal to keep her from coughing.

Nita's teeth clenched so tightly they creaked. Her gloved hands shook. Slowly, painfully slowly, the speed started to come down. The glow started to fade. After a harrowing minute, the cart bobbed to a stop. She opened her eyes. The runaway cart had traveled to nearly the center of the suspension cable. She'd traveled far enough into the fug that she was through the dense upper layer. The glow of lights below told the tale of just how far above the city she still was.

For just a moment, she eased the pressure on the cheater bar. Immediately the cart started to move. She leaned hard on it again and weighed her options. She couldn't risk letting the cart build up speed again. She'd have no chance of stopping it. Her only options were to try to bring it slowly to rest at the bottom, or hold tight and wait for help. Either way, it was going to be a *long* time before she could rest.

#

Dr. Wash stood on the service catwalk on the pulley tower for the funicular and scrutinized the main support wire. He'd rendered a hacksaw toothless in the process of sawing through the drive wire, but he'd gotten the job done. At first the wires had shaken chaotically, and he eagerly awaited the crash that would cripple Fugtown and cement his future as the linchpin of trade for the region, but now they'd grown still. No cacophonous smash, no plume of poison spreading through the city. He gritted his teeth and gazed back along the service catwalk.

"Just how dirty am I gonna have to get these hands..." he muttered, marching toward the maintenance shack tucked under the platform that hosted the station. "I pay the mercs, they can't get it done. I pay guards, they can't get it done. Am I the only guy in the fug who can finish what he starts?"

He thundered up to a man in a similar but less classy uniform to the funicular supervisor. He'd been sleeping in a leaned-back chair, something that was a genuine achievement considering the commotion going on. The depth of his slumber could probably be attributed to the empty liquor bottle set on the ground beside him. Wash kicked the chair out from under him, and he collapsed to the ground. The man sputtered awake.

"You got the keys for this shed?" Wash barked.

"What? Who're you?"

Wash dug out a sack of coins and threw them on the man's chest. "The one who's bribin' you. You got the key to this shed?"

The man groggily rummaged for his keyring and held it out, his sleep- and booze-addled mind grasping the prospect of a bribe with remarkable speed.

Dr. Wash snatched the keys. "Now get lost. You don't want to be around for this part."

"What's happening over there?" the man said, dull realization dawning that there was an event he'd been missing out on.

"Just get lost!" Wash snapped.

The man scurried away like a scolded puppy. Wash unlocked the shed and stepped inside. A saw had been easy enough to bring along. He'd needed it to help his boys sabotage the car. But to get through the main support cable inside of a week, he was going to need something more substantial. A cutting torch was waiting for him just beside the door, along with a mask and gloves that would be superfluous to his own. He strapped the torch to his back and marched back toward the strut for the main support wire.

The drive cable had been relatively easy to access. It was a moving part, in need of regular maintenance and oiling. The designers had provided a dedicated maintenance scaffold leading to the huge pulley above the station stop in Keystone. The massive cable that served as the rail for the cart to ride upon was another matter. It was far thicker, and if it were to fail, it would be far more disastrous. This cable ran down from the support strut that most first-time visitors to Keystone mistook for the boom of a crane lowering its hook off into the fug. The strut was massive, anchored into the stone of the mountain. It ran up through the platform and towered over the city, an artful construction clad in metal with strategic bits of timber bracing. Dozens of yards tall, just under four yards across, and leaning out over the cliffside. At its peak, the strut had something of an elbow so that it could leveled off and stretch far out over the fug. The cable it supported ran from its own anchor point, up the spine of the strut, and then out from its end like a fishing line cast out into the purple sea. A caged catwalk ran beside the cable for the length of the support strut, hanging rather precariously from the side like an afterthought. If he was going to be sure that the cable would release its payload, he'd have to follow the whole catwalk to its end and cut the cable where it left the boom arm. With the way things had been going for him today, if he clipped it at the mountain, the strut would turn out to be strong enough to hold the cart up on its own. He navigated a metal rung ladder to the base of the strut and kicked open the catwalk access door. Once he shut it behind him, he sparked the torch briefly and used it to fuse the hinges. No one was getting past that door. He'd have to cut it open himself when he was finished with the task at hand.

Wind whistled against him as he reached the point where the strut leveled off into the boom. His legs felt weak, but he pushed aside the reality of the swirling fug that was now the only thing that stood between him and the cruel cliffside below. The crowd on the platform swelled with shouting and panic. Perhaps they'd spotted him. It didn't matter. They'd all have something more to worry about soon enough. He'd nearly reached the end of the boom when he heard the rattle of the cage around the catwalk behind him.

"What *now?*" he snapped.

He turned, expecting to find the guard having a sudden bout of responsibility and trying to reach him. Instead, he saw a crazed-looking squarrel clawing at the cage. It managed to peel back just enough for a thin, pale woman with a fiery look in her eyes to hop from its back and drop through.

"So. Blanche. Fancy meeting you here," Wash said, gripping his torch tight.

"I don't know for sure if I really was Lil. But I'm *positive* I'm not Blanche," she said, stalking toward him.

"I thought you couldn't breathe up here. I guess the fug's finished running its course."

She pulled an empty glass beaker from her purse. "Guess again."

"What's that?"

"A gift from the *Wind Breaker* crew. The cure for being fugified. It works."

She stumbled a bit. The empty vial slipped from her grip and clattered through the slats to fall into the fug.

"You ain't lookin' so good. Guess it packs a punch."

"It ain't the only thing that packs a punch," she said, shaking off the bout of dizziness.

"I suppose your memories are floodin' back, then."

"My head's still fuzzy. So far, I only remember two things. The second one is, I owe you a long overdue beating."

"What's the first?"

"None of your business," she fumed, stalking toward him.

Dr. Wash took a step backward and grabbed the igniter for the torch. He sparked it a few times. "You need to know something about me, Blanche."

"Don't call me that," she rumbled, walking closer.

"I'm a survivor. I been around for as long as the fug has. Longer. I'm one of the few people who remembers things how they were. All this is me takin' one small step in puttin' them back the way they were. I'm takin' back part of the fug."

"From who? You *are* a fugger."

"I'm *not*! I'm not a fugger any more than you're 'Blanche.' That stuff changed how I looked, how I worked, but it didn't change what I am, who I am. The people who lost it all? They died. Most of the fuggers are just the corpses of real people, as far as I'm concerned. They belong in the ground, and I'm puttin' them there." He shrugged. "If I make some money along the way? Consider it payback for the time I spent havin' to live with 'em."

"I don't care. You held me prisoner. All this fightin' is your doing. And I ain't so sure you ain't done worse."

He clucked his tongue. "Grammar, Blanche. What would the other fuggers think?"

"Ain't *none* of my concern what nobody thinks except me and my crew. Now, I took my medicine"—she cracked her knuckles—"time for you to take yours."

Dr. Wash sparked the torch to flame and brandished it. "I'd like to see you try to take me out, all by your lonesome."

"And here I am thinking *I'm* the one who lost my memory. Seems like you forgot something that even *Blanche* worked out for herself. If you're fightin' a member of the *Wind Breaker* crew, you ain't never fightin' just one."

"You're trying to get me to take my eyes off you," Dr. Wash said. "We're hundreds of yards in the air, in the middle of a covered catwalk dangling over the edge of a cliff, and your crazy critter is too big to follow us in. You're bluffin'."

A vicious chattering screech behind him suggested he'd misread the situation. Before he could turn, he felt the scampering of little claws spiraling up his leg, then the slice of cruel teeth through his trousers. He cried out in pain, then huffed a groaning breath as his former prisoner torpedoed him in the gut. The still-lit torch slipped from his grip. Blanche tore the canister free from his back and heaved it back along the catwalk behind her. Wink scampered up to her shoulder, a shred of Wash's pants still in his teeth.

"You've had this comin' for a *long* time," she said, righteous satisfaction in her eyes.

#

Nita's eyes were shut tight as she did her best to keep the cart in constant, safe motion. A monkey-toe wedged between a friction-damaged wheel and an aging cable was not a precise way to control speed. She'd found that the best gauge she had was the sound of the metal-on-metal screech. If she kept the volume just below the threshold of pain, she was confident there wouldn't be a catastrophe when she finally reached the ground. But that meant she had easily a half hour of constant pressure ahead of her. She wasn't sure her body would hold out. Keeping her eyes shut both helped her focus on the sound of the steel and kept her from being tortured by the dizzying view and massive gulf she had yet to cross.

It thus came as a surprise when something clattered down on the top of the car beside her. She flinched and nearly lost her grip. In a panic, she forced her weight back onto the bar and brought the swinging deathtrap to a complete stop.

When she opened her eyes, she was face-to-face with Coop.

"You holdin' up okay, Nita?" he asked.

The deckhand was holding tight to a mooring rope that led up to the damaged scout with Gunner at the helm.

"I'm not," she said. "I'm really not. We've got to keep this thing from crashing down, or a lot of people will die."

"That's what we figured up there. We got the more ornery of ships knocked down or chased off, but we took a few hits more than we'd've liked. That scout ain't got the lift to keep this cart up all by its lonesome. Cap'n Mack thinks the *Wind Breaker* can handle it, though."

"The captain is here?!"

"Sure! Thing's been happenin' while you been down here tinkerin' and whatnot." He glanced around. "Didn't you have that critter with you?"

"Coop, I'd love to catch up on this chaos, but can we get something tied to this car before my arms give out?"

"I'm on it," he said. He flagged down the *Wind Breaker* and caught the dangling mooring line. "It's a pity Lil ain't here helpin' out. This'd be right up her alley," he said, deftly tying a hitch into the massive line. "Once her head's right, she's liable to be right jealous of us, hearin' what we got up to."

#

The battle on the boom raged on. At the beginning Blanche's desperate attacks were haphazard. The light-headedness that came with the antifug remedy wasn't doing her any favors. But with each passing moment, her combat became more akin to Lil's favored barroom brawl tactics. Indeed, with each exchange of blows, she was less Blanche and more Lil. Muscle memory, it seemed, was the most stubborn to leave and the quickest to return. Alas, Dr. Wash's full-body covering wasn't just useful for hiding his identity and filtering the air. It was a veritable suit of armor. Heavy layers of canvas and leather padded her blows, and her knuckles were bloody from bashing at that blasted mask. What it granted in protection, though, it cost in stamina. He was sucking wind through the restrictive filters and wheezing with each blow. One way or another, if he didn't do something drastic, Wash was not going to come out on top.

Dr. Wash was well aware of this fact, and just as Lil's desperate attacks were becoming more competent, his competence was becoming more desperate. He managed to kick her aside and dash along the catwalk. He was making a break for the cutting torch. Lil sprinted after him and caught his leg. The pair went sprawling forward. Wash's grab for the weapon turned into a swat that clanked the canister aside. It bounced against the side of mesh that enclosed the catwalk and rebounded, clashing with its own burning end. One of the fittings took to flame.

Lil's eyes widened. "Dang it!" she yelped.

She and Wink turned and ran for the far end of the boom. Wash followed. There was only so far they could go before they'd run out of catwalk. They didn't even make it that far. After a long, shrill whistle, the canister detonated. Burning fragments flew in all directions. The whole of the support strut rattled. Metal screeched. The midsupport of the cable sheared free. Without the balanced load it was designed for, the whole strut started to buckle and sag. The wood of the platform splintered, angling the boom farther and farther down.

Lil pulled herself up on her elbows. Her ears were ringing. Wink was missing. The last she'd seen him, he was bounding along faster than her. Knowing him, he was probably well along the cable, far safer than she was. Goose was gone too. She shook her head and tried to stand. The air stank of the fug. Gazing through the grating below, she saw the stuff swirling not far below. The failing strut was dipping the end of the boom down toward its roiling surface. The very tip of the boom was already starting to slip beneath the purple toxin. The strut's slow collapse had stalled for now, though that surely wouldn't last. It might take seconds, it might take minutes, but the whole structure was going to fail and take anyone unlucky enough to be clinging to it with it.

She got to her feet and started kicking at the cage on the catwalk. As precarious as the strut might have been, for the moment it was a good deal more stable than the shaky bit of rapidly failing iron she was standing on.

The silence of blotted-out hearing gave way to a loud hiss. The next clank, she heard as well as felt. Dr. Wash had climbed to his feet. His coat was smoldering. One of the lenses in his mask was fractured and mostly missing. But he was alive.

"Look, if you want to keep fightin', that's all well and good, but let's get on solid land first," Lil said. "I just got my second chance at life, and I ain't wastin' it clashin' with a man who don't know when to die."

He stalked toward her. He likely hadn't heard a word she'd said. Even if he had, she doubted it would have mattered. There was no mind left in the eye peering out through the broken lens. There was just fury.

A support bracket for the twisted catwalk snapped. The caged walkway shuddered. Lil's boots slipped. She scrambled to hold tight. Wash lunged at her and grabbed her leg. Another shudder and they both started to slide toward its sagging end. She clawed at the catwalk. The purple mist surrounded her as she slid to where the tip had submerged. When she finally got her grip, she was fully immersed in the fug and unable to see the man clinging to her legs. Unable to see the drop below her. Unable to see anything. She held her breath for as long as she could, but she lacked the strength to haul both herself and her assailant up. Finally, she coughed out a heaving breath and sucked in a lungful of fug. It tasted like ink. The stuff stung her mouth and burned her lungs. ... But it didn't kill her. Either the treatment had yet to fully take hold, or it never would. Either way, for moment, the fug was the least of her worries.

A few seconds after she discovered the fug hadn't finished her, Wash made the same realization.

"What does it take to *kill you*?!" he growled, clawing his way up along her body.

"You're one to ask. At least I ain't been kickin' around since the Calamity."

She planted a solid kick on his unseen body. He lost his grip on her and grabbed hold of the catwalk instead. Lil took the opportunity to pull herself up and away. She dragged herself along the catwalk. The damage Goose had done to let her in to the catwalk had been widened by the collapse. If she could reach the gap in the cage, she could get out onto the strut. Wash pulled himself along just a few slats behind.

#

Coop had tightened up the mooring line and was ready to call for Gunner to drop a line to pull him and Nita up. She was just easing her weight off the monkey-toe when the cable rattled with enough force to nearly shake both her and Coop free. He managed to hold the mooring line with one hand and Nita with the other. The trembling eased, but not before the line displayed a worrying amount of additional slack.

"What do you make of that?" Coop asked.

"Someone's trying to take the whole support cable down," Nita said.

"What happens if they do?"

"It goes down and suddenly the *Wind Breaker* has to support the funicular car *and* the weight of that massive cable. The *Wind Breaker* can't handle that."

"So what do we do?" he asked.

"You get up there and try to stop them. I stay here and dismantle the guards so we can get this free of the cable."

"Sure about that? You already almost fell once, I ain't too sure I'll... hang on, Nikita's tappin'."

He loosened his jacket and Nikita popped out. She drummed madly at one of his buttons.

Lil fought with Wash at the top. Wink on wire, tapping message. Wink heading back to help. All need help. Might die, she drummed.

Coop and Nita didn't waste any more words. He hauled himself up the line far enough to whistle to Gunner, then dove to the dropped ladder rather than waiting for it to align with him. Below, Nita spun bolts free and started fighting with a metal guard.

"What's going on?" Gunner called down to him.

"Get us up above the fug and heading for where this thing is hooked up. Nikita says Lil's up there." He tumbled over the edge and onto the deck. "You got a better spyglass than me? What about that rifle. It got sights that'll see better? I gotta see."

"We're not even out of the fug yet."

"I gotta see!"

"The rifle is the best we've got. Take it."

Coop snagged the weapon from Gunner's back and took aim to the west, waiting for the dense fug to clear. The seconds ticked by painfully. They could hear the cable twang and bounce with the weakening of the main support. When the air began to clear, Coop swept along the mountaintop. He scanned the skyline of Keystone, but the support simply wasn't there.

"The dang thing fell! It's gone!" Coop shouted.

"It can't have fallen completely, the cable hasn't fallen."

Coop scanned until he spotted the mostly demolished funicular platform. The strut was twisted and strained. The boom was almost completely gone from view. But there was motion at the edge of the fug. Two figures were perched on the top of the strut itself, beside a hole torn in the caged catwalk.

"It's Wash. Him and my sister are slugging it out. They're out on the edge of the arm. The middle part's all chewed up." He looked over his shoulder. "Get us there! There ain't much time!"

"Get on the helm," Gunner said.

"I gotta keep an eye on the fight! He's got his hands around her throat, Gunner!"

"You watching her isn't going to do any good. Me with a rifle in my hands just might."

"You been missin' an awful lot lately, and that's my *sister*."

234

"Give me the rifle," Gunner said, his tone dire.

"Fine. But you shout out what you're seein'. I ain't tryin' to sit back here wonderin' if I still got a sister."

Gunner took his rifle and steadied it on the railing of the ship. He focused on the support strut. Coop was right to worry. Lil was on her heels, being pushed back to the edge. She was fighting Dr. Wash's grip, and Wink was clawing madly at him, but he just kept bearing down on her. He didn't seem to care if he lived, only if Lil died. Every few seconds he would force her another step closer to the edge.

They were at the extreme range of this rifle in the best of conditions. A stiff mountain wind and the rattling motion of an airship moving at full speed were not the best of conditions. He worked the bolt.

"You ain't takin' a shot at this range," Coop said.

"We don't have a choice."

"He's got his *hands* on my sister. They're too closer for you to be takin' shots. You can't hit him from this far out."

Gunner squinted through the sight. "Like hell I can't."

He took a slow, steady breath and tried to force all the anxiety from his mind and body. He watched the motion of the fug to judge the wind speed. He measured the rattle and sway of the ship. He took a deep breath and held it…

#

Lil's vision was beginning to darken. Her struggles were growing weak.

The whistling wind in her ears joined the creak of failing steel. A sharp crack echoed across the cliffside, and the grip about her throat loosened. She caught a breath of air and shoved Wash away. He stumbled back and hit the top of the cage of the nearly vertical catwalk they'd narrowly escaped from. He held his hand to his side, where the bullet had found its mark.

"I told you," Lil gasped. "You fight one member of the *Wind Breaker* crew, you fight *all* of us. And we beat better than the likes of you already."

She grabbed the beak of the bizarre mask and wrenched it forward, yanking him off-balance. As he stumbled over the edge of the strut, the damaged mask came free, and he plummeted into the inky purple abyss below.

Lil allowed herself a moment of satisfaction with the victory and the souvenir before the shaky grip of an aye-aye about her leg brought her back to reality. The bad guy may have gotten what he deserved, but she wasn't out of the woods yet. She could hear the metal of the strut failing. Its steady collapse had left its length a jagged and impassible twist of torn metal and splintered wood. Goose was nowhere to be seen, scared off by the explosion.

She turned to the fug. Gunner and Coop's ship was getting closer. Just a minute or two more and it would arrive. By her estimation, that would be about thirty seconds too late. She turned back to the dangling catwalk. The section that should have led down through the platform was tangled up in the remains of the wooden planking. As the strut sagged down, the far end of the catwalk was tearing away. It might last longer than the strut would. She looked to Wink.

"What do you think, Wink? Think I can make it?"

Wink gave her an uncertain look, then bounded from her shoulder, deftly across the damaged patch of strut, and onward to safety.

"Thanks for the vote of confidence, fella."

The strut creaked and sagged.

"Now or never," she muttered.

She took a few steps back to the very edge of the strut and got a running start. Planting her boot on the last safe patch before the metal became too twisted to walk on, she vaulted forward and struck the roof of the dangling catwalk hard enough to shatter two more of its braces, which swung down parallel with the cliff and sent fug swirling around her. Hand over hand, clutching the mesh, she dragged herself up. It seemed like every tug upward yanked the catwalk farther down. It was anyone's guess which would come first: either she'd reach the top or the whole mess would tear free.

The metal screeched and rattled as the end of the strut finally failed. It clanked and smashed its way down the cliffside. The cable pulled free of its anchor and coiled off into oblivion. She felt the last few brackets give way. The catwalk started to slide.

"*Gotcha!*"

A hand grabbed the back of her dress and hauled her away from the catwalk. It tore away from the ruined platform and followed the rest of the mess into the fug. She looked up to find her brother hanging from the rungs of the rope ladder on the stolen scout ship.

"You sure do know how to get yourself into hot water, Lil."

"Learned from the best, I reckon," she said.

He pulled her high enough for her to grab hold of the ladder herself. She followed him up to the deck of the scout.

"How's everybody else?" she said breathlessly when she was finally stable on the deck. "Wink ran up along the arm. Critter's probably huddlin' down under what's left of the platform."

Coop gazed out over the fug. Lil matched his gaze. For a few seconds, there was no sound but the sputtering of the damaged turbines and the muted shouts of the crowd that had witnessed the whole thing from the far edge of the damaged funicular platform. Then the gleam of five pristine turbines could be seen slowly rising out of the fug. The *Wind Breaker* emerged, and after a length of mooring line, so did the funicular car, with Nita perched on top.

"Ha-*ha!*" Lil said. "There she is! Come on. Let's find a place to set down. I need a stiff drink. And it's long past due you caught me up on old times."

Joseph R. Lallo

Epilogue

Weeks passed. Despite the best efforts of the *Wind Breaker* crew, the fall of the funicular was not without its consequences. Hundreds of yards of stout cable and connectors can't fall from the sky onto a city without at least a little bit of damage. Fortunately, the sprawling city with its relatively small population meant little of the strip of Fugtown that was pelted with the support line was in steady use. Coupled with the raw spectacle of the battle that eventually brought the funicular down, the result was no casualties on the ground.

Far greater was the damage that would come in the wake of the funicular's departure. Without the swift, cheap, and efficient connection between Fugtown and Keystone, both cities were suddenly without a small but crucial piece of trade. The funicular had linked the fates of the two cities from the moment it was erected. It didn't take long before each learned that it had become an indispensable part of their day-to-day function. Keystone began to suffer many of the same shortages that plagued the other cities of Rim and Circa. They ran low of burn-slow. Phlogiston became a more valuable commodity. Similarly, Fugtown's downright luxurious lifestyle started to suffer. Foods and raw materials began to dwindle.

When the only two cities on a continent that haven't had to face true austerity in decades suddenly find themselves in the same boat as everyone else, two tasks of roughly equal importance quickly take precedent over all else. The second is to do whatever it takes to restore the lost way of life. The first is to find someone to blame for losing it. Dr. Wash received much of the blame, but there is something unsatisfying in pointing the finger at a dead man. Even if it *was* his fault, where was the righteous catharsis of making him pay? Clearly, a more visible, more lively, more *infamous* culprit would need to be found.

And so, the *Wind Breaker* crew found themselves in Fugtown, waiting to meet with a man they'd hoped they'd never have to deal with again.

The room was dim, lit by a single phlo-light in its center. Normally the city hall would be above resorting to the cheap and efficient phlo-lights that were so prevalent elsewhere in the fug, but it seemed the declining status of the city had even reached the mayor's office. No oil lamps. No gas lamps. Just the same pale green light as the commoners.

Packing the entire crew into the antechamber of the mayor's office left the place rather uncomfortably crowded. Captain Mack and Butch were seated in the only two chairs. Wink occupied the captain's shoulder and kept his eye locked upon the thin, stooped assistant mayor as he stood in the doorway. The rest of the crew milled about, each displaying varying degrees of restlessness or boredom.

"I don't like it," Gunner said.

"You been pretty clear about that," Mack said.

The captain had an unlit cigar in his hand, the filter mask preventing him from smoking it. At the moment it wasn't clear if the lack of a cigar, the general situation, or Gunner's disposition was most responsible for the simmering irritation that was painfully evident in his countenance.

"A man should have to work harder to get us into his clutches," Gunner said.

"You said that too," Mack rumbled. "And we ain't in his clutches. Fella sent out an invitation. Good and proper. You ask me like a gentleman, I'll answer like a gentleman."

"If we'd done that with Tusk or Alabaster, we'd be long dead."

The captain narrowed his eyes. He pointed at the carpet. "How's that rug look to you?" he asked.

Gunner glanced down. "Expensive."

"You reckon he wants blood on it? No, he don't. Because he don't do business that way. Ebonwhite don't make a mess in his own backyard. Now, you lookin' to defy my orders? You pickin' now to mutiny?"

"No, Captain."

"Good."

"But I still don't like it."

"Then you can just go on not likin' it. A crew's entitled to gripe. Just wait'll we ain't in the same room, because I'm sick of hearin' it."

Gunner tapped his foot on the plush rug. Nita and Lil were each admiring one of the pair of portraits hanging on either side of the entryway. Lil was looking a bit different these days. Her hair, which had once been golden-blond, had lightened to a platinum blond at its roots, contrary to Prist's initial theory as to how she might change. Her skin wasn't nearly the paper-white of the fug man quietly watching over them, but it too had lightened a shade or two. At the moment, the most glaring side effect of her misadventures was the simple fact that she wasn't wearing a mask.

"Darlin'? I can't quite tell if this here paintin's good or it ain't." Lil leaned closer. "I mean, it looks like the fella it's supposed to look like. I seen pictures back in Caldera that looked like what they were supposed to look like, same as these, but they looked... better. Didn't look *more* like the thing it was supposed to look like. Just looked… better."

Nita stepped over to Lil's side and cast a critical eye on the portrait. "It's a matter of inspiration. The skill is there, but I would say that the artist was not permitted to add any of their style or point of view to the piece. No flourish of creativity. Just a mechanical recreation."

Lil nodded. "I gotcha. Like how when Coop tells them stories about what he did when he gets back from Keystone. Ain't a lie exactly, but it sure ain't the way it happened neither. Just makes for a better story."

"Ain't nothin' fancy about the way I told it. Plain as day. The lady gave the money back," Coop insisted. "She said I was—"

"Coop, we all heard the story," Mack snapped. "Now ain't the time to hear it again."

A delicate knock drew their attention to the door between the portraits. The mayor's assistant stepped forward and opened it. Dr. Prist rushed through. She was breathless, and her hair was in an uncharacteristic state of disarray.

"I am so terribly sorry I am late. Things in Ichor Well have never been so busy."

"Ain't late. We're all still waitin'," Coop said.

Dr. Prist quickly turned to Lil. "And how are you? Any relapses? Odd symptoms?" the doctor asked.

Lil rolled her eyes a bit as Prist looked her over like a nervous mother.

"The fug still don't smell nice, but breathin' this stuff beats when I was sharin' a room with Coop and we got stuck with nothin' but beans for a couple weeks," Lil said.

"Hey! There was two of us in that room. You gave it as good as you got it," Coop defended.

"And your memory? How is that progressing?" Prist asked, nudging the corner of Lil's eye to get a better look at the white of it.

"Still feels a little muddy. Gotta work for it. But all the important stuff's there. I reckon I ain't got too many more knots to untie before I'm back to how I was. Or close enough so it don't make no difference. Just about the only thing that ain't so nice is the sun gets to me if I don't cover up. But squintin' and rollin' down my sleeves sets me straight, more or less."

"I would recommend a wide-brimmed hat as well. It is magnificent the treatment worked so thoroughly. Better than I could have hoped for."

The jangle of a soft bell filtered through the door to Ebonwhite's office.

"The mayor will see you now," his assistant stated.

He opened the door. One by one, the crew filed in. Gunner lingered behind long enough to accompany Prist through the door. What awaited them beyond the doorway was more of a library than an office. It was enormous, triple the size of the antechamber. Bookshelves lined the north and south walls. A picture window dominated the west wall, overlooking the dim lights and purple haze of the city beyond. A semicircle of chairs had been arranged around the large, antique desk behind which Mayor Ebonwhite sat with his sharp clothing and cool demeanor.

"Please. Sit," he said.

"Office is bigger than I remember," Captain Mack observed as he took his place in the center.

"Yes. There was some small amount of damage to the eastern facade. You no doubt noticed upon entering. I've had to move my office until it is repaired. A happy accident, as it has permitted me to provide you all with a more comfortable place to have this meeting. Refreshments?"

"I'm not fond of what passes for food here in the fug," Gunner said.

"Yes. It is an acquired taste. One that I wonder if the young Miss Cooper might have developed..."

"Keep my sister's name out of your mouth," Coop warned.

Mayor Ebonwhite tented his fingers. "A few words on diplomacy," he said. "Miss Graus, as I am sure you'll no doubt recall, we first met in this very building, if not this room. And on that day, thanks to a regrettable miscalculation on my part, we started our association in an adversarial role."

"You denied me the opportunity to purchase life-saving medication for my mother because there wasn't enough money in it for you," Nita said sharply.

"As I said, regrettable, but in line with what had until that point been our traditional means of interaction with the people of the surface. Following the alternate means you sought to fulfill your goal—"

"Still proud of that heist," Coop said.

"I utilized the means available to me to bring you to justice. The result was not just an escape from the prison two of your crew had been relegated to, but the destruction of that prison."

"Shouldn't't've tossed me in a prison that could fly if you didn't want me to crash it," Lil said.

"Following that, I learned from my mistakes and withdrew my direct dealings. Since then I've seen others make their attempts to deal with you. The results were the deaths of Ferris Tusk and Dr. Wash and the... I suppose we shall consider it an incarceration of Lucius P. Alabaster. In all cases, considerable devastation to their operations and surrounding areas. Which brings me to the purpose of this invitation.

"I suspect you are all self-aware enough to agree that you are, by no measure, saintly in your behaviors. Your profession operates entirely at and beyond the fringes of legality."

"Ain't our laws we're skirtin'," Coop said.

"We're smugglers, Coop," Mack said.

"Ain't any worthwhile laws that we're skirtin'," Coop amended.

"In just this most recent 'caper' of yours, you have caused the destruction of enough airships that I am still awaiting a complete tally. You have further caused the destruction of a not insignificant portion of the South Pyre facility."

"How come you didn't just say significant?" Lil asked.

"You ain't helpin', Lil," Mack said.

"And there is the matter of the funicular," Ebonwhite said.

"That wasn't us. That was Wash!" Coop said.

"It happened with us tryin' to keep you folks from gettin' a taste of that poison."

"The broad knowledge of the existence of which was also your doing."

Ebonwhite opened a desk drawer. He slapped sheaves of typewritten notes on the desk, one by one.

"I have done a tremendous amount of research. And what I have discovered his altered my opinion of you quite markedly. You are, by any measure, vectors of chaos and destruction. But you are *not* careless. You are not murderous. You seem to have mastered the art of slowly downing an airship. And you draw a sharp distinction between a mercenary hired to kill you and a simple worker doing his job. The former is fair game, the latter quite safe. And indeed, to all outward appearance and according to all reliable accounts, the whole of your actions surrounding the collapse of the funicular were dedicated to the preservation of both civilian life and the minimizing of property damage."

"This is all a lot of talk to say stuff we already know," Coop said.

"Forgive me. I lack your knack for brevity. I shall be direct. Fugtown cannot endure much more mishap or misfortune. The *fug* cannot. I am not entirely certain we can endure many more months without the funicular in operation. At least, not without intervention. And above all else, we *cannot* afford to run afoul of the *Wind Breaker* crew any longer. So here is what I propose."

He opened another desk drawer and removed two smaller stacks of papers. As he spoke, he handed them out. "A new funicular must be constructed. Until it is, at least a dozen additional cargo runs must be made per day between Keystone and Fugtown, dedicated to replacing the funicular's lost capacity. Additionally, multiple monthly trips shall need to be made from wherever it is you've been getting your burn-slow and phlogiston to make up for South Pyre's reduced output. I hesitate to think of what might happen if this crew is left to its own devices, and I'm not entirely comfortable having you unobserved. Thus, I extend the contracts to you. Both construction and shipping."

Captain Mack looked over the sheet he had been given. It was a detailed, and quite strenuous, shipment schedule. Nita, for her part, had been handed a set of engineering requirements. Each had a budget attached. Mack's eyes widened at the sight of it.

"You buyin' us out? Bribin' us?" Mack asked.

"Ha! We ain't doin' nothin' for no Ebonwhite. After what you tried to do to us? Ain't no way we'd work for you!" Coop stated.

Mack held up the contract. Coop's eyes found their way to the underlined figure representing the salary of each crewmember. He then glanced back to Ebonwhite.

"I reckon I might've been a little hasty just now," Coop said.

"One problem," Mack said, taking the page back and slapping it on the table. "This ain't a job for one ship, regardless of the crew. By my count, this here's a job for three. One doin' long-distance runs like we been doin', another headin' up a *crew* of workers puttin' up the funicular, and another just doin' runs up and down that cliff."

"That was my assessment as well. Given your obvious aptitude for procuring additional ships almost at will, I am confident in your capacity to divide the tasks adequately."

"How much time we got to decide?" Mack asked.

"I can give you a moment, but the need is rather dire. If you don't confirm today, I am afraid I shall have to seek aid from elsewhere. To the left, you'll find a door where you can privately discuss the matter." Ebonwhite set about returning his research to its drawer. "I eagerly anticipate your decision."

#

The crew filed into what turned out to be the archives of the library, a dim room filled with musty books. Gunner, Coop, Nikita, and Wink quickly swept the room to ensure they were being neither ambushed nor spied upon.

"What do we think?" Mack asked.

"I ain't one to trust that fella half as far as I could kick him," Coop said. "But that number's lookin' mighty nice. Wouldn't mind settin' up shop in Keystone for a bit, since it'd be the port of call."

"I think he's trying to split us up," Gunner said. "Separating us into different ships to keep us from presenting a unified threat."

"He may be, at that," Mack said. "But if that's what he's workin' at, he ain't got his thinkin' straight. You split the *Wind Breaker* crew, all you get is a whole new mess of troublemakers headin' every which way." The captain fiddled with his cigar tin. He glanced to Butch. "I reckon you and me're of one mind on this one, Glinda," he said.

She grunted an affirmative.

"So you all might as well say your piece."

"I've said it before, I don't trust him. But if we can string him along long enough to get our hands on a few well-armed ships in proper repair, whether or not he's trustworthy won't matter," Gunner said.

"That a vote in favor?" Mack said.

"It is," Gunner said.

"The way I see it, it's just us doin' what we always did, just on somebody else's coin for once. A whole heap of coins," Coop said. "I'm all for it."

"Not that I haven't enjoyed my time fighting the endless fight to keep the *Wind Breaker* airborne, but there is something genuinely enticing about engineering at this scale," Nita said. "It's much closer to what I'd been doing back at the steamworks in Caldera. I'd need a crew, but there is no shortage of capable workers both above and below."

"If I might make a suggestion?" Dr. Prist said. "If it is rebuilt, can we please designate it an aerial tram? Funicular seems a misnomer, and it has bothered me since I was a little girl. The pedant in me, I suppose."

Lil eyed Prist curiously. "Now when you say pedant, I reckon you and me are thinkin' two different things, or you wouldn't be bringin' it up. We'll settle it later though. Right now, seems like we're all for it. Which means we got a much bigger question what needs answerin'. Two ships means we're gonna need a new cap'n. Who-all's gettin' to wear the fancy hat?"

"Two," Mack said.

"Yeah, two ships," Coop said. "One extra cap'n. I ain't so sharp at figurin', but I can work that out."

"No. Two new cap'ns," Mack said. "Someone'll still need to do the Caldera run. I reckon I'll keep hold of the *Wind Breaker* and keep that run for myself. Glinda's got a taste for some of them spices, so she'll be comin' along. If there's one thing I learned tryin' to settle down for my golden years, it's that folks need somethin' to keep 'em busy if they want to keep their wits."

"The run between Ichor Well and Fugtown is going to be rather contentious," Gunner said. "A wartime commander is called for. I also, let us not forget, am the first mate and thus the next in line for advancement."

"Stands to reason," Coop said. "And ain't no one but Nita gonna be buildin' that tram." He leaned over to Dr. Prist. "Between you and me, I reckon tram's a better name just on account of it bein' easier to say. But that still leaves the short-run cargo haulin'. And if Butch is headin' back with the cap'n, that just leaves us Coopers with any time on the deck of a ship."

"I suppose so. I guess that settles things, then," Lil said with a shrug.

"Sure does," Coop said. "You reckon we're gonna find a cap'n's hat small enough for that head of yours?"

Lil gave Coop a dubious look. "What, me? You're the older brother. I worked it out a while back. Lil Cooper gets the hand-me-downs. I got cozy with that."

"It's a ship that'll spend most of its time under the fug, and there ain't but one of us that can breathe that stuff proper," Coop said. "Plus I ain't under no whatchacallits."

"Delusions," Prist said.

"Yeah. I ain't under none of them that I'm the smartest Cooper. A big fat cargo ship on a short run. You ain't gonna need much help anyways, and Gunner's gonna need all the help he can get."

"… You're sure?"

"If it ain't gonna be you, we're in trouble, because you're the girl for the job."

"Well… We'll—I'll…" Lil turned to Nita. "You'll be up and down buildin' that thing. And I'll be up and down deliverin' stuff. So it'll be you and me together, pretty much. And then spendin' our nights and our money in Keystone? Me bein' a cap'n and you back to bein' a free-wrench proper?" She hugged Nita tight. "What're we waitin' for!"

"If it's settled, it's settled. But for the time bein', I'm still your cap'n. So there's still some hagglin' that needs to be done to get us started right. So let's lay it all out…"

#

A few minutes later, the crew emerged from their discussion. Mayor Ebonwhite was still seated at his desk, industriously scratching at a ledger. He turned to them.

"So. Satisfied with your decision?" he said.

"We are so long as you're willin' to finesse it a bit," the captain said.

"If your suggestions are reasonable, I will certainly consider them."

"We'll need time to put together our crews and get our ships figured out."

"Of course."

"We'll need papers provin' we're doing a job for the mayor of Fugtown."

"I wouldn't have you under my employ without proper credentials."

"You'll need to get the rest of your fug folk cronies to wipe the prices off our heads."

"I believe I can persuade them to set their vendettas aside in the interest of continued strong relations with Fugtown."

"And you'll have to pay the first month's salary up front."

"May I ask why?"

"Because if this is the last night we spend as crewmates, we're gonna make it one to remember. Even if I mean to drink so much I can't remember it," Coop said.

"As we are presently cash rich and resource poor, I believe I can see my way to providing a stipend sufficient to ensure your morale and enthusiasm is properly lubricated with alcohol."

Captain Mack held out his hand. "Then you've got yourself a crew."

Ebonwhite firmly shook Mack's hand.

Coop marched up and slapped Ebonwhite on the back. "You won't regret it."

"I rather suspect I shall. But I am quite certain I will regret it less than any of the alternatives."

#

The crew stepped out of the city hall, each with very heavy pockets. They made their way to the *Wind Breaker*. It was in far better repair than when Captain Mack had piloted to Rim, but it was still not quite its old self. Lil and Coop unfastened the mooring lines. Mack took the ship up into the dull glow of the dense fug overhead. As the crew eagerly waited for the open sky to greet them, he looked to Lil.

"Lil, Nita, come here," he said.

"Aye, Cap'n," Lil said, trotting over. "What do you need?"

"You're about to have your own ship."

"I am, Cap'n. And awful big shoes to fill if I'm fixin' to be half as good as you."

"Flyin' straight and true means keepin' an eye out."

"I know it, Cap'n."

"The way the fug left you, that might be a mite uncomfortable."

"I'll manage, Cap'n."

He slipped the dark glasses from his face and held them out. "They're yours," he said. "A new cap'n with a future as bright as yours deserves to look at it with her eyes wide open."

"No foolin', Cap'n?" she said, reluctantly accepting them.

"Don't feel too bad you're gettin' somethin'. Gunner's gettin' the dusty old hat hangin' over my hammock." He turned to Nita. "Now you're headin' off in a direction I don't know the first thing about. But there's somethin' I been hemmin' and hawin' over for a while now."

He reached into his pocket. "Way back, when I was the fella in charge of navigation for a much bigger ship than I ever been the cap'n of, the first mate handed over his pocket watch. The thing ain't never kept good time, and it stopped tickin' about six years back. But it's pert near the only thing I got that's fancy enough that it might catch the eye of a Calderan."

He handed her the watch. Even through the patina of years on an airship, the skill and care that had gone into its creation was evident. The clamshell was engraved with a stunningly detailed moon with the silhouette of an airship drifting past. Nita clicked it open to show the motionless hands.

"Exquisite... And the watch stopped at twelve thirteen."

"That mean somethin'?"

"It's an auspicious time. On the first day of summer, that is the time that the shadow of Lo first touches Tellahn Temple."

"Well, if it's only right twice a day, may as well be a good time."

She clicked it shut. "I'll get it running again. A piece like this deserves to serve the function for which it was crafted."

"Then I hope it'll help you stay on schedule, fixin up that cable car."

He looked to the sky. The thickest part of the fug was just ahead. They were nearly to its surface.

"Been a hell of a ride since we took you on," he said. "Ain't all been good. But it took us a lot further than we ever would've gone. I hope it took you someplace you don't mind bein'."

"Captain Mack, I would not trade a moment of it." Nita put her arm around Lil. "This is where I was meant to be."

Mack fixed his eyes on the brightening sky. "Probably loads more to be said. But I ain't one for running my jaw when we got places to go. Run along."

Nita and Lil stepped to the railing. Lil hopped up to hang from the rigging. The *Wind Breaker* broke through the fug, streamers of purple trailing behind. It soared into the clear blue sky and aimed to the rising sun of a brand-new day.

###

From the Author

Thank you for reading! If you liked this story, or perhaps if you found it lacking, I'd love to hear from you. Leave a review, or contact me directly on social media or via email. You can find the relevant links (as well as my newsletter sign-up) at bookofdeacon.com/contact

Discover other titles by Joseph R. Lallo:

The Book of Deacon Series:

Book 1: *The Book of Deacon*
Book 2: *The Great Convergence*
Book 3: *The Battle of Verril*
Book 4: *The D'Karon Apprentice*
Book 5: *The Crescents*
Book 6: *The Coin of Kenvard*

Other stories in the same setting:

Jade
The Rise of the Red Shadow
The Redemption of Desmeres
The Adventures of Rustle and Eddy

The Big Sigma Series:

Book 1: *Bypass Gemini*
Book 2: *Unstable Prototypes*
Book 3: *Artificial Evolution*
Book 4: *Temporal Contingency*
Book 5: *Indra Station*

The Free-Wrench Series:

Book 1: *Free-Wrench*
Book 2: *Skykeep*
Book 3: *Ichor Well*
Book 4: *The Calderan Problem*

Joseph R. Lallo

Book 5: *Cipher Hill*

Collections:
The Book of Deacon Anthology
The Big Sigma Collection: Volume 1
The Free-Wrench Collection: Volume 1

CPSIA information can be obtained
at www.ICGtesting.com
Printed in the USA
FSHW010702220920
74001FS